Dangerous
Games

Dangerous Games

CHARLOTTE MEDE

BRAVA

KENSINGTON PUBLISHING CORP.
www.kensingtonbooks.com

BRAVA BOOKS are published by

Kensington Publishing Corp.
850 Third Avenue
New York, NY 10022

All Kensington titles, imprints and distributed lines are available at special quantity discounts for bulk purchases for sales promotion, premiums, fund-raising, educational or institutional use.

Special book excerpts or customized printings can also be created to fit specific needs. For details, write or phone the office of the Kensington Special Sales Manager: Kensington Publishing Corp., 850 Third Avenue, New York, NY 10022. Attn. Special Sales Department. Phone: 1-800-221-2647.

ISBN-13: 978-0-7582-2369-2
ISBN-10: 0-7582-2369-2

First Kensington Trade Paperback Printing: April 2009

10 9 8 7 6 5 4 3 2 1

Printed in the United States of America

The Koh-I-Noor is at present decidedly the lion of the Exhibition. A mysterious interest appears to be attached to it . . .

—*The Times*, London, May 1851

Chapter 1

London, 1851

Isambard Kingdom Bellamy bit the inside of his cheek and tasted blood.

By the cold grate, eyes wide with fear, a young woman—hands, feet, and mouth bound—struggled like a trussed chicken. Her cap and soot-stained gown, the petticoats ripped in a brief but desperate scuffle, revealed her to be a scullery maid. The upturned nose and the plump cheeks were wet with panicked tears.

Bellamy bit down harder, savoring the metallic taste flooding his mouth. She would cry, then whimper before realization dawned that it was truly too late. His lips twitched beneath his luxuriant mustache. If Vesper really could make good on his promises, it would all be over too soon.

Dr. Aubrey Vesper stood with his hands tightly clasped behind his back, gaslight glancing off his wire spectacles. He was of slight build with the air of a scholar, the tightness in his narrow shoulders evidence of his unease with the sumptuousness of the salon. His reddish hair brushed back from a high forehead, he contemplated neither the quivering mass of muffled sobs by the fireplace, nor Bellamy. It was the figure directly across from him who held his attention.

Well over six feet of lean muscle, the man in Vesper's view

sat insensate and passive as a string puppet, staring off into some unknown horizon. Despite—or perhaps because of—his preternatural stillness he was an arresting sight, Bellamy thought, following the doctor's gaze. He watched as Vesper took a step back to better study the relaxed features of his patient.

"You are remarkably certain that you can bend our guest here to your will?" Bellamy's challenge rang in the darkened shadows of the opulent drawing room of his Hampstead Heath mansion as he took stock of the physical specimen in question. A clock somewhere in the caverns of the house chimed midnight, punctuating the unusual stillness of the room.

"There is no doubt in my mind, sir." Vesper's voice was soothing in its professorial blandness. "He may appear to be a strong individual," he continued, his gaze glancing over the broad shoulders and long legs sprawled casually against the brocade settee. "But corporal evidence can be misleading."

"Given his history . . ." Bellamy didn't finish the sentence, thinking it both unwise and unnecessary at the moment. Instead, he stroked the silk of his mustache while eyeing the so-called doctor, noting his carefully erect posture. He could trust Vesper. Most certainly. He'd paid enough for his loyalty—and money did go far, that much life had taught him. And there were supplementary inducements, if required. Vesper's weaknesses, the result of a life carelessly lived in exotic places, were Bellamy's gain.

Bellamy understood weakness—he could smell it like a fox circling its prey. He liked to consider it an inherited talent, not that he thought often of his own desperate beginnings in the gutters of East London. Certainly his splendid house spoke otherwise, a direct rebuke to his humble origins. The acres of marble, the vast conservatory, the gilded music room that never heard a note. Waldegrave Hall was a pastiche of manorial Gothic, and no expense had been spared from the square-headed windows with double transoms and mullions of stone to the raised roofs and chimney staffs arranged in symmetrical stacks at each end of the building.

His money, and there was plenty of it, permitted every possible caprice and excess.

The whimpering behind him ratcheted up a degree, operatic to his ear. He permitted himself a careless glance over his shoulder to the huddled figure made small against the baronial splendor of the oversized fireplace. Soon the feminine sniveling would turn into outright hysteria, that last burst of energy that warred with the dimming of the light. Poetic bullshit. He'd seen rats struggle with more conviction than that ridiculous slattern.

He knew struggle, real struggle, the kind that burned acid deep in the belly. It was a corrosive appetite that had made him the major stockholder in the British East India Company, a mogul, a potentate in his own right, recognized by all who had both profited and lost by his efforts. That scullery maid quaking in the corner was hardly worth his attention, dead or alive. He commanded an empire, a vast commercial enterprise that ensured the sun never set on England. Not that the poor excuse for leadership, that squat little queen and her effete consort, would ever admit it.

The taste of blood on his tongue was dissipating. Alas. He smiled coldly at the doctor, watching as he extracted a silver watch on a chain from his vest pocket. He dangled it steadily, like a metronome going through its paces, in front of the heavy lidded eyes of the man who would see the British Empire undone but who at the moment seemed little more than a corpse, his breathing shallow, his arms slung untroubled over the arms of his chair.

Bellamy was bored, a feeling he had no taste for at all. The proceedings were becoming decidedly tedious. "What about this John Elliotson at University College London," he began sulkily, before settling himself into the wide berth of a rosewood balloon-back chair. "He was disbarred from the medical profession as a direct result of his demonstrations of animal magnetism."

Unlike Bellamy's servants in India, slavish and devoted to the end, this London doctor needed testing, and his reaction just might provide a mildly diverting sideshow. Bellamy scooped up an elegantly carved chess piece from the board displayed handsomely on the side table at his elbow, turning it thoughtfully in his broad hands. "I'm intimating that your approach is hardly original, Vesper. After all, wasn't it James Braid who discovered that his subjects could go into a trance if they simply fixated their eyes on a bright object? An object like a silver watch, perhaps?"

The doctor didn't turn away from his task, the watch firm in his slender hands despite the acid lacing Bellamy's words. Only the slight tightening of his shoulders revealed his disquiet at the challenge to his reputation. "Hypnosis is a component of medical science, a rigorous discipline. I'm not quite certain what you're expecting, sir, but I assure you this will not devolve into a tea party séance." He continued to swing the watch, from right to left, from left to right, in perfect metered arcs in front of the seated man's impassive face. "I explained to you from the outset, if you'll recall, that hypnotism is a neurophysiological process wherein a subject's attention is focused upon the suggestions made by the hypnotist."

"Ah, yes, the great god of science. I do so await with interest." Bellamy infused the statement with the right dose of ennui and double entendre. "Our association has been a long and profitable one for you, after all." It wouldn't hurt to remind Vesper of the largely transactional nature of their relationship. As for his other promises, they could easily be reconsidered.

The doctor continued to dangle the watch in front of the seated man's comatose gaze. Whether Vesper was thinking of India, his past, or his regrets, Bellamy could afford not to care. Instead, he spent the moment in private consideration of his perfect future, unfolding as it should thanks to the predator he was grooming like a hawk before the kill. Indulging in the reverie, he found himself unprepared for the doctor's next words, which caught him broadside.

"Why this man in particular?"

The audacity of the question was breathtaking and correspondingly, Bellamy's estimation of the doctor—never high to begin with—decreased fractionally. He caressed the fine elephant ivory in his hands before crossing one leg over the other, and said consideringly, "I don't pay you to make these types of queries, now do I, Vesper? Because what I do with this man at present, in this room, or later elsewhere falls entirely to my discretion and mine alone."

How calm Bellamy sounded, even to his own ears, when what he really wanted to do was kick the little bastard in the kidneys—is what he wanted to do. These middle-class snivelers, almost worse than the aristocracy, with their affectations and absurd sensitivities. His fingers tightened around the smooth ivory chess piece. For a moment, he considered giving in to his irritation. But then again—his eyes narrowed to take in his hawk held in Vesper's thrall.

A restrained cough from the doctor. "I didn't intend to be forward, sir, with my inquiries," he said. "It's simply that such delicate treatments require some sort of foundational underpinnings, the patient's history, for example, and not knowing very many details . . ." Vesper rambled and then stopped his rush of words along with the motion of the watch in midair with a tightly closed fist.

The figure remained immobile in his chair, oblivious to his role as the focus of the proceedings. As if to assure himself that he still had his patient under his control, Vesper peered intensely through his spectacles before taking them off and holding them up to the gaslight, as though inspecting for smudges that might impair his judgment. Finding none, he carefully donned them again, smoothing back his hair and his composure. "Very well then, sir. I am confident that he is properly primed and that we are prepared to begin." The words were neutral, the disquiet stored away in another place for another time. "I shall demonstrate."

"Really?" Anticipation rose in Bellamy's chest like heat from the Rajasthan desert. He leaned back in his chair. "You're ready, are you? But upon consideration, I don't think I'm quite prepared to proceed at this time after all." It amused him to keep the good doctor off balance. Besides which he knew it would be better if he could draw out the situation at least to some degree, like rubbing salt in a fresh wound. Because the little chambermaid snuffling in the corner like a truffle pig wasn't nearly as diverting as he'd hoped she'd be. Many years ago she, or many others like her, would have been cause for excitement. But he required more these days. Much more.

Vesper did a quarter turn to look at him with an expression Bellamy had seen before. Not relief at the thought of reprieve, but a combination of greed and self-loathing. Nothing new under the bloody sun, after all. Bellamy smiled benignly and glanced down at his hands holding the chess piece before returning it to its place. "So if we may digress for a moment, doctor, with your permission of course," he said with a disingenuousness that was almost convincing. He jutted his chin toward the chessboard at his elbow. "I can see that you're marveling over this wonderful East India chess set."

The doctor clutched the timepiece in his right hand, rooted to the spot, half his face in shadows cast by the gaslight, his confusion plain. "A thing of great beauty to be sure, but what of it, sir?"

Bellamy returned the watchful gaze. The set was carved from elephant ivory by craftsmen in Berhampore, northeast India, for wealthy officers, aristocrats, and politicians to take home as luxury souvenirs. One side wore East India Company livery, and the opposing pieces were depicted in Indian costume.

"One of my favored pastimes is chess, that game of strategy, as I'm certain you already know," Bellamy continued mildly and as if they were meeting over drinks at the club on a sultry summer's day and not in a darkened room, heavy drapes drawn against prying eyes. "A fundamental tactic is to capture the opponent's pieces while preserving one's own." He'd come to the game of strategy late in life, and as a man more accustomed to backstabbing and lynching in back alleyways as opposed to the subtleties of chess, something Vesper probably suspected. And feared.

The doctor glanced at the chessboard, carefully calibrating the mood in the salon, well aware who was paying his fare along the way. His expression was shuttered, the glass of his spectacles reflecting the gaslight and nothing more. "The queen is quite impressive," he said perfunctorily.

"But not as impressive as these two intricately carved juggernauts pulled by these oxen right here," said Bellamy, deliberately pedantic now. "Their role is not exactly known except that they relate to an old Indian custom in which pilgrims would throw themselves under the vehicle of the juggernaut idol to be crushed, thus releasing their souls." He asked casually, "Do you believe in the soul?"

Vesper said nothing.

"Neither do I." Bellamy looked past the doctor and to the man who remained immobile across from them. He hadn't moved, and appeared as though made of plaster, except for the barely perceptible rise and fall of his chest. "Nor do I believe in the power of the queen," he added, turning back to the chessboard and picking up the large white piece at its center. "Chess is all about middlegames and endgames. And if one is clever, the queen merely becomes a pawn that is easily captured and eliminated."

He tossed the piece carelessly to one side and rose from his chair, his extemporaneous lecture quite finished. "Thank you for indulging me, doctor, and now that we understand each other, let's see what magic you have wrought here." He smiled tightly. "Not that I am discounting the scientific nature of your enterprise, of course." And as if it had just suddenly occurred to him, Bellamy twisted around in the chair to gesture over his shoulder to the serving maid, who had stopped her keening.

"The little slut believes that if she's quiet enough, we may just forget about her," he said with bemusement. "She will learn differently in a few minutes, if your experiment proves successful. Which I trust it will, given the amount of sterling I've poured into your coffers of late," he added with enough casualness to emphasize the threat in his statement. "And that other matter you would prefer that I attend to . . ."

For the first time that evening, Vesper turned to face Bellamy directly, demonstrating that a man could hide from many things but not from himself. Shame warred with survival and, not that he was a gambling man, Bellamy predicted which side would win out.

"It is a most unfortunate situation."

"Indeed. Your unnecessary anguish makes it doubly so, Vesper."

"However, you may rest assured that I am grateful for your assistance and as such will endeavor to successfully conclude our dealings together." Vesper marshaled his credentials, in the event additional evidence of his worthiness was required. "As you know, although I believe it is worth reiteration, I have studied with Hippolyte Bernheim at the University of Nancy," he said. "And, as a result, I have every confidence the outcome here this evening will meet with your approval. As for the gentleman here"—he took a step back to take careful note of the strong but drawn features of his patient—"he is a curious subject, for many reasons which, as you intimated earlier, we needn't explore at the moment."

"I'm well aware of the curious nature of our subject. You have no idea how well aware," Bellamy said. He rose from his chair and sauntered to the opposite side of the room, positioning himself at an optimum vantage point to frame both their subject and the serving maid. From the periphery of his vision, he could see the mass of rags by the cold grate.

"The slut here has calmed down, so that should make things marginally easier for you." He cast the huddled form a contemptuous glance. A man should be able to expect some sport and he felt disappointingly calm. "Carry on," he directed Vesper with the crisp snap of his fingertips.

The doctor seemed to have recovered his confidence, having wrestled his conscience to the ground, but still studiously ignored the servant girl. From the first, Bellamy recalled with rising irritation, Vesper had refused to acknowledge the slattern in the corner.

"So what's your first trick?" Bellamy's insult was well aimed and timed. He tightened his cravat and his conviction to do absolutely nothing to salve the physician's no doubt unruly principles.

Averting his gaze and ignoring the taunt, the younger man slipped the timepiece back into the pocket of his jacket. "He's under my suggestion at the moment." Then he straightened to his full height, hands behind his back, good soldier he was. "However you would like to proceed, only say."

"No tea party tricks. Your idea, not mine, as you'll recall."

Vesper gave a tight nod.

Bellamy's pulse quickened. His eyes locked on the somnolent man in the chair. Brought to life, he knew exactly how dangerous—and skilled—the man could be. Bellamy shoved a finger into his high cravat to loosen the fabric. "The ultimate of course," he drawled.

Vesper, the limp coward, pretended not to understand. "You intend to have him assault her." He punctuated the statement by smoothing back his hair with surprisingly steady hands, again refusing to glance at the woman in question. Whether he was playing for time or genuinely perplexed was difficult to tell.

What was the physician's credo—*do no harm*? Bellamy smiled and crossed his arms over the superfine lapels of his chest. "Come now. You can do better than that, doctor." He leaned a shoulder casually onto the watered silk-covered wall.

To his left, the slut was stirring, a rodent twitching under a heap of rags.

"Surely you don't mean assault of a sexual nature?" The question was delivered halfheartedly. While not a tall man to begin with, Vesper seemed to shrink a few inches against the ostentatious proportions of the room.

Bellamy's breathing quickened. Things were becoming more interesting, what with the good doctor so studiously studying the patterns in the fine Oriental rug beneath his feet. And all the while Bellamy was beginning to feel the old stirrings again. His guts thickened like blood sausage, the back of his throat constricting with thirst. "What a lurid turn of mind you have, Vesper," he said, the temperature in the room rising a few degrees. "While molestation might prove a mildly entertaining diversion, I had rather something more challenging in mind."

The gas lamps hissed in the quiet of the salon. Stiffening his spine as though warding off a coming blow, Vesper summoned another barely perceptible nod, the fine furrows in his high brow deepening. It was inconvenient to have a conscience, not that Bellamy knew firsthand.

A second later, Vesper looked up from his meditations on the rug and, without glancing at Bellamy, turned his face to his subject. "Can you hear me, St. Martin?" His voice had reverted to its previous cadence, slow and calm.

A change came over the room, an energy slowly suffusing the four corners of the salon with a disturbing intensity. Bellamy's breath came faster. The figure remained still, relaxed as if in sleep, and then the heavy-lidded eyes opened. Dark as pitch. Like the chasm of hell yawning before them.

"Please answer if you can hear me." Vesper repeated.

"I can." The voice was low, more of a growl, as though the man hadn't spoken in years.

Bellamy hauled a breath into his lungs, preparing himself for the feast to come. He moved away from the wall, eager to get closer, listening intently for the doctor's next words. And the man's next actions.

"There is a young woman in the room with us. Please indicate that you see her, sir."

The figure flexed his hands, still suspended loosely from the arms of his chair. Strong, elegant hands. Deadly. Bellamy knew from experience.

The twitching by the cold grate had stopped entirely. Even for that pathetic creature of a slattern, now fully alone in her predicament, self-preservation was a stern taskmaster. Bellamy sensed the tightening in his chest, heat rushing to his loins, the harsh euphoria of power, ultimate power, within his tight grasp. He recognized the feeling and welcomed its resurrection.

The gaslight threw the doctor's shadow into sharp relief, a vibrating specter who knew enough not to hesitate. Because there was no turning back.

"That's very good. You can hear me then," he continued calmly. "And you can see the young woman by the fireplace grate."

The man nodded.

"What I am requesting of you, sir," Vesper said slowly, each word a nasty little pill, "is that you cross the room to her side."

Bellamy's gaze was fixed. He didn't move save to grind his teeth against the spittle that was forming at the corner of his lips. The pressure was building, a rising tide of excitement that threatened to tear his lungs from his chest.

The doctor continued, using the same mesmerizing monotone, distancing himself from what he was about to do. "Once you are at her side, I want you to," the barest of pauses that could not hope to bridge the reality of what was to come, followed by an inhalation as decisive as a knife's thrust. "I want you to," Vesper repeated, "kill her with your bare hands." He paused then, awaiting confirmation. "Do you understand?"

In response and in one fluid motion, the man came to life, rising from the chair. He looked neither left nor right, and Bellamy was reminded of a Bengal tiger he'd once hunted in the grasslands of Uttar Pradesh. The man and the animal shared the same studied calm. The same lethal, wholly instinctive intent.

The slut resumed her whimpering. Bellamy licked his lips again. The man loomed over her. The rag over her mouth was sodden with tears and sweat and terror, her swollen blue eyes shrunken in horror. She tried to make herself small, to disappear.

But those large elegant hands inexorably wrapped themselves around her plump neck. And squeezed with no more effort than a sleek animal in the wild shaking its prey between its jaws.

It didn't take long. Not long enough. The slut barely struggled, her face transformed into a caricature of a bloated balloon topped by a mop of tangled, matted hair. The scent of urine and feces filled the salon.

Through slitted eyes and short breaths, Bellamy watched the man drop the carcass of the girl to the flagstones in front of the fireplace.

And the stiffening, the hardening between his legs too quickly began to subside. Bellamy closed his eyes against the harshness of his breathing and bit down hard, saliva mingling with the renewed taste of blood in his mouth.

And against his closed lids, the image of Julian St. Martin burned. How easily he killed. Julian St. Martin, the cold-blooded assassin, who now belonged to him.

Chapter 2

"And what is your estimation of the situation in India at the moment, Mr. Seabourne?" Surrounded by six men, Lilly Clarence Hampton directed her question to the most senior of the gentlemen at her side. Having just returned from Lahore, Seabourne was a direct relation to the current governor general of India, Charles John Canning.

He eyed her speculatively before answering. "You do realize, my dear, that your interest in all things political and cultural is simultaneously refreshing and unseemly in a woman."

Lilly smiled, the evening candlelight bouncing off the jet beads of her black mourning dress. "Indeed. As though the behavior of a middle-aged widow indulging her harmless interests could be of concern to anyone." She tapped him on the elbow with her fan, pressing him further. "Or are you simply endeavoring to evade answering my questions, dear sir?"

The men chuckled heartily at her rejoinder. The Thursday-evening salons hosted by Mrs. Hampton had become one of the most coveted invitations in London society, each guest scrutinized by the hostess herself to ensure lively, engaging, and informed debate on the most compelling issues of the day. And while her town house in Mayfair was a modest affair, the company was always of the highest order, along with generous servings of food and drink to satisfy the most discerning guests.

Tonight, the room heaved with conversation, the latest rebellion in India taking center stage, while off to the wings, breathless discussion percolated about the arrival in London of the Koh-I-Noor, the world's largest diamond—destined to be presented to Queen Victoria and Prince Albert upon the opening of the Great Exhibition in one month's time. Conceived by the prince, the historic occasion would be held in Hyde Park in the spectacularly constructed Crystal Palace, designed to showcase England's and the world's advances in science and industry.

"Not at all, not at all, my dear Mrs. Hampton," Seabourne finally replied, clasping his hands behind his back and away from the tap of her ivory fan. "Your questions are diverting as always but never more so than the woman who poses them."

Lilly inclined her head toward him, raising her low voice slightly to compete with the surging exchanges going on around them. "Well, thank you, sir. But you must hasten to answer my question as the buffet will be served quite soon."

John Sydons, the former publisher of the *Guardian*, guffawed, his muttonchops bristling. "And we shouldn't want that, Seabourne. I just saw a spectacular Nesselrode pudding float by along with a platter of oysters swimming in cream. So let's move along. Respond to the lady's query—has the situation settled somewhat this past month?"

Seabourne nodded portentously, the horizontal lines on his forehead deepening. "The political expansion of the British East India Company at the perceived expense of native princes and the Mughal court has aroused Hindu and Muslim animosity alike, a complex situation overall which I do not think will be resolved without a Parliamentary solution."

"A tinderbox is what it is," Lilly murmured.

"Indeed," seconded the man across from her, Lord Falmouth, member of Parliament. Small and wiry, he barely filled out his impeccably tailored waistcoat and jacket. "It didn't help that our colonial government, in its boundless wisdom, furnished the Indian soldiers with cartridges coated with grease made from the fat of cows and of pigs. Ignorance and incompetence in one fell stroke. Amazing."

"The first sacred to Hindus and the second anathema to Muslims." Lilly splayed her fan in barely concealed annoyance. "We have an ineffectual and insensitive governor and of course, a historic series of blunders, beginning with the Kabul Massacre, that slaughter in the mountain passes of Afghanistan. I have heard it said that of the sixteen thousand who set out on retreat, only one man survived to arrive in Jalalabad."

"It was actually believed that the Afghans let him live so he could tell the grisly story—such a severe blow and bitter humiliation to British pride." Lord Falmouth jutted out his rather weak chin. "Reports from the Forty-fourth English Regiment are dismal. The troops kept on through the passes but without food, mangled and disoriented; they are reported to have knocked down their officers with the butts of their muskets. St. Martin is one of the few to have survived, if *survive* is the word one would choose to use."

"He's quite the loose cannon, or so one hears from the Foreign Office," Seabourne added. "Has publicly resigned his post, whatever it was, something to do with statecraft, certainly."

"You mean spycraft, surely," Lord Falmouth corrected.

"A shadowy figure one would assume and now one not to be trusted, given his precarious mental state," Seabourne continued. "The trauma and so on."

"My goodness. How clandestine and mysterious," Lilly said, frowning, only vaguely familiar with the St. Martin name. "One never knows what resentments these types of horrific experiences may nurture. I infer from your comments that loyalty is at question for these individuals who find themselves one moment at the service of their country and at the next entirely disengaged or worse. And what of his family?

The St. Martins have a seat in the House of Lords, if I'm not mistaken."

"The parents passed away some years ago and his older brother died of smallpox soon after, if I recall correctly. However, St. Martin has never taken up his place in Parliament, having instead disappeared for years to the farthest reaches of the globe. In Her Majesty's service, one presumes. Although one can presume no longer with his resignation." Seabourne looked pained.

"More of a dismissal is what I have gleaned," Falmouth said cryptically. "And the word *traitor* has been bandied about. Discreetly, of course."

The former publisher snorted derisively. "Not entirely surprising. With the Russians to the north and Britain to the south in India, Afghanistan is clearly the unforgiving landscape where empires collide and careers are made and sacrificed."

"Are you certain only political empires?" Seabourne asked the question as innocently as only a career diplomat could. "Might there be other concerns at stake?"

"Such as commercial enterprises? You are referring to the East India Company," Lilly said sharply, letting her closed fan dangle from her wrist. "I fear that behemoth has as much to answer for as our own governance structure and overweening imperial ambitions."

Seabourne narrowed his eyes, pursing his lips as though sucking on a lemon drop. "I find it curious that you mention the subject, my dear. Perhaps you might take up that very issue with your dear friend, Isambard Kingdom Bellamy. As it is, I'm astonished that he's not here at your side this very moment, given that he has hardly left your presence this entire month."

Lilly opened her eyes wide in feigned surprise, too experienced to blush or dissemble. "I didn't realize that you had such a firm grasp of my social schedule, sir. But in case you haven't apprised yourself as yet, Mr. Bellamy had other, rather urgent plans for this evening," she said, keeping a lightness in her tone.

She turned deliberately to survey the room with its tight clusters of guests in lively debate before continuing pointedly. "And as you can see by the wide array of company I keep, I can't possibly share in everyone's political perspectives. Although perhaps I do have an opportunity to shape the occasional opinion."

"Indeed, so it is, Mrs. Hampton," Sydons replied, taking two glasses of punch from a tray that appeared at his side and offering one to Lilly with a gallant nod. "Are you perhaps attempting to temper an unruly beast into something more manageable? There are those on Fleet Street who can't help but gossip, intimating that there may be nuptials on the horizon. What with your dear Mr. Hampton gone over a year now."

Lilly's fingers stilled on the stem of her punch cup at the mention of her late husband, Charles. A love match from the beginning, few could forget the steadfast devotion of the one for the other. All the more devastating was the tragic and untimely end of the marriage that had been seemingly made in heaven.

Seabourne cleared his throat to break the awkward pause. He patted her arm with avuncular affection. "Now, now, my dear. You do not strike me the melancholy sort. Charles would never have wanted you to mourn unduly but rather to get on with your life. You're a young woman with so much to recommend you. And certainly, regarding Bellamy, I say, eligible is not the word. The man *is* the East India Company. Enough said. And quite the catch."

"Enough said, indeed." Shaking her head, Lilly eyed each man in her circle in turn, her gaze finally settling back on Sydons. "You do prattle on, sir, like an old woman." She took a sip of the punch, wishing it were something stronger. "As if Mr. Bellamy would be interested in a nondescript widow of a certain age when he could have his pick of young, fresh girls on their first season."

Silencing the gallant denials with a graceful gesture, she motioned toward the buffet. "The food is getting cold, gentlemen, while we speak on of inconsequential subjects such as myself and Mr. Bellamy. In the interim, oyster a la poulette awaits."

The feint had its desired effect, as immediately Seabourne took her arm and led the group over to the mahogany table bracketed by two heavy silver candelabra. Amid sparkling chafing dishes swimming in cream and butter sat platters of delicious walnut-mayonnaise sandwiches, chicken salad, deviled crackers, and cream cheeses. Punctuating the savories was the Nesselrode pudding and a dessert of ice-cold coffee jelly smothered in whipped cream.

All of which was a feast designed to draw forth excellent stories and clever conversation, and, more important, create the most pleasant diversion, a nod to normalcy. Casting an experienced glance around the dining room, Lilly allowed herself to relax for the first time that evening, the tightness in her shoulders easing fractionally. Aware of Seabourne still at her side, his plate piled high with confections, she took a final sip of her punch, nodding to the various guests who made their way to and from the buffet.

Seabourne patted his lips with the heavy linen napkin. "Are you certain you will not have anything to eat, my dear?" he asked, the sharpness of his gaze belying the concern in his voice. He was a valued diplomat for a reason, his discerning eyes and ears absorbing the most subtle leitmotifs like a sponge.

Lily smoothed the rich bombazine of her bodice, the jet beads biting into her palms. She smiled brightly. "I had my tea earlier, realizing full well how time-consuming the preparations for the evening usually are," she said. "But thank you for your concern."

"I am concerned for you, Mrs. Hampton. Upon my return from India I was expecting you to be, if not fully recovered from the tragedy, at least somewhat more distant from it. But there are still deep shadows in your eyes, if you'll permit me to say so. I realize how much you cared for Mr. Hampton, but sometime the grieving must end."

"Again, your distress is not warranted, Mr. Seabourne, I am all but fully recovered, I assure you." She delicately relinquished her empty cup to the sideboard.

Seabourne could not be stopped. "A tragedy truly. And a crime, to which we have still to find a resolution. If you were to finally uncover the truth and apprehend the felons, I am certain that so much of your anxieties could be laid to rest." He raised a gray brow. "And then perhaps your burgeoning relationship with Mr. Bellamy might be allowed to flourish, free from the constraints of the past. And of course, Charles would want it so—to see his wife taken care of by one of his most ardent benefactors."

Lilly endeavored to look embarrassed. "Truly, sir, this conversation has become far too personal and at the expense of my guests. Now I must truly excuse myself and see to my duties as a hostess. And, as a matter of fact, I may see to having an early evening. The exertions of the preparations . . . you do understand."

Seabourne set aside his plate and napkin to lightly grasp her elbow before she could move away. "Absolutely understandable, my dear, but one last question, if I might be so bold." His voice hardened imperceptibly along with the hand on her arm.

Lilly gathered her skirts and turned to face him directly, her face smoothed of expression. "Of course. One last question and then you must promise to permit me to see to the welfare of my guests," she repeated her true emotions masked with a forced smile.

He spoke the words flatly. "It's about your late husband, Charles," he paused, and this time he gave the impression that the question was not of a personal nature. "And I hope it's not too indelicate for me to inquire whether you have chosen another architect to complete his final plans."

"For the Crystal Palace, you mean? And not at all, your question is not an imposition," she said evenly. "As you know, the major building has all but been completed. As for several remaining interior spaces for which very particular designs are still wanting, I have yet to make a decision . . . it is too painful, as you suggest. And yet I realize the urgency of the situation, what with the Koh-I-Noor."

He examined her closely, looking for the smallest fissure in her smooth façade. Then he nodded slowly as though suddenly understanding the meaning of an hitherto indecipherable text. "Surely I of all people don't have to tell you of the political implications of the diamond and its presentation to the queen." He grimaced at his own understatement. "Particularly given the unrest within the Raj at the moment. Security is of the utmost importance. I'm surprised the Royal Commission has not appointed someone to the project."

A rhetorical question, one she mercifully needn't answer. It was understood that the Crystal Palace would hold some one hundred thousand exhibits spanning the globe and representing nearly fourteen thousand exhibitors. It was the British Empire hosting the world in a huge iron goliath with more than one million feet of glass, a building both grandiose and innovative. "With the opening and presentation but a month away, they may well be pursuing the matter," she murmured, unthinking and incautious. Smoothly relinquishing her forearm from his grip, she looked down at the fan dangling from her wrist, choosing her next words more carefully. "I have had much else to think about these past months." They both knew to what she was referring. "The constabulary and their insistent questioning regarding Charles's death has been both painful and tiresome."

"Surely, they have given up making their ridiculous accusations, my dear."

"Let us hope so," she said abruptly.

"I heard that Bellamy came to your aid the other evening at Covent Gardens. I can't imagine that an inspector would have the effrontery to accost you in a public venue about a matter so indelicate. And with Bellamy as your escort."

Lilly was silent for a moment, but her downturned gaze indicated agreement. "Yes, if it had not been for Mr. Bellamy's astute management of the situation," she said finally, "I'm certain the gossipmongers would have gone to town with the incident. It's nasty enough as is. They so adore pursuing a juicy tidbit of rumor."

Seabourne harrumphed in sympathy, angling his head toward her benevolently. "Your continuing these evenings is very brave, my dear girl, in memory of your departed husband, if nothing else. He so loved society and debate and, of course, the opportunity to demonstrate his talents in the architectural arena."

"Indeed, he did," she murmured. "And I thank you for your sympathetic ear, sir." She summoned a smile. "As soon as the plans are completed, you will be the first to know. I shall apprise you instantly! And now back to my duties as hostess." Under the pretext of summoning the servants to begin clearing the sideboard, Lilly strode confidently to the adjacent clutch of guests, her head held high.

Hours later after the last of the guests had departed, she dismissed her housekeeper for the night and delved into the cherry wood wardrobe at the back of the narrow entrance hall for a thick cashmere shawl. From the mullioned window of her front door, she could see the first delicate snowflakes begin to descend from the dark and fathomless early April sky. It was nearly spring, the weather as unpredictable as her own fate, her life no longer arranged in neat geometric patterns with lines and angles colliding tidily. A decision made on a horrific night almost one year ago had consigned her to a purgatory without end. A decision, she thought with brutal honesty, that was hers alone.

She drew herself up sharply, burying her dark thoughts. It was likely close to one in the morning but the summons had been unequivocal, if not entirely unexpected.

Isambard Kingdom Bellamy and the Koh-I-Noor diamond

waited—for her. Anxiety, trepidation, guilt—there were far greater issues at stake than her ragged emotions. Perhaps she was condemned to hearing forever the ringing echoes of the gunshots on the night of Charles's death, shots that, she thought numbly, should have been aimed at her own heart.

Chapter 3

Built painstakingly by carpenters imported from Germany, the elaborately curved staircase wound its way to the second and third levels of Waldegrave Hall. King took one step at a time, the highly polished wood beneath his feet a reminder of how far he had come. Pausing on the landing, he inhaled deeply, the scent of beeswax and the rarest teak taking him back to the marshy landscape of Bombay.

So febrile and so fertile, and so ready to disgorge its riches, the insular archipelago had begun as his own private fiefdom and swollen to an empire that could easily compete with Russia to the north and, of course, with England, that juicy, lazy fly primed for swatting by a hard and heavy hand. His hand.

He smiled at the image before continuing his ascent to the second floor. The house was quiet, all the servants abed, the hallway unspooling before him with five bedroom doors, like soldiers, arrayed on either side. He stood absorbing the silence muffled by the cotton batten of luxury, a lifetime away from the heavy hum of bloodsucking insects, stifling destitution, and scraping servitude.

The distinction between east and west was the thinnest veneer. What was savage or primitive, after all? Between the willing Vesper and the groveling serf? Or the strangled maid heaped like so many discarded rags on his hearth and the Punjabi girl robbed of both hands by a machete for taking a scrap of left-over rice from the emir's plate?

The memories collided and coalesced, firing his blood, the heat chafing his overweening ambitions. He loosened his ela-borate cravat and began unbuttoning his waistcoat, pleased not to have his valet dancing in attendance and diluting his mood. Far too many servants in India, one more willing than the next to prostrate himself for the tiniest mercy. It really be-came quite tedious.

Much more challenging this evening with Vesper who had performed well, after all. As for St. Martin—

They had only met once, and briefly. Bellamy would never forget the encounter at the side of a rice paddy, the sun slant-ing hot and unforgiving overhead. Even then, the man was already a legend known to the barest few, his exploits whis-pered about in hushed undertones, one feat more unbeliev-able than the next. How much was true and how much was speculation? One of the advantages of coming from the stews, one learned quickly to distinguish the gold from the dross. Survival depended on it.

Few men could withstand the pressure forever. Even the seemingly indestructible Julian St. Martin. Particularly when it became personal, and Bellamy had guaranteed that it had. He narrowed his eyes. His sources told him that the man had become unhinged, unstable, the result of too much death and destruction, the stink clinging to him until it had become un-bearable.

But then again, instability could and would prove useful.

Shrugging his dinner jacket, he carelessly tossed it on the newel post before continuing his walk toward the master suite at the end of the hallway. St. Martin's weakness was the Crown's loss and his own gain. A deep satisfaction settled over him. The queen, her consort, and the entirety of Parlia-ment could go bugger themselves.

The gaslights had been turned down for the evening, bathing the hallway in a golden light. He wasn't tired in the least—the recent proceedings in his salon exhilarating, both fueling his nerve endings and his labyrinthine thoughts. He continued his slow walk toward his suite and then changed his mind, stopping at the second door on his left. He never hesitated but leaned in carefully, his hand on the polished brass knob, coaxing open the oak door on its four silent hinges.

Moonlight poured through the sheer curtains covering generous mullioned windows, revealing a slender figure lost in the amplitude of the four-poster bed.

She was asleep. The bottle of laudanum on the nightstand beside her was half empty, the silver spoon tossed on the floor. Her face was turned away from him, facing the window. But Bellamy didn't need the moonlight to remember those almond-shaped eyes shimmering with a combination of innocence and vice. He took a step closer toward the bed where Medusa slept, her serpents well hidden beneath a veil of virtue and artlessness.

A willing prisoner of his and of her own making, she did not stir under his gaze. He smiled at the thought of this graceful child-woman as just another weapon in his mounting arsenal. He raised his eyes to look out the window, the milky light a shroud for his poisonous deliberations. Out in the night, another woman waited for him. Lilly Clarence Hampton.

She would be disappointed or perhaps relieved to be rid of his oppressive presence this evening. He was under no illusions that the young widow in any way desired his company, other than for the protection he could provide. Not that it mattered. He released the band collar of his shirt and tossed it aside with the insouciance of the heedlessly wealthy. She needed him, just as her late husband had, and she knew it. Those wide eyes kept her secrets, or so she erroneously believed. An arrogant woman when it came down to it, with a keen intellect that would be her undoing. Probably at his hands, and as his wife, when he decided the moment was ripe.

He loosened the top two buttons of his shirtfront, moving closer to the window. From his vantage point he couldn't see the Tower of London or the Crystal Palace, its construction completed, but instead he traced the marshy landscape of Hampton Heath, the fields and ponds wending their way to the outskirts of the city. To the Koh-I-Noor and the fat little queen.

This night had been a fitting beginning, the savaged servant chit an early trophy in the stalk for much bigger game. There were so many traps to choose among, after all. India had been his playground with its rich diet of violence and degradation. His pulse rose in tandem with every option he considered. He had mastered ever-greater challenges on his way to this night, perhaps the apogee of his triumphant career.

Impalement via the use of sharpened poles. Mustard and latex combination to blind a beast and make it easier to run down. Or the raja's practice in Bengal of setting fire to grass ten miles around so beaters could drive fleeing tigers into a mile of netting.

His blood stirred at the memories. More wide awake than ever, he turned away from the window and strode across the room to the door, barely sparing a glance for the still figure on the bed.

Lilly Clarence Hampton would prove simple prey, but St. Martin was the real prize. He was without doubt the best living marksman in Great Britain, able to drill a gold sovereign from six hundred feet and hold off an army of marauding hordes for days. Who better to assassinate the queen?

And now demoralized and adrift, so far from the man he'd once been, St. Martin would blindly walk into the snare that had been set. And no one would question the outcome, accepting the fact that a madman, a former henchman of the queen, had simply come undone, unleashed his inner demons to accomplish the unthinkable. Regicide.

And the punishment would be death by hanging. So tidy. Even if St. Martin ever did regain his reason, he would tell no tales.

Bellamy sighed once again with satisfaction, closing the door behind him with a last contented glance at the still figure on the bed. He had traveled a long way, defeated insurmountable odds, committed unspeakable acts to straddle the pinnacle of an empire that spanned the globe. And no one would wrest that prize from his grasping hands. Hesitation, scruples, and conscience were for lesser men. Murder, torture, assassination conferred the levers of power—queen and Parliament be damned.

Aubrey Vesper regretted that he had never developed a taste for strong spirits. His hands trembled as he wiped the sweat from his brow with a damp handkerchief, despite the cold of the small parlor.

The fire in the grate of his modest home in Chelsea had reduced itself to ash and he could not bear to approach the hearth, the horrific events of the evening a bitter poisonous memory that he could not expel from his system. He startled at every sound, the wood of the staircase settling into familiar grooves, the night air whistling against the windows. Succumbing to nerves, that's what he was allowing himself to do.

Digging a footpath into the already frayed carpet covering the parquet floor, he couldn't hope to halt the images unspooling relentlessly before him. He shuddered, as unmanned as an unbreeched boy. Under his ministrations, St. Martin had become an unthinking, unfeeling, murderous machine. As for Bellamy, when Vesper recalled the unholy light in his eyes, the heavy breath, the obvious hunger for pain—

Crumpling the handkerchief in a fist, Vesper shoved it into the pocket of his jacket, his hand immediately recoiling from the cool metal of the pocketwatch, the instrument of his handiwork, nestled against his hip. A fresh layer of sweat beaded his brow.

If he was searching for justification of his actions, there was none. It was simple hubris and overweening pride that drove his insatiable desire for knowledge and experimentation. And like Faust, when the devil came calling, Vesper was ready to surrender for the opportunity of unlocking physiological and neurological mysteries that were perhaps better left in the realm of God. Bellamy had offered not only a handsome paypacket to do his bidding but also unfettered and unsupervised freedom to do what he wished with his patients—as long as the outcome proved ultimately useful. Vesper was wise enough not to inquire too closely as to the nature of Bellamy's plans. Knowledge was a dangerous commodity.

As for the personal events in India, he didn't know anymore. What was another child lost in the millions swallowed up in poverty and starvation and disease? Few white men would spend even an instant's time in consideration of a misbegotten by-blow, the sorry result of miscegenation. All he did know was that his nerves were nearing the breaking point, the enervation of fatigue overtaking him. What he would do to be able to drift to sleep, consoling himself that at least he had survived another day. He feared sleep now, his home too quiet. In the distance he imagined his neighbors, and some distance away, he thought he heard a woman crying, or perhaps it was a child.

He stopped his pacing, listening to the creaking of the floorboards beneath his feet. If he paid heed, he imagined that he could hear a low moan coming from the depths of the cellar beneath the kitchen. Cursing swiftly under his breath although there was no one to hear, he wondered if he was loosening his grip on reason. A story he had read recently came suddenly and annoyingly to mind, a tale that had conjured the specter of a telltale heart beating beneath the floorboards, the fretful conscience of a murderer.

Ridiculous, fanciful nonsense. Almost without realizing it, Vesper again found his clammy fist clenched around the watch in his pocket. He of all people recognized that the haunting was the product of a diseased mind, of a psyche overwhelmed with guilt and remorse.

Another low moan, like a branch listing in a heavy wind. It was quite impossible. He had given the man enough laudanum to keep him subdued. The gunshot wound had narrowly missed its mark, and the man had bled profusely before Vesper had been able to staunch the blood. The damp, cold cellar was not the ideal place for someone in his condition, but it was the only area in the house—containing his laboratory and medical implements—that was not open to his housekeeper and scullery maid.

The scullery maid. Dear God, Lizzie. He hadn't even inquired after her surname. His eyes filled from an excess of emotion and he removed his spectacles to wipe at them uselessly, smearing the lenses with his sweat and guilt. If she died, he would not see her in a pauper's grave and, if he had the chance, he would see to a proper burial. The very least he could do.

The moaning was more audible now, his punishment no longer the fancy of his imagination but the keening of a man in pain. His eyes darted to his doctor's bag, the leather scuffed and worn, sitting forlornly in the entrance hall. It held the instruments of his trade, a bottle of laudanum, and a syringe.

A few ounces more would surely not make a difference. And then he could get some much needed rest, far away from this inner torment whose tentacles were digging themselves, inexorably and relentlessly, into the innermost reaches of his increasingly febrile mind.

He shuffled to the narrow hallway and grabbed the bag. It felt solid and reassuring in his hands. Drawing himself up straight, he gripped the handle securely before making his final decision. Moments later, he disappeared down the darkened cellar stairs.

Chapter 4

Lilly Clarence Hampton was being watched.

Impossible. The barred windows of the Salt Tower, located in the Tower of London, reflected back only the darkness of the night and her bone-pale complexion. Iciness emanated from the worn granite beneath her feet, and behind her, obscured by layers of shadow, she had moments earlier discovered an antechamber, a small circular room with just one small window cut into the thick wall. It had stopped snowing, but she could not control a shiver against the damp and her knowledge of history. Queen Elizabeth had sent several Jesuit priests here to die, and if Lilly cared to look, which she didn't, their last desperate scrawls were inscribed in the cold and implacable stones just several feet away.

If she cared to look, which she certainly did not. Hundreds of years of history promulgated ghost stories, of course. She clutched her reticule firmly. So what that even dogs refused to enter the edifice? Ghosts, real or imagined—she'd had enough of them.

Ignoring the sensation of heat drilling through the cashmere of her shawl and directly through to the center of her back, she turned to the object in the glass case surrounded by thick iron bars. It glowed sullenly, a multifaceted ostrich egg to her eyes, a stone that very probably dated from before the time of Christ. And for which many had died for stakes that were entirely too high.

Because whoever owned the Koh-I-Noor diamond ruled the world. Or so it was said. Koh-I-Noor, Mountain of Light, the most famous diamond in history, in its original one-hundred-eighty-six-carat form, rested here now in the Tower of London. She read the inscription disclosed to the right of the display case.

The Koh-I-Noor. Its value is Good Fortune, for whoever possesses it has been superior to all his enemies.

Politics and power, always a dirty business, now allied with superstition in the wondrous form of a gemstone. How many more would covet it, die for it?

Pinpricks danced up her spine. The sensation of being watched. She pulled her shawl closer to her body and surveyed her surroundings for at least the tenth time. The blackness of the night, outlined by the lone window, couldn't hope to penetrate the circular room. She was in the third floor of the tower, at least two hundred feet from the ground. No spying eyes could possibly see . . .

Guilt was a toxic companion, accompanying her everywhere.

Lilly straightened her spine. A nervous disposition was definitely not permitted. She had no patience for weak, fainting women, their stays pulled too tightly for anybody's good, their minds closed to logic and good sense. What she needed was a vigorous walk through Hyde Park, a rousing debate, or perhaps another evening spent with Isambard Kingdom Bellamy.

The diamond winked back at her. Mockingly.

She resumed her pacing, making a deliberate circle around the glass case, restraining her emotions with the customary discipline that had become as necessary to her life as breathing. Every few steps, she looked over her shoulder toward the door, fighting a gnawing anxiety. Bellamy was to have met her here this evening, to show her the diamond personally, expound on its history, its infamous significance. When she'd first arrived, almost one hour after midnight, the guards at the entrance had been nonplussed, ushering her up the damp, circular stairs, no wider than a child's crib, despite her lack of illustrious companion.

She leaned in toward the glass case, studying the diamond closely. The architectural drawings of the Crystal Palace rose clearly in her mind, the soaring ceilings and the expanse of open space that were designed to welcome not only thousands of expectant visitors from near and far to London's Great Exhibition, but also the historic diamond.

The muscles on the back of her neck tightened. She tapped a tattoo with one finger on the glass case. Too accessible. That was the problem. While the building design, radical and revolutionary, echoed the diamond's faceted form, it would be next to impossible to protect the Koh-I-Noor and its presentation before the world to Queen Victoria at the opening of the Crystal Palace. It would be a historic occasion in commemoration of May 29, 1849, when the British flag was hoisted on the citadel of Lahore and the Punjab was formally proclaimed part of the British Empire in India.

As she had been apprised, the gem, which had been taken from Shah Shuja-ul-Mulk, would be surrendered by the Maharajah of Lahore to the Queen of England, by the hand of the chairman of the British East India Company, Isambard Kingdom Bellamy. A momentous event for the empire.

She continued her measured pacing. Other than the sound of her footsteps, the tower was silent. Yet her ears strained for what exactly—Bellamy's arrival? The sensation of eyes boring into the back of her head refused to relinquish its hold. She glanced at the darkened antechamber behind her and then at the door, a thick iron grille separating her and the sentry guarding the diamond from the outside world. She was alone and she was protected. Although it wasn't at all like Bellamy to allow himself to be delayed. He was prompt, attentive, and unfailingly courteous, a protective port in the storm that had become her life.

The face of Isambard Kingdom Bellamy momentarily blotted out the diamond encased in glass and iron. The other evening, at the Adelphi Theatre when they'd shared a glass of champagne, she had to admit that there was more to his attentiveness than simple friendship and that, somehow over the past year, they had been drifting toward courtship, their association taking on a new and stronger dimension. A long-time business associate of Charles's, Bellamy was not well known to her during the course of her marriage, other than in a social sense. But he had made himself readily available to her after the tragedy with kind words and a patient benevolence that she had never encountered before. Not that she had ever been a good judge of character, Lord only knew. After Charles, self-doubt was a troublesome attendant. The last thing she needed to do at the moment was to question why Bellamy would find interest in a widow, with an unimpressive family background, who had been absurdly and unfashionably in love with her late husband.

Her mouth thinned and she adjusted her shawl. Bellamy, for whatever reasons, demonstrated only the best of intentions toward her. He was a powerful man, and if she required further evidence, she needed only to remember how neatly he'd dispatched the inspector at Covent Gardens a fortnight earlier. Insistent, disrespectful, and very public with his inquiries, the inspector had made it clear that he was a terrier with a bone, ferocious and implacable. Until he had met with the wolfhound that was Bellamy who, with a low snarl, had sent the man packing. She had not been harassed since, not a coincidence, surely. Bellamy's influence reached to the highest corridors of government, and a single word could definitively halt an entire army on the other side of the world, not to mention an inconsequential investigation.

Marriage to him would mean she could continue her work discreetly. As with most men, he was vaguely supportive of her pursuits, and that was enough, more than enough. He spent most of his time with his vast business concerns in India, a situation that would translate into a measure of freedom for her. And security. No one would dare cast aspersions . . . the rumors would stop. She took a breath against the tightness around her heart. Then she—and the world—could forget the death of Charles Hampton.

The lights flickered strangely. A breeze perhaps snaking its way through one of the barred windows. The Tower was not yet outfitted with gas fixtures, the tall candles dripping wax on the cold stone floor. The outlines of her profile etched eerily against the glass case, she deliberately returned her attention to the diamond, shutting out memories, too painful and too dangerous. When she looked up again, she saw the face hovering over hers.

Haggard and masculine, stopping the breath in her lungs.

This was no ghost. A heavy arm roped around her neck and shoulders, pulling her back toward a hard chest.

"Obscene." The low whisper was hot menace in her ear. No time for thought, she clawed instinctively and ineffectually at the solid muscles of an arm. Reflected in the glass, his eyes glittered strangely, dark as onyx. Her head felt light, and her reticule, clamped in her hand, slid to the floor.

Her body frozen, her mind skittered with hundreds of possibilities. *Obscene.* Her eyes returned to the Koh-I-Noor. He was referring to the diamond. "What do you want?" The barely managed words were hoarse, strangulated.

He dragged her away from the glass case and toward the small antechamber behind them. Plunged into medieval gloom, she could make out three missing bars from the lone window in the room, weak moonlight the only source of illumination. Realization dawned, inconceivable as it was indisputable. The man had scaled two hundred feet in the dark.

She didn't know whether she'd cursed under her breath or aloud. "Let go of me—I can scarcely breathe." As if that should matter to him.

Trapped at such an awkward angle, her stays were gnawing into her abdomen, her breath coming in halting pants.

But he refused to relinquish his hold. Anger was beginning to replace the numbing fear in the pit of her stomach.

"See reason." Words were the only weapon she had, and she knew how to use them. "There's a guard standing outside the door and he's expecting me to emerge at some point." Her mind did summersaults. "And then there are the soldiers at the entrance of the Tower, and in all probability an even greater number inside."

"I know." The simple statement, filled with supreme unconcern, chilled her more than any knife or pistol could.

Her elbow jammed his ribcage, barely registering. There wasn't an ounce of padding on the man, save ridged sinew and bone separated by a few layers of leather and fabric. She took a ragged breath, his scent strangely neutral, soap and skin. Her careening thoughts slid to a halt.

It was the diamond he wanted. The diamond he believed obscene.

"Take it and see how far you get." She could not even sway her body against his, her arms pinned helplessly at her sides. Her anger burned brighter. "You must be a madman to think you could break into the Tower of London and make off with the Koh-I-Noor." She'd just sputtered utter nonsense. He'd already penetrated the Tower, beyond the phalanx of soldiers and guards who protected the Crown Jewels with their lives.

What kind of man was this? She commanded herself to be still, to tamp down her fury, marshaling her thoughts. Once long ago, she'd attended a naturalist's lecture, a scientist who had blithely categorized the human species as simply another animal. And at this moment, in the damp and in the dark, she knew his theory to be true. Because every particle of her being, from her cold skin to her rigid body, told her that she was a hairbreadth away from a death as meaningless as that of stalked prey on an open plain.

"You believe I want the diamond." The hot whisper in her ear again. The heavy walls of the small antechamber were suffocating, closing in around her, the stranger holding her so closely that she thought any moment their two bodies would merge. She shut her eyes against the renewed shock, and inexplicably, the image of Charles floated into her awareness. A harbinger of death. Her Charles with his soft brown hair and benign gaze. She had been so young when they'd married and he so poetic, so artistic, and so handsome. Dry tears burned behind her eyelids. The room around her faded away, the pain of the past smothering.

"Perhaps I want something else."

Charles vanished. Her eyes snapped open and the earth beneath her feet lifted as the band of steel around her neck and shoulder gave way. She struggled to recover her balance, legs unsteady, combs falling from her hair, one by one to the floor.

Her vision steadied, the chalky moonlight illuminating the small chamber. A few inches separated them. He stood almost a foot taller than she with broad shoulders and a hardened musculature that had only moments ago been pressed against her body. Clean shaven, sporting neither beard nor muttonchops, he pilloried her with his eyes, so dark and penetrating, Lilly took a step back.

"What is it that you want?" Panic crowded out the possibilities, one more horrendous than the next. Black breeches and shirt matched his expression. He was a fallen Lucifer, the hardened set of his jaw and the lines bracketing the sides of his wide mouth telling a story she didn't want to hear. A savaged, ravaged face, telling her he had nothing to lose.

He was no longer touching her but it didn't seem to matter. "What I require is you. Willing or not, is immaterial to me."

Without looking behind her, she sensed the door to the small antechamber would be closed tightly. "Me? Why me?" She repeated the words blindly, heedless now of the fall of hair around her face. She grasped at options, one more impossible than the next. "If you believe that I will help you with your foolish plan to steal the diamond, you're mad. And as though I even could."

He shrugged. "You can and you will."

She wiped a strand of hair back from her face. "Whoever you are—this high-handedness is positively risible, as though you could do, say, or threaten me with anything that would in any way assist you. I will not help you steal the Koh-I-Noor."

"If I wanted to steal it, it would be already gone," he said implacably. "Right out from under your superior nose." He advanced toward her in the already enclosed space. "I said it's you I'm interested in at the moment. The diamond may come later."

"You must have the wrong individual," she tried. "I am not the person you are looking for."

"I believe that you're deliberately misunderstanding me. For your own purposes. As though you may have something to hide. Am I right, Mrs. Hampton?"

She felt the blood drain from her face. He knew her name. She searched his expression frantically, noting the too-long hair, black as ink, scraped untidily back from his forehead. "What can I possibly provide you with?" she asked with a desperate tilt of her chin.

He pretended to smile, the flash of teeth white in the darkened room. "You have the plans for the Crystal Palace. The architectural plans."

She jerked as though she'd been struck, his statement taking her in an entirely new and even more dangerous direction. "What of them?" she asked, lowering her voice, rubbing her arms through the soft cashmere of her shawl. "And they are not my plans," she lied. "They belong to my late husband and are presently unavailable."

"Are they now?" His eyes, dark and fathomless, glittered with knowledge.

Suddenly, she thought of the guard behind the grillwork of

the Salt Tower's door, and desperately hoped he wouldn't intervene. Nor, dear God, Bellamy. It would only make matters worse, multiply the complications. She'd made her decision one year ago, lived with it, lived with the blood on her hands.

"It's irrelevant whether you believe me or not." She took a step backward until she was only two feet from the window, now stripped of its bars, and she had a wild thought that he meant to throw her over the ledge and onto the cobblestones below.

"This might be the time to tell you that I have a bad temper." It was as though he could read her fevered mind. For emphasis, he moved in closer, crunching one of her tortoise-shell combs underfoot. A gift from Charles, she thought wildly, irrationally. Now her only choice was to decide between the broadest shoulders she had ever seen and the window. Falling to her death would be preferable to meeting it at his hands.

Moonlight lit his face, throwing into sharp relief the hard plane of a jaw, the strong nose. A small scar sat above his right eyebrow. Backing up one more step, she felt the cold stone ledge through her shawl and dress to her corset and chemise.

She stopped breathing because she could go no farther and because something told her that he knew. *He knew*.

He smiled again, more chilling than the cold coming off the flagstone floor. "I see we've reached an understanding. How fortunate for you and me both."

She dug her nails into her palms in the vain hope she could keep the truth at bay. But she couldn't because he wouldn't let her.

"I will do anything," she whispered.

"I thought as much," he said, holding her gaze for the longest moment before nodding a grudging consent. "Yours is a perfectly reasonable response—for a wife who murdered her beloved husband. In cold blood."

Chapter 5

His skull hurt like a bastard. A thousand sharpened knives carved their way from the inside of his head out. St. Martin passed a heavy hand over his face, aware of the woman pressed up against the heavy stone wall regarding him as though he'd materialized along with the stench of brimstone.

At first he'd thought her plain in her stiff dress, spine pulled up straight like a marionette, her hair tamed into a strict chignon. But now, upon closer inspection and even through the blinding headache, he saw something else entirely.

Beautiful no, unusual yes. The lips too wide and full, the eyes with their elegant brows, clear and all too keen. And she was thin, from what he'd thought he'd felt when he'd hauled her up against him, beneath the myriad stays and crinolines of her mourning garb.

By this point, he'd have expected her to faint dead away. Lord knew, he was close to it, the hammer behind his head continuing its unrelenting blows. But then she was a murderess. And they clearly didn't succumb to the vapors.

"You were saying," he said with mocking gallantry, "that I could have anything."

Still pressed against the stone, she opened her mouth to utter something and then thought otherwise. Her face registered shock and the markings of desperation borne by guilt. About which he knew a great deal, the corrosiveness of its essence, how it could eat away at a life until there was nothing left save a hollowed-out bitterness.

Liberating in its own way, he thought cynically. Once the rubicon had been crossed, acts of duplicity and degeneracy became second nature, the devil as best friend. He wondered whether this was already the case with Mrs. Hampton.

"I find there's nothing like drama to focus the attention." Although it was impossible, she edged closer to the wall, the jet beads of her dress scraping against stone. "You seem distinctly uncomfortable given the circumstances. Perhaps we can discuss your options further elsewhere," he said.

Some color was returning to her face, now as gray as the granite behind her. "Of course. Elsewhere." The prospect of escape, when there was none.

He didn't care if his smile reached his eyes. "Your house in Mayfair comes to mind."

"You know where I live?"

"I know everything there is to know about you." Particularly the details around her dear, departed husband. The pounding behind his eyes increased, telling him to get the hell out of the Tower and back into the fresh night air. "By way of introduction, my name is St. Martin," he said, refusing to give into the pain.

Her eyes widened at the information as she attempted to place him and his family in the pantheon of connections that was London. She would glean very little of substance, the barest outlines, as he had made sure that most of his life was lived in the shadows.

"Lord St. Martin," she said softly, pushing away from the wall at last, as though his aristocratic associations, under the guise of gentlemanly behavior, should make any difference to her sense of safety. Lilly Clarence Hampton could not imagine the worst of it, he thought.

She seemed to be pulling herself together, restoring her sense of equilibrium, challenging a peer of the realm who would, after all, behave with a semblance of honor. The delusion was particularly pitiable.

"Why do you believe I murdered my husband?" In the moonlight, her hair shone a dark gold. She was younger than she'd first appeared, the angle of the light falling across smooth skin only lightly marred with shadows. "Surely you followed the investigation. An intruder entered our home and, upon Mr. Hampton apprehending him, he produced a pistol and . . ." She paused for a reason or effect, he couldn't tell.

"And shot him in the chest," he concluded for her. "Yes, I recall the details of the investigation, including the fact that there were no signs of forced entry, no footprints, and no proverbial smoking revolver."

Her shawl had slid from her shoulders to her waist, and she gathered it back up around her shoulders, her movements graceful despite her obvious fear. "And you dare to imply that I murdered my husband? And what evidence could you possibly have?"

He casually bent over to pick up first one and then a second of her combs from the floor, slipping them into his vest pocket. "Your reaction a moment ago, for one. As I recall, you said you would do anything. Not the response of an innocent woman."

"Anything not to relinquish the architectural plans, my lord." Her lips curled in annoyance. "You have misinterpreted my response."

"I'm not so sure. And you can jettison the honorific. St. Martin is enough." More than enough. "What if I told you that I had the pistol. Your pistol, to be exact. In my possession."

However fine a murderess she might be, she wasn't an actress. This time she came toward him, fear supplanted by anger. So close that he could see a fine pulse jump at the base of her slender neck barely revealed by a froth of black tulle. "I would say that you are lying," she said, scarcely a foot separating them. "I would ask you to present me with the evidence, is what I would say."

She was hardly the dry, brittle widow he'd anticipated. He wondered if Bellamy knew. "With pleasure. And with the full intention of relinquishing it to you in exchange for the architectural plans."

Her eyes captured his, a stunning, clear blue, and it occurred to him suddenly that Lilly Hampton would not be readily subdued. When it came to opponents, he was never wrong.

"Where would you like to make the exchange," she asked steadily. And he didn't believe her for an instant. She would return to look for her pistol, supposedly secreted away, only to find it missing.

He smiled grimly. "Tomorrow evening. At your home in Mayfair."

She swallowed hard and her breathing was heavy with a combination of impatience and fear. Pushing her hair back from her face, she said, "I have plans for the evening. It will have to be another time."

"Of course. How could I forget? Your assignation with Mr. Bellamy? Are nuptials in the offing or is this a simple affaire?"

Her eyes darkened, blue turning to a storm gray. He could tell that all she wanted to do was yell, throw something at his head, choke him with that ridiculous shawl falling across her shoulders. Instead, she took a steadying breath. "Your aspersions are reprehensible and not worth my consideration."

"Ah yes, the matronly airs." He wanted to see how simple it would be to provoke her. "Although it would only stand to reason that you would be prepared to spread your legs for his protection, one of the wealthiest and most powerful men in the realm, after all. And a close associate of your late husband's, if the rumors are correct." Despite the personal insult and stinging insinuation, his tone was as even as that of a barrister from the West End.

In an instant the tightly coiled, elegantly controlled widow was gone. She opened her mouth to scream, fingers curling into fists at her side. Her first mistake and he calculated that it would not be her last.

Before she could make a sound, he'd dragged her flush against him, his hand clamping over her mouth. The shawl fell to the floor as she shoved against his chest trying to break the contact. He lifted her off her feet and carried her back to the Tower room, pushing her up against the edge of the glass case. The diamond gleamed spectacularly as he enclosed her thrashing arms and legs with his torso. Avoiding her knee to his groin, he deftly shifted aside.

"What's the difference, precisely, Mrs. Hampton, between Bellamy and me? Between what he wants of you and what I want of you?" Not waiting for an answer, he lowered his face to hers, the blue of her eyes more vivid than the facets of the diamond behind them. He was strong, too strong, positioning his body over hers and pinning her hands over her head with one arm.

Her breathing was fractured beneath the heavy stays of her dress. "I don't believe it's a good idea, your screaming," he said, whispering a fraction away from her mouth, removing his hand. "You should know far better than I."

"You are disgusting." She hissed the words. "Leave me be. . . ." She attempted to scramble away but it was impossible. Her breath was warm against his skin, the scent of rosewater and fear a peculiar aphrodisiac. Not what he expected at all from the young widow, his reaction, this sudden and unmistakable hardening in his breeches. Even under all the ruching, the bombazine, the stays, and the corset, he could feel her body writhing against his. He saw her eyes darken a moment before he covered her mouth with his.

It stopped her words. It stopped her breath and he hoped it would stop her thoughts. His tongue slipped into the heat of her mouth while he ground his hips to push her roughly against the glass case. He felt the stays beneath her dress shifting as he slanted his lips to kiss her more deeply, more thoroughly, to obliterate her will.

He couldn't tell if she tried to pull away, because it was impossible, his weight holding her fast, his mouth an unrelenting assault. First hard, then soft, what began as an attack became something else.

The pounding behind his eyes receded as his right hand burned its way down her throat, the angle of a shoulder beneath the tightly sheathed fabric, the underside of her breast hidden away beneath the stiffness of an unforgiving corset. Her lips softened, a white flag, as his mouth continued its sensual assault, his hands his weapon.

She moaned, in desire or surrender, it didn't matter. Reason told him this shouldn't be happening, that this stiff, unyielding woman shouldn't be able to ignite mindless lust in a man who had given up on such things long ago. And yet he was feeding on her tongue, her mouth, her lips, ensuring she felt overwhelmed by his size, his power, his force.

Their desire mingled and St. Martin felt her chest against his own take several unsteady breaths as his lips wandered to her neck, the only exposed skin on her body, trailing heat just behind her left ear. She exhaled sharply, yielding to his mouth snaking along her jawline, brushing and then returning to hover again over her lips.

And suddenly he stopped, the silk of her hair roped in his palm, reminding him of something, someone. The ties that bind, he thought, the heavy pounding in his head returning with the steadiness of a distant drumbeat. He couldn't recall when he'd last been with a woman, or more brutally, he didn't care to remember. The heavy silk that he now gripped in his palm burned.

He wanted out and he wanted the cleansing breath of night air. Now. He let go of the woman in his arms but held her with his eyes, looking for submission of another kind.

She didn't make a sound. Slowly he moved away from her, still caging her body, still holding her prisoner. She stared at the profile above her, pale as linen save for the crimson of her lips.

When she still didn't move or say a word, he said, "I'll explain. Tomorrow evening," he added, reading her mind. "After Bellamy."

He stepped back and he could see confusion and fear imprinted on her face, wondering if she had hallucinated their embrace moments ago. The secretive and unbending widow and the savage and wounded man. He wondered himself.

The damp fetid air was a contagion in the enclosed space, the diamond glistening, overt in its shameless beauty, behind them. The widow licked her parted lips and he almost looked away.

Reason had reasserted itself. "You cannot have the plans," she said softly, decisively. Her trembling hands uselessly attempted to pull her hair back into place. "I won't allow it." A curtain of heavy gold obscured her face.

"We will speak of it tomorrow. Remember. You have no options." He shoved a hand into his vest pocket and produced two of her ivory combs. Without asking permission, he once again closed the space between them and, despite her startled gasp, pulled her hair away from her face. Exposed, she couldn't help but feel his gaze linger on her eyes, her lips, the curve of her neck.

She held her breath, watching as, with careful gentleness, he traced the outlines of her features, his long fingers lingering against her skin before anchoring her hair, almost reluctantly, with first one and then the second comb. The gesture more shocking than the violence of his kiss.

She stood motionless under his ministrations, eyes wide and searching, wariness shot through with distrust. For him, and most of all, for herself.

"Go," he said when he finished, pushing her toward the

door with its heavy grille, the soldier still positioned outside. "And remember," the warning deliberately cruel in cold contrast to the heat of his touch, "you're a murderess."

And before she could respond, he strode out the room and was swallowed by the doorway leading to the antechamber. The small window with its loosened bars beckoned, offering the solace of cold night air and unforgiving cobblestones two hundred feet below. He didn't look back.

Quickly securing the rope to the remaining bar, he leaped over the sill, not for the first time wishing for death but realizing fate was seldom so kind.

Chapter 6

The applause, a reverberating clap of thunder, rumbled and rolled through the Haymarket Theatre, the audience demonstrating its delight with *The Road to Ruin*, a farce that had most of London buzzing.

As the lights rose for the first interval, Lilly leaned back in the plush velvet seat of Isambard Kingdom Bellamy's private box, going through the motions of clapping, her hands cold in black lace evening gloves. She observed Bellamy's profile discreetly, the retreating hairline and the bold nose set above narrowed lips and full mustache. A handsome countenance all in all, she convinced herself as he met her gaze with a generous smile.

"Are you enjoying yourself, my dear?" he asked, once the thunder had subsided and the audience was beginning to shift from their seats to the splendid atrium offering champagne and ices and juicy tidbits of gossip. He took in her dark green satin dress with its flounced skirt and demure lace-trimmed neckline as befitted one in the late stages of mourning. Bellamy patted her hand approvingly, his touch dry and impartial.

"Wonderful play," she murmured. "And Sarah Woolgar's talents are quite remarkable." She had not been able to keep her attention on the farce, her own personal drama intruding—the searing memory of a man and a woman and a dia-

mond playing before her eyes on center stage. She'd imagined
it all, or so she wanted to believe. And yet when she'd returned to her townhome on Mayfair early that morning, her
small pistol was gone as promised. St. Martin had been in her
private rooms, finding the weapon secreted away up the fireplace
flue. The knowledge of a stranger rifling through her personal
things was beyond belief, and she shivered, despite the layers
of crinolines and chemises insulating her.

She wanted to forget that sharply planed face, haggard
and austere, and that tall, tightly coiled body whose imprint
still burned against her skin. There had been the touch of
demon in his stealthy menace, a trace of night and saltpeter.
St. Martin had looked as though he'd been to hell and back—
and eager to take her with him.

She unclenched her jaw. It was ludicrous. He had no
proof—even with the pistol supposedly in his possession.
And there would be no more opportune encounters, as she
had already instructed her servants not to answer the door this
evening or the next. It was simply a matter of avoiding the
man and his strange intensity that, if she was entirely honest
with herself, pointed to an unstable and eccentric character.
He was hardly reliable, as Seabourne had described him, a
man whose reason had become undone.

Lilly straightened a flounce on her voluminous skirts, wondering just who was the unstable one. She didn't want to remember those moments trapped in his arms. And, in particular,
she didn't want to remember her response to his mouth on hers.

Although her hands were cold, the air around her seemed
stifling. Suddenly eager to leave the privacy of the box, she made
to rise, the wide hem of her skirt impeding her progress. "I am
quite parched," she murmured by way of excuse to Bellamy.
"A lovely, cool ice would do nicely."

Bellamy rose in tandem, disentangling her skirt from the
curved legs of the settee. "I shall have it brought immediately." He was all solicitousness, a gleaming host in his dove
gray evening coat. Ruby cuff links shimmered against the

pristine white of his shirtsleeves as he gently but definitively motioned her back into her seat. He gestured to the major domo who stood behind them in the shadows, the young man disappearing an instant later.

"Thank you. You are too kind, Mr. Bellamy," she said, hiding her eagerness to quit the small space. "Truly, you do too much." From the carriage that had collected her from Mayfair to the best loggia in the theater, her companion had set about charming her with a businesslike ferocity that was his calling card.

He beamed, his ruddy face almost the same crimson shade of the red velvet that draped the private box. "My dear, all of what I have is nothing unless I have someone to share it with. And I must apologize again for not keeping our rendezvous yesterday evening at the Tower. Inexcusable on my part, but certain business dealings had to be attended to. I so much wanted to show you the Koh-I-Noor myself, given that our offices had it transported from India."

"You must be very proud," she said, her mind reluctantly returning to the Tower room.

"Indeed. The Koh-I-Noor left the shores of India on board the HMS *Medea*," Bellamy supplied, his barrel chest puffed with pride. "So shrouded in mystery was its departure that even the captain of the *Medea* did not know the precious cargo his ship carried. I ensured every possible security."

"Quite the responsibility, the British East India Company taking on the duty for such an important undertaking."

"All the more reason that I wanted to show the diamond to you personally. Before the hordes have their chance at the opening of the Crystal Palace." He paused. "And I believed, if you'll forgive me, that the venue last evening would provide us with a somewhat more personal, even, dare I say, romantic backdrop." He took a deep breath, the buttons on his waistcoat straining, waiting for her response.

For some reason that she didn't care to analyze, Lilly wished to change the subject, and so kept her expression deliberately vague, allowing his opening to slide by. A shrewd man, Bellamy let out a sigh, detecting her unease. "But enough of that for now. And by the by, you must call me King, what with all the time we've already spent together. Not to mention the good relations that I shared with your late husband, Charles."

Appraising him over the playbill in her hand, she decided that Isambard Kingdom Bellamy reminded her of the overstuffed, taxidermied bears that she'd seen in the collection of the Royal Geographic Society. Formidable and dangerous if awakened. Which was precisely what she needed. He had helped Charles in the past and now he would keep her own troubles at bay. "No apologies necessary, King," she said in a light voice. "We shall have another opportunity to view the gem together I'm certain." She sat back in her seat. Although he had made no move to come closer or to touch her again, she felt that they were sharing the same, all too intimate, breath.

Her response was irrational, irritating. She needed to defuse her tension by trying to focus on something else. "I adore this theater," she said, her gaze sweeping admiringly from the lofty ceiling with its sparkling chandeliers to the picture frame proscenium. "John Nash is one of my favorite architects, and I never fail to appreciate how he designed this area so that the front Corinthian portico can be seen from St. James Square."

Bellamy patted her hand and this time she almost flinched. "In any other woman less beautiful, such learning and preoccupation would render her a bluestocking. Of course, I understand your love of architecture comes from your association with your late husband, no doubt. He often shared with me the details of the various projects that required his prodigious and, might I say, passionate attention."

No doubt. Lilly pretended to concentrate on the coved ceiling with its classically strict lines rather than dwell on Charles and his passions a moment longer. Then laughing lightly and deliberately, she said, "I'm hardly beautiful, Mr. Bellamy—I meant to say, King," she hastily corrected herself. "And given your association with my late husband, I hope you don't feel compelled or obligated to spend time with me."

His brows raised in surprise. "Compelled? Obligated? My dear, I am most eager to extend any protection I can, given your situation," he continued diplomatically.

Protection. She looked away from Bellamy and over the balcony to see the last of the theatergoers filing from their seats, reassured that she had not glimpsed an errant inspector in their midst. She was jittery these days, a strange pattern of anxiety creeping into her mind and possessing it like a noisome disease. She would do anything to make it stop, to halt the guilt, to expiate her sins and do penance for her monstrous transgression. The monies from the Crystal Palace commission would be given to charity, and she would invest every ounce of her talent into ensuring the final design would honor the queen and her country.

Her eyes darted into the corners of the now-empty hall, looking for something that she could not see. Momentarily relieved, she forced herself to consider once again the man at her side. She arranged her face into a smile. "If I haven't said it before," she began, "I should express again my gratitude to your coming to my assistance at Covent Gardens. Had you not come to my aid—" The sentence remained unfinished.

Bellamy snorted, punctuating the air between them with a blunt forefinger. "The insufferable cur! Imagine the audacity, the temerity to accost a woman on my arm. And such slander! You may not realize it, my dear, but you do require a man's protection, as the last few unsavory incidents attest."

She actually envied Bellamy's confidence in her, so convinced was he of her innocence and so at the ready to use everything at his disposal to come to her defense. He was everything a woman could wish for and more, and yet her instincts contradicted her at every turn. Noticing that the major domo had yet to reappear with the ices, she felt they were more alone than ever in the shadows of the box, the intimacy strangely discomfiting.

Bellamy frowned dramatically. "You are a woman single and defenseless, and I know your departed husband would not wish you to continue without a partner at your side and what with these heinous accusations clinging to you like thorns to a rose. He would only have your best interests at heart. I had sincerely hoped that, given the appropriate amount of time, we would have more of an arrangement based on a burgeoning mutual respect and affection."

He continued making his case, settling his bulk in his chair more comfortably, warming to the subject. "And as you well know, a man like myself having spent many years in India overseeing the welfare of the British East India Company, well, I simply didn't have the time to turn my attentions to a wife and family. And you, of course, robbed of your husband at so tender an age . . ." He shook his head and turned to her earnestly, his delivery as smooth as an actor's final rehearsal. "We discover ourselves at a juncture," he pronounced grandly, "wherein we are fortunate to find salubrious companionship."

She didn't believe him, not for a moment. Although well into middle age, Bellamy could have had any one of the far more beautiful and malleable young girls on this year's marriage mart. There was something distinctly unsettling about his interest in her and yet, given her present situation, the fact should account for very little. Mr. Isambard Kingdom Bellamy could well be the answer to her prayers. Except that she didn't believe in prayer. Not anymore.

Out of the ether, she heard an echo of St. Martin's words. *What's the difference, precisely, Mrs. Hampton, between Bellamy and me? Between what he wants of you and what I want of you?* The question hovered intangibly in the air, but she knew she was right to be afraid of the answer.

"My dear, Mr. . . . I mean to say, King." She began feeling as though she should say something, not quite knowing what she wanted and why she was fighting so hard to keep this man—potentially her salvation—at a distance. "Perhaps we are advancing too rapidly, given my period of mourning is hardly at end."

Ironic that lately it was the specter of Charles she brandished whenever she felt too close to the precipice.

Bellamy raised his brows again. "We are both adults, are we not, Mrs. Hampton? Hardly in the first flush of youth and, therefore, it is entirely natural that we are eager to proceed with our lives." He cleared his throat importantly the way he might address his shareholders, leaning toward her to drive home his point. "I had wanted to delay this moment until a more suitable venue presented itself, but since we're hardly foolish young romantics, you and I, I shall come to the point."

Lilly held her breath, working her reticule between nervous palms on her lap while he reached into the silk-lined jacket of his evening coat. A small, velvet box emerged in his large hands, workman's hands, she thought irrationally, with their blunt fingers and broad palms. He opened the box.

It was a snake ring, set with diamonds and rubies the size of strawberries, the serpent symbol, she recognized, representing eternity. It was well known that Queen Victoria wore her own snake ring in recognition of her love for Albert. Each serpent, it was said, symbolized the bride and groom, intertwined and demonstrating the mutual communion of love.

Lilly swallowed and reluctantly looked up from the ring to meet Bellamy's focused gaze, his eyes almost lost beneath his heavy brow. She had to say something, to respond. It was expected, at the very least. "It's lovely. Wonderful," she said, licking her dry lips, foolishly aware that she should add something more. Her mind had stopped working.

"Not the Koh-I-Noor precisely." Bellamy barked a short laugh. He reached for her left hand and slowly peeled back the tight lace. His touch was strangely impersonal and her reaction just as cold. Perversely, the ring slid on her third finger perfectly.

"It's beautiful," she repeated, mesmerized by the winking stones now nestled against her skin.

"Are you accepting my offer of marriage, my dearest Lilly?"

She knew she should. Unbidden, another face lingered in her mind's eye. St. Martin. And his threats. His unreliable past and unreliable character. She didn't dare think about what this man wanted with the architectural plans for the Crystal Palace. To steal the Koh-I-Noor? Blinking, she looked directly at Bellamy, the man who would move heaven and Earth to protect her. As his wife.

She clasped his hand in her cold one. "I will," she said quietly as the air around them began to stir once again. Bellamy rose from his chair to bend down to kiss her lightly on the cheek, his cologne of bergamot and sandalwood enveloping her. So different from . . . She did not permit herself to finish the thought.

Efficient and purposeful, he launched onward, the argument won and the matter neatly settled in his mind. "A wedding breakfast, I thought, if that meets with your approval." The words drifted away into a fog. Bellamy was speaking, already organizing their lives, and she clearly wasn't following. Feeling momentarily lightheaded, she removed her hand from his.

"Whatever you prefer, King," she said, her mind closing off the future. How could she be doing this? Her work was important as was her freedom, but to marry a man one didn't love? The skin of her neck prickled. Of course, she thought she'd loved Charles and the results had been a catastrophe of historic proportion. Her stomach clenched at the memory. She would not risk again.

"I will leave the details to you. Something discreet," Bellamy continued, settling back in his chair. "We will have my cook oversee perhaps a menu of stewed oysters, galantines, mayonnaise of fowl, cold game, pyramids . . ."

She nodded mutely, the deed done, unaware until a moment later that the major domo had reappeared, without the ices, from behind the heavy velvet drapes cordoning the private box. He looked stricken and leaned over to murmur something to Bellamy.

The older man, palms on his knees, galvanized to his feet. Buttoning his waistcoat, he asked, "Why, that's impossible. Are you quite certain?" He frowned, watching the younger man back out of the box as quickly as he could but deferential to the last.

Something was wrong.

"Lilly—we must depart now." Without waiting for her reply, he stepped aside and ushered her from her seat and forward through the theater box exit. A quick glance told her that the audience had not returned to their places, and suddenly she knew why. She looked down from their second-floor balcony, where a crush of silk, satin, and organza transformed the atrium into a riot of color. The hallway was crowded with panicked men and women endeavoring to leave the theater.

"They've barricaded the doors from the outside," Bellamy said tersely, drawing her by the arm toward the central staircase. He buttoned his double-breasted suit coat. His mind was already elsewhere.

Cries and murmurs began wafting up toward them. "They? Who are *they*?" Trying to listen over the pounding of her pulse, she attempted to interpret what Bellamy was saying. Gone was the diffident gentleman of the previous moments, and in his place stood the major shareholder of the British East India Company. His eyes narrow slits and his lips razor thin under his fulsome mustache, he was considering his options. Aware that he was without his usual retinue of servants this evening, he appeared a man unaccustomed to being caught defenseless.

"The worst that can happen is that they set fire to the theater. It's happened before, once in Lahore, but the bastards didn't accomplish what they'd hoped." His fingers dug into the skin of her shoulder blades as he looked haplessly left and right to the front and rear exits, both of which were obscured by the throngs of theatergoers. Every moment or so, a shriek rent the air and several women had succumbed to the vapors, wilted flowers in their pale pastel dresses littering the lofty expanse of the grand center stairwell.

"Set fire . . . who?" Lilly demanded once again. She fought the impulse to flee, knowing full well that there was no place to go. The press of the crowd and the din of raised voices pushed in on her, making her head swim.

"I know whose work this is," Bellamy muttered to himself more than to her. "He is a favorite of Victoria." The words came out as an insult. "I'm sure you're familiar with his splendid country house Elvedon Hall in Suffolk."

She shook her head, confused. "You mean the exiled Maharaja of the Punjab, Duleep Singh? Whatever does he have to do with this? I should think the Chartists are more likely involved. There has been much civil unrest and rioting in London these past few months."

Bellamy snorted derisively. "And what you probably don't know is that Singh is in dispute with our government after his attempts to have his annual salary raised and to regain possession of the Koh-I-Noor, both of which were refused by the India Office."

Scarcely the reassurance she was looking for. "Why would they bring their troubles to London, of all places? This type of action will do their cause not a whit of good." She vaguely remembered a recent discussion with Seabourne around the matter.

Bellamy released her aching shoulder, his eyes darting to the bottom of the stairs. "This is hardly the time for discussion. Remain here," he said, and his tone rang with a possessiveness that was simultaneously unfamiliar and irritating to her. "I will make my way to the first-floor entrance and see precisely what's transpiring. With some good fortune, the constabulary will be here and apprehend the rioters."

Before she could reply, he'd disappeared down the stairs, his bulk melting into the throng. She cast a quick glance at the ring on her finger, the intertwined serpents coiled against her skin, and decided instantly that she would not wait for her betrothed to return and rescue her.

Betrothed. She didn't know which was worse. A future with Bellamy as her husband or being trapped in a burning building. She gathered up her skirts, convinced her ridiculous misgivings would prove her undoing.

She turned back toward the theater box, her knowledge of buildings and their structure telling her that there must be another stairwell where actors and stage workers could come and go unseen—used for far less grand purposes than parading about on opening nights. Already she imagined palls of smoke, an acrid burning in the back of her throat. Refusing to panic, she looked first to her right before picking up her skirts and breaking into a run to the end of the hall. If she found an alternate stairwell, she would return, signal the rest . . . the rioters could not possibly have secured all the doors to the theater.

Unease crawled over her. She was moving away from the crowd, in a direction opposite to everyone else. At the end of the corridor, more of a cutout than a proper door, she saw the faint outline—a small affair—with a low lintel and scuffed panels that could use a coat of paint. Hesitating for the briefest moment, she pushed her weight against the opening and moved from the light into the darkness.

Silence. The rising hum of terror receded behind her replaced by the beating of her heart as her eyes struggled to adjust to the darkness. Sure enough, a narrow flight of stairs led to a flagstoned landing. There would be a portal—there had to be. Stairs had to connect to something and somewhere, hopefully to the outside.

Halfway down the flight, a low whine of hinges moving reached her ears, another door opening below her. Before she could swallow her elation, a figure stepped from behind the entrance and into the faint radiance cast by the moonlight. He was short and strapping, and he pulled the door shut behind him to stand motionless, letting his own eyes adjust to the darkness.

Lilly froze, hoping the shadows would envelope her. The man looked up and pinned her with a gaze that communicated the worst of intentions. His stocky body blocked the narrow passageway and she took a step backward, up one stair. Hampered by her long skirts and stiff hoops, she couldn't risk turning her back, so she took one more.

A grim dance that seemed to take forever stretched time to the breaking point. He followed, swallowing two steps at a time until she could feel his breath, stale and menacing, on her face.

She had no choice. Jamming her reticule with its metal frame and gold and brass beads at his face, she hurled her body in his direction and down the stairs toward the door. She inhaled a mouthful of rancid sweat and, nauseated, edged her way past the bulky figure, the last of the stairs just a step away. Using her fists to rain blows on the man, she felt him grab a handful of her hair and twist.

She lashed at him with her feet, shoving her reticule at his throat, at his eyes. He managed to block her blows, but let go of her hair to do it. Breathing hard with defiance and fear, she threw herself down the last two stairs and out the door.

Cold air. A moonlit alley. And no rioters crowding her escape. If she could get past the stone wall to the front entrance of the theater, to the constabulary . . . away from her attacker. Looking up, all she saw was a night sky glittering with stars and not a wisp of smoke billowing from the building.

She couldn't breathe, couldn't think. Her heart was racing and her limbs tingled, almost entirely numb. If she could tear off her hoops beneath her wide skirts, she could run to the front entrance and summon help. But there was no opportunity to act on her next thought. Her head shattered, her vision disintegrating into shards of light. A hard shove between the shoulder blades and slowly she sank to her knees, skirts billowing around her. She closed her eyes, gorge rising against the blows she knew were coming.

But they never came. She remained kneeling for what seemed an eternity. At least the beautiful theater, the John Nash masterpiece, would not burn to the ground. At least the hundreds of theatergoers would not perish. At least death would come quickly when it did. Those were her last hopes.

When she opened her eyes, her assailant was crouched opposite her, focused on the moonlit pathway and at the man coming toward them.

His strides were that of a hunter, and a knife glinted in his hand.

Lilly choked back a rising hysteria, on her knees with the world swimming before her. Unable to focus, she was aware of her assailant panting heavily beside her. And then like a creature in the wild, he crouched even lower before jumping up and running to the back of the alley, away from the theater. He scrambled up the stone wall and vanished.

St. Martin lengthened his strides toward her, closing the distance between them. Her body refused to move, but head throbbing, she allowed him to pull her to her feet where she stood swaying, mesmerized by the knife in his hand and the hard glitter of stars overhead.

He folded it with frighteningly elegant movements and put it in the side of his boot. "Are you hurt?" he asked, his eyes glancing over her efficiently.

She backed away from him. Sickened, the blow to her head still ringing in her ears, she pointed feebly to the theater behind her. "We must alert the constabulary," she said as forcefully as she could. "The people in the theater still . . ."

"It's been taken care of. The rioters apprehended and the fire was a small one and already extinguished."

She stared at him in disbelief, still unsteady on her feet. Her neck hurt, but she managed to take in the high wall behind her, looking for her attacker. Her thoughts came in wild disorder. "Who was that man? Was he one of the rioters? Really didn't get a good look at him, although what does it matter now?" Her lips felt dry as sand. "And why are you here?" She didn't care whether the tumble of words made any sense.

St. Martin didn't answer and instead took her wrist. "I think I'd better see you home. You've had a shock."

Her lace gloves were torn, the diamond and ruby snake ring on her finger an incongruous shock to her system. Pulling back suddenly, trying to free herself from his curiously strong but gentle grasp, she shook her head. "Bellamy. My betrothed. I must find him."

He let go of her wrist, glancing at the ring on her finger before taking her arm. It was an impersonal gesture, a means of guiding her, yet she was aware of his touch immediately, intensely. Everything about the man set her on edge, magnifying her responses.

"I may have had a blow to my head, but I do remember our last encounter and I don't think I shall invite you to see me home." She pulled her reticule close to her body, the gold and brass beads loosened from their moorings. The bottom two flounces on her wide skirts were torn and caught on the low heels of her evening shoes.

"I'm sure your betrothed is well." He urged her forward toward the street. "And I suppose congratulations are in order."

Her head swam. "Thank you," she said as primly as she could under the circumstances.

"Although as you are newly affianced, I can't help wonder why your soon-to-be husband decided to leave you alone and defenseless in the midst of a dangerous melee."

She wanted to shut out his words but couldn't, trying instead to bring St. Martin into focus despite the blurring of her vision. Defending Bellamy, she said, "He was merely looking out for the both of us and thought it best to do the proper reconnaissance. And as though you would have anything to say about the matter, my lord." The cold air in her lungs did nothing to revive her. She took another cleansing breath, refusing to lean on him, although, inexplicably, she wanted to do nothing else.

She thought she saw a shadow pass over his face, the lines tautly drawn, his onyx eyes hooded. "You assume correctly, Mrs. Hampton. I know nothing of protecting a wife."

Suddenly, she was brought up close to his chest. He was tall. She had forgotten just how tall and how hard and unforgiving his arms could be. Charles had been elegant and fine. And Bellamy was corpulent and robust. But this man . . . Residual shock and overwhelming fatigue blurred her thoughts.

So when she found herself bundled into a hansom cab, its sturdy wheels and sheltering interior were a welcome respite. In the dark, she sank into the squab cushions and into another layer of lies building up rapidly around her. Beside her was a man who had threatened her yesterday and saved her life tonight.

And she was going home with him.

Chapter 7

Constance St. Martin shrugged off her wrapper with the insouciance of a concubine. Bellamy's pale gaze burned in satisfaction as he leaned back in his chair like a pasha prince.

She was stunning, with jutting breasts barely concealed by the satin rail that had probably cost him a king's ransom. His eyes tracked her languid walk, like liquid silk as she moved toward him across the floor, her narrow bare feet sinking into the luxuriance of the Indian rug. Hair the color of a raven's wing, she looked like a fairy-tale princess, but he knew differently.

"Darling," she purred, leaning over him in his chair, her musky scent finer than anything a Parisian perfumer could conjure. "You're a very bad boy expecting me to stay here, locked away, day after day, night after night." Her fine lips pouted her disapproval at the memory of the long days of her incarceration in her opulent palace. "And you had the temerity to go to the theater this evening without me?"

Bellamy shook his head as though dismissing a small child. His last hours at the theater still rankled. The impudence of that poseur, Duleep Singh, and the ultimately futile demonstration by his supporters on his behalf was beyond belief. A decade ago, colonialists would never have dared express their discontent with their rulers. And in London of all places.

He tightened the sash on his robe until it dug into his corpulent flesh. The pain was welcome, drowning out his frustration with that squat little queen and her even weaker consort who invited anarchy to their doorstep. The vote in Parliament loomed on his horizon, championed by Victoria herself, to take power over his empire and cede it to colonial government in India.

Unthinkable.

"You didn't miss much," he said, keeping most of his thoughts to himself as he had learned to do so many years ago. "The play was tedious and my companion even more so."

"What's she like, your companion?" Constance leaned closer, and he could smell the laudanum on her breath. She was usually not interested in other women, but her green, almond-shaped eyes narrowed further. Like the feline she was, she sniffed competition in the air.

Constance would soon learn her place, silly, demanding creature that she was, thought Bellamy. She was no different from the slatterns his mother had kept about. "Lilly Clarence is not simply my companion, she's now my betrothed," he said silkily, dangling the skein of wool before the cat, baiting for her reaction.

Constance raised her fine eyebrows mockingly. "You're taking a wife. How interesting and how terribly boring. You know how tiresome I found my own marriage to dear Julian. And you actually helped me do something about it, naughty boy."

Bellamy sat still, the mention of St. Martin a tonic to his system. That he held that man in the palm of his hand was galvanizing. And as for his wife . . . He could feel her breath. Warm, sultry. He reached up and squeezed her left breast, hard, like he was testing the worthiness of one of his polo ponies back in Lahore. Instead of reflecting pain, her eyes widened momentarily and caught the look in his. For a brief second it occurred to him that she was the ringmaster, not he, raising the curtain on their lust.

Impatient with his own weakness and yet fully aware of

her worth to him, he pushed her away. "Instead of talking so much, why don't you make yourself useful?" He jerked his chin in the direction of an exquisite Sheridan escritoire and the decanter of brandy. "I crave some refreshment."

Constance swayed away from him, peevish now, the cloud of laudanum still hanging over her, supremely unaccustomed to male indifference. She looked around the lavishly appointed room disinterestedly, barely taking note of the rich, watered-silk wall covering and the Louis quinze four-poster with its elaborate canopy.

She flicked her hair over her shoulders with an exaggerated shudder. "I don't think so, darling. I don't fetch," she murmured. He wondered briefly whether her reaction was part of the twisted game they both loved so much. "Why don't I assist you by calling in one of those burly guards that you keep posted outside this chamber day and night?"

Without waiting for his reply, she sauntered to the door and opened it wide. A moment later, a tall, heavyset man, hands clasped behind his back and eyes cast down, hurried over to the escritoire.

Bellamy's breathing quickened, the thought of a woman ordering about a man, any man, even a servant or guard, simultaneously arousing and revolting. Flynn was having difficulty focusing on his task, his large hands clumsy with the decanter, the crystal, his senses obviously overwhelmed by Constance who made sure she remained in his sight, tempting, seductive, and forbidden.

The whore.

The clatter of glass jangled his nerves. "Go now," he barked at Flynn, who fumbled with the crystal he was holding before awkwardly setting it down and backing out the door. It closed behind him silently.

"And you"—Bellamy rose from his chair and strode toward Constance—"you will remember your place. Which implies your wearing modest garb whenever you are with a man other than myself. I won't clarify again."

Constance took an affronted breath. "Are you completely mad? This isn't the benighted colonies. You've spent too many years with primitive savages, clearly." Rising to the moment, she reacted as though her world was coming to an end, waving her hands imperiously. "I've had enough of languishing away in a backwater for all those years with Julian. And I won't have it again."

"You came to me, as I recall, pleading for help."

"And you promised me that lovely major and all the diversions with Dr. Vesper that I wanted if I cooperated with your plans," she whined.

He could have her killed. Yes, right now, her body disposed of as quickly as the maid who'd met her own ignoble end at the dexterous hands of St. Martin the other evening. It had been decades since anyone had the temerity to ask inconvenient questions of Isambard Kingdom Bellamy.

But much as he would like to squeeze the life from her deceptively fragile form, he would have to wait. Bellamy smoothed the arms of his chair with open palms, conjuring one of his most delectable fantasies. He imagined the lengths St. Martin would go to see his wife raised from the dead and returned to him. For a price of course.

His momentary anger with this whore had to be managed, leveraged, when there was so much at stake. Constance St. Martin was his guarantor—in the eventuality that her husband decided to continue drowning in his own guilt. Highly unlikely. Constance's high whine momentarily shut out, Bellamy stretched his thin mouth into a smile, a smile of anticipation.

The whore's voice interrupted his thoughts.

"There's nothing to smile about, darling, surely. Why did you have me join you and Vesper if you were not intending to treat me well?" She stood in the center of the room, hands on hips. Her voice was petulant, a little girl who demanded constant indulgence.

Bellamy crossed his arms over his chest to contain his emotion and stroked his mustache. He should have asked Flynn to bring his cigars, his urge for tobacco doing nothing to temper his mood.

"You've erred," he said slowly, allowing the storm clouds to gather, "if you believe that I have your best interests at heart. I'm not like your husband." His gaze flicked over her like a whip. "And tell me, did he ever discover that you kept a retinue of lovers, ranging from stable boys to gardeners, while he was away on his various assignments for the Crown?"

The beginnings of anxiety tautened her lips. Constance was shrewd enough to turn things around while she could. Her nostrils flared at the slight. "You're speaking nonsense, darling, and you well know it. Julian ignored me, if you can imagine, so what choice did I have? He deserved it," she said, her fine features collapsing, looking like she suddenly needed a dose of laudanum to soothe frayed nerves. Her eyes darted around the room to settle on the bedside table where her tincture was customarily found. Bellamy made sure she had a ready supply. "I come from one of England's best families," she rattled on, moving toward the bed to begin opening drawers and rummaging through their contents.

"Such a lofty tone coming from a whore."

"Go sod yourself." She slammed shut a drawer triumphantly, small glass bottle in hand.

"Not while I have you about." Bellamy rose from his chair and made his way toward her. She raised the bottle to her lips just as he grabbed her arm and flung her into a chair. Seizing the bottle from her hand, he hurled it to the floor. The bottle smashed, leaking oily liquid, a bitterness perfuming the air.

Not about to be cowed and deciding she could do better by heightening the atmosphere of violence, Constance smiled slyly. "Your accent is thickening, King, my darling, along with your bad, bad temper," she taunted, crossing her legs as though she had all the time in the world, and making sure that one of the thin straps of her silk rail fell alluringly from her shoulder. "Are you reverting to savagery, having spent all that time with those primitives?" She shuddered delicately.

Bellamy heard the gathering thunder in his ears, and his hands itched to encircle her white neck and slowly, oh-so-slowly, strangle the life from that exquisite body. How he wanted to hurt her, to slap that delicate face, to shatter that sultry, knowing expression. He wanted a whip in his hand, to lash her until her smooth skin oozed welts, to give her over to his men to ride until even she would scream for mercy.

How unfortunate that he had to keep her intact. For St. Martin.

He jerked away from her as though she were filth. "I could call for the guards right now. . . ."

Constance's eyes narrowed, sensing an opportunity for advantage despite the lingering haze of laudanum. "But you won't because you want me all to yourself, don't you? And you adore taking something from a man like St. Martin, a man whom you could never be. Have I ever told you what my dear husband was like in bed?" She paused for a heartbeat. "No. I don't recall that I did. Quite superlative, if you must know. And I would know . . ."

"You're simply goods to him, as to me."

"Is that so?" she asked, a sharpness to her face, leaning forward in her chair. "What am I worth then? To my husband who believes me long dead? Tell me!"

If only she knew. Bellamy exploded in guttural laughter. "You bitch. I cannot believe he was dimwitted enough to make you his wife, despite your aristocratic pretensions. Imagine, the clever, strong, brave Julian St. Martin." He looked down as she sat languorously in the chair, her hard green eyes challenging him. "You can only hope that he is mad enough with guilt to take you back in spite of the fact that you spread your legs more easily than a mongrel in heat."

"He will," she purred knowingly. She rose from the chair until they faced each other, an orgy of danger surrounding them. He approached, moving closer, the arrows of fire once again piercing his belly.

"Look what I can give you," she crooned, "and look what you've taken from him."

Constance knew that he wouldn't resist. She felt through the opening of his robe while he grabbed her other hand and put it open-palmed between his legs, pressing it until he was sure she felt what he wanted her to feel.

"You adore taking something from St. Martin. And even more," she said throatily, intensifying her caress so he was unable to answer. "You're addicted to the way I spread my legs for you."

The aristocratic whore was right on both counts, Bellamy thought, looking forward to another descent into hell, moments before he surrendered, once again, to her depraved hands and mouth.

Chapter 8

The diffuse light stung through her closed lids. Moaning silently against the stiffness in her neck, Lilly moved tentatively against familiar, crisp linen sheets that released a faint rosewater scent.

Slowly, her own room swam into view, the bedside lamp throwing wild shadows against the walls and on the man whose broad back was turned away from her. Fighting a combination of shock and nausea, she catapulted into a sitting position.

"How dare you—get away from my desk." The world reeled on its axis, forcing her to slump back against the pillows. Shaking, she pushed away the sheet covering her, prepared to accost St. Martin, who was rummaging through her private papers and heaping them haphazardly across her blotter.

"How dare you," she repeated, at the moment not knowing how else to express her distress, short of throwing, if she only had the strength, the bedside lamp at his head.

He didn't seem the least alarmed. Taking his time, he turned slowly toward her, and in the low light, she was struck again by the severe lines of his face behind which she sensed lay a fearsome desperation. The man had a history, one she didn't care to learn. Particularly here in her bedroom.

St. Martin looked at her with single-minded intensity. "I dare—and I don't think there's much you can do about it."

Her response was to shove the bed linen covering her aside only to discover that she was, mercifully, still fully clothed. "I want you to remove yourself from my house, my lord. Now," she said belligerently, using her most confident tone. "Or I shall summon my housekeeper to escort you out personally."

Despite her bravado, she privately hoped St. Martin hadn't yet caught a glimpse of Mrs. Worth's generous and aging backside. Hardly intimidating. She was most probably snoring heavily in her nightcap in the attic, useless to all but those in her dreams. And Lilly's two footmen and maid had returned to their own homes earlier in the evening, ironically as it turned out, as she had not anticipated needing their services.

She stood up in her stocking feet and the world slowly righted itself. Someone, she hoped it wasn't St. Martin, had removed her evening slippers.

"I'm surprised, Mrs. Hampton, that you're reluctant to show appropriate appreciation for my coming to your aid this evening." There was no warmth in the dark eyes, and the statement did nothing to alleviate her growing unease.

The events came flooding back. "What were you even doing outside the theater? In the midst of a riot?" she asked, deciding that a display of aggression would do her the most good at the moment. "I shouldn't suspect that you have taken to following me about London." She shook out her skirts, and a glimpse in the oval mirror informed her that she could do nothing about her hair, an unruly mass falling to her shoulders, or the stiffness in her muscles, slowing every move. With little dignity to draw upon, all she had at her disposal was a low, simmering anger. "I am willing to forget your lapse in judgment last evening at the Tower. You were obviously in some type of distress. But this unseemly pursuit and the groundless threats . . ."

"And you without your pistol," he interrupted nonchalantly, inserting the non sequitur as though she hadn't spoken.

She stiffened. The man had been in her home before and without her knowledge, that much was clear. The thought that he could move about undetected and against her wishes filled her with renewed dread. "I could summon the constabulary and have you arrested, sir. To have invaded my home and my rooms and taken my property, to follow me to the theater . . ."

He smiled cynically, or to say, his lips curved in the approximation of a smile. Lilly sensed he would have more willingly growled. "You won't call the constabulary and you know exactly why."

Her head suddenly cleared because his expression was both cool and deadly. The dramatic events at the theater faded quickly until only a lingering stain remained. St. Martin was a different story, flesh and blood in her bedroom, demanding something she could not and would not give. They were entirely too close, here in the intimacy of rooms that she had not even shared with Charles. After his death, she had moved her belongings from the master suite into a guest room.

She would try an alternate tack. "I'm not feeling quite myself, given the events of the evening, Lord St. Martin. You are probably quite correct that I should take to my bed."

"St. Martin."

Lilly nodded and placed a palm on her forehead, feigning a headache. The room with its chintz wallpaper and flowered bed canopy seemed far too small to contain him. "Of course. Forgive me for forgetting your preferences," she said with what she hoped was her most conciliatory voice under the circumstances. "Perhaps we can continue this conversation when I am fully recovered and in the bright light of day."

He shrugged, his lean body taking up more of the room than was fair. "I don't think so, Mrs. Hampton." Gesturing toward her desk, he said, "Obviously, you keep the architectural plans for the Crystal Palace elsewhere. And I refuse to leave until I have them in my possession."

Her feint clearly wasn't working. She threw up her arms in exasperation, suppressing a gasp at the ache in her neck. "You found the pistol by ransacking my home, so what is stopping you from tearing apart my home once again? This is hardly the Middle Ages, sir." Her voice lowered in an attempt to swallow her pain and her annoyance. "I refuse to relinquish my late husband's work to you to use for your own, no doubt disreputable, purposes. You can hardly imprison me in my own home, surely, or threaten my person." Once she'd completed the sentence, she immediately doubted the veracity of her own words. He could and he would. Anyone could see the man was single-mindedly obsessed.

"You forget—I still have your pistol." The darkness of his eyes matched the inky sheen of his hair.

She moved away from her bed, skittish. "A purloined pistol—what of it? Having it in your possession demonstrates your guilt, not mine."

"You appear pale again," he said calmly, leaning against her desk. "You should be pleased that I decided to keep you company here in your rooms. A blow to the head can have serious consequences," he continued conversationally. Her eyes helplessly traced his long, muscled legs, crossed casually now at the booted ankle, his composure rattling her more than any demonstration of violence could. "Please don't stand on ceremony if you feel you must lie down."

"I am perfectly well." Lilly raised her chin and glared, refusing to move an inch toward the bed.

"Suit yourself, although once you hear what I have to say, you may find yourself requiring additional rest."

"Thank you for your concern." Acid tinged her reply. "Say what you must and then be done with it."

St. Martin looked at her for a long moment and then nodded amiably. But she wasn't fooled for an instant. "Forgive me then if this appears discursive, but I don't believe you may have heard of Sir William Herschel, Chief Magistrate of the Hooghly district in Jungipoor, India."

She frowned. "No—and what of him?" she asked impatiently.

"On a whim—imagine—he decided to use fingerprints on native contracts for personal identification. Herschel had a local businessman impress his handprint on a contract, the first of many as it turns out."

She kept her expression cold and hostile, pretending not to understand the implications of the anecdote.

"As his fingerprint collection grew, Herschel began to note that the inked impressions could, indeed, prove or disprove identity. Unique to the individual."

Lilly said nothing, her legs weakening at the knees. He shoved away from the desk and closed the distance between them, taking one of her clenched fists in his. Long fingered, strong and elegant, he had beautiful hands, she thought absurdly, refusing to pull away.

He turned her palm upright and traced an unhurried line from her wrist to the tip of her ring finger, now adorned with serpents and rubies, the sensation causing a heaviness in the region of her belly. "One of a kind, Lilly Clarence Hampton."

Somehow she found her voice. "You will give me some credit. I see where you intend to take this evidence of my guilt, imprinted on the pistol, to the authorities."

"Not necessarily," he said lazily and stepping in closer so that, looking up, she could concentrate on the small white scar atop the slash of an eyebrow. "Give me the plans and I shall never darken your doorstep again." He dropped her hand abruptly.

"That's simply not possible." She was saying no, again. Refusing him, despite the fact they might as well have both been naked, she thought wildly, his nearness causing her to take shortened breaths, the proximity of his hard body an as-

sault on her sense of self. He was as intimidating as an invading army. To move away from him meant backing up toward
the bed—an option beyond contemplation.

"I don't want to hurt you, Lilly." It was the first time he'd
uttered her first name. She took a small step back because it
was all she could do, aware of the simple dark jacket and
white shirt he wore, skimming the tight muscles of his torso,
the corded shoulders and the elegant strength of his forearms. She couldn't stop looking at his hands, large, beautifully formed. Those calloused, yet sensitive fingertips tracing
her palm.

She swallowed nervously. "Then don't." Looking over his
shoulder, she focused on a beautiful urn, a gift from one of
Charles's many aunts, decorated with grapes, leaves, and frol-
icking nymphs. And despite concentrating with every fiber of
her being on the beauty of the piece, she couldn't block out the
memory of St. Martin's mouth on hers, his body caging hers.
It hadn't been a kiss in the Tower, it had been an assault, hal-
lucinatory moments when she had no time to draw a breath
because she had all but ceased breathing.

And it couldn't happen again.

St. Martin watched her with unnerving stillness. And as
though he felt nothing at all. "You're making this more difficult than it need be, Lilly. Your secret will go with you to the
grave. Simply relinquish the plans."

What was he doing, offering her temporary respite? Mesmerized by the low velvet of his voice, she knew she couldn't
hide from the truth forever. He was unlike anyone she had
ever before encountered. With his sensual mouth and the
hard eyes that missed nothing. He *knew*. And it was his intention to use it to his advantage.

"And if I continue to refuse?" she whispered.

"I also know the man from whom you purchased your
weapon." His voice came low and quiet. "Two days before
your husband was murdered."

Lilly closed her eyes. She was mad to think she would survive this, let alone bring St. Martin to heel. But she couldn't relinquish the plans simply for her own immediate benefit. This man was unstable, untrustworthy, someone who could easily make off with the diamond so important to the queen and to the maintenance of peace within the empire.

He was still there of course, his breath warm on her hair, when she opened her eyes. They were not touching, but if she swayed so much as an inch ... she refused to complete the thought.

He shook his head. "You have no choice, Lilly." Then he lifted his hand and drew it across her cheek to her chin and, with pressure, tipped her head toward his.

Burning at the touch, she forced herself to steady her focus by continuing with her questions. "At least tell me why you want the plans so desperately. There are those who say that you have lost your reason, that you are not to be trusted, that your service to the Crown is under dispute."

His eyes met hers and his smile was flinty. "Is that what you've heard? Do not expect me to confirm or deny rumor. Not in my repertoire, Mrs. Hampton. I just want you to understand."

Suddenly, Lilly didn't know what she was being asked to say yes to. Her breathing came faster, yet she was powerless to slow it. It came to her that he was trying to seduce her, that this was part of the game, to see how far she would go to save her soul.

"I am a widow," she pointed out needlessly.

"A grieving one at that," he said, making sure she did not miss the irony in his voice. For a long moment, his eyes bored into hers and she sensed that he had come to some manner of decision. St. Martin's hands slid slowly down her arms to her wrists, tracing her racing pulse. The pads of his fingers moved slowly over the thin skin, and she bit her lip as he wrapped his hands around her wrists. Like a manacle, shackling her as much to her past as to her future. She should pull away but didn't. And it was as if he knew, the corner of his mouth lifting in an almost smile.

"Frightened?" His eyes were dark and intense. "You should be."

Lilly managed to control her breathing, to try to understand what was happening, this deliberate seduction. But for what purpose? Her arms held stiffly to her sides, she watched as he lowered his lips to hers. He kissed her hard and deeply, sending an unmistakable message with his lazily thrusting tongue. Mortified, she heard herself moaning into his mouth as her body shook with a combination of dread and desire.

Hot, urgent, demanding, he let go of her wrists as his arms slid around her. She felt his power as he held her against the unyielding strength of his body, his arms locked around her waist, his erection hot against her pelvis. She shuddered, mind and body, fear and desire, warring inside her.

The moment was more raw, more real than any in her life. Even the smoking gun, the metallic scent of Charles's blood at the moment of his death, could not compare to the savage intensity of St. Martin's body pressed against hers. At the thought of Charles, she momentarily stiffened, remembering the first years of their marriage, their romantic coupling, all sweet words and honeyed kisses.

But this . . . St. Martin's hair was thick beneath her fingers although she didn't know the exact moment when she had reached for him. She didn't care. This was a battle she didn't dare lose, a fight to the finish. And it had begun the moment he'd entered the Tower and pinned her to the glass case containing the gleaming Koh-I-Noor.

Retreat was not an option, never had been. So she clung to him as his tongue thrust and thrust again, stroking the roof of her mouth, skimming her lips. His large palms cupped her breasts, the whale bones of her bodice crushed beneath his grip, and desire tore through her.

"Persuasion comes in many forms." His voice was rough and urgent. The craving was deep, almost painful. Her stomach muscles tightened as his hand skimmed the bare skin of her neck, his fingers quickly making their way down the fan-fronted bodice of her dress, loosening the eyelet closures with sleek efficiency.

"You mean coercion," she murmured, dishonest with herself and with him. His lips were hot through the fine muslin of her chemise held fast by a stiff corset. With deft hands, he made short work of the back lacing and the front busk closing, slowly bunching the fabric up around her torso. She arched her back as he ran his hands over her distended nipples still covered by the thinnest silk.

"Lie to yourself if you must," he said with a small smile. Pushing her back toward the bed, he eased her onto the buttery duvet, sliding his mouth over the sensitive nerve endings, butterfly kisses suddenly gentle on her heated skin.

"Remove your chemise for me, Lilly." His voice was a low, soft contradiction to his hard gaze.

She didn't know herself any longer but she knew she couldn't refuse him. She didn't want to. Lifting shaking hands, she began gathering the fine silk in her fists, first removing her arms and then pulling the material over her head to sweep it aside.

His jaw clenched and she felt cool air and those dark eyes on her naked breasts.

"Thank you," he said, his voice deepening before he dipped his head, trailing his lips up her waist to the underside of a breast. She closed her eyes as he latched onto the nipple and rolled the other between his fingers. The hard pull of his mouth, every sensual lick of his tongue, sent a bolt of pleasure low in her body.

Her pulse raced as he released the aching point and moved to the other breast, plying it, laving it into swollen stiffness. As though her body had been taken over by another being, her hips began to rock and her arms came around his shoulders, so hard and warm beneath his jacket. Suddenly, she couldn't get enough of touching him, losing herself in the rhythm of his mouth on her breasts, desperate, hungry, aggressive.

Her voice shook, along with her hands burrowing under his shirt to meet the warm skin of his chest. "This is impossible. . . ." Her heart beat so hard she could hear it in her ears, feel it in the tips of her fingers. She felt his lips leave her breasts as he brought his mouth close to hers.

"What do you want? Tell me. And don't lie."

She met his dark gaze, scared by the power of her own need, afraid to analyze its source, petrified that she could never turn back. She closed her eyes, unwilling to say the words.

"Please fuck me," he said, finding the words that she couldn't. Her ears, skin, and heart burned. "That's what you want, isn't it?"

Still not answering, she sucked in her breath as she felt his hands skim the tapes of her skirt, warm and persuasive, tugging aside two layers of petticoats. She heard the snap of her corset, the stiff contraption pushed to the far side of the bed. Leaning over her, he tugged the remaining fabric of her drawers down her length and off her ankles.

"Spread your legs."

And she did, opening her eyes to the acanthus frieze circling the ceiling above her. Barely breathing, she felt the heat of his gaze before she felt his hot touch, parting her flesh, exposing her.

She felt drugged as his fingers slid between her wet folds. She was dripping and she had never been so drenched, so weak with need as when first one finger slipped inside. She gasped. And then another, as a trickle of moisture seeped out of her. Pressure, sweet pressure, against the spot that throbbed and ached.

"This is what you get when you don't say no." His touch scalded the inside of her thighs. "You're so wet," he said, more to himself than to her. In response, she lifted her hips toward him and he sank another finger into her.

Lilly's blood rushed to her core. The tight, throbbing spot pressed to the heel of his palm was like the primitive beating of drums. He lowered his mouth to hers and she groaned as his hand continued to stroke in tight, firm circles. Her body tightened and her fingers curled into the hardness of his shoulders.

"Don't hide anything from me, Lilly. Ever." His breath was hot against her mouth, the tender skin of her neck as she writhed against his hand. "Show me. Show me everything." The thick column of his arousal lay heavy against her bare thighs.

She didn't want to look at him. She didn't want to think. Everything drew up tight inside her, a place where the past, present, and future didn't exist. Her body was everything, wanting too much, wanting him. Arcing her head, she cried out, her hips moving convulsively as she clenched around his hand and fingers, her blood rushing to her center. The torturous pulse between her legs erupted, exploding with violent streams of sensation that pounded through her body.

Panting hard, it seemed an age before she came back to Earth, her arms still looped around St. Martin's strong neck. Slowly her mind became unfrozen, a horrific reality rearing its ugly head, refusing to go away. She didn't want to meet his eyes but concentrated instead on the feel of hard muscle beneath her hands, the acanthus leaves above her, his breathing, disconcertingly even in her ear.

She couldn't, wouldn't think about this now. She'd done many regrettable things in the past, but never this. Never this. And now it was too late.

He rose from the edge of the bed, taking the warmth with him and, reflexively, she grabbed the tousled sheet at a feeble attempt at modesty. "This was a mistake. . . . I don't know what happened." She addressed his broad back, her knuckles white from clenching the linens. "Why I let it happen . . ." She drew the linen over her breasts and sat up against the cushions.

St. Martin turned around to look at her, shockingly at ease. She expected at least some emotion, vestiges of embarrassment or awkwardness. Even his jacket, his shirt—he'd remained fully clothed while she . . . Her stomach dropped, suddenly aware that he was unmoved by their recent exchange, his expression registering calm and calculation and anything but lust.

This was part of his game. And she, damnably weak and confused, had succumbed.

Her mouth was dry, her skin paling beneath his gaze, agonizing regret more punishing than anything he could say or do. She had no intimation as to what his response would be, other than a deep-seated conviction, a piece of hot burning coal in her stomach, that it didn't bode well for her at all.

His smile was cool and his movements nonchalant as he tucked his shirt, the one she'd clawed at moments before, back into the band of his trousers. "A mistake? I don't think so." His tone was mocking.

"Please leave now." Her voice shook.

He merely shrugged. "If you like, Mrs. Hampton." The formal use of her name threw into sharp relief her utter carelessness moments before and the dire seriousness of her miscalculation. "I can see myself out to give you all the more time to dwell on the prospect of your fiancé, the proud and wealthy Isambard Kingdom Bellamy, learning of your recent adventures."

Her stomach clenched. "You would use this against me. To get the bloody architectural plans—to steal a damned diamond!" Beneath her anger, mortification swamped her. This was all so transparent, so simple. He hadn't even desired her. He had forced himself to pleasure her, forgoing his own satisfaction, simply to ensnare her further in his plans. Anger and humiliation, a potent combination, coursed through her veins.

"I should think the damned pistol would be incriminating enough. You need not have troubled yourself further," she said, ice dripping from her words. Wrapping the sheet around her, she unfolded herself from the bed. She was not going to reveal how shaken she really was. "Get out!" she said in a low voice barely above a whisper, although not caring if she rose the household and half of Mayfair. "Now!"

"This doesn't sound like the reasonable, intelligent woman I know you to be," he murmured. "What would the guests of your Thursday-evening salon say if they suspected?"

"You know nothing of me, nothing," she said, trying not to trip on the linen under her feet. She advanced toward him, lowering her voice even further. "You accuse me of murdering my husband, do you? Well I shall tell you that I am capable of murdering once again—if you don't leave my sight this instant."

"Forgive me if I'm not overly concerned."

"Go to hell."

"I intend to, thank you. But I'll be back."

She glared at him, knotting the sheet decisively over her left shoulder, eager for her hands to do something other than reach out and strangle St. Martin. Or pull him toward her. Not for the sweet lover's kisses that she'd once known. But for a rough, hard, deep . . . She stopped short, backing away from him.

"Don't return here. Ever."

He shrugged. "Here. There. I will find you, Lilly. And if you believe this to be the last of our encounters, don't be too certain."

She felt herself pale.

"Because I will seduce you again and again, wherever I find you, until you give me what I really want."

Cold settled into the pit of her stomach. Her lips thinned and she angrily pulled the hair back from her face, raising her chin. "A momentary lapse on my part, I assure you. You value your amorous skills much too highly."

"The parched widow who hasn't felt a man's touch in a year? I don't think so," he said musingly. "You're a passionate woman who doesn't seem to be aware of it. I suspect the late and great Charles Hampton didn't know the half of it." He let the words sink in before continuing. "And so I've decided, to amuse myself if nothing else, to keep your pistol and its incriminating palm print, in my back pocket as it were."

For a moment she was speechless and all but naked with nothing but a thin sheet protecting her from this mad stranger.

"Instead, I will sniff at your skirts like a determined hound, unrelenting until you ultimately collapse with pleasure and beg me to stop." He paused with a wintry smile. "I think next time I fancy taking you up against a wall, perhaps at one of the Royal Geographical lectures you're so keen to attend. Perhaps have you service me below stairs at one of the social teas you frequent. Or better still, in Bellamy's box at the theater, splayed across a plush, red banquette . . ."

She would hear no more. "Get out," she hissed.

And when she turned around, he was gone.

Chapter 9

St. Martin was covered with dirt, his mouth filled with grit, silt in every crevice of his body. He hugged the bank of the ravine until he found a rupture in the wall. Keeping low, he crawled out through a collapsed wash and onto the slope of a red knoll.

The valley was steeped in a uniform ochre with the occasional shade of dark crimson. Scattered boulders flaunted the dark varnish of time, and the denuded hills were brick red, not a scrub brush marring the harsh contours folding into flat planes.

Some craven god's idea of hell on Earth.

The craggy, barren mountains with their steep climbs, descents, and hairpin curves along narrow roads presented St. Martin with his own personal nightmare. The terrain was all too familiar now, the cluster of hills, smooth mushroom-shaped rocks fusing into neat concentric lines. Rugged, unwelcoming as Dante's seventh ring, a range of forbidding stone hills came into his view.

There was no breeze. Only the stench of death.

He checked his Enfield, a caliber muzzle-loading rifled musket, anticipating that the ubiquitous sandstorms had already seized the rifle cartridge. On a good day, and the current moment hardly qualified, the black powder could be driven out at about nine hundred feet per second. Raising the rifle to his shoulder, he felt for the adjustable ladder battle-sight range of four hundred yards.

Eyes narrowed, he scrutinized the slope, automatically adjusting the blade sight to more than one thousand yards. With practice, a good marksman could hit a man-sized target at about half that distance.

He forced himself to move again, keeping low, pausing behind rocks to survey the crest for anything still breathing. The stench grew stronger and he wondered whether there'd be anything left alive.

He raced to the next boulder. A musketball screamed off a ridge to his right, leaving a shower of red dust and black soot in its wake. He cut away and moved up the slope to stoop behind another outcrop while looking in the direction the fire had come from.

A man, his features indistinct in the distance, reared up from his cover. A British officer, his red uniform impossibly neat and clean against the backdrop of dust and death. In his arms, a young woman, her raven dark hair glossed by the harsh sunlight, the barrel of his musket caressing her forehead.

St. Martin stepped from behind the boulder and aimed carefully with his Enfield. The range was ninety yards below. He was holding his breath, controlling the pulse that beat beneath his temples, a band across the back of his neck tightening like a noose. He poured shots down the hill, absorbing the recoil, listening. But no sound came.

The woman's forehead bloomed crimson, her eyes flying open. She fell to the ground, a small bird felled by a stone.

The pounding in his head increased, a ricochet of silent explosions, sweat now mingling with the sand and grit coating his body. The harsh landscape spun and then fell away, narrowing its focus on the still body of the woman. If he looked closer, he would know the face, the turn of the cheek, the silk of her brow. If he looked closer—

St. Martin awoke with a start. The empty tumbler of

brandy slipped from his nerveless fingers to the floor with a hollow thud. Weak morning sun saturated the heavy curtains shuttering the room, made ghostly white by the drop sheets covering most of the furnishings.

His butler, Williams, stood awkwardly in the doorway of the library, hesitation marking his usually expressionless face.

Fortunately, despite the nightmares, St. Martin came awake instantly. The pounding behind his eyes was as infernal and relentless as a blacksmith's anvil. He shoved himself up from behind the wide mahogany desk.

"Yes, Williams."

"I was reluctant to interrupt, sir." The butler didn't quite know what to make of Lord St. Martin who had spent most of his adult life away from England and the family's London house on Berkeley Square. And now, keeping odd hours, a haggard appearance, and idiosyncratic behaviors, the man who was his better did nothing to boost his confidence.

St. Martin actually preferred to have his routine nightmares cut short. "No worries. What is it?" he asked abruptly, retrieving the crystal tumbler from the floor and setting it on the desk. It was a reminder of how much he'd had to drink last night.

And it was a reminder of Lilly Clarence Hampton.

He wasn't quite sure what happened, or why it happened. He had not let himself since—He cut off the thought ruthlessly. Williams advanced into the room, bearing an envelope on a silver palaver. "A message for you, my lord," he intoned.

Something about the smooth, ivory vellum set his hackles rising. Often when he blanked out, lost track of time, lost himself in the nightmares, his instincts jagged to knife points, excruciatingly sharp.

He ripped open the missive and quickly scanned the contents. A moment later, he looked up at Williams. "Thank you. That will be all," he said cursorily.

"You will not take breakfast, sir?" the butler asked, exceeding his station, overruled by the concern that the master of the house rarely took meals, at home or seemingly elsewhere.

"Black coffee. Strong. And anything else you have at the ready. Please don't trouble Cook." He'd lived long enough on his wits and little else and couldn't accustomize himself to having several large homes, an even larger estate in Devon and the Cotswolds, rounded out by a fleet of servants to do his bidding.

"And water for a bath," he amended, giving in to his useless craving to wash the metaphoric sand and grit of Afghanistan from his body and his memory.

A scant half hour later, he climbed onto his horse, the glare of the morning light doing nothing for the pounding at his temples. He welcomed the pain, drawing it in close to himself like a long-lost child.

The missive hadn't been signed. Not that the detail mattered. He was long familiar with rendezvous and assignations, their authors shadowy and nameless. If his demise was assured, he no longer cared. No longer afraid of mortality, no longer afraid of much at all, he rarely thought about his death other than longing for it.

Which was precisely why he was the right man for this particular assignment. Because he would be dead at the end of it.

He urged his horse along the cobbled streets behind Drury Lane, the detritus of raucous nights staining worn walls that crumbled under the weight of poverty and disappointment. The haunt of pickpockets, hucksters, and prostitutes, the alleys were empty, their denizens long retired to bed, the poor house, or prison.

The world was not a pretty place, by and large. Unbidden, the image of Lilly Clarence Hampton rose in his mind. The murderess, he thought with an inward smile, and strangely, his spirits lifted. Murder was familiar to him in all its evil permutations, as was human nature. And Lilly was not a murderess, no matter what the evidence might demonstrate. He also knew very well that he could have simply pressed the matter of her incriminating pistol and the demise of Charles Hampton to its logical conclusion. And departed with the architectural plans in hand.

He was reminded of a cat playing with a mouse. Or more accurately, a lion with a gazelle, the process simultaneously cruel and pleasurable. And he hadn't felt the siren call of pleasure in years. Even before Constance's death.

Guilt was useless and perhaps that was the reason he'd found respite in Lilly's unexpectedly and easily released desires. Images flickered through his mind, the young widow sprawled in carnal abandonment, her surprisingly long, smooth legs, her shock at her own highly responsive body. It was liberating to create passion rather than pain, and it provided him with a small and curious glimmer of hope. Instead of his usual stratagem, he would be kind to himself for a change, and yet still do what was needed through rather more gratifying means. Lilly Clarence Hampton was simply a minor tale in a much larger story, the plot of which, if life was fair—which it wasn't—she would never need to know. Because the end, when it came, would be ugly enough.

The alley narrowed and he made a quick turn into the back of the tavern, hitching his horse to a scarred fence post, casting an experienced eye over his shoulder before lowering his head to walk through the small back entranceway.

The odor was instantaneous, the reek nearly closing his throat. It took St. Martin a moment to adjust his sight to the dimness, where after a few moments, three men emerged from the gloom. The shortest, with a bullet-shaped head, spoke first.

"We're apologizin' for the short notice, my lord." He chuckled with grim humor, keeping the jest close to his chest. "The guvnor simply thought you jes might be needin' remindin'. You haven' been to see the good docter in a while."

"Much appreciated," he drawled, keeping his back to the

doorway and facing the men. A large-sized gunnysack sat between them. The odor stung his eyes. "I didn't realize that my health was of such concern. Refresh my memory, gentlemen, as it gives me trouble these days from time to time."

By the looks of it, the room was some type of a storage area with dust-encrusted barrels lining the walls and a dirt floor. Other than a low bench behind the three men, the space was empty.

The shorter man, clearly the emissary, grinned, displaying raw gums and a mouthful of missing teeth. "The King thought jes that." He nodded sagely. "Sometimes when somethin' is taken away, the wound is open and superatin'. Nothin' like a spot of revenge to heal things over."

"Your philosophizing is lost upon me, gentlemen." St. Martin was growing impatient both with the summons and the company. The gunnysack between the two men sat heavily on the floor, strangely vying for his attention. "I have other matters to attend to, so I would request that you get on with the matter."

"Arrogant isn' he?" the stout man said to the others, who laughed as though on cue. He was obviously the ringleader and accountable to Bellamy, a familiar type from Adelaide to Lahore and points in between. "These aristos too big for their fine silk britches, I'll be thinkin'. Specially given these types here"—he gestured largely toward St. Martin—"who didn' do much but flee them Indians and Arabs. We heard the story, *my lord*. And it wasn' much of one."

"Your insights into the British Army's retreat from Kabul are without doubt fascinating. But I'm certain Bellamy would have you dispense with the analysis."

"You're sure, are ye?"

In response, St. Martin moved closer, deliberately crowding the trio in the limited space. "I'm sure."

"When the time comes, he jes wants to know you'll get the job done. For a change." He paused deliberately. "We don' know 'xactly what yer doing for the King, but it seems important."

"Tell Bellamy he won't be disappointed." St. Martin narrowed his eyes and nostrils against the fetid tang hanging in the air. He wondered how much the henchmen knew about the diamond and Bellamy's plans for the queen. "I shouldn't expect Bellamy is the sort to confide overly much."

The stout man snorted, then wiped his nose with his sleeve in disgust. "The King only tells me what needs tellin' and he tells me you have a nasty bit of revenge burnin' in your gullet."

"I shouldn't let it concern you." He shrugged. "And if this is all that Bellamy wanted, a useless encounter with several of his minions, then let's consider the meeting concluded, gentlemen."

The dismissal was obvious. The stout man moved from behind the bench with a jerk of his chin to his companions. "Not quite so fast, guvnor. King had a gift he wanted passed along to you. A friendly reminder." Another gesture and the two men dragged the gunnysack across the dirt floor to the center of the room.

"Care to open King's generous gift, guvnor? We know he's expectin' you to."

The sack sat between them, the odor stronger now, almost unbearable, threatening to slam his lungs shut.

When he didn't move, the stout man motioned to the men behind him to unwrap the burlap. Dark matted hair spilled from the opening, followed by what was once a face, its previously feminine features now distorted by bloat and rigor mortis. It was difficult to discern how long she'd been dead.

If he'd been a decent man, he would have retched. Instead, he concentrated on the rivers of dry blood, coagulated under the blue skin of the young woman. If he focused even closer, he could make out fingerprints in the bruises ringing her neck like a macabre necklace. The stench was overwhelming, but he didn't care.

Because the victim looked nothing like his late wife.

However, he could never be accused of obtuseness. The message was clear, the gift received—a Trojan horse he'd been expecting and welcomed through an open door.

But as he'd mentioned to Lilly Clarence Hampton, he did have a bad temper—although not often on display. This was not one of those moments, however.

St. Martin moved quickly. The two taller men were suddenly face-down and grunting like pigs at a trough, eating the dirt floor while he hauled the stout man up against a filth-encrusted barrel. He pounded his bullet-shaped head once against the barrel's girding before cocking the pistol at the man's neck. They would both recognize the fatal cracking sound when it came. But first St. Martin rapped the man on the side of his forehead with the heavy weapon, delighting in seeing the whites of his eyes.

The man reared, helplessly choking back his shock. St. Martin raked his gun over his ear. "Tell Bellamy, I'm pleased to be of service. But you may also tell him that I don't like his coercive tendencies. I shall see Vesper when I please." The pistol dug into the fleshy part of his lobe. "You will tell him, won't you?"

Whimpering. St. Martin positioned the mouth of the pistol at the man's crotch. "I seem to have missed your response." Sweat bathed the man's mottled face, the scent of panic overtaking the stench of death. "I can do away with your manhood quite easily," he said calmly, although his blood was singing. "And then, if you live, I'll ensure you never walk again." He pointed the muzzle of the gun to the man's shaking knees. "So what shall it be, my friend?"

The man looked at St. Martin's eyes and started blathering. "I will tell him, certainly guvnor," he said hoarsely. "And anythin' else you be wishin'."

St. Martin smiled. "You do that." Then he let go, watching the man slide to his knees and to the floor in relief.

No need to kill him. His anger was quickly dissipating, replaced by the usual ice water pumping through his veins. He straightened and pocketed his pistol in the waistband of his trousers, concealed under his jacket. Without looking back, he moved out into the sunlight, the alley still deserted except for the slink of a cat silhouetted against a low wall.

He hauled a deep breath of London air, strong and pungent, into his lungs. The crunch of gravel beneath his feet almost obscured the sound of steps behind him. He turned.

The stout man careened toward him, pistol cocked and aimed. St. Martin smiled to himself philosophically before pulling out his weapon, shooting quickly and precisely. This time Bellamy's man slid to his knees permanently.

It occurred to him later that he'd actually performed a service for the bastard. Because Isambard Kingdom Bellamy would have been none too amused to have his choice assassin removed from this world unnecessarily and all too soon.

Chapter 10

Lilly pushed the papers around on her desk in the library. Her lunch lay untouched on a tray and she tried to ignore the ticking of the hall clock that told her she was already late for her fitting at Madame Bernardin.

Perhaps it was a mistake. A seven-hundred-seventy-thousand-square-foot, cast iron, and glass blunder.

Rubbing her inkstained fingers on her blotter, she peered more closely at the plans for the Crystal Palace unfurled on her desk. She did not need to clap eyes on the building behind large tracts of hoarding, which was all but completed in Hyde Park, because she'd committed the concept of the structure to memory. The modular construction system was radical with its prefabricated iron sections, and her idea was to have the interior volume organized into galleries that were alternatively twenty-four and forty-eight feet wide. The roof of the galleries stepped up by twenty feet every seventy-two feet and culminated in a central nave.

It was going to be a horrific challenge, and not simply protecting the Koh-I-Noor. At this point only she and a handful of the queen's closest advisers knew where in the building the diamond would be housed and where the ceremony would take place. The final interior finishings were a monstrous test in so many ways. The ridge and furrow roofing glazing system specially devised for the Crystal Palace required forty-nine-inch glass sheets capable of spanning between furrows several feet apart and with three ridges occurring every twenty-four feet.

Hellishly challenging, but beautiful. A glass house that would be widely imitated in Europe and America forever after, she was confident. And attributed to the late Charles Hampton.

Lilly threw down her pen in a combination of frustration and anger, forever humiliated at the thought of her late husband taking credit for her work. As for the protection of the diamond, everyone expected that as Charles's widow, with legal rights over his intellectual property, she would assign the final details to a draftsman of her choice.

Instead, she was the architect, laboring night and day to finish. She locked herself away in the library, lost in her vocation and as far away from thoughts of Bellamy or St. Martin as she could be. Intense concentration ensured that the flow of her ideas translated into the reassuring lines and shapes on crisp, white paper. It would work, she told herself day after day, hour after hour, confidence in her efforts steadily growing.

The exposition hall would be heralded as the first of its kind, never mind that Pugin had already called it a *glass monster* and Carlyle a *big glass soap bubble*. When first examining the plans, Ruskin had termed it a conservatory, which held an element of truth because the building had been designed using her experience in constructing the gigantic greenhouse for the Duke of Devonshire. It was her drawing of the building that was finally accepted by the Royal Commission with a vote of one hundred sixty-six against forty-seven.

Not for her the Gothic revival architecture with its feature arches, pointed windows, and other details borrowed from the Middle Ages. She wanted to create a new architecture for a bold new age. She'd argued at length with Charles about the direction her work should take, debating at length against the more popular and elaborate styles ornamented with towers, turrets, and other fanciful notions.

The memory of Charles still registered with a jagged pain in her chest. He had deceived her so, willing to sacrifice anything and anyone to his success. Even his wife.

His portrait hung over the fireplace, the only space on the wall not reserved for books. She didn't have to look at it to remember his delicate features, the warm blue eyes, and the light brown curls topping a high brow. Upon their first meeting she thought him to be Percy Shelley incarnate, a poet with a rarified soul, an unfettered spirit endowed with a higher, more refined understanding of the world.

Her father, a don at Cambridge, had warned her against throwing herself headlong at her tutor, but then, lost in his many projects and his eccentric pastimes, he had lost interest in her as well. And her mother had never approved of the private instruction and drafting lessons her husband had allowed, and was relieved to have her only child, a peculiar, bluestocking daughter, securely married and out of her home.

How hopelessly young and ridiculously enamored she had been of Charles's cultivated handsomeness and romantic nature. So much so that she didn't realize he had made her his wife for reasons far different from what she'd imagined or hoped.

And so it came to be that Lilly Clarence began working in secret for Charles Hampton.

The clock chimed three o'clock. She bolted from her chair and away from her bitter memories. Quickly rolling up the plans, she carried them across the room to the two wing chairs by the fireplace. Securing them quickly beneath a loose parquet floorboard, she paused only briefly to look up at Charles.

His benign features gave no hint of the ambitious and shallow nature that lay beneath. Herself a sheltered and bookish eighteen-year-old, Lilly had been enraptured with her new husband who indulged her in her passionate interest in drawing and architecture. And as Charles's commissions began to trickle in, he began to rely increasingly on her skills and brilliance to execute first the country homes and the conservatories and then the higher profile public commissions. Then two years ago, the colossal conservatory built for the Duke of Devonshire had solidified his reputation among merchants and royals alike.

Of course, no one ever suspected, considering Lilly only as the dutiful wife, eager for her husband's success. At salons and in drawing rooms, at balls and social teas to which they were increasingly invited, Lilly and Charles Hampton were considered the epitome of marital harmony. The ambitious man and his gracious helpmeet.

Lilly looked away from the portrait, unwilling to dwell on the night of Charles's murder. The days after his death remained a clouded dreamscape, a time when she careened between utter despair and extreme exhilaration. She had tasted freedom and yet she was still in chains, shackled by her guilt.

And St. Martin *knew*. Even here alone in the library, she felt as if the ground had shifted beneath her feet, testing the fragile normality she had built around herself. It had been nearly a fortnight since that chaotic evening at the theater and a lifetime since her outrageous lack of judgment and irrational behavior. She flushed at the memory, at her body's startling and unexpected response. Whether it had been due to the blow to her head, St. Martin's intimidation, or his uncanny ability to coax what was obviously a deep-seated carnality from her being—her actions had been both unconscionable and unforgivable.

She rose from her knees with a last glance at the floorboards, brushing out her skirts and straightening the stiffly boned bodice of her day dress now covered with a shapeless smock. Mercifully, St. Martin had not pursued her, and yet his words haunted her these past nights when she lay tossing under tangled sheets, sleep outside her grasp.

. . . I will seduce you again and again, wherever I find you, until you give me what I really want.

She harbored no illusions. No man in her circle had ever been rendered powerless by her beauty, and St. Martin was hardly a candidate for lovesick swain in any case. What he coveted were the plans for the Crystal Palace that would help him craft plans to make off with the Koh-I-Noor. His earlier admonition, whispered hotly in her ear at the Tower, was equally difficult to forget, a relentless refrain she wished desperately to banish to the nether regions of her conscience. *What's the difference, precisely, Mrs. Hampton, between Bellamy and me? Between what he wants of you and what I want of you?*

A sudden stray chill danced down her spine. She flushed at the memory and damned the man who had manipulated her with the precision of a renaissance master, releasing a flow of ungovernable passion that had left her stunned in its wake. His influence over her was inexplicable and unacceptable and she simply wanted it—and St. Martin—gone.

Wearily, Lilly untied the toggles of her smock and shrugged out of the garment meant to protect her gown from ink stains. Tossing it impatiently over the wing chair, she considered the unpalatable and sinister truth. *St. Martin was correct.* Charles had wanted something from her—her skills and talents to be appropriated as his own. Isambard Kingdom Bellamy now wanted something from her—and it wasn't her beauty or her reputation, the latter balanced precariously on the cusp of scandalous.

The damned diamond. It glittered dangerously in her imagination with its promise of riches and absolute power. Perhaps it glittered in Bellamy's imagination as well, although he had never once mentioned to her the plans for the Crystal Palace. And he'd had every access to the gem, she recalled, having had an emissary from the British East India Company transport it to London. Bellamy's ruddy features rose to mind, along with the memory of his barely suppressed fury with Duleep Singh, the Maharajah of the Punjab.

Questions continued to plague her in the hansom on her way to Madame Bernardin's for the final fitting of her bridal gown. Looking out the small window of the cab, tassels swaying in front of her vision, she wondered again if she was making a mistake in accepting Bellamy's offer of marriage, the date set two days prior to the opening of the Crystal Palace. From the window she could see that it was a gray day; the skies were heavily overcast for spring, echoing her volatile mood.

The cab rumbled over a deep rut, jostling her in her seat, reminding her—as though she needed reminding, dear God— that she had already been unfaithful to her betrothed, the ideals of fidelity going up in flames the moment St. Martin had come within an inch of her. Unforgivable, and one more heinous act that she would attempt to bury, at least six feet deep, along with Charles's murder. Clasping her gloved hands together fervently, she could only be grateful that St. Martin had reneged on his eccentric, outrageous threats.

That he was clearly unstable and treacherous, she knew to be true, the last person who should be entrusted with knowledge of the diamond and its security. And that he had already erased her from his mind and his body was something that she understood and accepted. It had been ten days. She was hardly the type of female whose allure caused men to banish dragons and overturn empires. Another rut in the road caused her to shift in her seat, and somewhere beneath her corset and crinolines, she felt a twinge of hurt pride.

They were nearing Madame Bernardin's. The cab window outlined the drapers, haberdashers, and china shops, along with a highly coveted jeweler, that dotted the small avenue off highly fashionable Curzon Street. Bellamy had insisted that his bride be outfitted by the most estimable but discreet establishment in London. Although the wedding would be a small affair, he was adamant that no expense should be spared.

Alighting from the hansom, Lilly hurried in through the front door of the shop with its elegant, bow-fronted window. Inside, amid the aroma of beeswax and exotic fabrics, Madame Bernardin swept out from behind an exquisite Louis Quatorze desk to greet her personally with her particular combination of avarice and bonhomie, waving aside Lilly's apologies for her tardiness.

"We have everything, *tout*, at the ready," Madame reported a little breathlessly, no doubt excited by the size and cost of the trousseau she was assembling. Her smile was expansive, her subtly kohl-ringed eyes lighting at the challenge. "Shall we begin with the wedding dress, the most important of all, *n'est ce pas?*"

Before Lilly could nod obediently, she was flown into the back dressing room, a jewel box of a space, and surrounded by three seamstresses and acres of pearl satin. "Nothing too elaborate, as we discussed, I trust," she began, stepping up on the cushioned dais and surrounded by mirrors reflecting her from every possible angle. She was quickly stripped of her bodice and skirts and left only her chemise before the new creation, including crinolines and hoops, captured her as surely as a cage. It was an alarming metaphor for marriage, she noted with rising anxiety and barely contained cynicism.

Why did she imagine the institution would be any different with Bellamy than with Charles? She realized better than most the uneven distribution of power that robbed the fairer sex of any advantage it might have. She frowned at her reflection in the mirror. At least as a widow, she would be able to keep her property, but otherwise legally and personally Isambard Kingdom Bellamy would have her in his grip. But he was generous and protective, and, she reassured herself, as a couple they were not prone to the emotional excesses that had doomed her relationship with Charles from the start.

They would be practical and respectful of one another, not blinded by unruly expectations of romance. She would welcome his anticipated absences, as would he, neither wishing to intrude overly much on the other. His power and reputation would give her the freedom to pursue her interests and to leave behind the past. He would travel to India, spend months away from London, but she would remain untouchable and virtually above the law. The ghost of Charles Hampton would finally be laid to rest. And perhaps, if they did get on well enough, she would accompany him to distant continents, far away from rumors and from men like St. Martin.

St. Martin. Even his name caused her pulse to jump and her body to stiffen in perverse reaction for a woman approaching her third decade.

"You'll recall," she said to Madame Bernardin as her words were momentarily muffled by a swathe of lace descending over her head and neck, "that I am a widow, barely out of mourning and of a certain age. I would prefer something restrained and understated."

Madame frowned but agreed automatically. "Certainly, whatever you wish!" She steepled her fingers together as she contemplated Lilly in her luxurious creation. She took a step back, a woman who kept strategic interests at the forefront of her business life. "Of course, your first marriage, when you were so very young—you must have been a beautiful bride."

Hardly, thought Lilly, remembering the confection with its fitted bodice, small waist, and full skirt. It had been made of organdy and tulle and her veil had been attached with a coronet of orange blossoms. Short white kid gloves, a handkerchief embroidered with her maiden name initials, silk stockings, and flat shoes decorated with bows at the instep completed her ensemble. All of it white, in the manner that Queen Victoria had made fashionable at her wedding to Albert in 1840.

Not this time, not so for the widow. She did not wear white, had no bridesmaids, no veil, and no orange blossoms, those symbols of purity. Lilly nearly choked at the thought. What she'd done with St. Martin . . . what he had done to her . . . If Bellamy so much as suspected . . .

She swallowed nervously, the reflection in the mirror revealing an appropriately sober figure, albeit in an expensive gown of pearl and gray satin trimmed with ostrich feathers.

"*Et voila;* you are once again a beautiful bride," Madame Bernardin enthused, instructing one of her acolytes to pin in the waist. Her hands fluttered around her shoulders, gesticulating her enthusiasm. "Such a splendid figure, such a tiny waist and beautiful bosom. Perhaps we shall lower the bodice a fraction, eh? After all, we are not a blushing maiden."

Lilly demurred, at this point believing she deserved a scarlet letter. "I think it is quite suitable as it is," she protested, alarmed at the expanse of skin already revealed by the square neckline. She was hardly buxom and didn't agree with Madame Bernardin's assessment of her obviously meager charms. "This is fine, just fine. Let us move on to the other items."

She was suffocating, a sense of doom slowly settling around her. Suddenly, she wanted to finish with the fitting, to flee the shop and the prospect of marriage to Bellamy. How foolish. Marriage to the man was her only recourse, her new and only reality.

She heard herself saying, "As I recall, thanks to the overly generous impulse of my betrothed, we have many other items that require fitting, but I shouldn't want to take too much of your time, Madame, so perhaps we can move along rather more swiftly."

Madame clucked disapprovingly, waggling her ringed fingers in protest. "Such a wealthy man, Madame, indeed. We must take our time. It would be beneficial to, how do you say, seek his approval and keep his attentions. Despite the great love between your queen and her consort—such a romance—I know you English have a different view of matrimony but perhaps a few lessons from the French would do you a ser-

vice." She smiled slyly before motioning her assistants to remove the wedding gown. "You will adore, *sans doute*, the
chemises and corsets we have assembled for you."

Smiling stiffly for the benefit of the couturier and her assistants who wrestled with the yards of fabric enveloping her,
Lilly was relieved when she could breathe again, a soft chill
sweeping across her exposed skin. Reflected in the mirror behind her she saw a young woman with a mob cap poke her
head in the doorway of the dressing room. "Madame, there
is a matter that requires your attention. I believe it best this
gentleman speak with you directly," she stammered, a blush
pinking her cheeks. "My apologies for interrupting."

"My attention, maintenant?" Bernardin asked grandly, an
artist interrupted at work. She turned to one of the seamstresses whose arms overflowed with wisps of lace and silk.
"I prefer not to interrupt Madame Hampton's most important fitting. Do you see how much we have yet to finish?"

"Please, Madame," pleaded the girl.

Pursing her lips and murmuring apologies, Madame puffed
up her chest like an indignant pigeon, directing her seamstresses to lay down their lacy burdens. Exclaiming to Lilly
that she would return in *un instant*, she clapped her hands
and turned on her heels, her acolytes following like ducklings
after their mother.

Thank God for the reprieve. Lilly shivered, clad in only her
chemise, corset, and white stockings, convinced that she
should gather her clothes and secure another appointment
for another time. And yet time was running out. The mountain of the finest lingerie mocked her, as did her reflection.
Not only was she a murderess, she was a hypocrite no less,
prepared to marry a man while inexplicably desiring another.

When she was a child and closed her eyes, she thought she
could disappear from sight. How she wished she could do
that now—close her eyes and vanish in a puff of smoke, spirit
herself away from this mountainous trousseau, from her

monstrous guilt, from the man who would make her his wife, and from the dangerous emotions left behind by St. Martin.

She should leave now, she thought, turning around to step down from the dais. Her eyes darted around the room looking for her clothes, one leg and stockinged foot poised over the floor.

Someone entered the dressing room. She cursed under her breath, rooting around for excuses she could offer the couturier or one of her many busy seamstresses. She turned abruptly expecting to face the Frenchwoman, but it wasn't Madame Bernardin after all.

Lilly stared up at St. Martin with mute shock.

"What are you doing . . . how did you get in here?!" Her face pale with astonishment, it was as though she'd forgotten she was almost naked.

Unfortunately, St. Martin couldn't. In her plain cotton underclothes, she was outrageously erotic, the bright lights of the dressing room blatantly revealing. He'd forgotten that mouth, sensual without any rouge, and the startled blue eyes wide-set with their flared brows. Her hands went up to the all but nonexistent fabric around her neck, the motion of her elegant body curving away from him. He could see the creamy whiteness of her fair skin, the flash of her backbone and hips, as she turned around to face away from him.

"It's a little late for modesty, I believe. Or would you like me to continue addressing your backside, wondrous though it is?"

"For God's sake," she whispered loudly over her shoulder. "How did you get in here and past Madame Bernardin? Or perhaps I shouldn't even bother inquiring."

No, she shouldn't. His late wife had spent thousands of pounds on gowns and fripperies, and consequently, a simple word from Lord St. Martin had vanquished difficult questions. A woman of the world with a sophisticated clientele,

Bernardin was accustomed to studiously ignoring indiscreet liaisons and alliances, buoyed by the men who spent so lavishly on their mistresses and paramours. If St. Martin preferred to remain closeted with Mrs. Hampton for an hour or a week in her jewel box of a dressing room, it would be so.

"I'm simply making good on my promise," he said, unable to take his eyes from her form reflected from every direction by the mirrors in the room. She was a goddess on the cushioned dais, a celestial offering, a Venus on the half shell. He couldn't recall why he'd ever thought her plain.

"This is preposterous, and you know it," she continued, making no effort to turn around and face him directly. "You cannot make good on your promise, as I am affianced to another man. Furthermore, I'm not interested in continuing this ridiculous association predicated on your outrageous threats that have absolutely no basis in reality."

He sat on a plump, overstuffed chair, the only one in the dressing room, before answering. "I thought we'd been over the specifics of your situation already, Mrs. Hampton. Surely you don't require another disquisition outlining your very precarious situation."

He may have looked more harmless seated because she finally turned around to face him. "You are not getting the plans," she said starkly. She'd managed to slip her arms out of each sleeve of her chemise in an attempt to hitch up the fabric to her neck. Ironically, the posture was all the more tantalizing.

He realized quite suddenly that he was enjoying himself, enjoying Lilly Clarence Hampton, like he hadn't enjoyed himself in a long time. Perhaps it was because he was courting death and the knowledge ignited whatever smoldering embers were left in his benighted soul. Fair enough. He wasn't a man to waste time on introspection.

"Your continued stubbornness suggests that I've not been persuasive enough."

She lifted her chin. "You'll discover quickly that your attempts at persuasion, if that's how you phrase it, are futile. Do us both a favor and exit as quietly as you came."

He rose from the chair with an exaggerated sigh. She took a small step back on the dais, her hands gripping the fabric at her neck. "I can do that if you kindly relinquish the plans but," he continued at the sight of her mutinous expression, "you don't seem prepared to do that at this juncture. Or perhaps you're actually looking forward to this encounter as much as I am."

"Don't be preposterous."

"At least we know you're not going to scream. Bernardin and her staff would pretend not to hear in any case." He moved toward her until his knees touched the cushions of the dais and the two were face to face. With excruciating slowness, he pulled the fabric of the chemise down, exposing her neat collarbone. When she didn't protest, he bared her shoulders, sliding the garment along until it snagged on the swell of her breasts, which were full but not large, filling her corset perfectly.

"What are you doing?" she asked with a barely perceptible quaver in her voice.

"Do you have to ask? Or were your relations with your husband so tepid that this approach comes as a complete surprise."

She stiffened beneath his hands. "You are being presumptuous to even inquire about my marital relations with Charles. It's absolutely none of your concern and an extremely private matter."

He continued his work unabated, unlacing her corset before tossing it aside. Underneath the sheer cotton of her chemise, her flat stomach was decorated by a tiny navel followed by white stockings and pantalets. He spanned his hands around her waist, her skin cool marble beneath the fine fabric. "I think I have the answer to the question," he said with a slight smile. Her unschooled and out-of-control response to his touch told him everything he needed to know. "Of course, if you'd like to stop now, please say so directly and I shall leave you to retrieve the plans for the Crystal Palace. Quite a simple solution to your current dilemma, would you not agree?"

While he said the words, he slowly pulled the sleeves of her chemise down her body until it pooled on the floor. Her perfect breasts shone in the light. The high, upturned nipples of the lightest pink were set on her narrow frame. He forced himself to slow down, lightly skimming his hands along her smooth arms.

"As though I have any choice," she said quietly; but there was anger and something else in her voice that he recognized. Desire.

He shook his head, his hands tightening around her wrists. "Don't lie to yourself, Lilly. You don't have to do this. You want to do this. Otherwise, you would comply with my request and be finished with it."

She hesitated, her eyes flashing frustration and need. "Why are you pursuing this course of action? You could go to the constabulary with the incriminating pistol without having to pretend . . . go through the motions . . . as though you enjoy . . ."

He raised his eyebrows inquiringly, enfolding her hips with his hands and gently turning her away from him. "What makes you think I'm not enjoying myself?"

The words were muffled. "You didn't take your pleasure. That last time."

He focused on the nape of her neck laid bare by the upsweep of golden hair, his hands still for the moment. The question reverberated in the small space and in the dark corners of his mind. It hit close to the mark, too close, and he wondered at its source—whether she knew or simply intuited that he was punishing himself by lacing pleasure with pain. He brushed his lips lightly against the soft skin of her neck and felt her shiver.

"You are to be forgiven if you believe that men are simply concerned with satisfying their own desires. Oftentimes, the journey is as interesting as the destination," he said, the statement hot against her skin.

"I somehow doubt that assertion. In my experience, men expect to have their expectations fulfilled." Lilly said the words over one slender shoulder, her profile turned toward him. Several strands of her hair had escaped her chignon, arcing toward her mouth, the full lips pressed tight.

Her back was beautifully naked, the delicate indentations of her spine a magnet for his lips and tongue. "You know my expectations then, Lilly, and they have everything to do with the plans for the Crystal Palace. My pleasure, that you're seemingly so concerned about, is in your hands." He trailed a languorous kiss down her back, his palm pressed into her buttocks still covered by her pantalets. He would expect that she could feel his shaft now, thick and heavy against her. "You know exactly what it is that I want."

Her lips parted in shock and with a little hiss of breath as she felt St. Martin pull down the last barrier between them. When the pantalets were at her ankles, he lifted first one slender foot and then another as she stepped out of them. Refusing to let go of the scrap of cotton, she turned around, inch by inch, holding the piece of cloth between her legs. He smiled darkly, his hand forcing hers away to reveal her most private place.

The mirrors gave him Lilly Clarence Hampton from every glorious angle. White stockings held up by demure garters were her only decoration, save his dark hands against her hips and then against the whiteness of her breasts. Lowering his head, he lightly nibbled her navel before trailing slowly up to her left breast, blowing lightly on the pink areola before working his tongue on her nipple. Her back arched against his teasing and he watched the pulse jump in her neck as she struggled to withhold her groan of pleasure.

His tongue continued to draw tiny circles around the pinkening areolas. The nipples hardened to attention as his mouth sucked and his hands kneaded the firm rounded flesh. "Just say when, Lilly," he said hotly against her skin. "We can stop anytime you wish."

He thought she choked back a sob and he dropped his hands from her body, moving away from her. "Is that your answer?"

Lilly shook her head mutely, looking back at him with expectant eyes. Her breathing was rapid, her body torpid as her expression. He shrugged his shoulders in confusion, feeling the muscles rippling over his lean body. She could see the movements through his tight breeches and thin, tapered jacket. And he knew she was watching. "You know what you have to do."

"Very well," she said slowly. Her tongue licked her lips. "Both of us can play this peculiar game of yours, St. Martin." Her stockinged thighs clenched in need.

It was all he needed, her acceptance hardly a surprise. He didn't want to inspect too closely the satisfaction that settled low in his gut. "I'm pleased you see it that way." He leaned toward her and took her shoulders with both hands.

The kiss began slowly, sensitively, probingly. His lips moved over hers, committing her mouth to memory, his tongue sliding in gently, firmly. As if they had all the time in the world and she wasn't half dressed and Madame and her seamstresses were not waiting outside, their ears pressed to the door. Her lips moved beneath his own, tentatively at first, and then more demandingly, her fingers curling tightly around his shoulders. He slid his hands up her waist to her forearms and his thumbs reached out to stroke the sides of her breasts.

Dragging his mouth to the side of her neck, he broke contact and met her gaze. Reaching behind her, he pulled the pins from her long hair, stroking the silken fall as it tumbled over her shoulders. Leaning in again, unable to resist, he kissed the curve of a high cheekbone before pulling her down to a seated position on the dais.

"Incredible." St. Martin looked at her, boneless and pliant

before him. Her small rounded breasts with their areolas, wide and pink, opened for him, the nipples raised like ripe raspberries. Bending his head, he separated the breasts with his hands, holding them apart while he ran his tongue up and down the shallow cleft between.

Lilly's hands cupped the back of his head, tangling in his hair. She bent one leg at the knee, resting the heel on the edge of the dais instinctively, helpless need drowning out anything else. He pushed her gently onto her back and then raised one of her breasts and caressed it with the other. He stroked the underside, traced the curve, thumbed the nipple. He bent again and trailed his tongue over the pinkness before touching the very tip with his fingertip.

She bucked under his ministrations, her nails digging into his arms, her thighs rubbing together as though outside her control.

He kissed her again and his hand moved down over her stockinged legs, caressing them up and down, working his way to the inside and gently soothing the clenched muscles.

"This is madness," she said, staring at his hand playing between her slender thighs. "I can't believe this." Her voice shook and she closed her eyes, shutting him out.

"You wanted to play," he warned. Before she could respond, he was kneeling over her and kissing her again. His tongue moved in and out of her mouth rhythmically, in tandem with his hand between her legs and then on her buttocks. His palm was pressed against her dampening curls, her hips writhing hungrily. She had long forgotten that they could be discovered in flagrante delicto at any moment for the whole world to see. Her hair was splayed over her breasts with her nipples sharp points peaking with passion. He registered the scene with less dispassion than he cared to, suddenly and irrationally angry with himself for what he couldn't precisely define.

He separated her legs, pushing them farther apart, exposing the lips of her apex, pink and wet and hungry. His erection throbbed in his breeches, mocking his parody of self-control. Slowly, he slid a finger into the tight, wet, clutching tunnel, moving in slow, excruciating circles.

She moaned once, twice as he continued to work his way in and out, and around and around. "Dear God," she gasped as her eyes opened to dart from her hand to his erection tenting the fabric of his breeches.

God had nothing to do with it, he wanted to say, but didn't. Instead, his head swooped down and licked the folds opened to him. He tongued her gently in tiny circles, her cleft against his insistent mouth, cupping her firm buttocks in his hands. It didn't take long. She tightened like a bow, her spine arcing and thighs spread wide; then it came, wordless, sobbing, and ecstatic.

He felt her shatter beneath him; then the panting subsided to cede to the hush of luxuriant satiation. When he looked up, the mirrors reflected the carnage. Lilly lay limp against the cushions, exhausted limbs splayed in surrender. The goddess, pale and golden, fallen from her pedestal. Tearing his eyes away from the image, he did not want to catch a glimpse of the man next to her. Still fully clothed, with a painful erection and wearing a dumbfound expression, he was unrecognizable to himself.

Lilly Clarence Hampton was not the only one playing dangerous games.

Chapter 11

Constance St. Martin exhibited an amazing appetite for pain.

Smoothing his waistcoat pocket inside his long frock coat, Isambard Kingdom Bellamy prepared himself for dinner with his betrothed. While Constance slept hours away under her usual fog of laudanum, he would be playing court to Lilly Clarence Hampton in the enormous dining room of his Hampstead Heath home.

Satisfied that the world was ordered to his liking, he straightened his shoulders, cursed the corset cinching his waist under his long frock coat, and made his way down the elaborately curved staircase of Waldegrave Hall. He shook his head admiringly. Constance's performance, and that's what it had been, with not one but two of the brutish louts from the stables, would have made the most experienced harlot take note. Quite the delicate aristocrat, my arse, he thought. He liked to watch and to remember, to replay every last decadent, lascivious scene, a predilection he had perfected in the backwaters of Lahore. Not that he chose to admit the fact to himself very often, but such brutal encounters harkened back to his tender years as a child when his mother would entertain in the one room shanty sentimentally known as home.

Stopping briefly on the newel, he absorbed the high-ceilinged splendor of the entrance hall. First impressions were all important and Waldegrave Hall had to impress visitors with an insistent proclamation of social status. The floors were inlaid with encaustic tiles in a medieval design leading to highly polished mahogany wainscoting. A great believer not only in ornamentation but also ostentation, Bellamy had personally overseen the selection of the oversized chandelier with matching wall sconces, the ensemble featuring crystal icicles dripping in profusion and lavishly embedded with golden beads.

He'd hoped the widow he was about to marry did not harbor any ridiculous ideas of changing the decor of Waldegrave Hall, his masterpiece. That was the difficulty with modern women, their headstrong and willful tendencies so much at odds with the passivity of their more primitive counterparts. In India, the female body was a place where imperial power was imagined and exercised. Bellamy smoothed the heavy silk of his cravat while his free hand lingered on the polished newel post. Of course, the British aristocracy abhorred Oriental practices as being beneath their moral virtues and social superiority. And those practices adopted by the British East India Company servants were considered disgraceful, all the more so because he knew that at the center of their icy hearts the English aristocracy was threatened by the influx of new wealth from the East.

His wealth and power, to be precise.

Besides which, there was nothing like a tasty morsel—weak, begging, and helpless—to pique a man's appetite. British men take note, he thought with dark humor. The good Dr. Aubrey Vesper had lived and learned and presumably enjoyed, despite the fact that his ridiculous lack of judgment had culminated in a muddled affair, thus delivering him to Bellamy's doorstep, hat in hand.

Vesper's by-blow was probably an ugly, diseased little thing, he thought absently, consigned as a leper to a life of misery, despair, and servitude. If she survived infancy, and escaped her leprous legacy, she might find her way to a brothel outside one of the military camps, he mused. Bothering with the survival of a mixed breed was beyond his ken but nonetheless, if Vesper performed well, he would make certain that she ended up in one of the stews surrounding Calcutta. It was the least he could do.

At the bottom of the hallway, he saw his butler waiting for him, his usual hauteur broken by a pained expression. "What is it, Croft?" Bellamy asked without looking at the man, instead concentrating on the fit of his low-cut patent pumps with their large flat bow of grosgrain ribbon, the latest fashion nuance courtesy of Bond Street.

"Your guests, sir." Croft pointed his nose higher in the air, his expression one of forbearance. Bellamy suspected that his questionable pedigree was not lofty enough for the butler's taste, but then, there was keen satisfaction to be had in the knowledge that he had purloined the servant from one of London's many delinquent and financially desperate noblemen, the Duke of Wilmington. Everyone could be purchased, even Croft.

"I have one waiting in the drawing room, the other in the conservatory."

"What do you mean by *guests*? I was expecting my betrothed, Mrs. Hampton, to be alone." He shot his cuffs, starched white against the dark wool of his coat. "It's not as though we're in need of chaperones. The lady is a widow after all and hardly a maiden requiring a vigilant eye," he muttered to no one in particular, quite deliberately. Servants in India knew enough to keep their eyes cast down when speaking to their betters. Would that Croft would do the same.

"If I may, sir." Croft flicked a nonexistent speck of lint from Bellamy's lapel before continuing serenely. "Dr. Vesper is in the conservatory. Mrs. Hampton is in the drawing room."

Bellamy looked up from his cuffs, eyes narrowed. "The

doctor here? Now? You should have asked him to return at a more convenient time. You knew I was taking dinner with Mrs. Hampton."

"He insisted, sir."

"Then insist that he leave. I have no interest in meeting with him at the moment." The directive came moments too late because the hallway echoed with hurried footsteps, a staccato of demand to Bellamy's ears. The muscles at the back of his neck tightened in irritation.

Aubrey Vesper, coattails flapping in urgency, scrambled down the hallway toward them. Bellamy's eyes shot back and forth between Croft and Vesper, his exasperation clear, before coming to rest unpleasantly on the doctor. He held up his hand, preempting discussion.

"Now is not the time. Croft will see you out." Bellamy spun on his heels, the fine leather of his shoes squeaking against the floor.

Vesper hovered uncertainly, blocking his exit. He hadn't shaved and there was stubble on his face that added years to his appearance, along with dark circles under his eyes attesting to a serious lack of sleep.

Bellamy stopped. He turned to face him directly because it was clear the man was losing his bearings. *Fuck him* to hell and beyond. Dismissing the butler with a flick of his hand, Bellamy unlocked his jaw and said evenly, "I will give you five minutes to state your purpose here this evening, doctor."

Vesper's eyes burned into his, as far from the rational medical man as a preacher in a brothel. "I want your promise," he said, his voice low and hoarse.

Bellamy's eyebrows rose at the effrontery. The man was obviously close to losing his wits if he was demanding promises. From him, of all people. "I don't believe I heard correctly."

Vesper looked startled as though he wasn't aware that he stood in Waldegrave Hall confronting the major shareholder and chairman of the British East India Company. Oblivious that a corner of his shirt had come loose from his waistband, he shifted his weight from one foot to the other, a schoolchild asking for the impossible. "I want your promise," he repeated.

Bellamy had once seen a leopard savage an antelope on an open plain and quelled a similar urge to dismember the trembling figure before him. "Doctor—I urge you to heal yourself." He attempted to keep his voice even. "If you have in any way lost your way or your purpose in this shared endeavor, I suggest that you quickly regain your bearings. You have everything to lose."

Vesper scrubbed a hand down his unshaven face. His voice cracked. "I am well aware of that fact, sir, and the reason that I am here—"

"I don't want to hear it."

Vesper seemed to rebuild his indignation, shoring up his defenses. "The other night. I began to think and then the man in my house . . . keeping him alive . . . it's too much to ask."

Frozen silence.

"But my daughter. Surely." The words were a mere whisper.

"Daughter!" Indignation welled like a tide, causing the ivory buttons on Bellamy's waistcoat to strain perilously. "You dare question my plans because of your maudlin concerns over a bastard child who, as far as you know, may not even be your own? And a female creature, a diseased creature at that, the product of an ill-considered liaison? A by-blow, for Christ's sake?" Bellamy's vision blurred red. "Are you completely mad?"

"The money means nothing to me," the doctor quavered.

Bellamy spat nails. "Spare me the noble attempts at reclaiming your conscience, Vesper. Be a man once in your sad life and deliver on your promises, or that scrawny offspring of yours won't live long enough to find her way into a ditch in Calcutta. Which would probably be a blessing. Do I make myself clear?"

The words rang ominously in the corridor, the lights seeming to flicker at the released venom. It had been a long time since Bellamy had to actually articulate his threats. His presence was usually enough to send the most stalwart men scrambling like ants at a picnic.

Vesper appeared startled, his pale lips forming a silent plea.

Bellamy showed no mercy, eyes narrowing ominously. "I urge you to dismiss these ridiculous notions as I shall give you the benefit of the doubt and am prepared to forget this unfortunate incident." He lowered his voice. "As for the plans in place, I trust that all is well and that you are ensuring the world unfolds as it should. The process worked exceedingly well in India with Lady St. Martin and it will work with *the man,* as you refer to him, who is at present a guest in your home. Alive and reasonably well, I trust." He stepped back, smoothing the superfine of his waistcoat. "You will depart now. And you will ensure that St. Martin is at the ready. At this point, I shouldn't think that I must articulate the consequences should you fail me in this directive." It was a good thing that this worthless little man would never glimpse the historical implications of his plans, or he would dissolve with fear into the imported Italian tile beneath his feet.

Spineless sniveler. Fuck him to hell and back, Bellamy thought again, feeding from the anger in the pit of his belly. He took a deep, restorative breath, the corset punishing his expanded girth. He ignored the pain, aware that, mercifully, he was a strategist with several rooks and pawns on his chessboard. The woman upstairs and, of course, his recently betrothed, formed a neat if unwitting rear guard should St. Martin prove reluctant. He would bring the dead back to life—with Vesper's cooperation.

Like a lost child, Vesper stared out at him from behind his spectacles, marooned in the center of the vast hallway beneath the giant, glittering chandelier. "St. Martin, yes, of course." The monster he'd helped create. Vesper shook his head, rubbing a lock of red hair on his forehead as though the thought had just occurred to him upon waking from a deep sleep.

Before Bellamy could turn his back and walk away, the drawing room doors burst open.

"I was wondering what has you delayed, Mr. Bellamy," Lilly Clarence Hampton said. She sailed toward the men with characteristic quiet grace, her presence as unwelcome as the last dregs of whiskey in a glass. Bellamy felt his usual low-grade irritation at the keen intelligence shining from her gaze. She was dressed in one of the new gowns recently ordered from London's most fashionable dressmakers, as per his instructions he noted grudgingly.

The wide mutton sleeves, the square-cut bodice, and the deep wine color were all bolder than her customary choices. He regarded her carefully, noting the subtle changes with a jaundiced eye. There was something more, something out of place. He'd always considered her looks indifferent, but this evening her skin had a creamier texture, her lips were fuller, and there was a languor about her movements that contrasted markedly from her usual formal elegance.

Suspicion rose in his mind, but he dismissed it for later inspection. He gave a theatrical bow. "My apologies, my dear. Please allow me to introduce Dr. Aubrey Vesper."

The man was disheveled, his hunched shoulders communicating a deep-seated unease. Lilly had seldom seen such misery etched upon a high, intelligent brow. "Good evening," she said, taking in his nervous glance as he sketched a brief bow and began backing his way toward the door.

Something tugged at the corner of her memory. He was familiar to her, the features sensitive and fine. She was usually good at remembering faces, her years hosting salons and cultivating Charles's benefactors honing her skills.

Bellamy turned toward the slighter man before facing her again, clasping his hands behind him, belatedly and reluctantly calling upon proper form. "My dear, may I present Dr. Aubrey Vesper. And doctor, my betrothed, Lilly Clarence Hampton." He watched with narrowed eyes as Vesper fumbled in his haste, taking his coat and cane from Croft who had magically reappeared.

"Pleasure, Mrs. Hampton," he murmured, shrugging on his coat with help from the butler. "My apologies, my manners are remiss. To have interrupted your dinner this evening was inexcusable."

Lilly inclined her head. "No apologies necessary, doctor. As a matter of fact"—she turned to Bellamy inquiringly—"might we not share a glass of sherry with our unexpected but welcome guest? Surely dinner can be delayed another half hour or so?"

Bellamy's smile was far from genuine. Lilly waited expectantly, Vesper's face tantalizingly familiar yet out of reach. She watched the two men with keen interest, the name St. Martin still ringing in her ears. Their argument—and it had been heated—had floated through the closed double doors and into the drawing room. There she had been waiting and sipping tepid tea with a lump in her throat, halfheartedly admiring the silk panels and curtains that Bellamy had once assured her had been woven on seventeenth-century French handlooms.

At first Lilly thought she'd misheard the intense exchange. Her thoughts, dreams, and senses had been full of St. Martin, full of the man whose presence haunted her every waking and sleeping hour. Exquisite anticipation warred with intense disquiet, and she imagined he might make good on his promise and materialize at every turn.

Even here. In the house of her future husband.

Her stomach plunged. And then, worse still, suspicion congealing into a hard reality, she'd heard his name. The feeling of his presence was palpable as a hand on her shoulder while she slept, shaking her awake.

"I shouldn't like to presume on Dr. Vesper's time," Bellamy continued smoothly, every inch the gentleman. "He's an enormously industrious man entirely and continually in demand. We shouldn't like to keep him from his numerous patients."

Vesper blinked behind his spectacles, eager for permission to make his escape. Murmuring several more niceties and with another bow for Lilly, he broke for the door held conveniently open for him by Croft. A sharp blast of night air and the clatter of his walking stick against the tile floor punctuated his exit.

Lilly stood awkwardly in his wake, her mind working restlessly now, endeavoring to connect St. Martin with Bellamy and the obviously agitated doctor. Some inner pulse kept time with her cogitation as she groped for the key that would pull together the unrelated pieces of the puzzle. She glanced up at the elaborate chandelier casting fractured shadows along the watered-silk-patterned walls of the corridor, looking for a connection where perhaps there was none. However, coincidence required a faith she didn't have.

"It's a shame he doesn't have time to join us," she said carefully, pretending to admire the crystal and gold beads of the ostentatious monstrosity while staking her ground, keeping her inquiry cool. "I hope you're not unwell, King, and seeking medical attention." She frowned deliberately. "And where does Dr. Vesper practice? His name is not familiar to me."

Holding out his arm to escort her to the dining room, Bellamy looked entirely nonplussed by the encounter, leaning toward her with the attention of a besotted suitor bathing in the sunlight of wifely concern. "Somewhere off Harley Street, to be sure, although he calls on his patients so I cannot claim to have ever visited him at his rooms. But no need to fret, my dear, over my health," he said, patting her hand nested in his arm. "I am in the best of spirits, mental and corporal. Vesper and I simply became acquainted in Mysore a few years back."

"Of course, India."

Entering the dining room on Bellamy's proffered arm, Lilly

deliberately held back her questions, struck by the elaborate guilloche design on the ceiling. The result was dizzying, a pattern of repetitive geometrically interlocking loops that repeated in the moldings of the doors and shutters. The windows facing onto a courtyard were of medieval design flanking a table that could comfortably seat forty.

"And while we are speaking of health and well-being . . ." Bellamy continued, interrupting her appraisal and pulling out a mahogany balloon-back dining chair finished in petit point embroidery. Lilly took her seat across from stuffed birds in cages, a small village of fine china figurines, and several exotic potted plants standing sentinel at the oversized sideboard. "Might I mention that you are looking exceedingly well this evening, my dear? Why you positively glow, a condition I must attribute to your excitement over our upcoming nuptials."

Her anxiety froze to shock. She wondered whether her illicit encounters with St. Martin were writ directly on her skin, a brand visible to the human eye. Unable to respond immediately, Lilly deliberately counted seven pieces of stemware at her place on Bellamy's right, consciously slowing her racing thoughts. She tried to calm herself, wondering desperately why she could not reconcile her reaction to the man who would be her husband and her overblown response to St. Martin. The one was her savior, the other her nightmare.

Her stomach constricted at the thought. "Very kind of you to say," she said, giving her hands something to do by spreading the crisp linen napkin on her lap, her engagement ring winking at her determinedly. "I am feeling quite well," she lied. The day of their wedding was quickly approaching like a heavy cloud looming on the horizon—a cloud she hoped would miraculously lift along with her dark thoughts.

Bellamy motioned a footman to pour the wine, and the sight of his florid face with its luxuriant mustache gave her pause. She didn't want to think about it, what it would mean to go to the marriage bed with Bellamy after the decadent, illicit hours she had spent with St. Martin. Even considering going ahead with the union was monstrous after what she had done, and yet she was hesitating still, looking for a safe haven in this powerful, if inexplicably repellent, man. Her first marriage, disaster it had been, had begun with infatuation. She knew enough not to repeat the mistake. This time, she counseled herself sternly, she would make a decision based on reason and practicality.

Pushing herself to relax over the next two hours, she tried to enjoy their desultory conversation that began with the first course of pheasant soup and segued to a turbot in white sauce before finishing with a saddle of lamb. Moving the food around on her plate while she discussed wedding details, drinking too much of the wine that was continuously on offer, she admitted that she and Bellamy could settle blandly into a cordial domesticity. He was clearly not enamored of her, instead patting her arm absently from time to time as though he might a favored pet.

So far away from what her relationship had been with Charles. And fathoms away from what she'd experienced with St. Martin.

Meeting Bellamy's gaze, she smiled automatically for what seemed to be the hundredth time, her cheekbones aching and her teeth grinding. They would get along well enough, she repeated to herself, and if she had to do her wifely duty occasionally, she would bear it. He hardly seemed the amorous sort and would most likely request little from her in terms of wifely duties. As for her recently discovered sensibilities, she would bury them away, immerse herself once more in her work, play hostess in the appropriate social and political circles, and become, once again, the admirable helpmeet of a highly successful man.

And she would be safe. From accusations of murder. And from St. Martin himself.

She finished the last drop of wine in her glass with an unnerving thirst.

Bellamy was talking, his lips moving. "And what have you been amusing yourself with, my dear, these past few days, other than your fittings for your trousseau?"

She clenched the fragile stem of the crystal wineglass, hoping it wouldn't shatter. Her body tightened at the memory of her *fitting* at Madame Bernardin's, heat immediately chafing her skin so ridiculously sensitized by St. Martin's touch. She was a credible liar, she'd learned this past year, and she only hoped her talent for deceit and mendacity, not to mention de facto adultery, would survive.

"The trousseau is all but complete," she said, "and the arrangements for the wedding breakfast all but finalized." The reality was that she had been fornicating with a traitor and working clandestinely on the final drawings for the Crystal Palace. The very least she could do amid the wreckage that was her life was to protect the Koh-I-Noor to the best of her skills and abilities.

"Of course, you may begin to have your possessions moved to Waldegrave Hall in anticipation of the wedding," Bellamy said, resting his elbows on the table and interrupting her thoughts. "I will have Croft and Flynn look after the necessary arrangements."

A fresh surge of panic shot through her. "Foolish of me but I hadn't really thought that far ahead," she said carefully. The idea of losing her home and residing with Bellamy was becoming too certain, smoke and mirrors coalescing into a hard reality. "Everything is transpiring so quickly, the wedding and then the opening of the Crystal Palace two days later. I believed you said that we might delay our wedding journey until after the event that is so important to both of us."

"Indeed, my dear. So important to both of us. For you, the culmination of your late husband's efforts, and for me, to finally see the Koh-I-Noor in its rightful place."

The last phrase hung in the air heavy with implication. Unable to hold back, her nerves making her bold, she said, "Quite the honor for you, King, to present the diamond to the queen."

"Representing the very height of my ambitions," he responded grandly.

"Indeed," Lilly murmured, wishing for more wine to wash away the unwelcome dread that threatened the carefully planned future she'd envisioned. "The diamond has such a history."

"Quite right." Bellamy nodded condescendingly, already practicing husbandly airs. "There are ridiculous tales and superstitions attached to the gem, the idea that the Koh-I-Noor brings misfortune to its possessor when, in reality, it is symbolic of our empire's power—in our ability to wrest riches from the East." His barrel chest pumped up at his own statement. "The ceremony a few weeks hence will demonstrate our unimpeachable power. We will have the diamond surrendered directly from the hand of the conquered prince into the hands of the conqueror."

Lilly was not certain of Bellamy's meaning, her instincts telling her she was wading into dangerous waters. She persisted against her better judgment. "The conqueror being the queen or the British East India Company?" she asked.

A dull glint of avarice, already uncomfortably familiar to her, lit his eyes. "An astute question, my dear lady," Bellamy said. "As a matter of fact, I did take possession of the diamond from the conquered prince until such time that I was instructed by the Crown to relinquish the gem into the guardsmanship of the governor general, whose lackeys, I might remind, were transported with the diamond on one of my ships. With full protection of the Company."

Bellamy glowed with a barely concealed combination of pride and possessiveness. Lilly moved back in her chair, surrendering to an acute need to move as far away from his physical presence as possible. She forced her fists to unclench, her engagement ring biting into her skin as she moved deeper into the breach. "I have heard it said," she murmured carefully, casually, "that Parliament is seeking to nationalize the Company, a political act that would entail its forfeiture of all administrative functions and all of its Indian possessions, including its armed forces."

His bark of laughter made her jump. "That will never happen. An impossibility. I shall never allow it."

She trod carefully. "But if unrest in the colonies continues, what choice would the queen and Parliament have? Even the other evening, at the theater, when the protesting mob reaches the very doors of London?"

"This is positively beyond your ken, my dear." Bellamy pulled himself up importantly. "Despite your charming Thursday-evening salons and your dabbling in politics, you fail to understand that it was the aggressive policies of Lord Wellesley and the Marquis of Hastings that led the Company to gain control of all India, making the Indian princes vassals of the Company. At the present time, our rule—and by that I mean the Company's—extends across most of India, Burma, Malaya, and Singapore with a fifth of the world's population under our trading influence." His complexion reddened further. "And nothing will alter that fact, not Duleep Singh and his ridiculous band of riotous men and not the queen, not as long as I draw breath!"

It was happening again, a curious and frightening reprise. She hadn't really known Charles and she was beginning to fear that she didn't know Bellamy any better.

"Your late husband would agree with me entirely," he continued. "We had many discussions regarding the subject."

Charles again. There was so much that Charles had kept from her, the details of his association with Bellamy stoking her rising anxiety. "I realized you were well acquainted as you graced us with your company many delightful evenings," she said, taking another drink of her refilled wineglass to keep her hands from trembling. Of course, Charles had made it his business to frequent the most influential circles, but he

had never mentioned Bellamy in any way that was conse-
quential. Her mind raced.

"We even discussed his plans for the Crystal Palace, for his
ideas to showcase the diamond to the world. The Koh-I-
Noor will decidedly be the lion of the exhibition. Because of
the enormous interest in the gem, the late Mr. Hampton made
known to me that there will be many challenges attending its
inspection, with importuning crowds necessitating police at
either end of the covered entrance to restrain a struggling and
impatient rabble."

Lilly's lips were dry and she had difficulty forming the next
words. "I had no idea."

Bellamy's eyebrows rose. "And why should you, my dear?"
He patted her hand, clenched around the stem of her wineglass. "However, you are now the keeper of the flame, are you
not? The keeper of the late Charles Hampton's papers and
drawings. Who better than his dear helpmeet to understand
and cherish not simply his ideas for the Crystal Palace but
also its execution? And I shall be by your side to ensure his
great dreams are realized."

Lilly had the sensation of a door slamming shut.

Undaunted by her stillness, Bellamy continued. "You need
me in so many ways, dearest Lilly. I hesitate to even mention
the encounter with the constabulary and their outrageous al-
legations, which, I should add, I did my best to silence and
will continue to silence, if need be. And you shall be free to
continue in your dabbling, of course. All the sketching and
drawing you desire." He smiled beguilingly, a corner of his
mustache coated with a trace of lingering white sauce. He
dabbed at it with his napkin. "We shall get along very well,
my dear Lilly."

He could not have said it more clearly. She turned the ring
around her engagement finger with obsessive concentration.
"Without doubt, we shall carry on very well," she said, suddenly convinced that she was making the gravest mistake of
her life.

He offered a knowing, pitying smile. "Now let us discuss our wedding breakfast, shall we? I thought the grand salon would be ideal for the ceremony and reception as the space is suitably imposing what with the windows and the elaborate balconies overhead. It will be quite impressive."

Chapter 12

Lilly alighted from Bellamy's gleaming black carriage with its prominent crest and hurried up the front steps of her town house in Mayfair. It was ten in the evening, although it seemed much later, the dinner hours with her betrothed having stretched her to the breaking point. No moonlight illuminated the impenetrable fog covering the street in a blanket of eerie white.

Hesitant to summon her housekeeper, she searched her reticule for her key, hands unsteady against the gnawing sensation that someone was following her. Like a child running from the night, she pushed the door open and slid hurriedly inside. Slamming it behind her she then shot the lock with a reassuring snap.

She leaned her back against the door, her mind a disconnected jumble of thoughts. The entire dinner with Bellamy, beginning with the overheard conversation with Vesper, drove her into a deep anxiety that made her question her own judgment. Something had warned her not to mention St. Martin's name directly, but the knowledge that Bellamy and he were somehow connected shook her to the core. It was difficult to believe, a staggering possibility, but then again, she'd also learned that Bellamy's relationship with Charles went much deeper than she'd ever imagined. It was unnerving—everything seemed to revolve around the Crystal Palace and that cursed diamond, but in a way that made absolutely no sense. Her worries trailed her up the stairs, to her rooms and into her dreams beyond.

That night she'd dreamed of St. Martin again, about his warm hands arousing the wickedness beneath her skin, about her own body, heavy, languid, and desperate to have him in her, around her. She luxuriated between sleep and fitfulness, her dreams a chaos of potent emotions causing her to thrash uneasily amid the damp sheets. The night seemed to go on forever, a twilight that hovered between fantasy and delirium, leaving her drained and enervated. Throwing an arm over her eyes, she tried to block out the morning sunlight that came too soon. Feeling drugged and heavy under the warm weight of the bedcovers, she gave in to an unusual lethargy mixed with a rising anxiety. She wanted to hide deep in the feathered mattress, to regress into a heavy sleep that shut out a stinging reality.

Not possible. She sat up in bed to find that Mrs. Worth had already delivered her breakfast. Moments later, she gulped her scalding tea, sitting back amid the covers holding out against the morning's chill. As the liquid burned down her throat, her thoughts began to right themselves. Bellamy, Charles, Vesper, and St. Martin. The names looped relentlessly through her brain, tantalizing and terrifying at the same time. She nibbled halfheartedly at her cold toast, watching the steam rise off the basin of water on the washstand. The names formed a refrain, a pattern that refused to give in to meaning. She was on unstable ground, accustomed to working with right angles and geometric shapes, and with reassuring logic. That was the world she knew, she thought, placing her bare feet on the cold floor and rising from the bed with reluctance.

She pressed a hand to her forehead and squeezed her eyes shut. Still no answers. All she was certain of was this peculiar madness, a disease that manifested as an incomprehensible, feverish need for St. Martin's touch. Suspended between wanting and fear, she thought she saw him in every room, around every corner, in the dark recesses of carriages, remembering his fathomless eyes and his rough demands. He colonized her every waking and sleeping moment, robbing her of control, exactly as he'd promised.

Yet she refused to give in. She'd never been a coward and she would not begin now. She would admit to the carnal weakness that St. Martin tried to use against her. And in her admission, she could disarm him, partially at least. She wasn't that much of a fool. After tossing and turning half the night, she needed the sting of the bright light of day to bring her back to her senses. She felt an overwhelming urge to see her completed plans, to evaluate them one last time in black and white, to remind herself of who she was and what she needed to do.

The library was cold, the hearth mounded with yesterday's ashes. Hurrying to the settee near the fireplace, she sank to her knees to the floor and slid aside the loosened boards. She carefully lifted out the plans and unfurled them beside her, staring hard at the dense marks on the pages, smoothing them over with her fingertips. The drawing was solid, but she skimmed over the diagrams nonetheless, mentally ticking off the important components: the dimensions, site, floor and roof plans, and then scrutinizing the details that would make all the difference, the wall sections and stair details.

The diamond would be protected and the queen would make her entrance from the secret staircase that Lilly had incorporated into the otherwise open, crystalline design.

The idea had come to her the night the Haymarket was attacked by the mob. Had she not been able to find the hidden stairwell, she would have been trapped in the building with the rest of the theater patrons. And ironically, unwittingly, Bellamy and his association with the British East India Company had also figured prominently in her solution. Her fingers quickly traced the lines on the parchment. This is what she did best. She was talented and skilled, and it would do for her to remember it. And damn St. Martin—who could go back to hell on his own without her.

Lilly pictured the design in her mind's eye. The queen entering from the main atrium of the Crystal Palace through the undisclosed stairwell, effectively cutting off access to the diamond save one clandestine and easily secured route. And all of it hidden from the naked eye.

A surge of elation swept through her as she rolled up the plans and replaced them underneath the floorboards for possibly the last time. No matter what happened, she would see this done right, and she would harden herself against St. Martin, make herself impervious against his arrogance and command over her. She needed to regain control, to take the offensive, to stop gambling with her future. She would persevere and she would allay her suspicions of Bellamy—and marry him in under a fortnight's time.

Seabourne could wait until later in the afternoon, because first, she had another visit to make. Scribbling a quick note to the diplomat, Lilly sealed the envelope hurriedly and grasped the bellpull in the library, summoning the housekeeper to deliver the missive and secure a hansom.

Her mind focused on the very odd, very disheveled, and strangely familiar looking Dr. Vesper. Ensconced on the leather banquette of the cab, she turned the piece of paper with his address over in her hands. He was listed in a ten-year-old medical directory in her library, despite the years he had spent in India away from London.

The history of Harley Street had begun in the early part of the previous century when the land between Oxford Street and Marylebone Road had been developed in grand Georgian style. Lilly quickly assessed the broad avenue from the window of the carriage as it lurched to a stop. Not waiting for the driver's assistance, she all but leaped from the hansom in a combination of eagerness and dread. The April sun was blinding, glinting off the brass shingles announcing the surgeons and physicians who plied their trade in one of London's most fashionable districts. She remembered from her studies that architect John Prince, supported with capital and enthusiasm from the second Earl of Oxford, had originally created this abundance of highly vaunted property at the center of Cavendish Square. Very quickly, the area had become highly fashionable, drawing in a number of wealthy and well-placed residents.

Lilly did not have the hansom drop her directly at Vesper's address, preferring to walk instead. She proceeded briskly, peering at the brass shingles decorating the handsome façades, the impact one of prosperity and quiet confidence. It felt like a spring morning, with a mellowness in the air, green buds entangling wrought-iron fences, harkening at better days to come. With each step, she was stronger, more in control, closer to regaining what she needed most—a sense of certainty that she was making the right decision in marrying Bellamy.

She strode determinedly on, intently examining the doors of the fine homes that lined the street, but as she neared its end, she realized that she was not going to find Vesper here. She'd reached the corner of Weymouth Street and, first tugging her locket watch free to determine the time, she made a right turn.

It was already close to noon. An unexpected gust of wind blew up a small maelstrom of winter's detritus along with her deep-seated doubts. She squinted against the mild onslaught, her thoughts returning to Dr. Vesper, his agitated state, his unkempt appearance. Perhaps he had contracted a disease such as malaria during his time in India, conspiring to weaken his mental and physical condition. He hardly exhibited the temperament typical of the surgeons and physicians of her acquaintance, although admittedly she didn't know many. The man who had attended Charles the night of the shooting . . . She forced herself to remember his serious, coolly rational mien.

She didn't want to think about how quickly and efficiently they'd taken away the body, insisting the coffin be closed at the funeral to spare herself and Charles's relatives any further grief at having to view his disfigured remains. She shook off the memories before the familiar shroud of guilt could settle over her shoulders.

Weymouth led to a narrow mews that gave way from Georgian elegance to a tumble of homes, a gap-toothed assemblage of buildings that cried out for care. Lilly glanced at the paper in her hands, confirming the address. No brass plaques here, their numbers beginning to dwindle, until she stopped in front of a tall, narrow house, its two-story structure setting it apart from the other rambling buildings in the block. A small plate, corroded by soot and damp, declared it to be the home and offices of Dr. Aubrey Vesper.

It took several determined raps of the horse-head knocker before a thin-faced, mob-capped woman answered the door. Her faded blue eyes swept Lilly up and down, seemingly startled to see a patient at the doctor's door. The strong odor of ammonia seeped out of the darkened hallway beyond.

Lilly proferred her calling card. "I should like to see Dr. Vesper, if he is available." Without taking the card, the older woman squinted at her suspiciously.

"I don't believe he's expecting you," she said, wiping reddened hands on her apron. The doorway refused to ease open.

"How is it possible that you can determine whether Dr. Vesper is expecting me without looking at my card?" Lilly persisted, the bite of ammonia at the back of her throat. "He's in I presume. These are regular doctor's hours."

There was something not right here, besides the hardened, mistrustful housekeeper and the blinds tightly shut against grimy windows.

"The doctor is not seeing patients no more."

More than not right. Once again Vesper's troubled visage appeared in her mind's eye. She slipped her calling card back into her reticule. "I am simply concerned. As a friend. Last evening when we met briefly, he seemed deeply distressed." The servant was clearly not the empathetic sort, particularly when it came to her employer. When the woman looked about to close the door in her face, Lilly asked, "Might I at least leave a message?"

Tempted to wedge her booted foot in the space between the stoop and the housekeeper, Lilly sensed rather than saw movement behind the older woman. Against the sunlight, the interior of the hallway was dark, outlining a slight figure with stooped shoulders.

"Of course," Lilly expounded with a wide smile as she confidently jammed her shoulder in the narrow space, prodding the door open farther with her gloved hands. "I see for myself that Dr. Vesper has come to renew our acquaintance. How charming of him." She nodded expansively at the older woman, slipping past her and taking a confident step into the house. "And thank you so much for your assistance."

Moments later she was perched on a creaking, high-backed chair, counting the dust motes floating through the air of Dr. Vesper's small and neglected parlor. In contrast with the spring warmth outside, the atmosphere was thick with damp and ammonia, a faint scent of bodies and cooking grease adding a noisome undertone.

Vesper appeared only slightly more robust than the previous evening, having shaven and combed his hair. However, the frayed cuffs of his shirt still exposed bony wrists. "Thank you for taking the time to see me," Lilly improvised, surreptitiously taking note of the room that did not feature any of the usual doctor's implements. No pewter tray with a row of forbidding instruments. No padded examination table. She could count on one hand the times she'd needed a physician's care and now wondered what imaginary symptoms she could conjure that would be convincing.

"After having met ever so briefly yesterday evening at the home of my betrothed, I had thought that I might consult with you over a health matter," she began, surveying his face for clues to a previous acquaintanceship, but finding none.

Vesper looked astonished. "I beg your pardon, Madame, but whatever gave you the idea that I am taking patients?"

"You're not?" The chill in the room deepened.

Vesper stepped back and crossed his arms over his chest. "I practice medicine of a different nature, Mrs. Hampton," he said uncomfortably, still not having taken a seat. "And as a result, I cannot help you directly but could perhaps recommend a physician who specializes in female disorders." He walked over to a massive desk at the far end of the room, its surface piled high with papers and books. Rummaging through the chaos, he gave Lilly an opportunity to think of another ploy to further the quickly dying conversation. Vesper wanted her gone.

"It's not woman's troubles, actually," she said, improvising. "It's rather more a problem with dyspepsia, a certain type of indigestion that I find is interfering with my ability to get a good night's rest."

He looked up momentarily, the eyes behind the spectacles owlish. "I still cannot help you, Mrs. Hampton, and as a result, I should not like to keep you any longer than necessary."

Lilly shifted in her seat, sweeping up a few more dust motes with each movement. She gave a conciliatory smile, smoothing the skirt over her legs, her eyes downcast. "If truth be told, doctor, you've caught me in a small lie because I am really here out of concern for Mr. Bellamy and his health. The moment I saw the two of you together, I was beset with concern over his well-being, certainly understandable given that we are to be married a few days hence." She looked up from her lap to regard Vesper's curiously blank stare. "So you see," she continued lightly, persistently, "no dyspepsia, no women's problems. It's a concern for my betrothed that brings me to your doorstep."

It was clear Vesper did not have the slightest idea how to smooth the progress of her exit. She took the opportunity to look beyond the salon to the darker hallway that led to the front door. To the back of the house lay the kitchens, she imagined, and she'd detected no foot treads coming from the upstairs rooms. Other than the servant woman who had made her feel so welcome earlier, she and Vesper appeared to be alone in the house.

She watched as the doctor played with the spine of one of the books piled high on his desk. "My association with Mr. Bellamy is not of a professional nature," he said briefly.

"I see."

He looked absently at the coating of dust on his fingertips, then fished for a handkerchief in his breast pocket. He seemed dumbfounded when his search produced a silver watch instead. He handled it as though it were a glowing piece of coal, depositing it quickly on the desk. Then Vesper looked at Lilly distractedly before saying, "I am sorry if I cannot be of more help to you, Mrs. Hampton."

Rudely, stubbornly, she refused to move, the silence between them widening uncomfortably and the quiet of the house holding her in its thrall. Somehow she expected to hear something, anything—footsteps, the clatter of a char woman going about her business. Out of the corner of her eye, she saw rather than heard Vesper's servant—scowl planted on her face—move heavily to the front door. Footsteps on the front stoop, a sliver of light, and then a low voice.

"Tell Vesper I'm here."

Lilly froze as a perverse mixture of anxiety and pleasure arose at the sound of St. Martin's voice. It was too fortuitous, coincidence stalking her at every turn. She stood frantically, experiencing a ridiculous urge to hide. She wasn't a two-year-old, for God's sake. Other than the huge desk in the corner, there was no refuge available to her.

He strode into the parlor just as the serving maid was wringing her reddened hands and making her excuses. Vesper jumped from behind the desk, his eyes tacking between his now two unexpected guests. Despite the size and shabbiness of the room, Lilly looked up at what seemed to be an impossibly long distance and caught sight of St. Martin's face. And it occurred to her, ridiculously, that she and St. Martin had only ever been alone together.

And that was a big problem, at least hers. Trying to slow the incessant pounding of her heart was proving impossible. Yet, if she looked at the situation logically, she was in control and St. Martin the one who was caught off balance for once. He was surprised by her presence—he had to be, even though his typically shuttered expression gave nothing away. This time there was a witness, Vesper, and the demanding, heavy handed St. Martin could do little more than play along with her charade.

The very notion was liberating, particularly so when she took in his tall, rangy frame that filled the shabby parlor. "Lord St. Martin." She greeted him summarily with a regal nod before she sat back down. Something blazed to life in those dark eyes, but vanished a moment later. Whether he was angry or pleased to see her there, she still could not tell.

"Mrs. Hampton," he said seamlessly, as though his curricle had just passed hers in Hyde Park. Bareheaded and in a coal gray suit coat and trousers, he sketched a quick bow before turning to the doctor. "Vesper."

She fixed her eyes on St. Martin, measuring his smallest reaction. The momentum had swung in her direction and she waited to see what evolved between the two men—and what she could possibly learn. Her eyes flicked to Vesper.

"I was expecting you earlier, my lord, as was arranged." The doctor ran a hand through his thinning hair. "And, as you see, instead of your visit I was graced by the presence of Mrs. Hampton"—he cleared his throat nervously—"quite unexpectedly."

St. Martin's expression tightened as he turned to her, the stale air crackling with tension. "Indeed."

"An amazing coincidence," Lilly responded, licking her dry lips. He was dressed as somberly as usual, the black and deep gray of his coat doing absolutely nothing to obscure the lean outline of his physique. She remembered the feel of those hard muscles beneath her hands and wondered distractedly what he would look like naked. She had never seen him naked, she thought unaccountably, her heart drowning out any other sound.

"There's a reason for everything and coincidence has little to do with it," he said. He shed dark leather riding gloves, as though planning to stay awhile. Lilly thought quickly, smothering her wayward thoughts and trying to focus on keeping the man in front of her on edge. It was a dangerous game she played.

"I do so hope you're not ill, my dear sir," she said in her brightest voice that sounded a false note and almost made her wince. "Particularly, as Dr. Vesper just explained to me that he is not seeing patients. He's quite in demand, is he not, for a physician who is not practicing medicine at the moment?"

He pretended not to hear her. Instead he surveyed the room with a sweeping glance, resting momentarily on the desk and the silver pocket watch that Vesper had discarded moments earlier. Then he looked quickly away, his expression impassive.

Her gamble was not yet paying dividends, because St. Martin clearly was not ready to show his hand. Although he could be forced to, Lilly was beginning to think. Her eyes darted to Vesper and then back. She was beginning to enjoy herself, in control for once where St. Martin was concerned. He could hardly throw her on her back and ravish her here in Vesper's sad, neglected parlor.

More's the pity, a small voice mocked her.

She straightened her spine, the chair creaking beneath her. Vesper appeared as though he was attending the theater in a foreign country, anxious and confused. He leaned toward her expectantly, peering out from behind his spectacles. "Mrs. Hampton was just on her way out," he offered in a feeble attempt to usher her from the sad little parlor. She pasted on a brilliant smile and settled back more comfortably into her chair.

"Absolutely not!" She pressed her elegantly gloved hands to her chest in dismay. "As a matter of fact, I don't recall your offering refreshment, doctor. Perhaps your housekeeper could see to some tea, which, I'm certain, would sustain Lord St. Martin here as well. Am I not correct, sir?"

"Tea?" Vesper repeated as though she'd just requested that he pull a rabbit from a hat. Both men regarded her as though she was a babbling idiot. Lilly forged onward, playing the role of established matron with relish.

"And furthermore, I refuse to depart until I ascertain for myself that Lord St. Martin is in the best possible health. It would seem that these men, my betrothed included, seek to shelter women from some of life's harsher realities. All together unnecessary, I might add."

"I did not realize the two of you are acquainted." Vesper appeared bewildered.

St. Martin had not moved, keeping his eyes locked on Lilly. A knowing smile on his lips, he tilted his head slightly to the side, prepared to raise the stakes. "I'm touched," he said, "by your concern."

Lilly responded by nodding primly. "Although I appreciate your sentiments, my lord, I am still without an answer, waiting here in the dark with regards to your well-being and the overall state of your constitution."

He took a few steps back to lean a shoulder against the doorjamb, the picture of ease. "Very well," he said, responding to her ante with the negligence of a consummate gambler. "I am here to consult with Dr. Vesper regarding rather vicious headaches that have been attending me since my return from India. And since the two of us were fast friends in Asia for many years, he was kind enough to offer his assistance, despite the fact that he is no longer practicing medicine but spending his time on research."

"Headaches?" Her eyebrows rose delicately. "How distressing for you," she said, not believing a word. He was the smoothest of liars. "My late aunt Emmaline suffered from the worst of migraines, although her smelling salts always brought her great relief, as well as a poultice made from lavender and rosemary," she added innocently, smoothing the fine leather of her gloves. "I'd always thought headaches a particularly female affliction." Sliding her eyes over him boldly, she concluded, "Obviously, I was mistaken."

She wondered if she would pay for that remark later, but the flush of power was well worth the risk. St. Martin's smile deepened.

Vesper interpreted the undercurrents as best he could. Adjusting his spectacles nervously, he said, "I should not like to comment on Lord St. Martin's current condition as it violates the confidentiality between patient and doctor." He glanced at the taller man like a pupil looking for approval for having recited his lessons correctly before continuing. "However, since he has already revealed his situation, I would concur that he is doing well with our continued therapies and should make a slow albeit complete recovery."

Vesper nodded for her benefit before adding, "It was probably a touch of malaria that set off the episodes, I should think."

"Contracted in India?" For the first time in St. Martin's presence she felt safe, with Dr. Vesper as the bewildered and unwitting chaperone. She allowed herself a sly smile. St. Martin's hands were tied and it would be a challenge even for him to coerce or seduce or manipulate without revealing his strategy.

He straightened away from the door, his fluid movement startling her. He moved so well, so differently from any other man she'd ever known or seen. Like liquid mercury, with rapid, tensile strength.

"All these questions and all this concern over my welfare. I'm beginning to believe you care, Mrs. Hampton." His tone held a hint of humor detectable only by her.

She held up both hands in protest. "As one would. I nurture a great concern for all my acquaintances and friends, Lord St. Martin," she said sweetly. "And only think that I heard your name mentioned, in relation to Dr. Vesper's, last night whilst dining at the home of my betrothed. So you must forgive me my disquiet over your welfare."

She watched him, unafraid, despite the smile fading from his lips. "My welfare," he repeated softly, and then nodded as though coming to a decision. Ignoring Vesper hovering behind him, he strolled across the small space, drawing closer until he stood within a foot of her. Aware that her breathing was coming fast and erratic, she focused on the innocent scar just above his right eyebrow.

For a moment, they were alone, Vesper all but disappearing.

"I think we should be going," St. Martin said, the statement unequivocal as his posture. "I shall escort you home, Mrs. Hampton, as any good friend or acquaintance should. And we shall have further opportunity to discuss the state of my health."

She restrained herself from bolting away from him, clamping down on her contrary thoughts. It was as though every decadent fantasy was revealed on her skin. Seeing him up close— the austerity of his face, the wicked mouth, the dark eyes— reminded her of each and every fiendish way he'd touched her. And worse still, reminded her of what more she wanted him to do—to her.

Her pulse kept up a rapid staccato, fueling the mad and ridiculous fight unleashed inside her. His shoulders were impossibly wide, looming over her, and she crossed her arms over her chest defensively.

"We can discuss the state of my health in my carriage waiting outside, given it's of such concern to you." His hand, large and strong, cupped her elbow to help her rise.

Her arms tightened against him. "I shouldn't think of it, sir," she said, taking a resolute breath. "Please complete your session with Dr. Vesper and I shall see myself home."

"I don't think so. It would be too rude of me," he said, this time not bothering to hide the mockery in his voice. He cocked his head in Vesper's direction. "Another time, then, doctor."

Vesper bobbed in the background, just outside her line of vision as St. Martin effortlessly drew her to her feet. She shook her head mutely and took one step back, throwing up her hands to hold him off. "I am leaving without your assistance, sir. Alone." Fired with self-consciousness, Lilly tugged her reticule onto her wrist and made for the door.

St. Martin was right behind her.

"Leave me be," she hissed over her shoulder, pulling on the tarnished knob to pry the door open. If she took a step back, her body would collide with his chest, and she knew he wanted to press her hard against him.

"You are the one who took it upon herself to make unnecessary inquiries."

She stopped in her tracks, incensed. Without turning around, she said, "You are the one who has been following me about London, need I remind you, making these insufferable demands of me."

"This is the first time I've heard you complain. Not that you haven't been vocal at times."

She understood his meaning, doubly so when her body stumbled into his as he tugged her backward. He tightened his hold and pressed his mouth to her temple. "For all your innocent exterior and wild protestations, I believe there's more to Lilly Clarence Hampton than first meets the eye. A black widow, very nearly charged with the murder of her husband, and now a little spy, prying into affairs that are none of her concern."

His accusations stung. "I have made them my concern however you might wish otherwise." And his hand wrapped more tightly around her waist.

"Not very wise, Lilly."

"You simply don't care for the fact that, for once, you are not the one who is directing this ridiculous farce. I suspect that there is more to Lord Julian St. Martin than first meets the eye and I intend to prove it. "

"At your peril," he said softly.

Lilly jerked from his grasp and pulled open the door wide. The light flooded the dingy hallway and she took a deep cleansing breath, exhaling the dust and the lingering sting of ammonia from her lungs. Her every instinct warned her to run away from this man who was as much dangerous as unyielding in what he wanted from her, a man continents beyond her range of experience.

Halfway down the stairs, steps of uneven stone, she felt his hands slide beneath her shawl, grasping her around the waist from behind. In front of her, in the innocent spring sunshine, she saw the carriage waiting for him. For her.

"I am not going with you—"

Too late. It was always too late when it came to St. Martin. He lifted her easily and her hands grabbed reflexively at his shoulders, their bodies entirely too close, her nose buried in the wool of his coat, enveloped by the feel of him, the scent of him. She could not pull away if she wanted to. And she didn't want to, the heat of his hands burning through the layers of clothing separating them.

He heaved her none too gently into the carriage, depositing her on the plush velvet seats. The fine aroma of rich leather filled the comfortable interior and, once she dared open her eyes again, she saw him slide opposite her after giving the driver terse instructions.

She drew herself up against the cushions. "I am not going to your residence," she said haughtily, well aware that she could do nothing about it at the moment. "And you certainly can't be seen outside my home."

He studiously ignored her, the slant of afternoon sunshine bisecting his face and glancing off the strong nose and prominent brow. At least he hadn't drawn the curtain; for agonizing moments, they sat in silence with only the turning wheels of the carriage punctuating the tense stillness.

She couldn't stand it. Swallowing hard, she examined his passive expression, endeavoring to read something out of the dark line of his eyebrows, the set of his mouth. As the carriage lurched away from Weymouth Street, she choked back panic at being alone with him in such a confined space, once more tormented by torturous thoughts and the potential for a reckless response to his nearness. She braced herself for his attack, but none came, and she slowly settled into the strange feeling that she held some small power over him.

Surreptitiously, like a prisoner planning escape, her eyes tracked his long, muscled legs that rested scant inches from her own. She could lean over if she desired and trail her hands over that hard chest, feel beneath the linen and the wool to explore the bone and muscle, before gliding lower over the strong thighs and to the bulge between his legs. He would tense under her touch, his muscles straining against her agonized stroking.

Her hands tightened on her lap and she stopped breathing.

Lilly had a chance if she dared take it. Her throat closed. Instead of merely submitting to his games, she could become a willing participant, leading the play, robbing him of any advantage.

Then it would stop. He would stop. Yes, he could go to the constabulary with the pistol as evidence—and she would deal with the consequences as Isambard King Bellamy's esteemed wife. And in the interim, he would desist in playing her like an unschooled virgin, because the rules of the game would be changed. And she would be the one to have changed them.

No more games.

It would take courage but what else did she have at the ready, other than her wits? Until her encounters with St. Martin, her experience of the marital bed had been circumscribed, to say the least, defined by furtive, intense couplings, awkwardness mixed with misplaced romanticism. With St. Martin . . . She flushed in the dimness. What he had done to her, his hard, searching hands, his mouth between her legs . . . Her cheeks warmed and she hoped he couldn't detect her rising color, the swiftness of her breath. She could imagine reaching for the placket of his breeches, opening it, taking out his manhood, dropping to her knees, parting her lips . . .

Her body thrummed. She felt herself settle back into the sensuous softness of the cushions. His voice cut off her heated thoughts.

"We aren't going anywhere. We will keep driving around the city of London in my carriage until you relinquish the plans."

She gathered up her courage. "You're angry. I can tell."

He laughed, the sound harsh. The coach leaned around a corner and she could see the neat row houses of Belgrave Square. He slid his gaze in the dimness to meet hers, the focus of his dark eyes unnerving. "You don't ever want to see me angry, believe me." He leaned back into his seat and turned to the window.

Indifference. It filled the carriage, draining away her confidence. "You are unaccustomed to the turn of events, I'd wager," she continued undaunted. "Finding yourself the hunted rather than the hunter for a change."

"That's what you think you're doing?"

"Isn't it?" she challenged.

"We could find out," he growled. Turning away from the window, his eyes once again watched her closely.

And then she did the impossible. She rose from her seat and neatly slid to sit next to him, her billowing crinolines the only buffer between them. "We could find out, indeed," she said, her voice surprisingly steady even to her own ears. "So if the world has not been turned upside down, and you are still the hunter, isn't this where you begin your seduction of me, sir?" She turned to him with a half smile on her lips. "And then I demure, of course, resist, importune and all the rest, but you," she paused, laying a gloved hand on his arm, "continue on with manly fortitude, breaching my feminine defenses with overwhelming amorous finesse."

The silence was ominous, only the crunching of the wheels and clatter of traffic infecting their intimate cocoon. There was no point in wondering if she'd gone too far because the words had been said, never to be taken back. She sensed a rising intensity despite his lack of direct response other than his eyes roaming her face. "And of course," she finished with nothing else to lose with the exception of her tattered pride, "I finally succumb and blithely relinquish the plans, conquered by lust. Have I summarized adequately?"

He looked down at the hand on his arm before pinning her with his gaze. "Is that a challenge, Lilly? Because if it is, I would be very careful."

"Oh I'm careful," she said, fisting her skirts in her free hand so their thighs touched. Even such slight contact stopped her breath. The muscle of his thigh clenched. "Careful because I need to be, because I know you to be up to no good, along with that shambles of a doctor."

"Believe what you will," he said, turning his profile, limned by the sun, away from her. His features were hard, still and remote.

Her corset was too tight, squeezing her, and she wished desperately for false courage, a big draught of brandy. He was so indifferent, as distant as the farthest star from Earth. She took a deep breath, her hand sliding to his thigh, the skin scorching through the leather of her gloves. Her instincts sharpened. Her wager, suicidal although it had been, had yielded results.

Because the bulge in his breeches was undeniable and from her unobstructed view was growing heavier and larger by the second.

Her pulse drowned out any other sound. Lord Julian St. Martin was not as indifferent as he appeared. She spared a quick look at his eyes gazing down at her, the clean jaw tense. He didn't have to say anything, the challenge was clear in his dark eyes. Her lips were dry and she licked them nervously, a spiral of alarm slowly transforming into aching anticipation.

His manhood was straining outrageously against the confinement of his breeches. Her mouth watered and she didn't dare meet his eyes.

"Do you think this will change anything, Lilly?" His voice was mocking. It was as though he'd known all along what she was about to do.

She didn't answer but slid slowly from the bench to her knees, her skirts billowing out around her in the small space. Sliding her gloved hands along his strong thighs, she pressed her cheek against the bulge in his breeches. The smell of starched linen and a subtle hint of soap. She remembered what he had done to her and, screwing up her courage, began nibbling and sucking a little on his hardness through the material of his breeches. Almost instantly, he pushed aside her skirts and she felt his hot hand impatient against her bottom. Her pantalets were thrust aside and he was stroking her skin as she crouched, touching between her cheeks, tracing the moist and aching distance between her core and her bottom and back again.

She stopped thinking now, a fierce heat overtaking her. She was immediately swollen and tender, and she wished he would put his fingers into her, but instead he continued playing, teasing, instant wetness drenching his hand.

Emboldened, she shook as she unbuttoned his breeches, pushing the fabric aside to release him. She had seen a man before, but never like this. He was big and thick and hard, and instinctively, she licked him, savoring the sensation like rich cream.

He rose up in the seat so that her tongue might lick deeper under him while his hand loosened the fabric around her core, his fingers sliding into her wetness easily, seemingly all the way to her center.

She was melting. Her corseted breasts, squeezed between

his leg and the banquette, were heavy, the nipples hard and sore and straining. Her entire being centered on the shaft beneath her tongue, hard and thick and angry, a velvet patina of fluid already anointing the broad tip. Instinctively, she caressed it clean with her lips and pushed her tongue over the silky yet rigid head.

It was like nothing she had ever experienced before. Panting softly, she took the head between her lips while she clutched at the fingers buried inside her. Slowly, inch by inch, she took him into her mouth, devouring his shaft. The delicious hardness in her gloved hand and mouth was hers to do with however she wanted.

She had him. For what seemed like hours, she slid her mouth up and down his iron hardness, while he kept the rhythm with his fingers, pumping hard in her mouth and then slicking his thumb over her center. She relaxed her throat muscles, taking more and more of him in, sucking harder and deeper.

And when she finally raised her eyes to look up at him, she knew she had won her prize. She drank in the taut stomach level with her cheek, the rise and fall of his chest, his eyes heavy lidded against the sensual onslaught. And she felt powerful.

It was as though he knew, his hand cupping the throbbing between her legs, the slightest pressures of the heel of his palm making her gasp. The pressure was building, his and her own, and she writhed madly over his knowing, skilled fingers buried deep inside her. She continued her licking and her devouring, rising up so she could get even more of him into her. It was a battle, wondrous and to the death, the tension between her thighs a torment that wouldn't let her go, wouldn't let her explode.

She didn't know where his body ended and hers began. The spasms of pleasure increased, an intensifying dance that rose to a feverish pitch, her skin on fire. His hands cradled her head, his fingers threading through her hair as spasms of pleasure drowned her. And then it came, the darkness closing around her, igniting a firestorm that consumed everything in its path, raging onward so she barely noticed when he quickly withdrew from her mouth.

She slipped from his hands, a shuddering heap on the banquette, her sightless eyes staring into oblivion shaped by deep, desperate breaths that went on forever. Her face burned against the rough velvet of the squab cushions, her limbs floating on a current of emptiness. They were locked in the carriage destined to go around and around, their destination elusive.

How much time had passed, she couldn't say. St. Martin remained still as she rose to a seated position beside him, surprised to find her skirts miraculously rearranged around her. At some point, he had rearranged himself, his long legs stretched out, simultaneously relaxed and remote, an all too dangerous man. She wouldn't look at the place where her mouth had been a few moments ago.

He appeared brutal in the harsh sunlight pouring through the carriage window, and her eyes numbed in disbelief. He had proven his point masterfully. The man was unmovable, fixed as stone, allowing her not even a modicum of control. Humiliation washed over her in a wave and she couldn't find her voice or utter a word.

"The plans, Lilly," was all he said. And it was enough.

She pulled her face over her hands, unable to absorb what was happening to her. When she looked up again, she locked on the passing buildings framed by the carriage window, anything to avoid his eyes. "This is impossible." Her voice was stiff. "You are not getting the plans. Not now. Not ever. And you will stop! You cannot continue to haunt me as you do, right up until the day of my marriage, for God's sake!"

She might as well have been shouting in the wind. He shrugged indifferently. "It's your decision entirely. Although I suppose a quick romp before one's wedding ceremony is not as unusual as it might seem."

She couldn't help her sharp intake of breath. At that moment, she wanted nothing more than to kill him, to feel her pistol in her hand, heavy and cold as she squeezed the trigger. As she'd warned him, she'd done it once and she could do it again.

She gritted her teeth against his coldness and his control, staring straight ahead. "In less than a fortnight I marry Isambard King Bellamy, a most influential man, who, if he discovered that you are unduly harassing me, will ensure you are sent to the worst hellhole in the British Empire." Anger surged through her, burning away any lingering traces of arousal. "And if I were you, I should be very prudent, St. Martin, as you are simply compounding an already difficult situation. I have heard talk about your history, about your instability, your dismissal from Her Majesty's service, and even"—she paused with a quick breath, her anger ruinous—"rumors of treason. So it would seem, you have much to lose, even more than I."

"You sound very certain," he murmured. His body pressed against hers, his arm against hers, his hip against hers. She wanted, needed, to get away from him, to be free of the intimate darkness of the carriage. But if she stood up and moved across to the opposite seat, she would be admitting defeat.

"I am certain."

St. Martin shifted, his shoulders turning toward her and, ridiculous woman that she was, she waited for his touch.

"Certain about marrying Bellamy two weeks' time? You know nothing of the man."

"And you would tell me all, of course, and most of it lies," she snapped. "I know everything I need to know about whom I am going to marry. He will care for me as I shall care for him." She stopped, horrified when her voice broke over the next words. "And he will protect me . . . from brutes like you, from . . . you have no idea, could not have any idea." She trailed off helplessly. And she was so tired of being helpless.

His eyes were dark, clear, steady in the changing light. "Don't fail me now, after putting up such a valiant fight,

Lilly," he said. "I'd say you were supremely capable of looking after yourself. You're intelligent, quick witted, beautiful, and, as a widow, independent most of all. Why you should want to compromise your status, I can't understand."

The carriage turned a corner and she was almost flung back into his arms. Sitting rigidly on the banquette, she straightened her spine against him. She was a few rumors away from being charged with the murder of her husband, and he was asking her why she felt compelled to marry a man whose name and position would protect her. "Bellamy will defend me," she said, clearing the last bit of emotion from her throat, "against men such as you"—she repeated stubbornly—"who would try blackmail in order to achieve their own ends."

"Relinquish the plans and the pistol disappears. You need not marry a man out of desperation."

A bone thrown her way but *how* she didn't trust him. She eyed him disbelievingly. "And why are you so concerned about my personal situation? I cannot fathom that you're feeling sentimental all of a sudden."

"I'm simply pointing out the obvious. You're entering into an arrangement for entirely the wrong reasons."

She wanted to cry out, throw her hands up in frustration; her throat was aching with pent-up emotion. Instead, she said deliberately, "Oh please, as though marriage at best isn't an arrangement predicated on the practical and mundane. You, Lord St. Martin, should know well enough, although I suppose as a younger son you never felt the yoke of dynastic expectation. All aristocratic unions are based on family name and money."

If Lilly was expecting St. Martin to unburden himself, she was sadly mistaken. Instead, he did what he did best, aiming his focus at her with a marksman's unwavering precision. "What about your marriage? Your relationship with Charles Hampton."

She froze, then clamped her jaw tight. Although she had

explored the most intimate moments with this man, the question still shocked like lightning on a hot day. Closed off like a crypt, this was the last place she needed St. Martin to trespass. "None of your concern," she managed to say.

"You loved him then."

"I beg your pardon?" He was trespassing into an area that she had closed off with a stone wall. She didn't flinch but pretended to neaten her skirts, tucking an errant flounce back into place. A quick glance out the window revealed Trafalgar Square, Horatio Nelson forever on guard for the empire.

From the corner of her eyes, she saw that he nodded, as though she'd given him the answer he expected. Turning to face her directly, his face was in the shadows backed by the bright afternoon light. "And yet you murdered him. Why?" His voice sounded sure and calm.

As though she could ever hope to answer that question honestly, even to herself. She remembered the pistol in her shaking hands, remembered how she'd hated Charles at that moment, hated every last minute of the last five years together, hated what he was asking her to do. But even in her worst nightmares, she couldn't remember squeezing the trigger or releasing the hammer. She couldn't recall the slow, flat seconds that she had her husband in the crosshairs of her weapon. The grip on her lungs hadn't eased, but somehow the pistol swung away from her. And before she could breathe again, before she could groan a protest, three red holes flowered on Charles's still immaculate shirt.

And for countless moments, he stood that way—surprised and suspended between life and death—before collapsing to the floor.

Lilly blinked, her head reeling. She wanted to let go, to try to free herself from a prison of her own making, but the reality of murder, and her part in it, had trapped her more easily than iron bars ever could.

"Are you all right, Lilly?" His question came from far

away, from the shadows that obscured his features. As though she could ever answer . . . She shook her head mutely; her face was numb, her neck and shoulders stiff as a corpse.

"I'm fine," she whispered, shocked that she could even manage the empty words. He made no move toward her. Not that she deserved mercy or comfort from a man who was doing everything in his power to see her undone. With the added humiliation that she still knew nothing of him. She heaved a deep breath, bracing her gloved hands on the cushions beneath her. "If I were to answer that question, St. Martin," she said slowly and carefully, testing the strength of her voice, "then I would expect you to answer mine."

What would it take for him to respond honestly, to strip away his defenses and let a glimmer of truth shine between them? She was destined to be disappointed in this man who withheld his very self from her at the most intense, intimate moments. Intense, intimate moments that he used against her. She bowed her head expecting defeat and saw his strong shoulders rise in a shrug, cynical to the last.

"Then we are at an impasse." It was entirely her imagination, but she thought she detected a hint of sadness in his tone. Impossible. And it occurred to her that they were in the midst of a conversation, an actual exchange of ideas, rather than the usual heated argument that quickly escalated to— she could not complete the thought.

"I am tired," she said at last. "And I should like to go home."

He turned his profile to the window, the light revealing his eyes that wouldn't let her go, demanding answers, demanding her response while giving her nothing in return. "Ah yes, go home to Bellamy, the solution to your predicament. A man who is known for his unbridled ambition and equally unchecked brutality." He crossed one booted foot over the other, his body relaxed despite the tenor of their exchange. "While I should like to spare you the details, I know firsthand, having spent time in the colonies, what your future husband is capable of—and it isn't remotely nice."

He had never spoken about himself before, and she was suspicious, as always, of his motivation. "Where in the colonies?" she asked. "And doing what precisely?"

"It's not important. At least not anymore."

"Of course." She tried not to sound bitter at his reticence. "So now you are spending your free time not rusticating at one of your estates but in London trying to get your hands on the Koh-I-Noor. I hadn't realized the St. Martins were quite so destitute as to have to resort to thievery. That would explain your unceasing and relentless quest for that damned diamond. What will you do once it's in your possession? Carve it up into a hundred pieces and sell them one by one? Or," she asked as though the idea had suddenly come to her, "are you doing this because someone is paying you handsomely so that he can have the diamond in his own personal collection?"

His eyes remained the same, shuttered and closed to her, the carriage wheels rolling on inexorably beneath them. A kind of purgatory. "If that's your assessment of my situation, then so be it," he said.

"And your assessment of my future husband, so be it."

He seemed to be studying her, as he had many times before, his mood distant. All the more surprising when he shifted in his seat toward her, his hand nudging her chin up. His fingers lingered there, sending waves of heat into her skin. "You are making a mistake, Lilly."

She jerked her chin from his hands, scalded. "As though I should believe you. As though we've ever had one moment of honesty between us. Why should I take your advice about Bellamy? For God's sake, give me one reason." Her desperation was raw but she didn't want to plumb its depths, to discover why exactly she was looking to St. Martin, of all people, for help out of her predicament, and not to her future husband.

"Don't look to me, Lilly," he said brutally, his hand falling to his side. "I need not remind you again that you're an intelligent woman who, if she cared to look honestly about her, would discover that Bellamy is not what he seems."

The irony was too rich. Here was the man, she was convinced, who was not what he seemed. "Enough talk of my betrothed," she said. Her body grew stiffer and straighter as each second passed. "I find your reasoning ridiculous, particularly when I know you to be a liar who finds recourse in dishonesty and treachery and seduction. And from this man you expect that I would take counsel?"

Flushed, Lilly found her face inches from his, the pain of the truth rooting her to the spot. She didn't move, numb and silent, staring at the small scar above his eyebrow. It hurt her more than she wanted to admit and more than she ever wanted him to know. It wasn't the fact that St. Martin wanted the diamond, that he was blackmailing her in the wickedest way possible. Nor was it that he would turn her over to the constabulary if she refused to do his bidding.

It was something else—the shameful and indisputable fact that she liked being devoured by him, craved his touch like a drug, panted like a wanton whenever he so much as came near. While he—

He inclined his head closer to hers and she breathed in his scent like an opium addict. The question emerged with a will of its own. "Why, St. Martin, why?" The words were out before she even realized. Mistrust scented the air between them, revealing her weakness to the bright light of day and leaving her as vulnerable to him as if she were splayed naked on the banquette to do with as he wished. "Why? Why will you not take your pleasure?"

His face, spare and drawn, betrayed no emotion, empty of shock or censure. For a moment, he looked as though he meant to lower his mouth to hers, and her stomach bottomed out. But then he only said, the words close against her lips,

"So many unanswered questions between us. Perhaps it is to remain so."

Lilly felt hot tears behind her eyes, the emotion unaccounted for and somehow magnified by the endless swaying of the carriage. He leaned away from her finally, his back to the window, although she wanted nothing more than to draw him closer.

"I'll take you home," he said.

Chapter 13

St. Martin cursed in every language he knew.

Unlike him, late afternoon in Mayfair was an oasis of calm. Lilly's town house stood off Berkeley Street, a relatively modest address when compared to the spacious mansions that surrounded it. It made sense that Charles Hampton had wanted to be in the heart of the city, the neighborhood made famous by architecturally opulent homes such as Aspley House at Hyde Park Corner and Devonshire House, which, it was said, rivaled the palaces of the royal family.

Rapping impatiently on the roof of the carriage, St. Martin watched the door into which Lilly Clarence Hampton had just disappeared recede in the distance. The carriage clattered on, turning around in the direction from which it had come. He rubbed the side of his jaw, trying to ignore that he still had a cockstand that could hold up the archway of Kensington Palace itself. He'd been so caught up in Lilly's reactions, in prolonging her endless orgasm, that he'd never been closer than losing that last bit of control. He couldn't remember the last time he'd climaxed with someone, and didn't want to.

What he had wanted was her panting, shaking, ready to explode. She'd been lost and helpless and on her knees from the response he'd drawn from her body. He remembered the feel of her beneath his hands as she sank slowly down onto the banquette beside him, a tangle of arms and legs and re-lease, and he'd left her there.

She'd shocked him. Yes, it was still possible. When she'd slipped to the floor and had taken him in her mouth, his body had nearly arched off the seat. It was obvious to him that it was about taking control, wanting more, about the fierce power of having him vulnerable to her hungry mouth. She'd shaken him more than he ever wanted to acknowledge to himself, a fight to the finish waged by a comparative inno-cent, and a valiant attempt at breaking through his every last defense.

He'd come close, right to the edge. He would have given anything to raise her in his arms, to put his mouth to hers, to be inside her, but he couldn't have what he wanted. To have had her astride him, her hands splayed on his chest—it had taken everything to keep him from rubbing his iron-hard cock against her wetness and surging hotly into the sweet tightness of her body.

Fuck. His hands were shaking when they never shook. He should have seen it coming and, better still, not care. So what if the sexually sheltered widow Hampton discovered her re-pressed carnality thanks to a few sordid encounters. It should have meant nothing to him and everything to her.

And now she'd found her way to Vesper. He swore again. Indulging in pleasure to hold his own demons at bay had ex-acted a price. Because he'd kept the game going when he could have ended it that first night in the Tower, she was fur-ther away than ever from relinquishing the plans and uncom-fortably close to unwinding a dense tissue of deception.

It was his fault and it had to stop now. Death was on his doorstep, and dallying with a confused widow would not delay or soften the inevitable. So Vesper was his first destina-tion. And afterward, he would have to find a way to prevent Lilly from marrying Bellamy. Even if he had to kill her.

The idea was disorienting, aberrantly so. Killing was what he'd been doing for the last ten years of his life, most of the time discriminately, he'd hoped, but often, as life would have it, not. He wondered if he was truly losing his way, distorting what should have been a straightforward liaison, satisfying but ultimately useful, only to find it twisting out of his control. Getting what he wanted from someone as harmless as Lilly Clarence Hampton should have been child's play but then again. . . .

Naïve of him to believe that women were actually the weaker sex. Far from it, as his late wife was fond of demonstrating over and over again. Why would Lilly, who was indulging in sexual congress with a man while intending on marrying another, be any different from Constance?

The carriage heaved to a standstill, and he stepped from the conveyance into the cool shadows of the afternoon. Vesper's rambling house was less welcoming in the waning sunlight, a stern taskmaster that reminded him of what lay in store. After half a dozen sessions with the doctor, he had no inclination to prolong the relationship beyond its ultimate usefulness. Vesper was expendable as anyone else. Looking up at the residence, he saw the housekeeper behind the twitching curtains. Partially obscured by the frayed lace, she watched him with something like fear yet didn't move when he took two stairs at a time to arrive on the stoop.

This time, the door opened magically before he even had the knocker in his hand.

"You here to see him?" the wary voice demanded, making way for him as he strode directly into the hallway. A medicinal pall hung in the air, closing St. Martin's throat. Vesper might as well have been a witch doctor what with the dust and grime that coated the interior of the dismal entranceway. Other than a few faded prints hanging crookedly on the wall, neglect permeated the atmosphere, along with a potent mix of ammonia and despair.

The housekeeper, Mrs. Gant, had kept her head down on his previous visits, studiously ignoring the goings-on in what must have been an unusual household. Something had changed, because today her eyes met his as she crossed her arms and raised her chin a little higher. St. Martin was accustomed to noticing details, every wrinkle and nuance that could make the difference between life and death. He glanced behind him before shutting the door firmly. Mrs. Gant's cap was askew and her eyes were as reddened as the chapped hands she twisted reflexively in front of her.

Sometimes it was more effective remaining silent. He felt himself calm, the influence that was Lilly Clarence Hampton drying off like mist in the sun, his instincts clicking back into place. He'd been correct in returning to Weymouth Street.

"You're here for your session," she repeated with a mixture of wariness and despair.

He nodded, his back to the parlor, which he sensed was empty. Either Vesper was in the kitchen in the rear of the house, highly unlikely, or on the second floor. He listened for footsteps overhead but heard none.

"The doctor is in," the housekeeper said, answering his silent question but clearly leaving more out as she swayed with what he interpreted as indecision. Her back was to a small door, which he assumed led to the cellars.

"Shall I wait as usual in the parlor?"

Her chin rose again. "No . . . not exactly."

The woman was holding back, refusing to retreat behind habitual subservience. St. Martin waited patiently for her to go on, watching as she looked away to fix her eyes on a grease spot on the wall beside him. He gave her time, pretending to focus on an uninteresting watercolor to the right of the cellar door behind her. The watercolor depicted a clutch of lemons, leafy branches still attached, filling a worn ceramic bowl. The artist's signature was indecipherable. In the background, a clock kept time, the relentless ticking a powerful reminder that the hours were running thin.

He tugged his own watch free from his waistcoat before allowing himself another glance at the watercolor and then down the narrow hallway. The housekeeper shifted, thin shoulders lowering, every line in her body communicating uneasiness.

"Where would you like me to wait then, Mrs. Gant?"

Her head bobbed twice before she replied. "If you could wait jes a second."

"Certainly."

She mumbled a reply and he understood her perfectly.

"Did you say that you would like me to see something?" he repeated, rendering his tone and posture as unthreatening as possible.

Her double chin wobbled. "But you can't say it came from me, or let the doctor know, see . . . I could lose my position." She smoothed the wrinkles in her apron, her worn hands moving obsessively.

"Of course," he said without elaboration.

She took a step away from him and toward the cellar door. "None of this is right. All these goings-on, even if it is a doctor's residence."

"How do you mean?"

"The patients and such." For the moment, she refused to be more specific. "Too much death." She shook her head worriedly, the thin gray curls that had strayed from her cap trembling.

Any lingering softness he harbored hardened around the edges. "Whose death?" he asked carefully.

For a moment, she appeared to consider taking the words back. Her reddened knuckles whitened against her apron. "Jenny's."

"Go on." His tone suggested that her response was important to him. He let another moment pass before asking, "Who was Jenny?" As though he didn't know.

Wrapping a fist in her apron front, the housekeeper shook her head. "The scullery maid. Jes' a young thing and the doctor bringing her home in such a state and then she jes disappearing like that. Without a trace. Terrible, it is."

Like a bolt sliding into place, the jagged images in his mind merged. The night at Bellamy's—Vesper's scullery maid and this woman's friend. For anyone else, the dichotomies would have been overwhelming. But he only saw opportunity.

"I'm so sorry. You must have been close, working together here."

The apron twisted in her fist. "That's why this is so bad."

"What precisely is so bad?" he asked, seizing on the critical point. "If you don't wish to, you don't have to tell me directly," he continued, attempting to strike an empathetic tone. "Simply point me in the right direction and I shall do fine. And no one else but the two of us need know."

Her fist stilled at her side. Her eyes watered at his offer or at the memory of the missing Jenny, it wasn't clear. She took his suggestion literally and gestured behind her.

No need to ask for permission. His instincts sharpened as he opened the door to find a stairwell leading to the cellar. Someone was downstairs, judging by the wavering light, but there wasn't time for speculation or hesitation. Silently he moved down the stairs, two at a time, brushing against stone walls that had been whitewashed, dripping moisture. He rounded a corner and into a narrow hallway. Then he heard it. A moaning, low and keening, coming from the farthest corner barely delineated by a faint halo of light.

A slight silhouette kneeled by a low cot, a bag and flickering oil lamp by his side on the dirt floor. St. Martin closed the space between them just as Vesper looked up from the ground and caught sight of his face.

He scrambled awkwardly to his feet, fumbling with a syringe before throwing it haphazardly back into the worn leather bag. A mound of stained, rumpled blankets shuddered at his feet.

"This is interesting," St. Martin said, stopping a few feet away but close enough to study the face of the man, barely conscious, roiling on the cot. He nudged the mattress with his foot. "Another patient? I'm afraid I must agree with

Mrs. Hampton that for a physician who is not practicing, you have an intriguing number of clients strewn about. This was not part of our agreement."

Gin fumes permeated the fetid basement air the moment Vesper opened his mouth. "None of your concern, Lord St. Martin." Clipped tones with just a hint of an alcoholic slur. "I suggest we move back upstairs to the parlor. No questions asked would be my advice."

The liquor had clearly given Vesper false courage.

"I'm in no particular hurry." St. Martin nudged the patient again, and the man turned his sweat-matted face to the wall. A good shake would rouse him, he guessed, watching his eyelids flicker. "I have the impression that I interrupted this man's daily dose of opiate."

He leaned in to get a closer look. "Who is he?" The back of his neck tightened, sign of a headache ready to descend. He suddenly wanted to get the hell out of there, the combination of gin, stale sweat, and presentiment conspiring against him. The man's thin chest rose and fell in shallow gusts, a gray bandage encircling his upper torso. "Can't be doing his health much good down here in the cellar."

Vesper picked up the lamp, encircling them in a halo of light. "Inquiring too closely will do you no good."

St. Martin ignored the exhortation. "Another of Bellamy's protégés, then?"

Vesper held the lamp higher. "And if I said yes, you would hardly be surprised."

St. Martin shrugged, wondering if he should drag the patient from the bed and up the narrow stairs. Fresh air and a few gallons of coffee would get to the truth faster than this dance with Vesper. The doctor had deteriorated since their first meeting two years ago in Bombay, the nervous gestures and disheveled appearance hinting at deep fissures not far beneath the surface. St. Martin had seen it before, the symptoms of a resurrected conscience. Bloody convenient, if mined correctly.

"I should ask you that question. Why a physician would keep an injured man drugged and imprisoned in his cellar. Makes one wonder."

Vesper switched the lamp to his other hand, licking his lips as though needing a drink.

St. Martin continued, his booted foot kicking the bedpan farther beneath the bed. The noise was jarring and Vesper jumped, his face chalk. "Wonder all you'd like, sir," he managed, "but it's in your own best interests to leave this alone."

"It's my business to ensure I know of everything you do, doctor. As you well understand."

Vesper's features radiated self-righteousness, not entirely immune to the sarcasm despite his inebriated state. "You are the one who approached me," he said, voice rising accusingly and echoing off the low cellar walls.

"But Bellamy had you in his employ from the first. So you can appreciate my concern. Hypnotism, opiates—your medical repertoire is amazing and useful. Particularly to Bellamy."

"And to you."

St. Martin nodded, a low pounding behind his eyes beginning its relentless rhythm. The man at his feet moaned feebly. "Although your patient here is clearly not thriving under your ministrations."

Vesper looked away and then back again at the figure huddled beneath the linens. They had reached a stalemate, a draw that St. Martin was willing to prolong until Vesper broke like the thin wire he was. St. Martin could smell capitulation in the dank air heavy with gin and desperation. He'd smelled it in Bombay and he smelled it now. "If you feel the need to unburden yourself, Vesper, I would advise you to give in to the weakness. We don't have time to waste. You can wrestle with your demons another time."

If anything, Vesper appeared more ill at ease at the offer, his fears surfacing to tighten his fine features, all signs of inebriation suddenly gone. "There is nothing you can help me with here, St. Martin."

"Help? I'm not here to help. We had an agreement. I'm expecting that you keep it and that includes telling me about any extracurricular projects that Bellamy has you involved in."

"It's not that simple."

"Never is." As if on cue, St. Martin felt the throbbing at his temples. He shut out the pain reflexively. "Playing two sides is never wise."

"You do."

"All too well. And that's my point."

The dark shadows under Vesper's eyes made him appear far older than his forty years. He placed the lamp on the floor at his side and glanced at the man on the bed who snored fitfully, the opiate clearly having taken over. "It's not as though I have many options. I must continue to convince Bellamy that my loyalty lies with him, despite the fact that he threatens to crush everything I hold dear."

St. Martin's shoulders tensed. The weakest were always the most unreliable. "You received the money you needed in Bombay. It was part of our agreement."

Vesper nodded desperately. "But ultimately, the money was not enough. I'm afraid no one can protect me against Bellamy."

"And that's the reason you're keeping this man drugged in your cellar?"

"It worked with Jenny."

"But that was at my behest. You're quite adept at bringing people back to life," St. Martin said dryly. "But it appears that your magic is dissipating. This man doesn't look well."

Vesper glanced at the bandage that had come loose with the man's thrashings. His lips tightened. "He won't die. He cannot die." He added cryptically, "And yet he can't be allowed to live either."

"I wish I could say that you're speaking sense."

Vesper scrubbed a hand through his hair, debating with himself. His eyes behind the glasses looked old and weary. "I really haven't much choice."

"I'm offering you one, doctor. As I offered you in India."

"Why should I trust you?"

St. Martin's tone was reasonable. "We've worked well together up until this point in time."

It was the opening he needed, a veiled reference to the charade they'd been enacting for months—those sessions of hypnosis in the parlor upstairs, culminating in the harrowing events at Bellamy's residence at Hampstead Heath. Vesper needed to be reminded that he could rein in or cut loose his patient, if required, by the simple sway of his pocket watch. In theory at least.

Vesper's eyes glimmered with something like hope but his voice was tentative. "I don't know quite where to begin. It's a baroque affair and I don't understand exactly how I became so deeply involved." The comatose man at their feet stirred, but they both chose to ignore him.

"Try simplicity then. Tell me what you need in the starkest terms possible and I'll see what I can do."

"I wish it were that simple."

"It can be. I can make it so." Vesper was a desperate, albeit intelligent, man, and he sensed the power behind St. Martin's stark proposition. He sensed what he really was, an assassin whose loyalty was questionable at best.

He sighed deeply, the sound like a death rattle coming from his throat. "I hope you can perhaps use your influence," he said, coming to a decision. "In effect, I would require assistance in the colonies, to secure medical care for a loved one and possibly emigration papers to London." He pressed his lips tightly together waiting for St. Martin's response.

So that was the knot that tied Vesper to Bellamy. "Done."

The doctor appeared first surprised and then momentarily elated as though he'd received an unexpected gift. His shoulders straightened as if from under a burden. But his eyes flicked to the cot again and instantly his face clouded over. "It can't possibly be that simple. I do realize that your position, however compromised at the moment . . ." He trailed off, gathering his thoughts. "But no one can know, you understand. This man is to remain dead, for the time being at least."

Just as Jenny the scullery maid was to remain dead.

St. Martin's gaze narrowed on Vesper. "You have my word."

Bellamy or St. Martin? A student of human nature, Vesper intuited who was the more dangerous of the two men.

"Of course, we shall continue our sessions," St. Martin continued, the tempo behind his eyelids amplifying. He glanced down one last time at the cot. The man's head was still turned to the wall with its seeping moisture, jerking restlessly with every rise and fall of his chest. "So who is our patient?" he asked finally.

Vesper hesitated for a moment, perhaps regretting his intemperance and his decision. He opened his mouth and closed it again. The aroma of juniper and spirits did nothing to dispel the winch tightening around St. Martin's forehead.

"This is horrendously difficult—I really shouldn't say. Can't say."

"You've come this far. Giving up the name won't make that much of a difference. And think of what you'll gain in return. You're not asking me to move heaven and Earth—your request is relatively simple to fulfill."

The lamp by Vesper's side cast outsized shadows on the moist walls. He looked down at the cot and straightened his spectacles, peering through the fog of his conscience. "The famous architect murdered in his home over a year ago," he said finally. "Charles Hampton. That's who he is."

Chapter 14

"And to what do I owe this unexpected pleasure, my dear Mrs. Hampton?" Richard Seabourne asked, his outward graciousness masking a veiled but pointed curiosity. He smiled broadly from his wing-backed chair.

Lilly tried to relax under his sideways glance. She was stiff, clutching her bulging satchel with one hand and bracing herself on the arm of her chair with the other. Her mind and her body were in turmoil, the terrain of her life upended by the disorder Julian St. Martin had left in his destructive path. She wanted to be done with him and done with it all—and Seabourne, diplomat and confidant of the queen, presented the only recourse.

She could no longer think about what had happened in St. Martin's carriage earlier in the day, the torrent of emotion that had led to actions so uncharacteristic as to truly cause her to doubt her sanity. Not to mention that her ruse had failed. St. Martin had remained supremely untouched and completely out of her reach and more dangerous than ever. Grasping the satchel tightly to stop from shaking, she pretended to return Seabourne's smile.

"You are very kind to see me at such short notice," she said brightly, hoping the underlying brittleness would not break through. "You have always been so generous in your support, given my recent difficulties."

"All of which are quickly receding into the past, as I understand it. I saw the banns in the papers announcing your upcoming nuptials and offer my heartfelt congratulations." Seabourne settled back in his chair, his hand hovering over the bell that would summon servants. "May I offer you some refreshment, my dear?"

"No, please. Do not trouble yourself." The thought of food was repellent; her nerves, raw and exposed, were close to shattering. She was going to marry Bellamy in two weeks' time, and there was only one way of ensuring that she would rid herself of St. Martin's frightening hold on her life. The satchel sat heavily on her lap, all the while she was forced to go through the motions of a normal conversation. Her life, it seemed, would never be normal again.

"I received the invitation to the wedding," Seabourne continued, "although I regret that my wife will not be in attendance. She is in Jaipur at the moment, awaiting my imminent return. But of course, I will make it my priority to be in attendance."

"Wonderful. It's to be a small affair. Mr. Bellamy and I both wish it so." She paused deliberately. "And both Mr. Bellamy and I wished to ask if you would be so kind as to accompany me down the aisle, as my father and mother passed away several years ago and not having any siblings, male or otherwise—"

Seabourne beamed his enthusiasm at the invitation. "Why I should be honored, my dear, you need only to have asked. You are aware of my great affection for you and your late husband. I should be eager to have such a beautiful bride on my arm."

Lilly wished desperately to share his unbounded fervor, her throat constricting at the prospect of marriage to Bellamy. She made an attempt at normalcy. "Thank you again. And please assure Mrs. Seabourne that her presence will be missed."

Seabourne waved an elegant hand. "She is accustomed to

the rhythm of our lives abroad, necessarily so being married to a diplomat. Of course, she wishes desperately to see the opening of the Crystal Palace."

"As do we all," Lilly responded tightly.

Seabourne, she understood all too well, was a man who spoke between the lines, a diplomat whose knowledge of the internescine affairs of state was legendary. He could be counted upon for his discretion, leaving no fingerprints behind. Dread pulsed through her heart at the thought of her pistol, with its incriminating evidence, in St. Martin's hands. If she could dispatch the completed plans, he would no longer have any reason for his pursuit of her and, more important, she could take steps to ensure the safety of the diamond and the queen.

Seabourne nodded thoughtfully and said presciently, "The opening is but two days after your wedding. I might suggest that you are here with me this afternoon to confer about more than simply your upcoming nuptials." He eyed the satchel on her lap. "Anything specific you would like to discuss?"

"I would."

"I thought so."

The silence lengthened because she did not know exactly where to begin. Although she didn't have the time to spare, the burden on her lap growing heavier by the moment, she automatically took in the architectural details of the drawing room, noting the spaciousness of the high ceilings with their elaborately carved moldings. The tall windows were draped in velvet and adorned with scalloped valances to better frame the deep buttoned medallion and serpentine-backed upholstered sofas. Altogether, a graceful, elegant design. She shook her head. What she once thought beautiful had suddenly become meaningless.

"Mrs. Hampton," Seabourne interrupted her wanderings in an expectant tone bordering on exasperation. "I appreciate your willingness to cooperate with the Royal Commission in this matter, particularly when the situation with your late husband clearly still resonates so deeply."

"It is the least I can do," she replied honestly, forcing herself to look at the older man directly.

Ever helpful, Seabourne continued relentlessly. "And am I to understand that you have found an architect to complete the drawings, someone whom you would like vetted perhaps, to preserve the clandestine nature of the assignment?"

"Not precisely." Her teeth clenched and her jaw tightened.

"We understand the sensitivity of the situation, my dear Mrs. Hampton, and your unwillingness to see your late husband's work completed by someone who does not comprehend the uniqueness of his vision. However, should you find yourself at an impasse, and given that perhaps you would like to close this chapter of your life, we should be only too pleased to offer our assistance."

Lilly jumped at the opening. "Yes, that's quite to the point. I would like to end this chapter of my life and look forward to beginning a new one with Mr. Bellamy." The sentiment sounded as flat as a piano out of tune. Nevertheless, she removed the satchel from her lap and placed it to the side. "You see, I have the completed plans in my possession."

Very little could surprise Seabourne, but he gave her a hard look from beneath bushy brows. "How can that be? Just a few weeks ago at your Thursday salon, you'd informed me that you were still hesitating over the choice of an architect."

"And you pressed upon me the urgency of the situation. We must protect the Koh-I-Noor."

"And the queen," Seabourne finished.

Lilly flinched at his words, hoping to conceal her unease. "Yes, of course, and the queen." Once again, she picked up the satchel in both hands and held it out to Seabourne.

"I'm giving you the completed plan." Her voice held a sad finality.

He rose from his chair to remove the package from her

open palms. Immediately, she felt lighter, the anxiety coursing through her veins diluting with the act of relinquishing the satchel to the diplomat. Seabourne paused, weighing the bulk in his hands. Then he frowned.

"I still don't understand how the plans for the room were completed so quickly or by whom."

Eager to dispel the suspicion in his voice, the lies coming rapidly to her lips the result of old habit, Lilly said, "No one completed them. Charles had finished them before his death, and unbeknown to me, secreted them away because of their confidential nature. And I," she said with a slight pause, "in preparation for the wedding, moving my things, you understand, found them yesterday, quite by accident."

Seabourne turned away from her suddenly and faced the tall windows framed by the heavy velvet drapery, clearly eager to conceal his expression. She waited for him to turn back around but he didn't, instead setting the satchel down carefully on one of the settees. "Have you taken a good look at them?" he asked.

Lilly compressed her lips, preparing herself for another lie. "I admit that I did only to discover that Charles's design reveals a quite clever intricacy. The stairway is quite hidden you see, undetectable despite the open nature of the main building and the transparency of the glass walls. And there is a specific mechanism incorporated in the design in order for it to be accessed."

At last, Seabourne turned back to her and raised his hand to his forehead, digesting his thoughts. "Quite ingenious I'm sure, judging by your description. And perfectly able to seamlessly accommodate the passageway from Apsley House." In his eyes, Lilly saw genuine appreciation leavened by a growing urgency. "Amazing for him to have had the foresight to secret away the plans. Not that he could have foreseen his premature death, or taking the secret to his grave."

A chill settled over her. Until this moment.

"Until this moment," Seabourne echoed her thoughts uncannily. Her guilt was transparent as the glass walls of the Crystal Palace. "And a good thing it is as the building is nearing completion. We shall endeavor to work as quickly as possible to incorporate this important modification. As a matter of fact, the longer we waited to implement the final modifications, the less likely we were to have had the knowledge fall into the wrong hands."

The wrong hands. St. Martin's hands. Lilly rose from her chair, eager to be done with the whole business and salvage what was left of her conscience. First murder, now adultery, and very possibly if she was not careful, she would add treason to the list. "I'm pleased to have found the plans in time," she said, reaching for her reticule.

"Of course, Mr. Hampton would have wanted it so," Seabourne said, rising instantly to her side and touching her elbow to escort her from the room.

Lilly hoped with desperation bordering on insanity that Seabourne nor anyone else would ever realize the exquisite irony of his statement. "Indeed," she murmured.

"Your late husband would have been very proud of your fortitude, my dear."

The blood drained from her face. "That's kind of you to say."

Seabourne patted her arm good-naturedly, genuine affection shining from his eyes. "And next I will see you at your wedding! So much for you to look forward to and a chance to put the darkness of past events behind you. You still look much too strained, my dear, for my liking. A fresh start is what you need. And Mr. Bellamy, whom I'm looking forward to getting to know on a more personal level, is the man to do it."

"Mr. Bellamy is a fine man," she forced herself to say, hoping to convince herself as she and Seabourne made their way through the large double doors of the drawing room. "I should have thought that the two of you would be better acquainted, given your posting in India."

The diplomat smiled broadly. "Now we have the opportunity—through you, my dear. I know you were somewhat concerned about his politics," he continued, "but I assure you there is little to be concerned about. Parliament will soon assume the more onerous tasks of governing India to leave men like Bellamy and the British East India Company to do what they do best—trade."

Lilly returned his smile woodenly. "I have every confidence in your political appraisal of the situation, Mr. Seabourne. As I'm sure my future husband does as well."

Seabourne beamed his approval, escorting her down the long hallway with its black and white tile floor, an infinite journey that Lilly hoped would never end. "And then we can all look forward to the opening of the Crystal Palace," he continued, "which you and Mr. Bellamy will be attending as husband and wife. So exciting for you, such exhilarating times, my dear Mrs. Hampton."

Lilly felt as hollow as a china doll. It wasn't excitement she was feeling. Only dread.

Isambard Kingdom Bellamy hauled long and hard on his cigar. The genteel women of London detested the habit even when they retired to their drawing rooms, but he was alone now and so he didn't have to care. It was a habit he'd indulged in India, along with many others, and he wasn't prepared to stop for any reason.

He rang the bell at his side and instantly one of his men appeared. His voice was all attention. "Yes, sir, what can I do for you this evening?"

He dispensed with the niceties. "Mrs. Hampton. I want to know where she is at all times, is that clear?"

"Absolutely, sir."

Bellamy exhaled a curl of cigar smoke. "I want every minute of her time accounted for before the wedding. Do you have anything of import to relate?"

"She is currently visiting with Richard Seabourne. And earlier today, a hansom dropped her off on Harley Street."

Bellamy grunted and then set down his cigar. He glanced up at his man, one among many in his retinue. Flynn was his name. Silent and loyal to the grave. He made sure of it. "Harley Street? What—is my betrothed beset with female troubles?"

At his elbow, Flynn said quietly, "We assume it was a doctor's visit, sir."

"Brilliant deduction—precisely what I pay you for. Now tell me something I don't already know."

"We saw her enter Dr. Vesper's residence."

Bellamy's eyes glowed red like the lit end of his cigar. "Visited Vesper, did she?" He didn't wait for confirmation. "Don't appreciate that bit of news at all, Flynn. Now if any other woman of close acquaintance decided to seek out my physician and friend, I shouldn't be concerned. But our dear Mrs. Hampton is quite another matter." He flattened his fleshy hands on the armrests of his chair. Mrs. Hampton was entirely too clever, devious, and as it turned out, bloodthirsty to be trusted. He was certain that she hadn't sought Vesper's company to verify the condition of his health.

He snorted derisively. "As for Seabourne, it's to be expected that she would run to him." He answered his own question, impatience his constant companion these days. "No news there, I suppose. He's a friend of the Hamptons', Charles Hampton, to be more precise, albeit a well-connected one." Seabourne was just one of many in his paypacket, convenient to have on hand. From an old family, although without title, Seabourne had spent most of his life currying the favor of his betters. But before long, men like Seabourne learned that their political maneuvering didn't count for much at all. There was a better way. An easier way.

Flynn cleared his throat. "One more item, sir."

The vacillation in the Irishman's voice was unusual and raised Bellamy's ire. "Why the hesitation?" He preferred his underlings to be direct.

Flynn rolled his heavy shoulders like the boxer he was,

clasping his hands before him. "We saw Lord St. Martin follow Mrs. Hampton into the doctor's residence and then depart with her in his private carriage."

Bellamy took no more than an instant to digest the news. Resisting the urge to reach out and strike something, Bellamy stroked his mustache to calm himself. Perfection. St. Martin and his betrothed. She was feeling the pressure as he'd intended, from every direction. He fingered his lower lip. One way or another, his seemingly prim but devious future wife would succumb to his demands. St. Martin had stared death in the face too many times to count. Lilly Clarence Hampton was a fragile sapling in his experienced hands. Easily broken. He'd learned long ago, early in his rise to power, the importance of preparing for any and every eventuality. Throwing Lilly in St. Martin's path was just one in the many layers of deception he'd constructed to ensure a satisfactory finale.

He was about to dismiss Flynn, when a disturbance at the far end of the library stole his attention. He grunted his disbelief. Constance St. Martin wearing a white robe, her black hair hanging to her waist, was framed against the double doors of the library. She walked toward him, her cheeks flushed pink, eyes filmed by clouds of laudanum. Swaying dreamily on her feet, she was more beautiful than she'd ever been, a vixen disguised as an angel. But before she was halfway across the library, he expelled a curse because he'd already had enough.

"How did she get out of her rooms," he barked at Flynn, who quickly went to stand behind Constance like an oversized attendant, prepared to catch her if she fell.

"I don't know," Flynn stuttered, grasping the woman's waist from behind. "I'll return her immediately and it won't happen again, I assure you, sir."

"Darling," she purred, not bothering to struggle against her captor, straining toward Bellamy. "I need more of my lovely tincture, you know that I do." Her soft voice whined annoyingly. "Dr. Vesper promised. He was much more generous in India. And you promised."

Bellamy ignored her, spinning around in his chair so he wouldn't have to face the virago that she would quickly become. Toying with St. Martin's wife had become wearying at best, and he knew she should have remained in Vesper's hands. But it was one thing to keep her hidden away in India and quite another to keep her buried in London. Vesper was having trouble managing Charles Hampton these days, his backbone weakening with every day.

"I deserve it." The three words uttered at his back grated, taking him away from India and back to the East End, reminding him of his whore of a mother and her addiction to gin.

"You deserve something else entirely." He spun around slowly in his chair. Wild eyes flashed in her pale face, her lips a livid red mark. Only a few hundred thousand pounds separated this creature from the dregs of London or Lahore. "I don't ever want to hear that tone of voice again." But then again, he did, relishing the opportunity to see that pale face covered in a bruise the size of a fist, his fist, from cheek to eye to mouth.

And Flynn was well trained enough to recognize what was coming. Instead of dragging Lady St. Martin back to her room, he dropped his arm, not bothering to interpose himself between the woman and the older man.

Constance tossed her hair over her shoulders. "No one orders me about, the least likely someone from your unfortunate station in life, Bellamy." She smirked defiantly, the haze of the drug lifting from her eyes. Spite cleared her head before it began pouring forth from her lips.

His blood began to simmer, a not unwelcome sensation. He watched her performance unfurl under Flynn's vigilant eye. No stranger to violence, his henchman stood a few feet away, arms crossed over his barrel chest.

She laughed hysterically and pointed directly at him, her pale hands clawlike in their intensity. "What dung heap did you emerge from, hmmm, Bellamy? What cesspool, what ditch, what whorehouse did your bitch of a mother call home?"

Bellamy stared up at her with murder in his eyes.

Unafraid, she shook off Flynn's imaginary arm, advancing toward Bellamy. "You can't hide from me," she said in a trilling voice that was simultaneously girlish and rasping. "You come from nothing and you are nothing, despite your affected airs. It's little wonder you spent years in that primitive backwater consorting with servile beasts that hardly qualify as human, never mind civilized." She paused to catch a breath, eyes narrowing. "Oh, don't look at me that way. I know what you're made of and it's not much. You fault me for my appetites and yet look at your own."

He reared from his chair and slammed the back of his hand across her face. Even before the first contact, she began screeching uncontrollably, lunging for him with her nails before Flynn grabbed her from behind once again.

"You coward, you cur," she spat, struggling, a rag doll come to life. "You don't even do your own fucking for God's sake, preferring to watch what you yourself aren't capable of." She heaved frantically, her black-spun hair falling over a face that was reddening rapidly where his hand had struck. "We had an agreement, you bastard," she screamed, a vortex of invective flowing from her mouth. "I want"—she kicked uselessly at Flynn—"my tincture, and I want it *now*."

"I didn't hit you hard enough, clearly," Bellamy said.

The tendons in her neck straining, she snarled her reply. "I won't cooperate with that whelp of a doctor or help you with St. Martin unless I get what I want and when I want it."

"You will do as I say, when I say it," Bellamy corrected her mildly, anger suddenly draining from him. For some unaccountable but deeply familiar reason he lost interest, the brief spark of rage extinguished like a candle in a cold draft. Constance was tedious, finally, rather than electrifying, and just another in a long line of females who failed to sustain and ultimately slake his insatiable appetites.

"That will be all." He dismissed Flynn and his burden with an impatient wave of his hand, the tendency toward feudal fiat difficult to abandon. Constance had already ceased to exist as far as he was concerned. He had learned to shut out his whore of a mother with equal efficiency. "Make sure Vesper doses her thoroughly. She was calmer in India, and I don't want another scene such as this."

Screams receding behind Flynn's burly back, Bellamy picked up his cigar, put it back down, and took stock, the cold trader who had clawed his way from the stews to the pinnacle of the British East India Company. Constance was quite correct in her estimation of his raw beginnings, but she was ultimately useless to him if his future wife somehow undid all his carefully laid plans. Despite her histrionics, St. Martin's wife was as manageable as a doxy with her sailor compared to Lilly with her shuttered gaze and controlled manner. To be saddled with that clever, cunning widow, even if for a short time . . . How long before he could dispose of her without alerting suspicion? Perhaps a mysterious fever contracted in the tropics might exacerbate a supposedly fragile constitution. Bellamy pictured her walled up in a rice plantation, far from home, as strong as she was vulnerable.

In the interim, Vesper would tell her nothing. *He would not dare.* And St. Martin would reel her in. Impatiently, he swung his chair around and picked up his glowing cigar. The hot smoke filled his mouth, a combination of pleasure and pain. He felt his old needs rising to the surface and replayed in his mind the images of Constance with the two stable brutes. It wasn't nearly enough, a mere shadow of what he had become accustomed to in the hinterland where life was cheaper than a bottle of gin, to be consumed and thrown away without a second thought. No difficult questions asked.

But for now, he would have to quell his unusual appetites and play the role of besotted betrothed to get closer to what he wanted—the plans for the Crystal Palace. Designed by none other than Lilly Clarence Hampton.

That no one else had recognized the deception was rich. He'd known the first instant upon meeting Charles Hampton that he was nothing more than a shallow fool, mincing about with thoughts of fame and fortune far beyond his meager talents. It was his wife, with her careful eyes and composed demeanor, who hid a prodigious gift that even the most elevated and refined of London society were unable to recognize. It took a Shoreditch bastard to see the truth.

However, he had been prudent in keeping Charles Hampton alive, in the event that Lilly proved particularly recalcitrant. Much like St. Martin, consumed by guilt, she would do anything to expiate her sins. He fingered the hull of the cigar thoughtfully. Knowledge was incriminating. Once Lilly was married to him there would be no way out, just as there had been no way out of her marriage to Charles—other than murder.

They had two whole days before the opening of the Crystal Palace, if he sensed she would not go easily. Secrets would be divulged, pleasurably, if she insisted. Subservient she was not despite the façade of good breeding and manners. A surfeit of education and inappropriate exposure to masculine concerns did not bode well. Those Thursday-night salons, for example, would come to a swift end.

Women were ultimately tiresome creatures. Even Constance St. Martin was no different from his whore of a mother and her pack of half-wits and strumpets. At least the prostitutes in India knew their place, their subservience running like sluice from an overflowing ditch. The sexual antics of St. Martin's wife were initially mildly entertaining but had become predictably dull. Even the brutes from the stables thought so. If it were not for Vesper's steady supply of laudanum to keep her in hand, Bellamy would have had her disposed of already. Maybe even have had St. Martin do the deadly deed.

Cigar smoke burned his lungs. The idea had a compelling symmetry. Under the influence of hypnosis would St. Martin realize he was snuffing out the life of his wife? Yet again? Even Bellamy had to appreciate the horror.

He rose from his chair and surveyed the sumptuousness of

his drawing room and the now cold stone fireplace where he'd witnessed St. Martin cut short the life of a scullery maid with the dispassion of an animal in the wild. He eyed the chess set on the side table reminding himself that Vesper had completed his assignment even if the man had looked frayed at the edges the other night. To barge into his home unannounced and make unreasonable demands—Bellamy's teeth clamped hard around the nub of the cigar. It would not happen again.

True, Vesper had been fundamental to the success of his strategy, keeping Constance St. Martin and Charles Hampton in a twilight, balanced usefully between life and death. The demise of both individuals had been necessary, giving him ultimate control over St. Martin and Lilly. Then again, everyone was replaceable, even the doctor. Bellamy weighed his many options. Perhaps he would have to use Constance sooner than planned. If Vesper and the hypnosis scheme failed, there was always the wife brought back from the dead. A death for which St. Martin felt ultimately responsible.

Leave nothing to chance, he repeated to himself, a lesson he'd learned long ago at his mother's poxed knees. In one week he was to be wed. And then the future would be his.

He crushed out his cigar on the side table's fine oak finish, careless of the priceless chess set and the acrid scent of charred wood.

Chapter 15

Charles Hampton's Crystal Palace, to open within four weeks, owes its aesthetic qualities to factors hitherto unrecognized—the repetition of units manufactured in series, the functional lace-like patterns of crisscross trusses, the transparent definition of space, the total elimination of mass and the sense of tensile, almost live, strength as opposed to the solid and gravitational quality of previous masonry architecture.

Lilly threw the newspaper with its critique of her creation onto the bench beside her. Overhead the sky was a flawless blue, framing the cast iron and glass building rising before her eyes in Hyde Park, its reality and beauty humbling all at the same time. Tears blurring her vision, she reveled in the building's strength and elegance. She remembered Charles telling her that the Royal Commission had reviewed nearly two hundred fifty submissions from architects, but none of them would have been constructed in time or within a reasonable budget. The commission was looking for strength, durability, simplicity of construction, and most important, speed of execution.

And she had created all that—and more. She'd sketched the original drawing on a blotter and drew up the plans in fewer than ten days. The idea of a giant greenhouse, an enormous flower, had come to her in a dream, after which she'd worked feverishly, closeted in the library with only tea and biscuits to fortify her and an agitated Charles to urge her on.

She wiped the moisture from her eyes and focused on the reality—her reality—planted in the middle of Hyde Park. Although she had yet to tour inside, she knew that full-size living elm trees were enclosed within the central exhibition hall near the twenty-seven-foot-tall Crystal Fountain. Charles had also told her that the close to one million square feet of glass necessary to gird the structure had been provided by the Chance Brothers glassworks in Smethwick, Birmingham, the only glassworks capable of fulfilling such an ambitious order.

The park was deserted at such an hour, late afternoon but with a spring sun still high in the sky. Tender green buds sprouted on the forsythia bushes, veiling the now emptied pathways in a gossamer cloak. Tulips bobbed beside her at the foot of the bench, each nod of their heads mocking her for the undeniable fact that her wedding would take place in the morning. A wonderful time for fresh beginnings indeed, she thought, rubbing uselessly at the newspaper's ink staining her pale, satin gloves.

She wondered if she would ever see St. Martin again and fought a shock of panic at the idea of his simply fading into her past, along with his dangerous games and outrageous demands. Foolish, foolish woman. She tightened the ribbons of her bonnet more tightly beneath her chin. St. Martin had not set foot in her presence since that unfortunate incident in his carriage, if that was any way to describe the most appalling encounter of her life. And she should be pleased. Relieved. The past was behind her once she had delivered the final plans to Seabourne, and now she was about to embark on a marriage with a powerful man who would make everything go away. Including Charles's murder.

Then why did she feel like a fist was closing around her heart, cutting off her blood, her thoughts, and her spirit? Over the last week, she'd hidden behind wedding plans, in fittings with the dressmaker and in conferences with Bellamy's cook and the special chef imported from France. And seemingly a thousand decisions had to be made despite the small but lavish ceremony. Should the servants and horses wear flowers? What should the arrangements be—potted palms, festoons of evergreens, or blossoms? She had refused any extravagant display of wealth, including Bellamy's offer of a diamond tiara for the ceremony. An avalanche of other myriad details consumed her attention. Something old was often a family heirloom and the bride's link with the past. Something new could be her dress or a gift from the groom. Something borrowed was to be of sentimental value such as a veil or headpiece, eventually returned to the owner.

And something blue was often the garter or an embroidered handkerchief, symbolizing faithfulness.

Dear God, fidelity. She swallowed hard, her head falling to the back of the bench. She closed her eyes, blotting out the hard blue sky and the memory of St. Martin, a fever in her blood, a disease, a contagion that would not be cured. Marriage to Bellamy was the antidote, she was convinced, precisely what she required. And yet her pulse continued to beat madly in direct and careless counterpoint to her feeble attempts at reasoning.

When she raised her head again, she jumped, although she knew she'd secretly conjured him, Julian St. Martin, sitting there waiting for him to appear. And so he had. A stranger who was not a stranger.

His body blocked the sun, a silhouette in black, a fallen angel, the hard lines of his face giving nothing away. His face was composed of shadows and she couldn't see him clearly. He moved too quietly and she wondered how long he'd been standing there watching her.

Shielding her face with the brim of her bonnet, she broke the lengthening silence and spoke first. "I cannot seem to shake you from my path, my lord." Relieved she could not read his expression, she refused to think about those moments in his carriage, memories so torrid as to make it impossible to go on.

His hair, black sable, stirred in the faint breeze. "It doesn't have to be this way," he said as his eyes roamed the pathway, the bushes, and the park bench before coming back to rest on her, calibrating her acute mortification with a careless glance.

"You lie. I have no choice in the matter. You've tried to make sure of that." Lily hated him for the glitter in his dark eyes, the calculated gaze that took stock with the eyes of a marksman, insensitive to the calamity he believed he was about to unleash. Sod him—she could not allow herself to dwell on what had passed between them. As though she would give him access to the diamond, or to the queen. She had sacrificed too much already, a sacrifice that would mean nothing at all to him. She adjusted the rim of her bonnet, hands shaking, pretending concern over the sun.

St. Martin took an agonizing amount of time to finish his examination of her. He stared at her, deep in some type of deliberation. She was cornered in the trap of his gaze, looking for escape where there was none. Above them birds sang, but all she heard was the beating of her heart. She heeded the urge to strike out.

"Big, brave man. You've come to take me away then, armed with the incriminating evidence." There was challenge in her tone and her eyes darted around his person, attempting to discern whether he carried her pistol, the one she'd murdered Charles with.

Looking down at her, he offered a pitying smile. "That's clearly what you want to believe, Lilly. I wonder why it is you won't take the opportunity when it is presented to you."

"To which opportunity do you refer? I see none." A robin darted through the forsythia bush, a momentary diversion. She watched as it rested on a perch, shook itself, and fluffed its feathers before lighting out once more.

"You could flee," he said quietly, following the direction of her gaze. "I would help you."

She continued to look away from him, following the bird's path. "Of course you would help me if I relinquish the plans. As though I ever would. I simply wonder how often I must refuse you before you go away."

"You misunderstand. I am offering you a way out."

Her head snapped to attention. His mouth was as hard as his eyes. "I'm not interested."

"Perhaps you would hear me out."

"Please proceed as there's nothing I can do to stop you," she said with a combination of weariness and impatience. At least she was no longer terrified, secure in the knowledge that her upcoming nuptials would offer her safe haven from St. Martin and his terrifying demands. Now if she could only stop wanting him with a reckless and irrational hunger that she was helpless to appease. Those moments in his carriage, at Madame Bernardin's, in her own bed— She banished the images, her nails biting into her palms.

"You don't have to marry Bellamy." For a moment she wondered if she'd just imagined the impossible. The words were as wickedly enticing as he was, standing there in front of her, tall, strong, and obviously unhinged.

The temptation was nearly unbearable. In two breaths, Lily had lost her patience. "You followed me here to tell me this? Are you quite mad? Not marry Bellamy?" And do what? Run away with you, her mind taunted her.

He was seductive as sin, brandishing his ridiculous offer that was made worse by her blindingly irrational response. She could not go with him, never, it was beyond hopeless. So she forced herself to wait quietly for his next maneuver, certain that if he spoke further, she could convince herself and him that there was no escape for either of them.

St. Martin bowed his head and his voice held an unfamiliar warmth that pulled her toward him like a riptide, false though she knew it to be. "You can't marry Bellamy, trust me."

"Trust you?" Dry-eyed and miserable, she fought the urge to throw herself in his arms, an impulse that made her hate herself even more. *"Damn you,"* she ground out, "you don't care for me or my welfare, despite the intimacies we have shared. Just your accosting me here in public—" Panicked, she looked up and down the secluded pathway before lowering her voice. "Simply accosting me like this could jeopardize everything I hold dear. Anyone could see us and make unreasonable conjectures." A chilling thought reared its head. "You are doing this quite deliberately, aren't you? You would like nothing better to have our liaison out in the open. So I would be unable to marry Bellamy."

He raised an arrogant brow. "One of my many options and one that I choose not to exercise. After all, I could have brought you before the magistrates yet I did not," he reminded her.

"Instead you chose to toy with me."

"Perhaps. But you can forgive a man his weaknesses."

"None that I can detect," she whispered with bitterness on her tongue.

He meant to draw out the torture, tempting her by intimating that their moments together had been more than pure stratagem on his part. But she knew differently. She had detected it in his response, in his inability to simply share his body with her, let alone his mind or the contents of his conscience—if he had one. She scrambled to cover her emotions, fumbling with the newspaper bulked under her arm.

His voice was calm. "Lay your guilt aside, Lilly." The words were neutral and yet cut her to the core. He knew everything, had flushed out her deepest secrets.

"None of it is of your concern," she said stiffly.

"So you think." The statement was clipped and he glanced at the bench. When he dropped beside her, she realized how determined he was, and that there was something else, something new, hovering in the shadows between them. Tensing, she moved her skirts away from him.

"Why do you feel the need to punish yourself for Charles's murder?"

Her head jerked as if avoiding a blow. His black eyes were shielded but she could detect a glimmer of emotion. Pity, perhaps. "You continue to pry, sir," she said, affecting disdain, but as the moments passed the pretense grew more difficult. She was reflected in the darkness of his gaze, her pain and her guilt and, most of all, her duty. Eyes that would not let her go.

"Believe it or not, I am trying to help you."

"Why such a sudden change in disposition? Please don't expect me to believe that you somehow care. You are after one thing only and the specter of my marriage is one more insurmountable challenge to your accomplishing your goal. Do not try and tell me differently."

"Lilly—"

She tossed the newspaper under her arm aside. "Nothing you can say will make a difference, so I suggest you simply leave me alone."

"Tell me why you did it." His low voice broke through her tirade. "I need to know."

She froze. "Know what?" A strange fog penetrated her mind, images of Charles the night of the murder. The door in the sitting room opened, and she could hear his breathing amid an insidious silence, the staccato of a pistol shot, one or two or three and then a pounding of drums, her own heartbeat. A scream of desolation rent the air, stretching toward oblivion, and she couldn't remember if it came from her or Charles or a dream.

Guilt shone from her eyes. "I cannot recall," she lied softly.

"Were you defending yourself?" His shoulders were nearly wide enough to block out all the light. St. Martin faced her directly, twisting away from her on the bench. "You can tell me."

"I don't recall," she repeated.

"It would make a difference in a court of law." He didn't say that no court in the land would believe her, find it credible that the gentle and gentlemanly Charles Hampton physically abused his wife. Besides which, it was patently untrue.

She shook her head mutely, not quite knowing what she denied. "I will marry Bellamy tomorrow, regardless." She forced the words out, blood from stone.

"You cannot," he said simply. His strong shoulders simultaneously barred her way and invited her to lay down her burden.

"I can and I will," she said again. Other than spiriting her away to another life, there was nothing he could do to stop her.

"You don't know what this marriage entails."

"And you would tell me." Her heart was squeezed by an enormous fist. She wanted him gone, before she broke into a thousand shards of glass. The sun behind them was beginning to set, the hours and the minutes before morning disappearing like grains of sand in an hourglass.

"I can't," he said brusquely.

"The answer I expected." She gathered her skirts in her free hand and rose from the bench. He stood immediately but made no move to touch her. Thank God.

"Please," she said, the one word inchoate with need. Afraid of revealing any more, she straightened her bonnet, hoping to hide her expression. "Please do not come after me any longer, I beg of you." Her voice quavered but she would not grovel. "I will marry Mr. Bellamy tomorrow and, as a gentleman, I would hope that you discontinue your relentless pursuit of the Koh-I-Noor." And of me. Three silent words torn from her.

He rose from the bench and she could not stop him, her body leaning toward him despite her mind's screamed warnings. His hands rose to cup her face, the heat of his strong fingers a mark on her skin. She closed her eyes against the coming assault. "I can't explain it to you in full, Lilly, it's not possible, but I'm warning you not to go through with the wedding tomorrow. You are placing yourself in grave danger."

The last word breathed close to her lips. Then he said her name before brushing a soft kiss onto her mouth, his lips offering a lingering, seductive taste.

If only she could believe . . . if only she could imagine her life any other way. Before she allowed herself to sink into his arms and her delusions, she jerked back and pushed him away. "No. Stop this." If she pretended enough, she thought she could see a hint of warmth in those dark, devouring eyes. It was all pretense, she knew, and the pain of it threatened to swallow her whole. She took a deep breath and stepped back, putting several feet of distance between them. "You menace me. You seduce me. And now you condescend to me," she said. "The last is perhaps worst of all."

"Is that what you think?"

"It's what I know." She watched the trace of warmth in his eyes fade away, if it had been there in the first place.

"You are making an enormous mistake." The sun burned orange behind him.

"It's mine to make. And it won't be the first time or the last," she managed to say. It was all the more brutal, the strange sense of yearning that sparked between them. A moment later it was gone. And then she walked away, leaving him and her emotions behind in the glowing haze of dusk that would herald night and then the dawn of her wedding day.

Lilly.

St. Martin pushed the name away, sinking more deeply into what these days passed for sleep. He sat upright in a chair in the small dressing room opposite the cavernous master suite, a place better suited to suppressed emotions and intrusive dreams. He had only a few hours until dawn, the low drum of a headache a familiar jailer, but he imagined that he could smell the ripe opium buds, like wet grass. Not unlike the wet grass of the perfectly manicured lawns of his childhood.

Yet the scene behind his closed eyes was as far away from England as humanly possible. The denuded hills were brick red, not a scrub brush marring the harsh contours folding into flat planes of brightly nodding flowers. His horse turned a corner sharply. Impossible to avoid the ruts in the roads pockmarked by centuries of war. Soldiers climbed like rats all over these provinces. St. Martin swallowed a curse.

His mount ascended to a craggy, barren mountain, negotiating steep climbs, descents, and hairpin curves along a narrow road. The terrain was familiar, etched by years of warfare, with its cluster of small red hills, smooth mushroom-shaped rocks fusing into neat concentric lines. Rugged, unwelcoming, another range of gray forbidding stone hills came into view.

He slowed his horse to a halt in front of a small granite building in the middle of a field sheltered by two walls of rock. After the bright light of day, the interior of the small building was dark. All he could smell was earth until his eyes adjusted and he saw the two men in the corner.

"*Salaam.*"

St. Martin approached and knelt down onto the cushion on the dirt floor. To his right was Nazir Ghalib, a local warlord who held a clay pot on his lap between his flowing robes. Just before reaching maturity, the poppy plant produced a flower. After a week, the petals fell off, leaving a capsule. Raw opium gum was harvested from this capsule, about a hundred of which nestled in the earthenware container Ghalib cradled between his hands.

Ibrahim Azhar, with a full beard and flowing robes, nodded approvingly. His eyes glistened as he listened to Ghalib with the attention he would have given the prophet Muhammed.

Azhar stroked his beard, leaning forward to invite further

confidence. He watched as the other man ran his fingers carefully through the buds like they were the finest jewels.

"So what do you wish—more money? *Chand affhaniy? How much?*" St. Martin began without preamble.

Ghalib raised his eyes expectantly and then shook his head. "No money."

"If not money, then what do you desire?"

Azhar watched the exchange, raisin eyes glinting in his sunburned face. Then he said, "No more English."

St. Martin bit back a reply, although knowing it was time to assert control. He rose from the floor and signaled that the meeting was over before it had even begun. The older man shuffled to his feet, still cradling the bowl, bowing to Azhar although there was a set to his shoulders that was anything but respectful.

Desperately poor, ravaged by war, these tribes didn't know loyalty. Azhar watched as Ghalib left and then motioned St. Martin to return to the cushions. Then he spat off to the side and wiped the corner of his mouth as though what he had to say was particularly unsatisfying.

"No more English."

"You know I cannot guarantee that." Azhar didn't trust him, a rogue Englishman who played too many sides in a battle no one was destined to win.

"Too much European ways, European women. Resist temptation. Do not allow yourself be corrupted."

"She is my wife," he said simply.

"Just a woman. One woman."

The damp earth beneath the cushions seeped into his bones. "It should be enough that you negotiated a treaty to have the English withdraw from Kabul." And what St. Martin didn't mention were the thousands of soldiers and their families who came under attack and were massacred when they reached a mountain pass, the Khurd Kabul. "That should be enough for you."

Azhar's look was dismissive.

St. Martin's spine tingled,though not from the cold. "You don't have her but you do know where she is and who has her."

Settling his hands on his thighs, Azhar looked to the east, his expression impenetrable. *"Ensa allah*, God willing, it will all come to pass."

He had stopped believing in God, any god, years ago. "Who has her?" he asked again.

Azhar smiled knowingly, clever, determined, and as hardened as the hills that comprised his ancient land. "A doctor. A western doctor."

"His name. And with whom he is allied."

Azhar frowned. "What do you give in return? For his name and his place?"

"More money."

"No more English."

It was a large price to pay and they both knew he wouldn't pay it. Constance St. Martin would be sacrificed to the greater gods, corrupt deities who rolled the dice for their own pleasure and gain. In the distance, two explosions. Dynamite or gunfire going off across the length and breadth of the country.

St. Martin jolted awake, not by the din of cannon fire but by a piece of coal shifting in the small ceramic stove in the corner. He jerked upright in the chair, the dressing room coming into focus. His mouth was full of ashes, his limbs stiff. Diffuse morning light slanted in the doorway, obscuring the edges where his nightmare ended and his life began.

Lilly. For whatever benighted reason, the thought of her was a shock to his system, and he didn't shock easily. He scrubbed a hand down his face now roughened by a faint beard. Her husband was alive and she didn't know it. Ironic that both of them had the blood of their spouses on their hands.

He groaned, shoving a hand through his hair. Lilly should

have been taken care of a long time ago, and he wasn't sure why he hadn't simply forced the plans from her hands. Instead, she was ready to walk down an aisle this morning and into the arms of a man who would take them from her. A very dangerous man. He closed his eyes again, listening to the sounds around him, second nature to him as he first identified and then dismissed each noise. The beginnings of traffic, horse hoofs, creaking carriages rolling on the cobblestoned streets below, the mutter of the wind and the steady beat of the pulse behind his temples. He sat perfectly still, aware of what he had to do.

How would Lilly react when she discovered that Charles Hampton still lived? That she hadn't murdered him as she'd obviously intended? That Isambard Kingdom Bellamy had kept him from her—had kept him alive?

It was the last piece of the puzzle, why she had decided to take his life. She was not a rash woman. There had to be a reason, a damned good one. And what would she do when fate intervened in the form of her resurrected husband in a few hours' time, and prevented her from marrying the man she thought was her savior?

Not that it mattered. The goal was to flush out Bellamy, even if Lilly paid the price in a hard bargain. Actions he would take this morning would join a rich history of difficult choices, ones he took without hesitation. In the interim, he had to forget Lilly's wide and questioning eyes, the bleakness in her voice, the unwelcome desire she engendered with nothing more than a look or a touch. Forget that what he really wanted to do was wipe away both their pasts and begin again.

Fuck, he was getting weak. He couldn't afford to be sentimental, never could. Then again, not everyone lasted as long as he had, doing what he did.

Chapter 16

Exactly one hour later, St. Martin stood at the kitchen entrance of Waldegrave Hall. He listened intently, not yet ready to make his way into the residence until the time was right. His pistol was pressed hard against Charles Hampton's neck where the skin was pasty and the pulse hammered in his throat. Risen from the dead, his eyes were bloodshot, uncomprehending but somehow still watchful.

Vesper had given over his charge almost eagerly earlier that morning in a fair exchange, the use of one man for the return of his family, and protection against Bellamy. He didn't know much, didn't care much about either Bellamy's or St. Martin's motivations. It was safer that way. He'd carefully dosed his patient so that he would tread the careful line between sleep and wakefulness. St. Martin was absurdly grateful.

A thin, weakened man hastily dressed in clothing that hung on his emaciated frame, Hampton was not fit to be Lilly's husband. The thought came out of nowhere, irrational and entirely beside the point, and St. Martin had no business thinking it. Yet, he'd experienced a visceral dislike for the man, sensed it in every muscle and fiber of his body, convinced that Hampton had never been any good for Lilly.

"What do you want from me?" Hampton croaked, trembling in his grip.

"Absolutely nothing. Just try to remain standing wherever I put you."

Hampton attempted to ease away from the pistol muzzle digging into his neck. "I don't understand."

"I'm sure you don't." St. Martin had sorted through the possibilities and had quickly concluded that Hampton was no simple victim trapped by circumstances beyond his control. He exuded a lack of character, a deviousness like a bad aroma. It wasn't difficult to imagine Lilly training her pistol on the man. "We are going to a wedding and you are simply to appear as a special, albeit unexpected, guest."

Hampton made a sound like a whimper. "The bitch tried to kill me," he said as though he'd just remembered. St. Martin leaned him not gently against the doorjamb, peering through the edge of the high window alongside the door.

"I'm sure she had her reasons," St. Martin said neutrally, making note of the circle of servants bustling about the stove in preparation for the wedding breakfast. "And by the way, if you're referring to your wife, I'd advise you to speak of her only in the loftiest terms." He dug the pistol deeper into the pale flesh of Hampton's neck. "I'm certain I won't need to remind you again."

Even the slightest threat was enough to cause Hampton to shrink back in fear. St. Martin eyed the coal chute, deciding it wasn't big enough to allow them into the house. He recalled the interior of Bellamy's huge drawing room with its massive fireplace and crisscrossing balconies overhead. To gain entry undetected and then let Hampton do his work would be a challenge.

Although nothing compared to what he'd faced before. To disrupt a society wedding by bringing a murdered man back from the dead was sleight of hand.

It was a beautiful spring morning in Hampstead Heath. The ponds at the back of the house glistened in the morning sunshine, precise and deliberate replicas of the thirty or so ponds punctuating the parklands surrounding Waldegrave

Hall. Helpfully, the elaborately pruned bushes around the back of the house provided adequate covering from prying eyes. St. Martin shoved Hampton onto the ground beneath a flowering shrub, the man collapsing readily under his hands to the soft earth. Adjusting his peaked cap over his face, St. Martin looked up and down the narrow path leading to the kitchen door. In the past fifteen minutes, no one had come or gone, the servants otherwise occupied at the front of the house where the bell chimed incessantly to herald yet another arriving guest.

"I feel ill," Hampton said from under a low-hanging branch. He looked green, not yet fully recovered from the regular measure of laudanum at the hands of Dr. Vesper. It was the last thing he needed or wanted, the man sick at his feet. St. Martin crouched down next to him, sheathing his pistol in the waistband of his breeches.

"No time to be sick. Work to be done."

Hampton looked at him through bloodshot eyes. "I don't understand what you want of me." St. Martin really didn't have an answer, wondering what Bellamy ultimately had planned for Lilly's husband.

"Just be happy you're alive." For the time being at least, he thought uncharitably. He'd hated the man on sight, from the first moment he'd laid eyes on him in that damp bed in Vesper's cellars. As though what he felt should matter. He couldn't afford the luxury of emotion, an indulgence that had led him to dallying with Lilly Clarence Hampton instead of doing what he did best. The worst wasn't that he was paying for his lack of discipline but that the whole empire might pay the price because he'd wanted a diversion from the specter that was his own death.

It had to end. "You're staying here until I get you. Understand?"

Hampton looked back with uncomprehending eyes when St. Martin took out a hank of rope from his pocket. St. Martin quickly and efficiently tied Hampton's wrists to his ankles and placed a loose gag in his mouth before dragging him to the coal chute. Heaving him over his shoulders, he bundled him unceremoniously inside, making sure he rested at the top of the shaft. Vesper's dosage of opiate was perfect because the man protested very little, his eyes drifting closed.

The coal dust fell from his hands like chalk as he made his way back to the tall kitchen window. He was looking into the scullery in the foreground, the site where the scrubbing, washing, and food preparation was done. It was empty, the plain plaster white-washed walls polished clean. A bag of laundry blue in a paint bucket set to the side had clearly imparted a faint blue tinge to the walls. He rattled the pane of the window gently, easing it open with the skill of a thief. The lintel was tall like most kitchen windows, designed not to keep servants from daydreaming or spying on their betters as they took walks in the garden, but to assist in ventilation of the heat built up by large, open ranges.

He leveraged himself up and through the opening in less than an instant, thinking back for a moment to the night at the London Tower, the first time he'd clapped eyes on Lilly. She'd served simply as a means to an end, and now—he took a quick look around—she was forcing him to take unreasonable risks. Rapidly taking in the deserted scullery, he eased himself down from the joist and onto the glazed brick floor.

The murmur of voices from the kitchen reminded him that discovery could be an instant away. He strode silently to the partially opened door and slowly pushed it closed until only a sliver remained ajar.

His eyes were drawn to Lilly like a magnet. He watched as she moved easily through the kitchen surveying final preparations, clad in a simple day dress even though her wedding ceremony was only a half hour away. Dark circles smudged her eyes, her normally serene features pinched and pale. She turned toward the housekeeper and then nodded, ready to excuse herself before gesturing to the chef who was himself gesticulating wildly over the complicated terrine he was assembling on a tray. Her back was turned away from the scullery, her trim waist and slender shoulders a vulnerable and distracting outline. Murmuring the correct platitudes to calm the domestic upheaval, she raised her head to look beyond the housekeeper, only to meet St. Martin's eyes.

She rocked on her feet, as though the room spun and her blood turned to water. He continued to hold her gaze with absolute command, compelling her to move closer. Her breath came faster and she opened her mouth to say something, and then suddenly thought better of it.

"Madam," the housekeeper said, fortunately not following her gaze but noting the sudden pallor of her skin. "Are you feeling quite yourself? Perhaps it is merely bridal jitters. You should be getting dressed, not wandering around here in the kitchens tiring yourself to the bone. I can assure you that Mr. Bellamy has every trust in me to oversee the details of the breakfast."

Raising a trembling hand to her forehead, Lilly said, "Of course I trust you, Mrs. Pettigrew, but I can see that I have just one more detail to look after before I promise to ready myself for the ceremony. If you'll excuse me."

St. Martin watched as she moved toward him, and for one moment he thought she was going to give him away. Her hand had been shaking like a victim of ague, and her face had gone so white he thought she was about to faint. If he was brutally honest, he hadn't been prepared for her, either, from the moment when his eyes had locked with hers. Her body had already marked his, scarred him as permanently as a knife's score.

All he wanted to do was put her down on the parquet floor, raise her modest skirts, part her smooth long thighs, and lay his hand on her moistness. He turned abruptly aside, stepping back into the deserted scullery, certain as death was around the corner that she would follow.

Her hand on his back burned through his coat. "I asked you not to come," she moaned into his shoulder. "I begged you to leave me alone."

Then why didn't you give me away? He didn't bother to ask when he turned to face her in the revealing morning light and she flung her arms around his neck.

He wrapped her in his arms, lifting her off the ground as their lips met, crushing her against him. "You can't marry him," he said, closing the door behind them softly with a spare elbow while bearing her backward, pressing her against the smooth wood wainscoting. His tongue drove into her mouth as he bent her body backward the better to devour her. For once, he couldn't stop. He wanted to keep on and on, to fill her mouth, her body, to take everything and damn the consequences. With her skirts already up to her waist, he traced the delicate silk of a stocking as his flat palm pushed up inside the leg of her drawers. There was no leisure this time, no repeat of the discussion in Hyde Park, but a rough and urgent invasion demanding surrender.

Damp and aching against his hand, she groaned against his mouth. "I must do this," she said, her confusion plain, and he didn't know whether she referred to marriage with Bellamy or this present, more insistent, desperate need. She bit his lips as his fingers delved deep within her, pressing her abdomen against his hardness.

"I need you inside of me," she urged. "For once. This only time, you must. Now."

The words were desperate and he responded. Nothing mattered right now but the need to take her body into his own, to echo her murmured words of wanting. He had to yield to the hungry, rough demands of passion, to feel her, to touch and probe and explore. In his mind her thighs parted for him as he unfastened his trousers and pushed them off his hips. He held her against the cool wall, her pelvis tilted to meet his. And he entered her, penetrating to her core in one deep thrust. He wanted to let go of the prison of control, of his self-imposed punishment, thrusting up into her. He further imagined his hand fisted in her tumbled hair, pressing her face against his shoulder as he lost himself in her.

The clatter of pots crashing to the floor. The interruption was the purest agony. He wrenched himself from his reverie and from the warm body that clung to him. The last bit of strength deserted him, leaving him stranded in a desert far less forgiving than any in the world that he'd ever crossed. What had happened to him? He was groping a woman in a scullery before her wedding like a puerile adolescent driven by unschooled hunger. And with someone he couldn't afford to give a damn about. If he were not so angry with himself, he would laugh at the absurdity. Instead, he withdrew his hand, pulled away, and gazed at Lilly in the harsh light of day.

She was beautiful and she could never be his. "Give me what I want," he said, his voice thick, knowing what the reply would be.

She sagged against the wainscoting, falling backward away from him, her eyes closed against his demands and the unpalatable reality she faced. He had his answer when her breathing slowed and her hands no longer clung to him. She straightened her skirt, careful not to touch him, as if he were a hot brand that would set her afire.

"You know I can't do that," she breathed finally, her voice small and precise.

"You won't heed my warning?" he said with soft urgency.

She shook her head as if the physical effort was almost too much for her.

"Then you leave me no choice."

Her eyes met his, a clear blue in the late-morning light, her honesty desperate. "There is no way you can expect me to base decisions on the ramblings of a man I hardly know." She sounded forlorn, lost. "You speak of warning me against some kind of imminent danger when you have spent the past weeks doing nothing but ensuring that I remain in danger every moment that I'm with you and every moment that I don't give in to your demands." Sun through the scullery window dusted her hair, reflected it so that she seemed to glow. "And now I am to be wed to a man who will protect me, and you insist that I am making a grave error." She paused, lowering her gaze and her voice to a whisper. "Don't ask me to trust you one more time, because that is quite impossible under these or any other circumstances. Explain yourself, sir, or finally leave me in peace."

It was as he suspected. Nothing had changed and it was probably for the better. That he even attempted to alter the situation rankled, particularly when he knew what had to be done. He was risking too much—not his life, which was ultimately negligible, but far worse. And if Lilly Clarence Hampton was felled in the cross fire, so be it. He'd known long ago how it would end.

It was time to spare her and, most of all, himself. He gave in to the urge to hurt. "Yet you seem eager to couple with me. Despite the fact that you're about to marry another man."

The insult was like a fist to the face, deliberately so. He waited for her protest, but none came. Clenching her hands at her sides, she stiffened—a combination of fury and sadness lighting her features—and she looked as though she was about to strike him or cry. "This is over," she said in the softest undertones, "and I regret that it was ever begun."

It was no answer, but it was all she could give him. Then she left, just like that, gliding out from the scullery, closing the door softly behind her, about to wed another man. Leaving him with excuses that he couldn't swallow and lies that he couldn't afford.

It took less than several strikes of the clock in the house for him to recover. He was practiced enough. And it was easier, a far more familiar habit, simply not to care—about himself or about the slender woman with the clear blue eyes. Down the long, narrow passage that was his fate was only darkness. There were things he had to accomplish before time ran out, and that required his undivided attention and a cold, still heart.

The clock struck noon and a glance out the door confirmed that the kitchen had emptied, the servants having moved to the front of the house to bear witness to their master's imminent marriage.

Hollowed out, his mind and emotions blank, St. Martin drew on years of experience. He knew how to make himself invisible, a decade in foreign climes and unfriendly lands forging an ability to become one with his environment. Although he'd been in Bellamy's house only once before, he'd deftly memorized its contours, hallways, and stairwells, the likely routes to make a quick escape. He entered the back of the grand drawing room, keeping to the far side and quietly climbing the spiral stairs leading to the balconies overlooking the cavernous space. Bellamy's paean to his own hubris now buzzed with suppressed chatter, the men in their morning coats conversing politely and the ladies glittering tastefully, plying their fans vigorously in the overheated rooms as they cast sharp, assessing eyes at their peers.

It was the perfect vantage point. He could see but not be seen. The grand drawing room was filled to capacity, a string quartet perched in the corner softly playing music. A profusion of white and purple flowers adorned the doorways, balustrades, windows, and fireplaces.

A few of the faces were familiar. Richard Seabourne, John Sydons, Lord Falmouth, and their wives. After a few moments, Seabourne disengaged himself from the group and shouldered his way to the back of the room. Several of Bellamy's cronies, including what clearly passed as his personal military, kept a discreet watch on the proceedings.

Bellamy played the impeccable host and eager groom, standing aside during conversations, rarely participating beyond making a few opinionated statements. Flushed red, his barrel chest straining his elaborate morning coat, the whitetails giving him the unfortunate profile of a penguin, he vibrated with self-satisfaction at the coup only moments away. Stroking his mustache with deceptive idleness, his eyes roamed the room before resting on the wide double doors.

Behind him appeared a man in an ecclesiastical gown, clearly the minister who would preside over the ceremony. After a few exchanged words, the two men began to make their way to the front of the wide space to stand at the side of a lectern encircled with the same white flowers that were artfully placed around the room. The clergyman whispered something in Bellamy's ear and then gestured to several gentlemen standing to the side. Another rustle of movement, and guests turned their heads toward the wide double doors where, suddenly, Lilly Clarence Hampton and Richard Seabourne stood.

The string quartet immediately took the cue and changed smoothly from a Bach fugue to the wedding march, the music accompanying the slow glide of the bride as she walked down the makeshift aisle on Seabourne's arm. She smiled stiffly, acknowledging the guests to her left and right.

Appreciative murmurs rolled through the room. The bride wore a pale oyster gown, opening over a half-slip of gray Valenciennes lace, her hair pulled back and held in place with a silver fillet adorned with a few simple feathers. Pearls encircled her throat and wrists, their opalescence blending with the transparency of her skin and accentuating her wide eyes and the gold of her hair.

St. Martin froze, his reaction to watching Lilly about to marry another man a fist to his gut. She remained very still; he looked down at her through the noonday light filtered through the stained glass windows as she stood tall and straight ready to give herself away. He allowed himself a moment of uncharacteristic indulgence, narrowing his eyes until he had the groom in his sites, a perfect target, if he so wished. And he never missed.

"Dearly beloved," intoned the clergyman, raising both hands to symbolically embrace Lilly and Bellamy who now stood side by side. "We are gathered together here in the sight of God, and in the face of this congregation, to join together this man and this woman in holy matrimony."

Not that he remembered the words to the cursed ritual, but he sensed he didn't have much time. Edging his way along the back of the balcony, he kept to the shadows, choosing the right moment, with all eyes on the blessed couple, to edge down the spiral staircase and out the side door. His body moved quickly, automatically, through the narrow hallway leading to the kitchen and servant's entrance until he was outside in the back garden, hands opening the coal chute, ready to jerk Hampton from the enclosed space.

Except that he wasn't there. The dark space yawned empty.

Cursing fluently under his breath, he didn't stop to think, a more primal urge taking over. His hands itched for his revolver under his jacket. The wedding had to be stopped—with or without Hampton.

He flew, rather than walked, back into the house, through the narrow hallways and into the grand drawing room. This time he didn't care who saw him. As it was, it took entirely too long, the droning minister's voice coming closer by the second.

"Therefore, if any man can show any just cause why they may not be lawfully joined together, let him now speak or hereafter ever hold his peace."

The Reverend. The couple. And the assembled guests. All held spellbound by an apparition in the balconies overhead. The regular rules of time and space, heaven and earth, were suspended. It happened all at once, in a disjointed, incoherent series of motions that defied logic.

Charles Hampton had anticipated his role, taking to the stage with aplomb and requiring little direction. Leaning over the balustrade, shirttails waving, he bellowed his message to the assembly below. *"That's my wife."* An unholy silence followed. "The murderess!" he spat, the reverberations of the word bouncing off the high walls in a seemingly never ending echo.

*   *   *

For the second time that day, Lilly questioned her sanity. It was an hallucination, like sinking to the depths of a cold sea—her dead husband come back to life. The fault line running through her mind pried open fissures that revealed her worst fears. Craning her neck upward, she saw Charles's twitching face, his hands trembling at his sides.

His chin quivered. "You," he sputtered with a single explosive syllable and an outstretched arm and pointed finger, indicting from beyond the grave. An unnatural silence descended like a bell jar as the assembly, in strange unison, watched the unkempt, trembling man, accusations on his lips, make his way across the balcony, stumbling and falling, barely able to descend the spiral staircase at the back of the room.

Pure terror washed through Lilly's veins, and she didn't have the courage to look to her left where Bellamy stood rigidly by her side. Charles, arms waving, muttering under his breath, danced toward her, a gremlin released from hell. How could this be? She had seen him die. She had witnessed the doctor taking his body away. Another wave of horror washed over her. It was only then she noticed Seabourne and Flynn, out of the corner of her vision, appear at Bellamy's elbow.

She squeezed her eyes tight in disbelief, breathing in the scent of sweet cologne as a hard hand clamped around her waist and the sharp edge of a knife jammed into the flesh right where her corset left off and the thin lace of her bodice began. Flynn dragged her up in front of him, making sure he stayed behind her, his weapon scoring her flesh.

What was he doing—protecting her from Charles? A fog of confusion, then panic, as understanding set in.

And yet no one noticed. Each pair of eyes was fixated on the uninvited guest, staggering his way through the crowd. On each of her frantic exhalations, the knife pried deeper. She didn't struggle, aware that her life depended on it.

Charles lurched toward her.

Her breath rushed back into her lungs. She winced as her head was forced back in a brutal grip. The room blurred, faded, and then righted itself again. There was no logic to any of it, most of all why Flynn was ready to slide a blade between her ribs. She couldn't look to the balconies overhead or to the garland of flowers that swathed the elaborate drawing room. Or to Seabourne who stepped away from her. Charles's bizarre smile held a demonic intensity as he rushed straight toward hell. Toward her.

His words sailed over the collective hush of the assembled guests. *"Dearest wife,"* he sneered. "The truth will out. Did you think it wouldn't, that you would get away with murder?" Without taking his eyes from her, he gestured to the guests shrinking away from him. "And now they will all know—that you, my dear loving wife and helpmeet, shot me in cold blood in our own home."

The spell was broken. The assembled guests stepped out of the picture frame, gasps, hisses, and shocked murmurs rippling through the silence. The grip around Lilly's waist didn't ease, but a small pistol poked its head from behind her, effortlessly thrust in her lace-gloved hand. Before she could breathe again, before she could groan a protest, three sharp blasts rent the air and almost simultaneously three red holes flowered on Charles's shirt.

It was a dream, her recurrent nightmare. For countless seconds he stood that way—grimacing and accusing, suspended between life and death—before collapsing to the floor.

The knife twisted between her ribs and, before she could be sick, her arms were wrenched between her back, right before her last incoherent thought. Flynn dragged her through the hysterical din and out the broad double doors where she had made her entrance with Seabourne just moments before. Behind her she heard shouts and screams for the constabulary, for a surgeon to be called. The pounding of footsteps, the scrape of chairs, the outraged voices gradually receding.

Screams stuck in her throat as they moved down the narrow hallway toward the library, her slippered feet barely touching the ground. She couldn't begin to piece together what was happening and where they were going. The voices in her mind formed an incoherent jumble as she clung desperately to every echo. Then suddenly, miraculously, Flynn stopped.

"I'll take her now." St. Martin silhouetted in the doorway. Cold as ice. And without a weapon in his hand. The fog of confusion in her mind thickened.

Flynn grunted, shoving Lilly more directly in front of him. "I don't think so. She's Mr. Bellamy's property now."

"That's a matter of interpretation."

Fear blocked her throat. Bellamy's property? Or was Flynn intent on taking her to the constabulary on her betrothed's behalf? A combination of hate and relief turned her limbs to paper. St. Martin appeared entirely unconcerned despite the pistol that reappeared in Flynn's capable hand. *Don't do it. I'm not worth your losing your life.* She didn't know where the words in her head came from, but suddenly she didn't want to see him collapse in a spray of bullets, did not want to be responsible for one more death.

Flynn's eyes narrowed speculatively, like a dog sniffing out one of his betters, recognizing that he was dealing with someone of the upper orders. "Mr. Bellamy is not going to be pleased. And when he's not pleased, the outcome can be very ugly indeed." He tightened his hold around Lilly's waist. "Who are you anyway? Can't believe the prim widow Hampton had a lover. Though then again, perhaps we've all underestimated her." The knife twisted in her back as a reminder. "Murdering her husband yet a second time."

The nightmare wasn't over. It had been made to look like she'd killed Charles—again, she thought hysterically. The brightly patterned, silk-covered walls tilted wildly.

"Doesn't matter who I am. I want her." St. Martin's voice was calm and steady. The words barely had time to sink in, like water rolling off sand.

"Amazing how many people want the widow Hampton,

isn't it?" Flynn's voice taunted, his Irish brogue becoming more pronounced. Her pulse notched up several beats until all she could hear was a pounding in her head. Sweat rolled down her back and a fresh roll of nausea settled in her stomach—self-loathing, dark and thick. Her breath came in sickening gasps, the arm around her waist close to shattering her ribs.

St. Martin smiled innocently. "I don't like asking twice."

No response. Sounds of the wedding guests in uproar in the near distance while two men and a woman closed in on death. Lilly stopped breathing, expecting the worst. And it came.

A blast followed by muffled grunts and sickening smack of fists against flesh and bone. She was thrown to the floor, her face scraping against the cold tile, knees buckling under her. The walls closed in, suffocating, and she was afraid to look. When she did, the scene paralyzed her, wiping out every emotion but terror.

Flynn lying on the hallway several feet away, blood spurting from his left shoulder. And St. Martin, the one left standing. It wasn't a second later that Flynn pushed himself to his feet, the gun still in his hand. St. Martin tripped him and together they went down, a priceless vase on a side table behind them crashing to the floor.

Leaning on the wall for support, she tried to stand, the sweat on her body clammy cold, her mouth dry with fear. She watched as St. Martin went for Flynn's throat, grabbing handfuls of his shirt. Throwing Flynn down onto his hands and knees, St. Martin then tightened Flynn's arm around his neck, knee-knifing his back, grinding into his spine.

"Bellamy should be more discerning when hiring help. Not a good sign to be taken down by an unarmed man whilst shooting yourself in the process."

"You bastard." Flynn exhaled the words. "Who are you? Who sent you?"

"I thought by this time you'd appreciate that I'm not a

patient man." St. Martin tightened the grip around Flynn's neck, keeping him from getting the air he needed to speak. "I told you to release Mrs. Hampton. And I warned you that I wouldn't ask you a second time."

Flynn clawed ineffectively at St. Martin's face, struggling like a fish on a hook, his skin purpling as he gasped for air.

"You're fortunate that I've decided not to use your pistol, or my own," St. Martin drawled, casually picking up the weapon and pocketing it. "The magistrates need you alive to prosecute you for Charles Hampton's murder."

A grunt was Flynn's only reply.

This time St. Martin's smile was ugly. Lilly sensed what would come next. A brutal and efficient blow to the side of Flynn's head—followed by silence. She muttered a prayer, not because she expected divine intervention but because the rhythm of the words had, more than once, kept her from going mad.

When she looked up again, St. Martin turned toward her, his dark eyes daring her to back down. She heard a buzzing in her ears. She saw his lips move but she couldn't hear what he said over the thunderstorm inside her head. New pain blended with old. She never did remember his quickly taking her hand, stepping around Flynn, and then leading her through the hallway and out the kitchen door.

She only remembered the cool air on her face, the numbness, as she stumbled into the garden, shaking, to retch onto the hard earth.

When she'd recovered she followed him, docile as a child, as they moved toward the parkland across the heath, walking in concentric circles away from Waldegrave Hall. They were going nowhere and she didn't care.

After what seemed an eternity, her slippers sodden thanks to the tall, wet grasses, too weak to argue or even speak, she stopped and slid against the remnants of a garden wall for just one moment. Her mind reeled, flashing from point to point, keeping time with the somersaults in her stomach. Charles alive? And then murdered by one of Bellamy's own men? St. Martin squatted beside her, his face close to hers, and she averted her head to avoid his gaze. But nothing was ever simple with this man. He took her chin in his hand and forced her to face him. "Do you understand that you can't go back there?"

She found her voice. "I didn't do it."

"That's really beside the point. It appears as though you did."

She stared at him. "I know," she echoed in a whisper.

"It means you have to listen to me for a change."

"Where are we going?"

"You'll find out soon enough." He released her chin and rose to begin a renewed march. Without thinking, she followed, tramping through the tall grass, her mind a blank, refusing to function in a bid for self-preservation. One foot after another, occasionally stumbling, then righting herself, her eyes fixed on St. Martin's broad back, a false hope, she knew, but the only hope that had the power to keep her upright. After an indeterminate amount of time she saw the sign, Hatchett's Bottom, a small hamlet where East Heath Road led to a small lane. A black carriage, completely out of place, waited, its gleaming doors bared of a crest.

The coachman swiveled on the box and leaned out around the corner to address St. Martin. After an unintelligible exchange, the door clattered open followed by the footstep. She allowed herself to be bundled into the carriage like a portmanteau, not permitting herself to even think about the last time she'd been alone with St. Martin in an enclosed space. Too many threats, too many deaths, and too many lies had left her numb, drained, and unable to fight.

The coachman was obviously prepared for the unexpected when St. Martin closed the carriage door with a restrained slam and turned to survey Lilly. The conveyance began to move, possibly toward London, throwing her back into the padded squabs.

He looked more remote than ever, as far away from her as an alpine peak. And he had blood on his hands—hands now resting quietly at his sides. She stared at them, mesmerized, her eyes focused on the drying traces marking the long fingers.

Nausea rose in her throat once again, and she was cold, so cold, her muscles clenched tight against the fear that invaded her body. She didn't want to draw St. Martin's attention any more than she had to, afraid of where this was going, where he was taking her. More than ever, she needed to disappear, to vanish into nothingness. Once again, she recalled her favorite childhood game, the fantasy that if one closed her eyes, and didn't move or speak, the horror would simply go away.

"You're going to have to talk to me sometime."

Her muscles tightened against him.

"If we're fortunate, the melee we left behind will mitigate against anyone following us." He would have made sure of that, she thought, steeling herself against a fresh wave of panic. Other than Flynn, if he survived, no one could have known St. Martin had been in the house. Her mind flashed back to the moments in the scullery. They would surmise that she'd escaped alone, a murderess fleeing the scene of the crime.

"What are you thinking?" he asked in a flat voice.

She looked down at the carriage floor and at her now scuffed silk slippers and torn lace overskirt, the pathetic remnants of her wedding dress. Deciding to answer honestly, she said, "What I'm going to do next."

"Any ideas?"

"Whatever I choose will not involve you," she said bleakly.

He stretched his long legs, crowding the small enclosure. "I'm afraid that's no longer possible."

"I trust you know where we're going?"

He nodded. "We'll have enough time to talk about things we've been avoiding far too long."

She sighed wearily, letting her head fall back on the cushioned seat. "The diamond."

"Among other subjects." His voice was deep and unemotional. "And perhaps you can begin by telling me how your late husband happens to be alive."

Only to be killed again. If she had anything left inside, she would have laughed, a dry, heaving cackle bordering on hysteria. Instead, the madness of the situation dictated that she ignore the question. She sensed they were miles away now from Hampstead Heath and Charles.

"I wish I knew," she replied flatly. Suspicion flared in her mind, but as always, his expression gave nothing away. His long body was casually sprawled in the seat opposite her, as relaxed as she was tense. "This is what you were warning me about, weren't you? That somehow and for some reason Charles was still alive. Which leads me to ask"—she was on the edge of falling apart—"how did you come by the knowledge?"

"We'll get to that eventually."

"Then you admit to withholding the information from me." She sat up straighter, fresh anger taking the place of some of the numbness. "Dear God, had I married Bellamy, had the ceremony concluded, I could have been a bigamist!"

"In addition to being a murderess," he supplied with a small smile. "I don't know how anyone could have ever mistaken you for a modest, retiring widow."

She wanted to strangle him, wipe the humor from his too striking face.

"It's good to see some healthy color back in your cheeks. For several moments there I believed you were going to faint."

She clenched her teeth and her hands in her lap. "I don't faint—ever. And no gentleman would have referred to a lady's indisposition." He'd done more than that, actually, and she cringed when she remembered how he had held her, supporting her as she emptied the contents of her stomach. Too shocked to push him away, she let him hold her until everything was gone, finished. And even now, she wanted to die, both from misery and humiliation. Except that St. Martin wouldn't let her.

"We're almost there." He leaned forward to look out the window, brushing against her, so close she could conjure the familiar scent of his skin. She felt dizzy and this time it wasn't from nausea.

"You never did tell me where we were going."

"My home, here in London."

The dizziness evaporated instantly. "Oh dear God."

He raised an arrogant brow. "You have no other suggestions, you informed me earlier. Besides which, we require some hours as we're going to talk this time."

The statement was lightly delivered but she shivered nonetheless. She'd just seen him beat a man senseless with a dark danger and frightening skill that emanated from him like an aura. Images rolled through her mind's eye. The night at the Tower of London. The attack at the theater. Flynn. It was the way he moved, efficiently, effortlessly, that should have been warning enough.

She wanted to go home. Now. But knew it was out of the question. "Let me off at a train station. Any one will do," she tried impetuously, gathering her skirts in preparation, cursing the awkward hoops. North, south, east, or west, she simply needed to get away because at the moment, she didn't want to think anymore, about Charles, Bellamy, or St. Martin.

One look at him, at that cool, enigmatic face, and she knew it was hopeless.

"You have no money, no clothes, and no friends, not to mention half of London out looking for you by now. If you're half as clever as I know you to be, you will prove co-operative and I'll have the coach let you out at the rear entrance of the house. No one will have a chance of seeing the two of us together disembarking."

The instinct to get away from him was strong. "Very well," she lied. "I have no energy or will to argue with you at this time. And as you pointed out, I can't very well run away in a ruined wedding gown and not much else."

St. Martin smiled, a cynical curve to his lips. In the past, he'd had the ability to read her mind and she desperately hoped he'd forgotten how.

A dense and strained silence descended over them. She closed her eyes, the lurching of the coach and the shattered peace of the countryside eventually displaced by the rising din of the city. It was difficult to tell how much time had passed until they slowed and she realized they were close to their destination. Opening her eyes, she pretended to ready herself, deliberately looking away from St. Martin, careful not to meet his eyes for fear of what he would see in her own.

She waited until the carriage door closed behind him and the conveyance began slowly moving again. A quick look out the window told her they were turning into a mews where she could expect the coach house. There wasn't much time before they rounded the corner. Tearing the hoops from beneath her skirts, she struggled briefly before tossing them aside. Then opening the door carefully, she looked to the gravel-strewn ground below, cringing at the fall to come. The carriage slowed to take the corner and it was over in a moment, the hard ground biting into her shoulder before she could roll to a sitting position. St. Martin wouldn't know she was gone until the carriage spun into the coach house.

Picking up her skirts that now trailed behind her, she ran back around the corner to the entrance of the mews. She wanted to avoid Regent Street, much too visible, she thought, turning the opposite direction instead. Tall hedges beckoned, a place to hide if necessary.

The thought was barely completed when he caught up with her, a looming shadow blocking her body from view before she hit the ground a second time in less than a minute. He picked her up in his arms an instant later and she could feel his anger, silent and deadly. "You fool. You'll get yourself killed, or worse." His voice was cold. "The former will at least save me from having to do it myself."

He would do it in an instant, she realized with every beat of her sinking heart.

With typical efficiency, he'd had them both inside the house a moment later, an unflappable butler holding open the servant's door, watching coolly as his master ignored him to take the backstairs two at a time, despite the burden in his arms, to the second floor.

St. Martin deposited her in the middle of a bedroom, the late afternoon light pouring through the sheer curtains, the overall effect heightened by delicate gold and pink–hued wallpaper. Exhausted, resigned, and barely able to stand, she eyed the canopied bed piled high with pillows and crisp sheets. A rich Oriental rug, an armoire, and a chaise longue completed the decor, giving the room a jarring and unexpectedly feminine air.

He closed and locked the door behind them, then motioned toward the dressing room. "Hot water will be brought shortly and we'll talk afterward—as promised."

She ran a shaking hand through her tangled hair, her wedding coiffure, complete with drooping feathers and silver fillet, now tumbling past her shoulders. The last thing she wanted to do was talk. "Are you going to give me my privacy?"

"You don't deserve any," he said, leaning against the door, arms crossed over his chest. "You may use the dressing room."

A few minutes later she'd slammed the dressing room door behind her. A quick glance revealed a window, but it was small and high and even if she could get through, she was at least forty yards from the ground.

Eager to shed her clothing, along with her memories of the day's gruesome events, she struggled with the hooks down her back, finally tearing away at the delicate fabric in a bid to free herself from what exactly, she didn't know. Looking down at her left hand, she saw the serpent ring, the diamond and ruby embedded in her skin. Twisting the jewel from her finger, she threw it to the tile floor. She was bone-weary, frustrated, and terrified, and now, clad only in her chemise and pantalets, vulnerable and naked.

The brass claw-footed tub was steaming with hot water. Discarding the wilted feathers and bundling her hair on top of her head with the silver fillet, she eased herself into the soothing depths, letting it scald her and burn the anxiety from every tight muscle in her body. Picking up the soap perched on a marble-topped side table, she scrubbed, over and over again until the bar was half its original size.

Reluctant to leave the deceptive warmth of the tub and enter the real world again, she forced herself to rise dripping from the water, her skin red from the heat and the vigorous washing.

Unfortunately, she was not reborn. Drying herself quickly with one of the abundantly available towels, she couldn't bear to clothe herself in the wedding dress, now crumpled and damp on the tile floor, a reminder of what was past and a harbinger of the emptiness to come. After quickly running her fingers through her hair and shrugging into her pantalets and chemise, she grabbed a dry towel, unfolded it and draped it around herself.

St. Martin looked as though he hadn't moved from where she'd left him earlier when she finally emerged from the dressing room. If he was surprised to see her clad in little more than a length of linen, he didn't show it. She only needed to remember that he used intimacy as efficiently as a rapier and, recalling their last moments in the scullery, he was hardly overcome with lust for her. Nonetheless, feeling undignified and exposed, she pulled the towel more snugly around her, leaning her hip against the foot of the bed for support.

"Would you like to sit?"

"I'm fine," she said tersely.

"I can see that." The sarcasm was veiled but he still blocked the door.

"Not to worry," she said, matching his tone, "I won't try to run screaming out the door clad in little more than a towel."

"Or a wedding dress, as you'd declared earlier." He must have left the room at some point because he'd changed his clothing. His shirt was crisply white and his hair damp but his hard jaw was still dark with stubble. He hadn't trusted her long enough to have shaved. "Please forgive me if I don't believe you."

Tucking the towel even more tightly underneath her arms, she said, "Given the tumultuous nature of our association, it's fair to say that trust between us is scarce."

"And what are we to do about that?" He stepped into the room, closer to the bed.

"I have no idea that we need do anything," she answered stiffly.

"But you see, I do. Now get into bed."

She was stunned, the command entirely unexpected, signaling a dangerous rush of memories.

He pushed back the comforter and sheets. "Don't look so shocked, my not-quite-so-prim Lilly. I don't have any evil designs on your person, I'd simply prefer that you don't succumb to the vapors as you reveal all to me." The sarcasm was generous.

"I told you that I'm not prone to fainting spells," she said as he came closer, so close that she could see the small arced scar above his dark eyebrow. "And what makes you certain that I shall divulge anything worth hearing?" His hand on her bare upper arm stung, but she clamped down on her emotions, allowing him to slide her between the sheets. As indifferent as a nanny putting a child to bed, and not anywhere as reassuring, he tucked the comforter around her.

Then he pulled the small occasional chair by the door closer to the bed, gesturing to a tray on the side table. "Water, wine? There are also some dry biscuits if your stomach needs settling."

She was too suspicious to dwell on her earlier humiliation. "This gentlemanly concern is unlike you," she said, watching him settle his long frame into the chair, which seemed entirely too small for him. Feeling childlike curled under the sheets, she was robbed of most of her rapidly dwindling confidence.

"Of course, I'm concerned about you. It's not all about the Koh-I-Noor, despite what you might think."

The lie fueled her low simmering outrage, some strength flowing back into her limbs. "I asked you earlier today, an eternity ago it seems, not to condescend to me, St. Martin." She punched back the pillows. "I have had no choice but to accept your lies and obfuscations, but don't expect me to accept your palaver."

He crossed one muscled leg over the other, and she tried to ignore the sheer beauty of his body. "You misunderstand," he said coolly. "Without you, there is no Koh-I-Noor."

"Because I have the plans, allegedly, and therefore access to the diamond. Don't expect me to be flattered by your attentions."

"We'll get back to that point shortly," he said in a way that made her shift uneasily beneath the sheets. "But at this moment I'm more interested in this morning's events. Charles Hampton is alive, although everyone believes he was murdered over one year ago. And we cannot help but remember that he was the architect for the Crystal Palace."

His logic rankled in more ways than one. Never mind that the plans were never his—*they were hers*. But how had

Charles managed to escape death? Her head buzzed painfully as she tried to recall the night of the murder. The fog of memory had turned into a quagmire of doubts and misgivings. And if he now lay dead or dying—she bit her lip to control the turmoil of her emotions, a bitter brew of anger, guilt, and the remnants of deep affection. She'd loved him once, so long ago.

It was too much, the urge to have her sins explained and washed away. She couldn't decide whether to scream, laugh, or cry. The words escaped before she could hold them back.

"I didn't murder him," she blurted out, wanting to turn her face away from the truth and into the pillow. But she didn't, instead holding St. Martin's dark gaze over the gentle mound of white damask.

"I suspected that." He looked calm, controlled, and not in the least bit surprised.

"You believe me, then." Relief made her weak again. "How did you know?"

He didn't have to answer. As a killer, he recognized one of his own. And Lilly Clarence Hampton could no more take a life than fly to the moon. And if it wasn't precisely absolution, his silence was welcome and she accepted it with grateful hunger. "Thank you," she said simply.

He leaned forward toward the bed, persistent as a priest hearing confession. "What do you remember of that night?"

"Not much," she said with honesty, her voice faint.

"But the investigators found a pistol on the scene—and it was yours." And he could track her fingerprints on the weapon, if he chose.

St. Martin was the last man she should trust, an agent of the Crown, disgraced, untrustworthy, damaged everyone said—a would-be thief intent on stealing a diamond right out from under the queen and her government. Unfortunately, he was her only refuge as a fugitive, a woman with a price on her head, with nowhere to go or to hide. She'd come this far, the truth in all its ugliness all but revealed. She swallowed hard, the desire to confide, to set down her burden, impossible to resist.

She couldn't help but ask. "Do you believe he's dead— Charles that is?" The question preyed on her mind and on her conscience.

"I'd be surprised if he could survive three bullets to the chest coming from such a close range."

Her eyes welled with tears and she blinked them away, hoping he wouldn't see. It pained her still, what she'd lost with Charles and what, in the end, they'd never really had together. The bed dipped when he sat next to her, his thigh pressing against hers, the weight and heat of his presence magnifying her anguish and confusion. She curled away from him.

"You loved him."

The simple fact shamed her, as did her naïveté and innocence lost long ago to the desperate desire to be loved, at any cost. "I did." She couldn't respond any other way.

"Did he threaten you in any way?"

She sank deeper into the cushions. His strong hand with their sensitive fingers rested on hers.

"No . . . yes."

"You can tell me, Lilly. I'm the only one whom you can afford to tell the truth. Let me help you."

He was too close, to her body and to the truth. She focused on a fold of the heavy damask but she could still see him clearly, the planed austerity of his face, the lines bracketing his beautiful mouth, the eyes dark and enigmatic as always. No longer naïve, no longer so very young, she recognized him as the complex, dangerous man he was. A man who used his skill, like the darkest arts, to draw her out, to confide in him, and yes, to ultimately trust him. Through the pain and the confusion, she knew exactly what he was doing—and she was helpless against it.

His thumb caressed the back of her hand, the touch mesmerizing. "You're the architect behind the Crystal Palace."

The prudent thing would have been to stop him right there, but she couldn't, her salvation at the root of the paradox. A volley of bullets could not have hit their mark as precisely, and he knew it. She sat up, the towel twisting beneath her arms and falling away. Eyes widening in recognition, she struggled against the enveloping sheets, every instinct telling her to run away. But this time, she couldn't. Not from this man, not from the truth.

"Yes," she said hoarsely. "I am the architect of the Crystal Palace." She gulped in air, now that she'd begun, her heart pounding with something like hope, the words tumbling in a torrent from her lips. "I am the architect," she repeated, "and Charles took my work and made it his own. From almost the very beginning."

She pulled the covers closer to her chest. "But I loved him, would do anything for him, even lie and go along with the deceptions and subterfuge. He would not have it any other way." Curling farther away from St. Martin, she sat up on her knees, the need for confession and absolution acute. "But when he came to me about the Koh-I-Noor and the queen, you see"—she watched St. Martin's face, desperate for understanding—"and when I asked why, what purpose the additional plans served, then I knew . . ."

She broke off.

"What did you know, Lilly?" St. Martin was preternaturally still, his eyes fixed on hers.

Shaking her head, she pushed a hand through her hair. "Assassination." She licked her dry lips. "I discovered that Charles was part of a plot to assassinate the queen—and I was the only one who could stop him."

It was as though a cancer had been lanced, the malignancy burned away through an acknowledgment of guilt. Her guilt. And whether she would die from the treatment, Lilly no longer cared. She felt strangely liberated, lying nearly naked in this bed and with a man who showed neither shock nor disgust at her revelation.

Her need to explain was acute, to him and to herself. "He needed the plans, you see, which would allow the assassins access to Her Majesty. The Koh-I-Noor was simply a diversion."

He gazed at her over the rumpled sheets, and if she allowed herself, she could imagine compassion in his eyes. But then, after an entire lifetime, she was so very good at lying to herself. She sank back against the pillows and pulled the sheets up to her neck.

His voice was neutral. "Did you ever discover the motive behind the assassination plans—why someone would want to kill the Queen of England?"

"I hadn't a clue and sometimes I believe Charles didn't know what was behind the plot either. He was simply seduced by the promise of money and further, highly visible commissions."

"So you thought to thwart Charles's plans by buying a pistol and using it against him."

In retrospect, she acknowledged that her plan sounded hopeless and even now she had difficulty separating the strands of reality from fantasy. She shook her head in confusion. "But I swear to God, I swear to you, St. Martin, that I didn't release the hammer." *I could not have done it*, a voice inside her head insisted, *I could not have murdered my husband.*

"Whom else did you tell? Did you confide in anyone?"

She thought of Seabourne, and the many important friends and acquaintances who comprised their social circle. "That was precisely the problem," she said, her voice low with distress. "I did not know with whom Charles was colluding or even the details of the plot. I could not begin to question his associates without raising suspicion. I feared that I would make it worse, possibly fuel the plotters with my careless stumbling. All I knew, finally, was that my husband was a vain and superficial man who would go along with a heinous conspiracy simply to further his own ambitions." Her mind touched on the afternoon with Seabourne, the moments at the wedding when he'd moved away from her side and toward Bellamy. She had given him the plans. She pushed the doubts to the back of her mind.

St. Martin's weight on the bed shifted closer to her. "And to exacerbate the situation, Charles wanted to use you as an instrument in the conspiracy."

"He wasn't accustomed to my refusing him," she said, burrowing back into the cushions and into her years with Charles. "He had been passing off my work as his own for many years and I had gone along with the deception if for no other reason than I was desperate to continue to work and I could—through Charles."

He listened patiently, urging her silently to continue.

"I purchased the pistol, you see, not with any intention of actually using it but to simply and urgently state my case— that I would refuse to go along with him this time." She paused, the moment heavy with her guilt. "I could think of no other way of making my point. I would not take part in any plan that would result in assassination. In regicide!"

She hid her face in her hands. "And the rest I can't recall. I remember confronting Charles, his laughing at me and then—nothing."

St. Martin reached for her and she let him, hating her weakness, as she felt him gently move her hands from her face. His face swam behind her tears and she blinked desperately to hide the evidence of her distress. If anything, her confusion had intensified and she felt a nagging worry that confiding in this man would be her final undoing. Even if she wished for it desperately, it could never be. St. Martin was implicated, somehow, in the profound disarray that marked her life.

She swallowed the lump in her throat. "How did you

come to know that Charles was still alive?" She didn't try to hide the mistrust in her voice.

His hand tightened on hers. St. Martin was adept at sensing her reactions, knowing her better than she knew herself. It worried her.

"Vesper."

"Dr. Vesper?" She didn't know how many shocks she could absorb in one day. She looked at the man so close to her, wondering if she would ever see behind the dark eyes that watched her like he was one of those new factory machines she'd read and heard so much about. There was a connection, if she could only grasp it, but it dissolved like gossamer between her fingers. "Of course, your doctor. The headaches."

St. Martin nodded. "He'd kept Charles alive—for over a year."

"But why?"

"He didn't confide those details, other than to let me know that as a physician, with a commitment to saving lives, he couldn't let a man die under his care."

Her brow furrowed. "I see what you're thinking. That perhaps the associate Charles was involved with wanted to keep him alive—believing that Charles served as access to the plans for the Crystal Palace and to me."

His eyes glinted with admiration.

Her head hurt. "This is all too much, too confusing. I simply can't make all the pieces of the puzzle fit." And the more she thought about it, the more she wondered about St. Martin, a man all too close to the diamond, too familiar with subterfuge, and at the moment, too close to her. As always, his physical proximity was overwhelming, making it hard for her to think clearly. Misgiving shone from her eyes.

"Now it's your turn," she tried, pulling the sheet up to her neck. "I have been more than open, St. Martin."

"You've had no other choice. I'm your only option at the

moment." Arrogant man, she fumed despite her profound exhaustion, wishing that he would rise from the bed and return to his chair. "And I was, after all, truthful about Vesper and his role in keeping Charles alive."

And less than open about his relationship with the damned Koh-I-Noor. Tired but not weary enough for it to stem her impatience, she let out her frustration. "You're hiding," she said, aware that she was treading on dangerous territory. Beneath the sheets, she felt hot and cold all at once.

For once, he looked surprised, moving fractionally away from her. "From you—is that what you're suggesting?" As though the assumption was beyond belief.

"From me, among other things."

It was a bold statement, but she wanted to, for once, disturb the unfair balance between them. He had seduced her, not only physically but also morally, prompting her to confess what she had barely been able to reveal to herself. And somehow she resented him for it, resented him for his distance, for his refusal to disclose the nature of his true involvement with the diamond, and for his utmost determination to withhold himself from her.

He withdrew his hand from atop hers with a ghost of a laugh. "This is about the sexual nature of our association, I think, rather than about the Koh-I-Noor."

"Don't be absurd." She wished she could forget about how well he could read her, cold anger already beginning to war with hot desire low in her abdomen.

He leaned back on an elbow, the movement stretching the white shirt across his finely muscled shoulders. She shouldn't notice but she did, wondering how she had allowed herself to be ensnared by something as basic as physical desire, which, when it involved St. Martin, managed to trump all other concerns, ranging from larceny and adultery to murder and assassination.

"You speak of hiding," he said, "and you question my honesty. So while you find yourself in confessional mode, why not be completely honest, Lilly, with me and with yourself. It might prove cathartic in more ways than one."

She read the challenge in his eyes and met it by stretching out her legs beneath the comforter. He seemed immune to the outline of her long limbs, which she'd always thought lacked fashionable plumpness. She let the duvet, cocooned around her neck, drop a fraction. "Very well," she said, "why is it that you do your best to seduce me and yet hold yourself aloof, as though your response to me is only mildly"—she paused awkwardly—"diverting and all in a day's work?"

"Unmoved and uninvolved. That's what you think." He smiled pleasantly, irritating her to no degree.

"Precisely." Some instinct drove her to go on. "And you accused me in Hyde Park of letting my own guilt get in the way, coloring my decision to marry Bellamy. But I suspect, sir, that you are doing a version of the same, a variation on the theme." She let the sheet clenched in her hand drop lower. "I suspect that you are hiding some type of guilt, perhaps associated with your clandestine past, and that you are punishing yourself by disallowing yourself the pleasure of . . ." She broke off, unable to continue, momentarily staggered by the word that hovered on her lips.

His eyes darkened and she thought she'd gone too far. "Finish your thought, Lilly. You were going to say what exactly? That I am disallowing myself the pleasure of *sex* with you because I harbor a dark, unfathomable guilt?"

She pulled the sheet back up to her neck, her face flushed. Thank God he hadn't guessed at the word that had nearly tripped off her tongue. *Love* was what she almost said. As for lust, to which he was referring—

Already regretting her outburst, she attempted to paper over her blunder. "You misunderstand. I didn't mean to say that I would expect anyone to find me overwhelmingly desirable, far from the truth," she rambled, embarrassed down to her toes twitching beneath the covers. "I was merely suggesting that most men don't require, well, can find satisfaction in, with . . ." she trailed off hopelessly, looking up at the tall ceiling now colored gold by the late afternoon light.

He shifted on the bed and she returned her mortified gaze to the side of the bed where he began stripping off his shirt, shrugging out of it with his usual efficient movements to toss it on the floor.

"What are you doing?" she croaked.

"Proving you wrong," he said. He was as beautiful as she'd feared, his elegantly defined muscles spanning strong shoulders, a smooth chest and a delineated abdomen. She remembered suddenly that she'd never seen him nude before. "I am not punishing myself. Nor do I harbor deeply buried guilt." There was a belligerence to his tone that she hadn't heard before. "So do your best, Lilly, I challenge you." He tore the comforter off her body, tossing it out of reach on the floor.

Scrambling to make do with the scrap of linen towel wound around her like a shroud, she watched in disbelief as he began to unfasten his breeches. Her mind wrestled with the possibilities, that he was doing this out of a strange type of pity or that he was attempting to distract her because she'd struck a painful wound that rested too close to the bone. "You don't have to do this, St. Martin. I'm not expecting you to assuage my vanity, for God's sake."

"Is that what you think this is about?" A cold anger seeped into his words as he approached the bed, as naked and unforgettable as a pagan prince. He moved to her side, one knee on the mattress, looking down at her. "You can't possibly be that disingenuous not to recognize that yes, absolutely, you are a beautiful woman. Even though I must admit, you have the experience of a nun and the proclivities of a wanton. Did anyone ever tell you that?"

Her breath caught in her throat as he began slowly unwinding the linen from her body. She couldn't find anything to say, watching as his hands next moved to her chemise and her pantalets. The chemise was nothing more than a concoction of lace and wisps of silk and he unhooked it and pulled it away. Then he continued his work like a connoisseur, sliding the pantalets smoothly from her body, leaving her naked and exposed for his eyes.

"You're beautiful," he repeated coolly, his gaze moving slowly over her breasts, down her waist, and along her legs that she clenched together helplessly. "And don't ever think any differently."

"You don't have to . . ." She was repeating herself, but it was all she could do as he moved with lethal grace to stretch over her, touching every part of her exposed body, his erection at the juncture of her thighs, hard and full and indisputable.

He pulled her hand between them. "This is the proof if you require it," he said, his face hovering over hers, his mouth too close for comfort. Perhaps it was her profound shock mixed with the sparks already dancing low in her belly, but she kissed him. She kissed him, softly, sensitively, probingly. Her lips moved over his, catching his breath, wanton, hungry, and ready. She felt his tongue respond, slide in gently, firm but not demanding. Reaching behind her he stroked her hair, leaning in and kissing the taut skin over one cheekbone.

Then his breath was warm over her breasts. "Beautiful." The areolas were wide and pink, as if the kiss had caused them to bloom.

"You don't have to do this." Her hands tangled in the silk of his hair. "I can't do this if it's only about secrets and lies and coercion." Neither of them moved for a moment.

St. Martin pushed her gently back into the pillows. "I have nothing to hide and nothing to prove, Lilly." His hand moved down over her naked thighs, caressing them up and down, working his way to the inside.

"I hope so." She breathed, staring at his hand playing between her thighs, to the skin that suddenly felt achingly smooth. Before she could continue, he was kissing her again, his tongue moving in and out of her mouth rhythmically with his kiss. At the same time, his palm rested between her legs, pressing against her dampness.

His lips played her mouth endlessly until she was writhing hungrily, her hand still clenched around his hardness. "I hope I excite you," she murmured into the warm skin of his shoulder. "I want to excite you."

He didn't answer. Instead, his hands parted her legs, separating them until he could see the evidence of her lust glistening on her thighs. His erection throbbed against her as he slid a finger into her and up her hot, clutching tightness, moving in slow excruciating circles. And then without any warning, he pulled her legs apart, removed his hand, and pushed inside her with a force that stopped her breath.

"Does that answer your question?" he murmured.

She knew he was big, had held him in her hands, held him in her mouth, but the sense of having him fill her for the first time, the awareness of male with female, washed over her. His strong hands closed over her legs, pulling them around his hips. Helpless with need, she clutched the sheet beneath her while he bore into her, deeper and deeper.

Slowly, deliberately, he built up the speed and the pressure, each contact with her core sending a shock of desire flowing through her body. Then he pulled out, and she clutched at his shoulders, before he sank back in again with a clever movement that left her gasping for air. She arched her back so that each thrust of hardness brushed her fleetingly, teasingly, before sinking farther into her.

Then he changed the pace, moving slowly, insidiously, deliberately taking whatever she could give. She felt the first tremors begin but held back, wanting to fight the protracted buildup of response that would draw her to him more deeply.

She opened her eyes. His arms were braced against the wall behind them, his dark eyes heavy lidded, intent on something far away. But she wanted him closer, she wanted him to be part of the dangerous rhythm, the thick fullness of it that threatened to sweep her away.

"Come with me," she whispered. "Come inside me." Reaching between their legs, she found his heaviness, his vulnerability, as he pumped slowly and deliberately. She caressed gently, squeezing and stroking. He moaned and pushed harder, faster, deeper. She answered his every move with her whole body, every inch of skin on fire.

She watched as he closed his eyes, trying to shut her out, but she slid her arms around his neck, pulling him closer, wanting to feel him fully on top of her, their bodies merging. Beneath her hands his skin was hot and smooth, the strong line of his neck arched above her. This time he would not win, she would not allow her response out of her control without bringing him along with her. She bit her lip, releasing a low moan of pleasure. He was moving faster now and she was meeting his thrusts, his hands cupping her hips, pulling her against him so that he went deeper still, hot and strong and hard.

Pulling his face down to hers, she leaned her mouth into his, pushing her tongue in and out, meeting his movements again and again. She felt his hands under her naked bottom tighten as he pumped, and when their tongues touched she contracted, and their rocking became more of a grinding motion.

He rose up against her hard, then stopped for an infinitesimal moment, and she thought all was lost. His eyes were open but unseeing, and she sensed he was fighting a battle with single-minded intensity. But to lose him now—she would die. Clenching around him, buried to the hilt, she squeezed hard. She leaned back on her elbows and rose up, then moved down again, releasing the powerful pressure that had been building in his hard, powerful cock.

His expression was tortured, anguished, and then something inside him broke. The first stream exploded in her and she went suddenly weak and dizzy, clinging to him as her own orgasm took control, her hips bucking in wild frenzy. He gripped her waist, pulling her hard against his insistent, unrelenting, untiring erection. Her arms stretched out on the bed, clinging to the twisted sheets, her inner muscles gripped him with hungry power.

With every move he came, and she took him with her with every rotation of her hips, endless, hot, and wet until, after what seemed like hours, they collapsed onto the bed. And only then did he roll away from her, his ragged breathing music to her ears, his sweat-drenched body her prize.

And then with the profound exhaustion of a child, she slept.

Chapter 17

Isambard Kingdom Bellamy wanted to hurt someone. It gnawed at his innards like a long-toothed rodent.

Flynn's swollen lip bled from a fist to his lantern jaw that he'd absorbed like the good soldier he was. Bellamy's hand sung with the memory, the pleasure vibrating with the intensity of a well-tuned string instrument.

Flynn continued to stand while Bellamy lounged in his favorite wing-back chair in the library. On the floor were the useless contents of a leather satchel, the rolled sheets papering the rug like snow drifts. It was little wonder Seabourne had not risen very far, despite his lofty affectations. A poor judge of character, he had actually believed that Lilly Clarence Hampton had placed the safety of the queen and the Koh-I-Noor in his soft, white hands. The fool. She had held back one fundamentally important component—of course.

A quick glance at Flynn told him that his shoulder had been bandaged but it still seeped blood. Bellamy bit back a smile of profound pleasure at the thought of the pain.

It wasn't enough that he'd been publicly humiliated on his wedding day. But his lieutenant, the man who'd been entrusted with far more difficult assignments in godforsaken hell holes like Lahore and Bombay, had lost his bride. To a mystery man yet.

"Anything to say for yourself, Flynn?"

The Irishman and former boxer stared straight ahead, no doubt dreaming of the hundreds of other places he'd prefer to find himself.

Bellamy chuckled, but the sound was anything but joyful. He played with the chess piece from his favorite set. The white queen, an ornately carved portion of elephant ivory, glowed between his hands. "You know, Flynn, back where I come from we were plenty tough and yet we still believed that Irishmen were even a more durable breed. Close to bestial, as a matter of fact."

Flynn absorbed the insult, and if anything, his face hardened in self-abasement. Bellamy continued conversationally, one foot crossed over another and swinging to an inner rhythm all its own. "You did well eliminating that vermin, Hampton, as requested," he said, his white teeth bright against his mustache, "and making the deed appear to be the work of my betrothed, as I also requested. All of which demonstrates to me your continued usefulness."

Outwardly he appeared calm but inwardly his mind seethed with questions about Hampton, how it was possible that the man had escaped from Vesper. Charles Hampton was pathetic—worse than a nuisance—an albatross, a red herring, to be used when Bellamy deemed the time was right. He was merely a conduit to his talented wife who'd held the key to Bellamy's future in her talented grip.

But in his laudanum-laced stupidity, Charles Hampton had dared interfere with his careful arrangements. There was nothing like violence to concentrate one's ambition. So— Hampton had to die once more, seemingly in a public place and with his wife clutching the pistol. Turning the chess piece over and over between his palms, Bellamy didn't have to wonder overly much what Lilly would now choose to do given the chance. Because there was no choice open to her— other than relinquish the plans for the Crystal Palace or spend the rest of her life in Newgate.

And in exchange, Flynn would be made to confess.

It was a good thing, Bellamy congratulated himself, that he could still think quickly on his feet. The years spent in the humid, fetid backwaters of India had not diminished his powers for swift action. The millions of sterling that he'd accumulated over the years, the brutal business dealings, the hundreds of humiliations, large and small, meted out to those whose role was to crawl rather than stride over the earth—it had made him the man he was.

He was the major shareholder and chairman of the British East India Company, the man who had signaled to Flynn to dispose of Hampton in the most brazen, outrageous way possible. And the man who would send Flynn to the gallows if need be.

"Get me a cigar," he motioned to the Irishman. He adored the fact that the queen and her consort detested the habit, making tobacco an offense at Court. Flynn moved swiftly to the drinks table, fumbling to extract a churchwarden from the humidor before presenting it with a flourish, and cutters, to Bellamy.

Bellamy grunted his thanks, chewing off the tip before spitting it on the floor. The flare of a match held attentively by Flynn, then a rain of sparks, preceded a ring of smoke rising in the air. It was calming, the biting heat filling his mouth, but it did nothing to assuage the gnawing in the pit of his stomach.

Absolutely not acceptable. His plan had been simple, perfect, and unassailable, every nuance anticipated. He could not tolerate a mess. Chaos is what he'd left behind with that whore of his mother and her den of thieves. Order is what he'd delivered, like a Roman emperor of old, to the primitives that populated the colonial world. As a result, what he didn't expect to see was Charles Hampton's corpse dragged publicly and *a second time* to the undertaker's. Once should have been enough.

He took a deep breath and another haul on his cigar. And then there was Lilly, his eager bride, stolen from him by a mysterious stranger whom Flynn, somehow, was unable to identify.

"I want her back," Bellamy said in a flat voice. He bit the inside of his mouth, the metallic wash of blood a comfort.

"I apologize, sir, but I didn't recognize him." If standing with a suppurating wound was strenuous, Flynn didn't show it. "He was tall, well over average height, dark, an aristocrat—"

"And why would you say that . . . an aristocrat?"

Flynn shrugged, not wincing at the fresh spurt of blood seeping through his bandage. "As though he owned the world."

"You don't say." Bellamy digested the bit of information. He missed India, missed the slavish devotion, the intense unwavering loyalty of the natives who at least recognized that their lives depended on the higher orders. Here in England, it was a different story. Despite his wealth, despite his conquests, despite his power, he didn't have the pedigree, the patina that the effete rulers of Britannia demanded. The caste system in goddamned England was worse than any he'd seen among the flies and the dung of the colonies.

As though he owned the world . . .

Bloody hell—Bellamy did own the world. And he would have that fact acknowledged, if he had to bleed the empire dry.

"For a comparatively young and healthy man, your memory is severely lacking." He swung his foot to tamp down the fire in his vitals, demanding retribution, demanding attention, demanding anything that would assuage the burning in his belly. There was always the St. Martin bitch, but, then again, she'd drunk from the cup too deeply to provide any form of sport these days. Beautiful though she was, he required spirit to hone the suffering, an awareness of the humiliation, not simply the ability to absorb the pain. Constance would keep, until the time was ripe to return her to her husband. For a price.

The gnawing intensified. He drew on the cigar, his thoughts expanding. Constance, St. Martin, Vesper, and of course, Lilly. An unholy quartet, his unholy quartet. The links in the chain grew stronger and he paused.

And where does Dr. Vesper practice? His name is not familiar to me.

We saw Lord St. Martin follow Mrs. Hampton into the doctor's residence and then depart with her in his private carriage.

He roared to a standing position, clenching his cigar between his thumb and forefinger. "You fool, you son-of-a-whore, you mongrel!" He thrust his face close to Flynn's, snarling. "Did you not recognize Julian St. Martin when he was standing directly in front of you this morning? That's the man who managed to make off with my betrothed while you were busy shooting yourself in the shoulder."

Flynn shook his head like a sheepdog, momentarily confused, shifting anxiously from one foot to the other. "I don't think I ever . . . I never did get a clear look at him . . ."

Bellamy grit his teeth, resisting the urge to bite down harder. "You complete ass—you were the one who reported seeing the two of them leave Vesper's residence near Harley Street and enter St. Martin's carriage."

Flynn stuttered, holding out both palms in supplication despite the tight bandage winding around his shoulder. "I never did get a good look at him, sir, other than, now you mention it, the description fits. I saw a tall man, dark, but it was the doctor's housekeeper that confirmed it in the end."

Bellamy shook his head in disbelief, yet feeling a familiar calm steal over him. Like a fire burning down, he knew it burned hottest when the coals were white.

Not all was lost. Vesper had kept Charles Hampton alive. And St. Martin was with Lilly. The assassin—whom he held in the palm of his hand.

If anything, the game had just become more dangerous. Just the way he liked it. Not that it meant Flynn didn't deserve his punishment. Nor Lilly, once she was returned to him. He pursed his lips as though deciding between sweets for dessert. She had spirit and intelligence and talent, attributes he normally detested in a woman, unless he had the opportunity to beat them out of her.

And as for Flynn . . . Raising the churchwarden chest high, he moved the glowing tip until it just hovered over the younger man's chest. The Irishman stood immobile, only the faintest tightening of his muscles indicating awareness of what was coming. Smiling broadly, the gnawing in his stomach sharpening with every move he made, Bellamy placed the red glow of the cigar directly over the bullet wound, where the bandage was dampening with blood.

The contact made a satisfying, hissing noise—the only sound in the otherwise silent room.

And Bellamy was content. For the moment.

Chapter 18

For once, St. Martin didn't dream. Blackness descended and he welcomed it.

He awoke with a start a few hours later. Next to him, Lilly slept. He had wondered whether she was going to remain awake after the turmoil of the day, the blue eyes that saw all too clearly, continuing to probe deeply where they didn't belong, her beautiful mouth asking questions that he couldn't answer. He'd already gone too far, said and done too much.

Careful not to waken her, he stared at the ceiling overhead. Light from the moon escaped through the curtains of the tall windows, illuminating the delicate scalloped ceiling, a faint reminder of his mother's elevated tastes. He'd lost his family early in life and the result was that the house had never felt like home to him, the shadowed years away in foreign lands more familiar than London or the country estates could ever be.

He was good at what he did, even though what he did was often very bad. Lilly had come close to the truth when she said that it was guilt holding him back, keeping him in a half lit purgatory where human connection had no place. Holding himself away from her, confirming to himself that he could, turned out to be a fallacy. True intimacy had never been his forte, and denying himself sexual completion had served as a kind of penance.

Constance, his dead wife, was the sin he would carry with

him forever. Although forever was fast approaching. The outcome of his mission would be certain death and, until Lilly, he hadn't really cared, perhaps even welcomed it. The irony was that he wasn't expiating his sins, merely compounding them.

He could hear her breathing, sense her stirring, and he didn't want to look because looking would make him want her again. And what he wanted shouldn't count. The alluring, talented widow had staggeringly, overwhelmingly insinuated herself into what, paradoxically, passed for his life.

He choked back a laugh at his own expense. He deserved to die, for his arrogance, if not for his lack of humility. The hunter had become the hunted. Lilly Clarence Hampton had turned his strategy of seduction inside out. Difficult to believe that she'd ever shared a marriage bed, so little did she know about pleasure. He felt an unfamiliar surge of possessiveness, like an alpha wolf for its mate. He'd killed more often than he wanted to remember, carved unpalatable agreements from stone, lied to himself and lied to his countrymen. And in the end, he'd almost lost the game—and worse still, to an innocent.

Lilly stirred beside him, arms outstretched, the tangled sheets baring the length of her slender legs. Deliberately, he turned away, wishing her a deep sleep that would wash away the horror of what she'd witnessed earlier in the day. He couldn't afford to look and he couldn't afford to examine what, and more exactly, *why* he was feeling anything at all.

Constance had been the beginning and the end, a bright, scintillating gemstone so hard and sharp that she'd almost cut his heart out. Except that he'd never entirely given it over to her. He'd recognized that the sexual excess, her outrageous demands and the erratic behavior, later exacerbated by opiates and intemperance, would signal the end of a marriage barely begun.

Poor Constance. He understood now that it was the distance, emotional and physical, that he put between them that doomed them from the start. It was exciting for her at first. Julian St. Martin wasn't anything like the young bucks that curried the favor of the most coveted debutante of several seasons. Dark, dangerous, and ultimately, inaccessible, the man who was her romantic fantasy quickly became her worst nightmare.

He no longer permitted himself to think of the end. The dreams were enough, a continuous loop of self-reproach that went nowhere. It didn't matter. Constance or Lilly. Practicality and exigency would win out—they always did. Placing his hands behind his head, he cleared his head of sentiment and emotion. What mattered now were the next few days. The diamond and the Crystal Palace, Bellamy and the queen.

It wouldn't take long for Bellamy to discover who held his valuable betrothed—the assassin who had been sent to get close to Lilly and whom he believed was twisted enough to do his bidding. Besides which, Bellamy wouldn't necessarily want the local constabulary to know—Lilly was more useful to him as a fugitive desperate to exchange anything for exoneration. Not that he would allow that to happen. The least St. Martin could do was keep Lilly safe—precisely what he was unable to accomplish with his own wife.

Tomorrow he would see that she disappeared into the countryside until the opening of the Crystal Palace had passed. And tomorrow evening he had one last meeting with Vesper, this last time under the watchful and suspicious eye of Bellamy himself. By that time, he would have had Lilly disclose to him the contents of the architectural plans, exactly as he'd intended, at least two steps ahead of the chairman of the British East India Company.

Feeling in control once more, he sat up, putting his legs over the side of the bed, prepared to return to his room. He could walk away now as his barely resurrected conscience dictated or turn toward the warmth that lay just beyond

arms' reach. As though testing his resolve, Lilly kicked restlessly, murmuring in her sleep, a heavy lock of hair obscuring
her face.

He should walk away, ignore her. But he didn't, couldn't.
He sat back down on the bed and slid beside her, pulling her
restless body into his arms. Automatically as though nature
dictated, she leaned into him, her curved backside cool on his
heated skin as she buried herself against him.

His mind raced, all the while he wrapped his larger body
around hers, already hard. He was baffled by her ability to
arouse, her relative innocence and inexperience an unexpected aphrodisiac. He needed a reason to be doing this, a
reason for his wandering hands exploring her high breasts, a
reason for tasting the sweet skin at the curve of her neck.

She was his, and at that moment, in the dark, that was reason enough.

In the night St. Martin had turned to her time and time
again. His senses hammered with the knowledge of how
quickly he could excite her, how much more intense her next
climax would be. When she stopped trembling, still deep inside her, he sought the spot behind her core, his shaft rubbing, teasing to new heat, new sweetness. It didn't take long,
and Lilly leaned her mouth into his and kissed him and
pushed her tongue in and out in the way that he suddenly
couldn't get enough of. She slipped her hands across his chest
and played with his nipples. She clutched at his hardness,
urging him on with deep, soulful movements.

"Do what you want, what you wish," he told her, his voice
hoarse. His hands went under her flushed, naked bottom,
and he moved her over his legs without leaving her tightness,
shifting until she was sitting astride him.

"Like this?" Lilly swung one long leg around him so that it
curved behind his hips. His hands swept up her torso as he
watched the blond curls of her center where it joined with
him. She was seated on his lap facing him now, her slender
legs locked around them both. She clasped her hands at his

shoulders and looked down where they were inexorably connected, changing the rhythm of their lovemaking all together, rocking forward and backward.

St. Martin reached between them with both hands and played with her breasts as she rocked, thumbing the nipples and licking her cleavage, her warm tautness taking him to the brink.

She moaned her pleasure, leaning forward to run her lips along the bridge of his nose. "I love it when you're so deep inside me," she told him as she rocked backward and forward in a series of long, flowing motions as though she'd done it all her life.

"You like it when I fuck you," he teased, sensing her body flushing beneath his hands. She kissed him when he said the word, and when their tongues touched, she contracted and her rocking became more of a grinding motion as he let her take total control. "You're going to make me come again," she whispered hoarsely against his lips, arching into his hand as he deftly played with her.

"But not alone, never alone," he assured her, clasping both his hands over her smooth bottom and pulling her tightly against him, savoring the deep pull of her muscles when he came with her.

And so it went, into the stillness of the morning, until a shaft of sunlight pierced through the heavy drapes and he finally, desperately hoped he'd had enough. Drawing her toward him one more time, he acknowledged the biggest lie he'd ever told himself. Because with Lilly, it would never be enough. And he knew he was lost.

Tea, freshly baked bread, ripe fruit—the aromas enveloped her like a warm blanket. Lilly awoke slowly, her limbs boneless and relaxed, a satisfying and unfamiliar contentment settling over her. Every inch of her body purred and every inch of her mind was clear of the anxiety and darkness, her constant companions of late.

She stretched leisurely, pulling the tousled sheets over her naked body. For the first time in hours, she was alone in bed, without St. Martin. And, impossibly, she needed and wanted him again. After what he did, what she did . . . dear God, what they did together . . . Her body liquefied at the memory, the sensations rolling over her, chafing her senses when she'd thought there was nothing left to satisfy. St. Martin had left no desire unmet, urging and cajoling, accepting and demanding, opening a new world while opening himself to her.

She felt smug, even joyful, an emotion she thought forever out of reach. And yet she knew better, aware that the delusion wouldn't last. Just because he'd been with her, making love to her for hours, spilling deep inside her in endless release—didn't mean he was hers. He had told her that he used seduction as a weapon, and if she didn't believe his words, she should have believed his actions. Foolish woman. She still liked to pretend that last night she'd somehow broken through his defenses, when reality dictated that a deadly and treacherous man like Julian St. Martin could never be hers.

Sitting up in bed, Lilly slowly came back to Earth. Her eyes fastened on the tray, laden with the aromatic ingredients of breakfast. On the floor lay the lacy remnants of her undergarments, reminding her that she really had nothing to wear but the linen towel, an untidy heap at the end of the bed. Not that she regretted for an instant the ruinous condition of her chemise and pantalets. Her face warmed at the recollection of how St. Martin had stripped them from her body.

Swinging her legs to the side of the bed, she gathered up the sheet, covered herself as best she could, and gave in to her grumbling stomach. Padding over to the table by the window, she sat down and began to eat, the tea hot and strong and invigorating. For the first time in a long time, she felt calm and in control. With every bite of pastry and with every slice of fruit, she was arming herself for the battle to come, the battle she was finally prepared for.

She had never needed Charles and she did not need Bellamy. Most of all, she did not need St. Martin. Want him, yes. Desire him, certainly. And if he came into the room this instant, she would be hard-pressed not to push him down on the bed and make him repeat every last intimacy they'd shared over the past ten hours.

The thought gave her a strange confidence. As for her present predicament, she was the only one who could set things right. Charles was most probably dead, and she would stop feeling guilty over his death and mourning what never was. He had never loved her nor cared for her; instead he had been consumed by an overarching ambition that presaged a bad end. To cry for him would only mean continuing to cry for herself. And she had never been one for shedding tears.

No longer anyone's wife and no longer anyone's widow, she had freedom that few women of her class enjoyed. She would never marry again, and for the first time, her fate would rest in her own hands. Enough of hiding, behind Charles's public image or behind Bellamy's power and wealth. And enough, finally, of cowering behind a curtain of lies and fears that prevented her from living her life.

Knowledge was power—as evidenced by the many who wanted the architectural plans to the Crystal Palace. Discovering the source of Charles's involvement in the assassination attempt would not only clear her name but also bring to light the threat to the queen, the empire, and an international exhibition that could bring the world together. Of course, first she would have to see to some clothes.

Finishing the last sip of tea, she responded to the knock on the door. Rising to her feet, careful not to trip over her makeshift robe, she called for St. Martin to come in. Her stomach clenched in anticipation and desire, images of the two of them, entangled and entwined, rolled through her mind.

He had shaved; that was her first thought. Then her stomach dropped, his compelling masculinity overwhelming the feminine proportions of the room, along with her. Worse still, he looked at her from those dark eyes as though nothing had changed, nothing at all. Not that she was expecting an importuning lover, she reasoned with herself, trying to hold onto her newly discovered confidence.

Under his right arm, he carried a folio. She swallowed any disappointment, remembering that St. Martin was not hers to keep but rather hers to fear—despite the superlative intimacies they had shared. He wanted the Koh-I-Noor and he needed the plans to get it. Knowledge was power, she repeated to herself, and she happened to have it.

"Good morning," she said tightly. "And thank you for seeing to breakfast."

He didn't reply straightaway but walked toward the table, pushing the tray aside and replacing it with the folio. Intent on his task, he seemed unaware of the fact she was clad in nothing but a linen towel.

She squared her bare shoulders. "I see we're not going to indulge in any post-coital repartee," she said when he'd still not lifted his head. He pulled several sharpened pencils from the folio and spread several sheets of thick vellum over the table. Slivers of alarm pricked her spine. "I can't interest you in a cup of tea, then?"

"I've breakfasted already, thank you." The dark silk of his hair, bent over the table, uncomfortably reminded her of what it had felt like between her fingers. It was still damp and curling over the back of his strong neck, fresh from the bath. She forced herself to harden against him. If this is how he preferred to ignore their admittedly peculiar liaison, then that was his choice. She should not have expected any differently.

There were other, more important, issues that required her immediate attention. "I wanted to ask you, given the situation, if any clothing might be available."

"In good time."

"You mean to leave me naked." Her mood was changing rapidly, and not for the better. "How gallant."

"For the time being, at least." He finally looked up at her, obviously indifferent to her state of dishabille. Unlike last night. That at least she knew, the knowledge ridiculously rousing, confirmation that finally someone had wanted her for herself. "This house has enough cavernous wardrobes, so I'm sure we'll be able to find you something suitable."

For him, time was obviously not of the essence, and his lack of concern was vaguely alarming, as were the heavy vellum sheets splayed on the table like a winning hand of cards. She considered sitting down on the rumpled bed but decided to remain standing. "In the interim, what is it that you are doing exactly?"

He didn't answer for a moment. Then he straightened and turned to look at her as though seeing her for the first time since entering the room. "Because you're the architect of the Crystal Palace," he answered, "you have been provided with paper and charcoal to produce a rendering of the amended plans."

Of course, back to where it had all begun. She knew what was coming, all good feeling draining from her blood in an instant. Her mind steeled against the predictable onslaught. "The ones leading to the diamond, you mean." She attempted to keep her voice cool.

"I will have them." A thief, traitor, and probably worse, the man's arrogance still astonished.

Lilly had had about enough. In her bare feet, he towered above her, but he'd lost his ability to intimidate. He was no longer an angel fallen hard to Earth, but an ordinary man who had lost himself in her arms just a few hours ago. He had surrendered to her and they both knew it.

She allowed herself a smile. He would hear her words, because she meant every one. "Nothing has changed, St. Martin, for me, although perhaps it has for you. Do you think because I have slept in your bed, and I'll admit enjoyed the experience, that I will surrender so easily?"

He rounded the table but she did not step back. "It's not surrender that I'm asking for."

Her smile broadened. "I believe it is. And the answer is still no. Even if you keep me here naked and chained to the bed, it will always be *no*."

He looked as though the thought held some appeal. "Even if you do more harm than good with your stubbornness and pride?"

"This has nothing to do with my stubbornness or pride and everything to do with your twisted reasons for wanting the diamond." She threw her hands in the air, gesturing to the elegantly appointed room. "It's clear that you don't need the funds that the diamond could conceivably bring you, judging by what I see around me. Nor do I suspect that money is a prime motivator for you in any case."

"What do you believe, then?" He stood observing her, arms crossed over his chest.

She stopped her pacing. "Revenge perhaps. Or perhaps service to another master, another country? I have heard it said that you are not on the best of terms with Whitehall or the Foreign Office since your dismissal."

His smile chilled. "We're quite well informed. Must be the result of exalted company you invite to your Thursday-evening salons. Is that how you first managed to secure Bellamy's attentions?"

This was a man who didn't anger easily, but a tension radiated from his body nonetheless, a body that she suddenly knew almost better than her own. "You seem displeased. I should ask why."

She hoped to surprise him with her boldness, but his voice was totally without expression. "I'm not displeased, merely astonished that you still cannot see that Bellamy is behind all of this."

The audacity of his assertion was stunning. "We're going to begin that business again." She struggled to keep calm. "How Bellamy couldn't possibly want marriage with someone like me unless there were an ulterior motive? And of course, he's richer than God but he still covets the diamond, in your version of the story, because it just makes so much sense." Once more she threw her hands up in frustration. "Only think, St. Martin, it was his own company that transported the Koh-I-Noor from India to London. Had he wanted the bloody gem, it would have been so much easier to have it go missing than to go through all the gyrations, including the faux murder of a well-known architect, in order to remove it from under the Crown's nose."

It sounded right, and wrong, all at the same time, even to her own ears. But she was loathe to admit it.

"You're quite finished with your thesis?" he said mockingly. And she considered tossing what was left in the teapot at his head.

"I'm so eager to hear yours, particularly if it's a close approximation of the truth, which I highly doubt." She pulled the sheet more securely under her arms, all too aware that being fully dressed had its advantages.

He rewarded her sarcasm with a dark glance. "You don't find it strange that Bellamy had one of his men kill Charles yesterday?"

"How do you know it was at his bequest? That man Flynn may have been acting on his own volition."

"Very well. You choose not to believe me." St. Martin began pacing in the small space between them. "What about Bellamy's association with your late husband?"

Her chin notched up a fraction. "What of it? Charles had a myriad of associates." Despite her answer, she knew what he was getting at, the pieces of the puzzle taking amorphous shape.

"What of Bellamy's politics, of which you can't possibly be ignorant? Your interest in current affairs is well known."

What was it that Seabourne had said? The upcoming vote in Parliament most possibly spelling an end to the British East India Company's empire? Her mind circled around Seabourne and his unsettling behavior at the wedding, just moments before Flynn shot Charles.

Outside it was a glorious spring day, golden light bathing the room in its beneficence, and yet it couldn't hold the encroaching darkness at bay. She turned over the possibilities, unnaturally slow and reluctant to reach an obvious conclusion.

"And then," St. Martin continued his pacing, "there is Bellamy's courtship of you, Charles Hampton's grieving widow."

Why else would a powerful, wealthy man be interested in her? She'd asked herself that question hundreds of times and never allowed herself to guess at the answer. Because she knew it would be all too humiliating.

Her legs felt suddenly weak, and for once, she didn't know what to say. So she proceeded over to the bed in order to sit on its rumpled edge. It was difficult to meet St. Martin's razor-sharp gaze, but she did. "I see where you're going with this, although I don't like it," she conceded.

"The truth is rarely palatable."

But necessary, she thought bitterly, particularly if her fate, and the queen's, were to remain in her own hands. This time she didn't try to shut off the disloyal thoughts, the harsh judgments that seeped into her mind, in new and disturbing forms. "Bellamy knew that I was the architect," she began in a voice that was deadly calm. "So he had me believe that I killed Charles, to make me more vulnerable, open to guilt and his overtures. And he kept him alive with Vesper's help in the event that his resurrection could prove useful." She struggled to sit upright. "He's behind the queen's assassination, and he is, or was, Charles's mysterious benefactor." She felt hollow, emptied. "Have I understood correctly, tied together all the loose strings? Not that you will divulge your involvement," she said bitterly.

She waited in vain for him to deny her assertion. "It's better you don't know," he said. There was no missing the light of warning in his eyes.

"What about Vesper—and your association with him?" she persisted.

"He's a man with a complicated history, one that Bellamy knows how to take advantage of."

"And you—are you taking advantage of his complex history? I find it strangely coincidental that you would be consulting with him about medical matters." The image of the close, dark quarters of the house on Weymouth Street lingered.

This time he didn't answer but he did stop his pacing. "As long as you understand Bellamy's role," was all he said. Mercifully, he didn't offer her sympathy or pity. He knew what he wanted and didn't waste any time getting it. "Now you will draw me an approximation of the amended plans."

She steeled herself and took a deep breath. "Still no."

The silence stretched between them. She hated that he was correct, hated the fact that she hadn't seen the truth when it was right in front of her, her judgment clouded by fear, weakness, and need. And hated, most of all, that he remained so elusive, so far away from her. Their coupling had meant nothing. She hoped he respected her enough at least not to use the night they'd spent together as a bartering tool. She couldn't bear it.

"Even for a chance to flush out Bellamy?" It was a statement not a question.

Always so cold, so focused.

"Let me ask you this," she countered, for some reason undeterred, ready to hear the whole truth even if it tore her apart. "Does this have anything to do with my accepting the truth or did you expect me to relent because you think that after last night I'm in love with you?" She made sure to make a mockery of the last three words.

He never wavered, the bastard. "It makes no difference. I've warned you all along and last night was more of the same. My lack of self-control notwithstanding."

Because I will seduce you again and again, wherever I find you, until you give me what I really want.

She wanted nothing more than to crawl under the twisted

sheets of the bed. "Another stalemate, then," she said instead. The truth didn't matter. What mattered was that she would never give in to him.

His eyes were black ice. "No stalemate at all. You give me the plans," he shrugged philosophically, "or I return you to Bellamy."

If his threat unsettled her, she didn't show it.

"If I return to Bellamy, I return on my own." She looked small and lost against the rumpled linens, but her voice was strong. If St. Martin ever believed she would be easy to manipulate, Lilly had just proven him wrong. He regretted the night they'd spent together more than he'd ever regretted anything else. And that list of regrets was long.

He looked pointedly at the table, strewn with blank paper. "I don't think so. What you are going to do is sketch for me the location and the outlines of the hidden entranceway, and I will resolve the matter on my own."

Her eyes sparked fire. "And I just thought I heard you say that you would return me to Bellamy."

"If you don't relinquish the plans."

She rose with a huff and a swirl of linen. "It's too late. You've missed your chance."

His voice was deadly calm. "What do you mean?"

"Seabourne has them." The words were simultaneously triumphant and harsh. "I gave them to him several days ago."

At last, she'd managed to startle him. He smothered a curse. "I thought you said you couldn't trust anyone around Charles, so why Seabourne suddenly?"

She radiated tension, and possibly hatred, against him. "As though you need ask. Where else did I have to go? I wanted to rid myself of the plans—and rid myself of you, more specifically."

He could tell she was waiting, for his argument, for the anger, for reason, and for more threats, all designed to push her back into a corner. "Not a good idea," he said abruptly. "And all the more reason you'll now do as I tell you."

Her smile was cool and bitter. "We'll see who obeys whom."

"You seem to have given up on fear."

"Perceptive of you. I've lived with it far too long." He'd seen that look before, not on the face of a beautiful woman but in the eyes of a steadfast and committed opponent.

"You've lost, Lilly, you just don't know it yet." He was accustomed to keeping calm even though he was ready to walk across the room and throw her back on the bed and make love to her until she relented. There was no place for her to go. The door to the room was locked and she was all but naked as he was having trouble forgetting. Her golden hair tumbled to her shoulders, her skin was stained by the remnants of passion and more recent anger. He wouldn't allow himself to remember what lay beneath the linen towel.

He saw the angry light in her eyes at his words. She took a steady step toward him. "I don't see what more we need to discuss. Tell me, is this door locked or is my only freedom the dressing room?"

"Locked."

"Very well," she declared as though he wasn't there. "I intend to bathe and change my clothes, which, I trust, you will have provided me. After which, you may go about and return me to Bellamy. So you see, St. Martin," she said calmly, "I'm not going to burst into tears and beg you to spare me. I'm calling your bluff."

He knew what he had to do before she did. There was no more time for talk, the last thing he wanted to do. For a careful man, he'd already made too many mistakes. She had deliberately gone too far, baiting him the way a hapless rabbit baited a ravenous bear. He made sure to move so quickly that she had no warning. One instant he was standing by the table, in the next he was leaning over her on the bed, his hands landing lightly on the cool smoothness of her bare shoulders. He'd trapped her, his mouth dangerously close to hers.

"Believe me, Lilly, you don't know what you're doing."

She looked steadily into his face, trying to hide the emotion flickering over her features. "Don't I?" she replied before she pulled him down toward her, kissing him. Not a tentative, exploratory caress but a kiss that demanded, full of anger and frustration. She clutched the muscles of his upper arms, her fingers digging into his skin. And he couldn't stop himself from kissing her back.

Except that an instant later she pulled away. She was breathing hard. "You would not give me over to Bellamy. I know it."

How wrong she was. He would use any excuse to be rid of her because she represented the most frightening juncture of his life. Without her, his existence was meaningless, precisely how it needed to be. Now if he could only let go of her, remove his hands from the smooth contours of her face, leave her behind in a locked room. "You would have me believe that you have found a heart where none existed?" He moved her shaking hand over his chest. To prove to her, and to himself, that he couldn't care.

Fearlessly, she gripped his shirt in her palm and pulled him closer. For an intelligent woman she was astonishingly courageous. Perhaps because she didn't really know who he was. "I've never taken you for a coward, St. Martin."

He smiled a reply, sliding her hand beneath the linen of his shirt, where her small palm was hot against his skin. "A good thing," he whispered against her mouth, a breath of a touch. He traced his lips along the side of her neck, making sure she could feel his teeth against her rapidly beating pulse. She was tense under his touch, fighting herself as she fought him. "You think I won't do it?"

She pulled back, her eyes the color of a flawless summer sky. "I know you won't. Because you feel something, even if you're not brave enough to admit it."

He held her gaze. "And what if I were?"

"Prove it."

"I shall," he said.

He was as good as his word. Against all his better instincts, he hauled her up from the bed and propelled her into the dressing room before ringing the bell to have fresh bathwater delivered from the kitchens. Enough of his goddamned indecision. Never mind the plans. Lilly would take him to the Crystal Palace itself. And he would keep her safe—from Bellamy, Seabourne, and anyone else who dared come within an inch of her.

She didn't waste time and he studiously ignored the faint, self-satisfied smile that taunted him when she emerged from the dressing room. The boy's breeches that clung to her curves did little to improve his mood. And she knew exactly the effect the unorthodox garments had on him. His usual cold practicality faded away.

And it unnerved him as nothing had before.

"I'm ready," she said.

"No, you're not." He pressed the cold metal of her revolver in her hand.

Her revolver, the one with her prints, the one she had pointed at Charles Hampton over one year ago. Her eyes widened.

"Now do you believe me? That I'm brave enough?" He had given her back her freedom and she didn't know what to say. "In case you need it," he said gruffly.

She smiled at him then, a brilliant invitation to sin. And it was more than reward enough. "You know what this means, don't you?"

"That you'll shoot me the minute I turn my back," he said brusquely. "Never mind the gratitude. There will be enough opportunity for talk in the future," he lied smoothly.

Lilly cocked her head as though considering him for the first time, storing away her impressions for later. Her smile faded and she tucked the revolver in her bodice, well concealed underneath the looseness of her shirt. "Where are we going?" she asked. "Or let me surmise. The Crystal Palace? And I disguised as a young male servant." She waved the boy's cap in front of his nose. "That isn't what you'd led me to believe."

His voice was calmer than he expected. "Bellamy is still a possibility if you choose not to cooperate once we're inside the building."

"Of course," she said smugly, but there was light in her beautiful blue eyes. "I take it that you're not overly concerned about my escaping your clutches and returning to him on my own volition. And of course I have the pistol now." She patted the inside of her loose shirt, annoying him to no end.

"I'll take that risk." She still hadn't the slightest idea what he was capable of. And he prayed to a God he didn't believe in that she would never find out.

A half hour later, they sped through Hyde Park, having left the carriage behind at Edgware Road at the end of Oxford Street, close enough to the Marble Arch entrance. The flower gardens were already in bloom opposite Park Lane, but he kept up the pace, a firm hand on Lilly's upper arm. To the left were only a few desultory strollers along the Serpentine River and in the distance the Achilles Monument rose up in honor of the Duke of Wellington. A magnificent series of fountains, comprising almost twelve thousand individual jets, punctuated the area surrounding the Crystal Palace. It was said the largest of these threw water to a height of close to three hundred feet and one hundred and twenty thousand gallons of water flowed through the system when it was in full play.

St. Martin would have preferred the cover of darkness, but he would settle for a deserted construction site. The Crystal Palace loomed before them, a gigantic glass flower. It was a colossus, its girded sides strung with flags fluttering in the breeze, the Prussian colors entwined with those of Austria, the Russian eagle with the stars and stripes of America. Lilly had gone still at his side, her eyes wide with pride and something like trepidation.

He knew that they should simply keep moving, that this was not time for discussion. But something in her expression tugged at him. Going against his better judgment, he pulled her closer so no one could possibly overhear. "It's a noble and daring piece of work, Lilly. No one can take that away from you."

Her eyes remained riveted at the site, and for the first time, he knew what her work meant to her. "So much of me has gone into this structure," she said quietly. "And I'm still not entirely sure . . . and yet it is said that only recently Prince Albert observed to the Prince of Prussia that mathematicians had calculated that the Crystal Palace would blow down in a strong gale." She paused. "And that engineers had predicted that the galleries would crash to the ground."

"You know that's not true."

She turned away from the building to look up at him. "I know that's not true," she repeated, "because I know the rigor of my work."

His chest tightened and he didn't recognize the sensation until a moment later. It was pride and respect—for her. Physically slight, her golden hair tucked up beneath her cap, her mouth held in a tremulous straight line, Lilly Clarence Hampton was a colossus in her own right.

He slid his hand down her arm to squeeze her hand. "You should be immensely proud. Very few people in the world have been able to accomplish what you are now able to realize right before your eyes. I salute you, Lilly."

Her eyes told him that she didn't quite believe his words.

"Regardless of what's passed between us or what will happen over the next few days, believe that I am sincere in what I say."

Her lips turned up in a small smile. "Flattery won't get you into the building, nor into the hidden entranceway. But it's a valiant attempt, St. Martin."

His response was to pull her away and toward the exhibit entrances to the back of the building, which he knew to be divided into a series of courts depicting the history of art and architecture from ancient Egypt through the Renaissance, as well as exhibits from industry and the natural world. Rumor said that the world's largest organ was also contained in the Crystal Palace's center transept, which would also play host in the next several weeks to daring feats by world-famous acts.

But it was not the public spaces that vied for his attention. He surveyed three guards in the distance, all of whom were deep in conversation. The hum of their low voices told him that they were not interested in the two figures quickly approaching. He had given himself mere minutes to get inside without notice. Warm air from the late afternoon sun fanned his face as he picked up speed, Lilly following close behind, her hand in his.

Ducking behind one of the giant transepts, he couldn't believe that he wouldn't even have to pick a lock. On the second level, a pane of glass was either missing or yet to be replaced, a yawning opening that made its invitation clear. Good thing he'd made sure Lilly was wearing breeches. Scaling glass and iron would have been a challenge. As it was, a trellis with its convenient crosshatch design served as the catapult from which, St. Martin estimated, they could launch themselves into the building.

He pushed Lilly in front of him, ignoring her trim backside and urging her to place her foot into the first rung.

"I can't do this," she stuttered, her face flushed.

He didn't answer except to give her a firm push, and soon her long legs were making their way up the trellis. Once at the top, he didn't give her a chance to think. Grabbing her around the waist before she could protest, he launched them both into the air to land ten feet down on the outer edge of the main hallway.

He touched ground with a deep knee bend, Lilly toppling beside him. He didn't give himself more than a second to recover. Although the vast expanse was empty, he had a sudden feeling of being watched. He never ignored his instincts, particularly when every nerve and muscle in his body stood at attention. Pale and shocked at his side, but smart enough not to make a sound, Lilly was on her knees, still as a cat as she listened carefully for the slightest change in the air around her.

They didn't move.

The hair on the back of his neck prickled. A quick look at Lilly, who was taking in the splendor of the building's main hall, told him they didn't have much time. He had given himself approximately ten minutes to convince her. Failure was not an option.

This time he didn't have to take her hand. They sped silently down the great hallway, flanked with plants, trees, and exotic botanicals, he moving with his accustomed stealth. When they reached the end of the corridor, he watched her closely as she instinctively leaned to the left, following the directions imprinted on her memory. Dipping quickly into the passageway, they skidded to a halt, knowing instantly that they'd arrived.

The diamond wasn't there, of course. The iron cage, constructed by the renowned Chubb security company, sat empty. Though it didn't contain the Mountain of Light, it did feature the door that would keep it safe with its little aperture in the side of the basement of the cage. St. Martin already knew that an instrument like a bed key, turned around twice, produced an iron plate that would rise on a velvet cushion. This action would present the peerless diamond, thought to be the purest and most valuable in the world, tomorrow morning for Bellamy's presentation to Queen Victoria.

St. Martin surveyed the echoing space encased with reams of glass, his eyes darting into corners, unable to shake the sensation of being watched. With the transparency of the building materials, it was almost impossible to discern where Lilly could have possibly designed an unseen stairwell and entrance. A huge fountain, the water yet turned on, waited majestically, the only other structure in the room.

"It's not here," she said, referring to the diamond. Her voice was triumphant. "And this overly dramatic chase is all for naught, St. Martin. You can't steal something that isn't here."

"So you believe."

"And you are not intending to give me over to Bellamy," she continued, the startling blue eyes staring up at him, the anger that had burned there gone. In its place was a strange combination of confidence and vulnerability. "Actually, I'm waiting for you to begin tearing the place apart looking for the hidden entranceway. Let me give you a hint—there's no trapdoor or false bookcase." Her voice gently mocked him. "Or are you contemplating more dastardly ways of convincing me to give up my secrets?"

A faint sheen of perspiration marked her brow, tendrils of golden hair escaping from her cap. Her simple linen shirt outlined her slender shoulders, squared in triumph. Although she whispered, the cavernous space caused her words to spring off the glass ceilings.

He wasn't remotely disappointed, the last thing he wanted her to know. The passageway was lit by the afternoon light, etching her face, shining more brightly than a diamond ever could, forever on his memory. Strategy and tactics were forgotten and he stood there, suddenly an ordinary man, struck by an extraordinary realization.

He wanted this woman. No matter what.

The truth grabbed him by the throat. He wanted to grab her, hot, strong, and alive against him, to press her against him, taste her skin. Damn, he wanted her.

She was speaking but he didn't hear her, stunned by the fact that his life was forever changed. If he died, no, *when* he died sometime over the next few days, he would die with a huge regret—having to leave behind Lilly Clarence Hampton. And it made him angry, furious, that his coldly efficient existence, marked by solitude and duplicity, had been ripped away from him, leaving him vulnerable and exposed.

"Have you lost your nerve, St. Martin?" She repeated the sentence twice before he responded.

Her question cut too close to the truth. She represented the most danger he'd ever faced in his cursed life. He gave himself a mental shake. All he wanted to do was keep her safe—and get her out of the damned building before it was too late. "It's time we left," he said brusquely.

She assumed a boyish pose, hands on her hips. "I can't believe what I'm hearing," she said, playing with him, all too sure of herself and his feelings for her. "And here I was just about to give you a few clues."

The feeling of danger intensified. He was at her side with one lethal movement, just as he heard the footfalls. "Let's go," he growled.

"An exit is somewhat premature at this point, Lord St. Martin, wouldn't you agree?"

Lilly stopped trying to shake St. Martin's hand from her shoulder. Isambard Kingdom Bellamy, flanked by Flynn and four other men, blocked the passageway. It was not the Bellamy she knew, ruddy with benevolence and benign attentiveness. Instead, a harsh intelligence stared out through his eyes, vulpine and cruel.

Pure animal fear rushed through her.

"You're finally deciding to be helpful. You were just about to mention clues, my dear Lilly," Bellamy reminded, taking a step farther into the room, his retinue standing back.

"I don't know what you mean," she said, trying to control her voice. Her eyes darted to St. Martin, whose only reaction was to grip her shoulder infinitesimally tighter.

Bellamy admonished her with an upraised finger. "You know what Lord St. Martin and I require of you, my dear. Let's not play the innocent. It may have worked for Seabourne, but it won't work with me."

There was no trust left anywhere in the world. She didn't say anything for a moment.

Bellamy absorbed her reaction carefully before gesturing to the empty cage. "Do you know the story of the diamond?" he asked conversationally, his leisurely tone worse than any threats could be. "I think not," he answered his own question, "given our evening in the Tower of London never came about. But then again, it was an opportunity for you and St. Martin to become better acquainted."

Her stomach turned over, but she didn't trust herself to look at St. Martin, fearing that she would only see a darkness reflected in his eyes, her worst fears confirmed. A hundred cries of anger and despair rushed through her as she watched Bellamy's red lips beneath his thick mustache curl with disdain. "It's a good thing that for a remarkably, dare I say it, unnaturally talented woman," his eyes sweeping over her unusual attire with distaste, "you didn't see the obvious, that Lord St. Martin and I wish the same thing of you, Lilly." He turned to St. Martin. "Am I not correct, sir?"

For a brief moment, it was as if she hadn't heard the words, only blood pounding in her ears. *What's the difference, precisely, Mrs. Hampton, between Bellamy and me? Between what he wants of you and what I want of you?* Shock and confusion pitched her sideways. She wanted to close her eyes against the tears, but they threatened to come anyway.

"Absolutely correct," he answered. Through a blur she saw St. Martin's eyes locked on hers. Her newfound confidence evaporated, leaving a combination of terror and despair in its wake. This was a test, she lied to herself. This could not possibly be true. Even though it was.

"Now, Lilly," Bellamy continued, brandishing his walking stick for effect, "I know that you have absolutely no intention of relinquishing your secrets to me here in the Crystal Palace. Despite the fact that I am accompanied by these fellows here," he nodded perfunctorily to the men arrayed with Flynn against the entranceway. "It would not do to have a commotion in such an august place and I know you enough now, as my erstwhile betrothed, that you will not go easily. Why it seems that even Lord St. Martin has not been able to make progress with you."

Bellamy's eyes flicked to St. Martin and then back to her again. "Perhaps a history lesson regarding the Koh-I-Noor, by way of context, is required prior to our leaving to return to Waldegrave House. So that you understand its symbolic importance for me." He continued conversationally. "Legend has the stone dating back to the early fourteenth century when it was in the possession of the Rajah of Malwa. It then became one of the most coveted jewels of the Mogul Emperors until 1739 when Nadir Shah of Persia obtained the gem after invading Delhi."

Lilly wondered whether she was listening to a madman, her head spinning.

"The victorious Shah was said to have exclaimed 'Koh-I-Noor,' or Mountain of Light, upon seeing it for the first time. Following his assassination, the stone was fought over for years, finally ending up in the Punjab, and when the state was annexed by the British in 1849, the British East India Company took the stone as partial security for the Sikh Wars. Am I boring you, Lilly?"

She jerked away from St. Martin's hand on her shoulder. She could not, would not, think of him now. She concentrated her anger, her rage too great to let the fear back in.

"Fascinating," she said with contempt. "And I suppose that you will tell me next that therefore the stone belongs to the British East India Company and not to the queen or to the people of England."

"Well done."

"Why did you not plan to steal the gem while it was in transit and under your control?"

Bellamy pointed his ebony walking stick at her for emphasis. "You really don't understand the man you nearly married, Lilly, which is perhaps for the better. I could explain, and I will, but I fear we have overstayed our welcome. The good people of the Royal Commission gave me their gracious permission to catch a glimpse of this remarkable building prior to its official opening tomorrow morning. Unlike St. Martin, who clearly couldn't wait."

St. Martin had still not stepped away from her, his body shielding hers. Lilly knew that if she began to even contemplate his betrayal, she would shatter inside. Pulling the last tatters of her self-respect around her, she slammed a door on her rioting emotions.

"But then St. Martin will do just about anything in order to fulfill his objectives, even if it demands personal sacrifice or, dare I say it, involves treason along the way. He did not survive the Kabul Massacre playing by the rules. Am I right, my lord?"

St. Martin didn't respond.

"However, he has led me back to you. My runaway bride. Or should I say, my runaway murderess."

"I am not a murderess as you well know," she snapped. Not for the first time, she noticed Flynn glowering behind Bellamy. The bandage beneath his jacket visible, he had not removed his eyes from St. Martin, sweating barely repressed violence from every pore.

Bellamy tossed the cane from one hand to the other and back. "Tell that to the magistrates," he said. "Which just might come about if you continue in your stubborn ways. Even Lord St. Martin has not had much success with you, clearly," Bellamy continued leisurely, "even though I could have told him that this approach of his wouldn't work. It will take much more to convince you to share your knowledge with the outside world, so to speak." He sighed dramatically. "But then Lord St. Martin has not been himself of late, given certain traumatic events that even he has found difficult to overcome. However, that's where Dr. Vesper, unstable though he is at times, serves his purpose."

With the slowness of a nightmare, Lilly digested the information, forcing herself to think cogently in a world gone mad. Her mind screamed at her own unwillingness to see the truth, that the web of treachery starting with Bellamy threatened to undermine so much more than her own insignificant life. She should have known. *She should have known.* And she would never forgive herself if the very future of the British Empire were imperiled because of her own selfish and personal blindness.

Stone formed around her heart. St. Martin be damned.

Against the backdrop of the soaring glass walls, Bellamy turned toward his retinue. "To Waldegrave House," he declared grandly.

Chapter 19

Lilly remembered little of the ride to Hampstead Heath. St. Martin had disappeared into a separate carriage with Flynn, not that she cared anymore, her focus concentrated on a single outcome—defeat Bellamy or find herself lost.

As the conveyance rattled its way to the outskirts of London, she easily ignored the two men on either side of her and the gimlet-eyed gaze of Bellamy who was wise enough not to engage her in conversation. He probably thought she was close to surrender, frightened beyond belief and preparing herself for the tribulations to come. Far from it.

The truth, ugly though it was, had set her free. She had nearly made the mistake of trusting St. Martin, wishing desperately to believe in a lie, in a love that would not be. The same error in judgment had kept her in a marriage predicated on deception and deceit. She grit her teeth—she would never make that mistake again.

Gaslight illuminated Waldegrave Hall when they arrived just after dusk. The wedding decorations had magically disappeared, and Lilly wondered how she could ever have considered this monstrosity of a house her future home. Inside the front hall, the one she had entered as a soon-to-be bride a mere thirty-six hours before, the ostentatious chandelier cast its ominous shadows.

Bellamy dismissed his retinue with a flick of his cane. "Welcome home, my dear," he said. "And to think that you could have crossed that threshold as my wife," he mused. "Alas, not all is lost. As we speak, inspectors from the London constabulary are searching for your whereabouts, while I, the shocked and despairing groom, wait anxiously to hear the unbearable news."

"And what news might that be?" She endeavored to remain strong.

"Let me see," Bellamy pondered. "I think Mrs. Hampton, wracked with grief and remorse, came to a tragic end. Floating Ophelia-like in one of the ponds of the Heath, or perhaps laden down with stones in her pocket. In any case, I foresee a watery end to her life."

They would make it look like suicide. "Your imagination runs to the lurid."

He shook his head with condescension. "You mistaken reality for imagination."

She turned away to glance at the elaborately carved staircase winding its way to the second and third levels of the house. Bellamy had told her proudly, not so long ago, that as with the rest of the house, it had been built painstakingly from the rarest of Asian woods and by carpenters imported from Germany. And now he took her elbow, as though leading her in a farcical dance, urging her toward the stairs. He murmured, "It is indeed easier to rid oneself of a body in India, of course, but not having that particular recourse, we shall have to do our best with the marshes surrounding Hampstead Heath."

Preserving her strength for what was to come, she didn't resist, trying to keep him talking, hoping to glean something of use. "What would your plans for me have been had we married?"

"Actually, your late husband's impromptu appearance at our wedding, while inopportune, merely hastened your early demise, my dear. No need for onerous trips to India or exposure to foreign fevers that would heat your blood until you wasted away at a tragically young age. Instead, we are left with a clearly unstable woman who murders her husband and then regrets her actions." He paused with a foot on the first stair, as though just remembering something. "And by the way, not that you seem overly concerned, but he is quite dead this time."

She absorbed the news a second time. Having accepted Charles's death in her bones, having already mourned and buried him in her mind, she pushed away his unexpected restoration, refusing to allow Charles ever again to trigger any shred of emotion. Her rational mind needed to continue to work, freed from the delusions that had led her to this place—here with Bellamy and his web of power, greed, and ambition.

"Thank you for your condolences."

"I don't regard you as a sentimental woman. After all, you believed that you squeezed the trigger the first time, although obviously your aim would never have been good enough."

"But Flynn's was."

Together, like an absurd version of man and wife, they mounted the stairs. "Of course, given the drama of your heated exchange with your husband that night, Flynn had no trouble entering your home unnoticed and doing what was necessary and making it look like a burglary. What with all the ensuing hysterics, you never even noticed Dr. Vesper taking the body away."

"I thought he looked familiar when I saw him last week prior to our having dinner," she said, surprised at the frost hardening the blood in her veins. "You've been using him to keep Charles alive, although for some reason, he managed to elude his captor and interrupt our wedding."

"Obviously, Vesper miscalculated the dosage. His first and last mistake, I trust."

She doubted it. Her mind skipped ahead to the final horror. St. Martin. She couldn't trust herself to utter his name in Bellamy's presence, undisciplined emotion once again threatening to carve away at the stone forming around her heart. But she knew what was coming.

"Now of course, you're speculating over St. Martin's role in all of this," Bellamy said helpfully. They had ascended to the second floor, the hallway unfurling before them. Lilly counted five bedrooms, but she refused to speculate what awaited her behind any of the closed doors. For the moment, there was only silence and the workings of her heated imaginings.

"All in good time, this business with St. Martin," he promised. "But at this juncture, I believe it is better that you get some rest, Lilly, to help you decide how you would like to proceed. You can make things simple or difficult. Your choice." Unalloyed threat lay behind the words. Bellamy would expect resolution before the night was over.

He stopped at the first bedroom, opening the door silently. "There is paper and charcoal on the Sheridan desk. I need not tell you what to do with them. And don't attempt any of the ridiculousness you tried with Seabourne. He came to me promptly, by the way, with drawings in hand," he continued. "Clever of you to withhold that last, important component. I always knew you to be shrewd, my dear. Tell me, do you trust anyone at all?"

At first Lilly thought she couldn't answer. The only person she wanted to trust had never been hers to trust in the first place. "No one," she answered finally. "Not a soul."

There was something like begrudging admiration in his voice. "As I said, you're a shrewd woman, Lilly, and I trust you'll use that quality to smooth things along. It is ten o'clock now. I will return precisely in one hour."

Any lingering courtesies were dispensed with. Lilly heard the turn of the key in the lock behind her with a combination of anxiety and despair. She would forget him, forget her dev-

astation, forget that St. Martin was a cold-blooded bastard
and that she had seen him clearly from the first. It was all she
could do now, or lie down and die. If it were only her own
life at stake—

She surveyed the room quickly, already familiar with its
garish opulence from her last visit to Waldegrave Hall as a
prospective bride. Overstuffed and overdone, the bedroom
with its crimson watered silk wallpaper and marbled wainscoting closed around her. Shaking off the feeling of suffoca-
tion, she ran over to the shuttered windows, moving easily in
her trousers and loose shirt, only to find the shutters tightly
locked.

Her eyes skittered over to the desk, paper, pencils, and
rulers in place, as promised. Her mind considered the possibilities, none of them favorable. She wanted to jump out of
her skin, to turn back the clock. Instead, she was left with agonizing images of the time she'd spent in St. Martin's bed like
the ridiculous and hopeless woman she was, afraid to recognize the ruinous truth.

Even now she was wasting valuable time. She began pacing, sinking into the softness of the rich rug beneath her booted
feet, counting off a narrowing number of options. She could
produce a useless sketch for Bellamy, which would plausibly
satisfy him—for a time. Or she could simply refuse to cooperate at all. Her life was forfeit in any case, and she no longer
cared, if in exchange she could bring a halt to an assassination that would be heard across the world.

Tossing her cap onto the bed and scraping the hair back
from her face, she pulled out the chair and sat down at the
Sheridan desk. She picked up a pencil with surprisingly steady
hands and began sketching with a few loose, deft strokes. The
movements were familiar, reassuring, the motions balanced
and sure. For a moment, it was possible to forget—to forget
Bellamy, the Koh-I-Noor, and the queen. Only St. Martin's
image pulled at the corners of her mind, demanding her at-

tention, pulling her toward him with a twisted and hopeless longing.

How much time had passed she didn't know, when a grinding noise prompted her to lift her head. The key scraped in the lock of the door. A quick glance at the ormolu clock on the escritoire told her she still had thirty minutes. It was not time yet—she wasn't ready. Composing her features into a semblance of calm, she watched the door open.

Her suppressed agony flared to life. St. Martin. Her muscles clenched painfully. He moved toward her, closing the door softly behind him, and she saw the pistol in his hand and a body draped over his shoulder.

It was time to die. Bellamy had sent him. Her knees nearly gave way, but this last time she refused to let him see any weakness.

He threw down his burden, the heavy man sliding to the floor with barely a sound. A thin trickle of blood seeped from the back of the man's head as St. Martin pushed him behind the curtained bed. Her reaction was no more than a choke of horror, color draining her face. For the first time, she believed she might prove him wrong and faint at his feet.

Before she could finish the thought, she felt his hands, rough and impatient, pulling her from her chair. "He's dead, isn't he?" she asked, hopelessness in her voice. Not expecting an answer and knowing it was useless to scream—that no one would care to save her—she glared at him instead. "Have you come to do Bellamy's work for him? You bastard—give me the goddamned pistol and I'll end my life myself," she said, her voice raw. "Anything to get you out of my sight and out of my life permanently."

"I sensed this wouldn't be simple," he said by way of understatement. "If you can manage to be silent for a moment..."

"I will never be silenced again," she snapped. "When I told you earlier today, and you listened so quietly and so calmly, you bastard," she said on an explosion of breath, "that Bellamy wanted me vulnerable, you were part of that, working to get closer to me at his behest. And I was too besotted to realize it. So perhaps I deserve to die at your hands for my own stupidity." She straightened away from him to haughtily stare down the barrel of the heavy pistol in his hand.

He radiated calm while she was ready to explode. "Lilly, if you want to get out of this alive, we haven't much time. You're going to have to trust me."

She thought she was going to burst into flames. "Trust you!"

"It's either that or you wait for Bellamy and his men."

"I'm not sure which I prefer."

He glanced at the clock. "We haven't much time."

"And conveniently, we never have time for discussion, or I should say that we only ever have time for more of your lies and obfuscation." None of her hurled insults seemed to penetrate. He looked entirely detached, his dark eyes communicating nothing but cold competence.

"If you're looking for proof of my trustworthiness, simply glance at that corpse a few feet away under the bed curtains, the man who was guarding your door a few minutes ago."

She was reluctant to look and he knew it. "All that proves is that you can kill indiscriminately. I'm hardly surprised."

"There's nothing I can say to convince you."

"It's not what you've said, it's what you've done." She tried to keep her voice from trembling, placing her palms down on the intricately inlaid surface of the Sheridan desk.

His expression didn't change despite his next words. "I'm here to ensure your safety, Lilly, to get you out of this debacle and keep you safe. It's the least I can do."

She shook her head, disorientation taking over. "You expect me to believe you? Nothing has changed."

"You told me that everything changed just this morning." He paused. The shadows transformed his face into planes and angles, only the dark of his eyes giving life to his expression. "And now I believe it myself."

She shook her head slowly, her body sagging under the weight of disbelief. "These lies of yours are truly desperate. Your flimsy protestations of undying devotion leave me indifferent at best. It may have taken me long enough, sir, but I have learned my lesson and, therefore, this wretched scheme of yours will go nowhere."

"And last night?"

She crossed her arms over her chest defensively. "Means nothing, as you well know."

"Then why did you agree to accompany me to the Crystal Palace?"

She lifted her chin, incredulous. "You will at least admit you left me with little choice. What was I to do—remain naked and locked in your home or seize an opportunity for escape?"

His gaze locked on hers and wouldn't let her go. "You agreed to accompany me because you knew beyond a shadow of a doubt that I wouldn't return you to Bellamy," he said evenly. "I couldn't."

She refused to look away, his last two words a twisting knife. "You couldn't return me to Bellamy—are you quite certain? Because I find myself here, back at Waldegrave Hall at the moment," she said bitterly. "It was entirely too convenient to have Bellamy stumble upon us this afternoon."

She needed to close her eyes to shut him out. His words stung and yet she couldn't admit to herself why they cut her to the core. She wanted to believe him, wanted to believe that the night they'd spent together had meant more to him than simply a means to an end. But she couldn't trust herself, much less him, ever again.

She glanced at the clock. "I have fewer than twenty minutes to produce the draft that Bellamy is expecting. So I shall ask you to leave and take your false promises with you."

He still didn't move and it occurred to her that he would finish what he'd come to do. St. Martin was not an indecisive man, and he had probably not faltered once in his life. She wondered what it would feel like to die, to have a small neat hole drilled precisely into her forehead. At least it would be over, she thought wearily, and the world would be a safer place without her.

He raised the pistol, long, black, and comfortable in his hand, and she flinched before he tucked it into the waistband of his breeches. Then he leaned closer toward her, with only the small expanse of the desk separating them. His expression was composed and she thought she could see her reflection in the darkness of his eyes.

"I love you."

The sharp retort of his gun could not have shocked her more. Her throat closed in instant revulsion. "Don't do this," she said hoarsely, trying to get out from behind the desk and away from him. "Don't do this," she repeated, not caring if she raised her voice.

He reached for her but she brushed his hands away. "This is beyond insulting, to expect that I would succumb to such empty blandishments, such outright lies— Don't come near me. Don't even try."

She was afraid that if he touched her, her resolve would melt along with any trace of conviction she had left. And yet deep inside she was looking for an excuse, any excuse, to have his hands upon her.

"Now who's the coward?" he asked.

"You use intimacy as a weapon against me, as surely as you would use that pistol." Lilly was furious. She should run while she still had the chance and try to slip past him and out the door.

"Come here," he said. The room was quiet and still around them. She was reminded of the first time she saw him that night at the Tower of London—a ravaged man, the hardened set of his jaw and the lines bracketing the sides of his wide mouth telling a story she'd imagined she didn't want to hear. Yet she had listened and it had brought her nothing but bitterness that had turned her life to ashes.

"You know this is what you want." He stretched out his hands toward her. "And you know that what you feel is no lie." Her response was immediate, both horrifying and inexplicable, as though another woman had taken her place. He stepped closer and put his hands on her shoulders, sliding them behind her thick hair to rest at the nape of her neck. His dark eyes swept down her body, and his beautiful mouth curved in a smile.

It wasn't the kiss she'd expected, but it told her everything she needed to know. If time was running out, there was nothing in the slow, hypnotic rhythm of his mouth but all the time in the world. She barely drew a breath, her heart pulsing as his tongue played between her parted lips and his hand cradled the back of her head, leaving her no room for retreat.

She clung to him as he thrust and thrust again, hot, urgent, and demanding, no restraint, no pause, and no room for her to think. Drowning, she tasted him, her palms tracing the strong contours of his back through his shirt, her head spinning as she heard his low groan despite the rush of blood in her ears. His hand tightened in her hair while he moved to grip her chin with the other. He broke the contact and spoke against her gaping mouth, "This is no lie, Lilly."

She wanted to stay in his arms forever. Her mind groped toward reason, toward the force of memory. Her eyes were dry and raw, eager for a wash of tears to clear her head. Then her mind registered a sound, and, suspended between elation and despair, she stiffened away from him looking toward the door slowly easing open.

A vision stepped into the room, a beautiful woman with

raven dark hair, slanted green eyes, the dark pupils dilated and wide with surprise. Her full red lips parted in shock.

"Oh dear," she said in a tiny, breathless voice. "This is somewhat awkward, I should think." She swayed on her pink, bare feet. "I didn't expect to come upon my husband with his lover."

Chapter 20

Lilly stepped from the circle of St. Martin's arms. The woman was mad, she thought, the echo of the fine, refined voice lilting like a wondrous instrument slightly out of tune. Her mind groped for explanations. Bellamy's mistress, a sister, a distant relative—anything was possible.

Then she looked at St. Martin and she knew, not in any factual way, but in the heart of her being. She remembered yet again the first night she saw him, reflected in the glass case guarding the Koh-I-Noor. Only now she recognized the source of the pain etched on his face, the skin stretched impossibly tight over the sharp cheekbones and the shadowed eyes. She looked away, the knowledge too much for her.

"Constance," he said in a low voice.

The apparition floated into the room, closing the door softly behind her. "Now I'm certain you're surprised as I am, my darling." Her gown was of the finest white silk, flowing, unstructured and revealing. She moved with the seductive grace of a goddess, her eyes riveted on her husband. There were just the two of them now, alone in the room. The tall, compelling man and the voluptuous, exquisite woman.

Her husband, Lilly's mind screamed.

St. Martin made no move to deny the association, his eyes instead devouring the woman he called Constance. Lilly was almost convinced that she was dreaming, and that somewhere outside her hallucination there was order and reason, a world where normalcy reigned.

"I thought you were dead."

"Clearly, I'm not," Constance replied. She settled gracefully into the divan, a confection of silk and creamy flesh. "Although I'm sure, my darling, you're desperate to find out what really happened that day."

That day. They were speaking in a foreign language, a secret code whose solution was denied her. It was as though she were not present, absent from the reality of these two people whom fate ripped apart. Too shocked to react directly, Lilly watched the clock, frozen into passivity, aware that only ten minutes remained before Bellamy's return.

"And who is this lovely young woman?" Constance asked, her cat eyes suddenly narrowing on Lilly. Constance's eyes swept over the figure outlined in the boy's breeches. She made a moue of distaste. "My darling Julian, she is interesting in a diverting way, I suppose, but really, I would have thought someone a little more voluptuous would be to your liking."

Constance leaned forward, her low-cut gown displaying a generous amount of her ample breasts.

St. Martin's voice was a rasp. "Leave her out of this."

Constance arched a delicate brow. "Possessive are we? That's so unlike you, my darling. Why, I can recall several occasions where you had no trouble sharing me at all."

Lilly was stunned by the drama playing out before her eyes. Her mind worked swiftly, attempting to make sense of an incoherent spectacle, slamming the door shut on her emotions. It was as though time had collapsed, the conversation between husband and wife taking on a wild, disjointed immediacy. It was all she could do to remember just moments before when St. Martin—She could not complete the thought, forcing herself into a necessary numbness. To restore some semblance of calm to her thinking, she imagined her Crystal

Palace with its long shining triangles of glass, fanning out to embrace the sky, fading down to dusk.

It was all that mattered anymore.

As though coming from a great distance, St. Martin's voice was steady. "I think we have other, more important matters to discuss, Constance, such as how you survived, how you remained alive." He stood facing his wife, his arms held loosely at his sides. For some reason, Lilly focused on the pistol that she knew was holstered under his shirt.

"I thought you were dead," he repeated, his dark gaze unwavering, searching for certainty in a yawning abyss. The statement was stripped of emotion, searing in its boldness.

Constance shrugged, pulling up a rounded leg, a curved calf peeking out from beneath her nightgown. "I never thought you had much of a conscience, dearest Julian, so I assumed my disappearance wouldn't discomfit you in the least."

"It was more than a disappearance." The statement was flat.

She stretched out fully across the divan, her rounded figure displayed like a Botticelli nude. "We could quibble about details, but you know I don't like to do that."

Her words were slightly slurred, magnifying the relaxed sensuality of every move. Lilly was reminded of a cat that had had a surfeit of cream.

Constance eyed her once more before turning back to St. Martin. "I'm assuming you have fucked her, Julian. It's the least of what I'd expect from you. Tell me, do you still exhibit that marvelous stamina of yours?" She turned her feline gaze back to Lilly. "His staying power is incredible, wouldn't you agree? Now what is your name again? I don't believe we were properly introduced."

"Enough, Constance."

"Oh it's never enough for you, Julian, as I recall. Remember the night in Istanbul? I can hardly get it out of my mind." She all but purred at the memory.

Lilly was holding her breath, unable to assimilate what was happening. She desperately wanted to fight back, to tell them both to go to hell. But the waters were too deep, and she was caught in an undertow unable to rise to the surface, her lungs bursting. Too soon, those green eyes locked on her again.

"My husband is a marvelous lover, as I'm sure you know, and an even more incredible man," she said in her lilting voice. "Do you realize that he served as the Crown's assassin at large? No? Well, I don't believe that is common knowledge. Let's just say our Julian here can drill a dime at twenty paces, a crack shot is what they call it if I'm not mistaken. Correct me if I'm wrong, dearest." She barely paused to take a breath. "He's as good at killing as he is at sex. Maybe even better—killing, that is."

St. Martin was deadly silent. The clock shed another five minutes. *Bellamy.* And this madwoman. Lilly's mind was barely forming coherent sentences.

"Do you still dream about it, my love? Not the sex. The killing."

St. Martin still hadn't moved. "And are you still enamored of your laudanum?"

Constance laughed, the sound of a babbling brook. "You would not rob me of my pleasures? Certainly Bellamy doesn't, although he did try," she said slyly. She crossed one slender ankle over another. Her small, plump toes curled beguilingly. "You should try it, my love. Probably do wonders to salve your conscience. You do have me on your conscience, don't you?"

"I said that I thought you were dead. Clearly I was mistaken." St. Martin's eyes glittered strangely.

A surreal sense of horror broke over Lilly. Two minutes before the hour. She took a deep breath, beyond mere panic.

"Does your lover here know?" Constance asked innocently.

"She does not."

"I thought so."

"Know what?" Lilly spoke finally, moving out from behind the desk.

Constance laughed softly, as though at a private joke. "You devil, Julian."

Lilly's mind flashed back to all she knew about St. Martin. Emotion warring with logic, she grappled with her slim hold on reality. *Remember the queen. Remember the Koh-I-Noor.* It was all that mattered. The rest was madness.

But there would be no reprieve. At least the ormolu clock didn't lie. It was eleven o'clock precisely, the discreet chime seeming to invoke its master. Isambard Kingdom Bellamy suddenly stood framed in the doorway, his bulk blocking any possible notion of escape. A feral gleam in his eyes spoke of a heightened and malevolent interest. Voices echoed in Lilly's head, keeping time with the ticking clock, tearing her apart, consigning her to a hell she never thought existed.

"There you are, dearest." Constance looked up from the chaise, acknowledging Bellamy in a singsong voice, throwing back her thick black hair with sensuous abandon. "So pleased you could join us."

"I'm not pleased to see you here. You're wandering again, Constance," he said in a patronizing voice that was all too familiar to Lilly. "I thought I asked you to stay in your rooms." Bellamy had changed into a tartan smoking jacket, its shawl collar and turned-up cuffs adding an incongruous note to the proceedings. "And where is the guard that I pay an exorbitant amount to patrol these hallways at all times." His eyes were sharp, landing on St. Martin.

"He needed to use the privy," St. Martin supplied, his expression unconcerned. "I told him that I would assume his duties for the moment." He shrugged. "He's yet to return. And when I heard voices coming from this room, I thought it best to investigate."

Bellamy stroked the lapels of his smoking jacket, sauntering toward St. Martin. "Only to discover your long, lost wife." His eyes narrowed. "You don't appear overly shocked." He paused to consider. "But then again, a man of your background is accustomed to absorbing all manner of blows."

Lilly tried to make herself invisible, all the while attempting to piece together a shattered picture to make a whole. For his part, St. Martin ignored her entirely.

"My memory may be at fault. Again," he replied cryptically, appearing indifferent to the rising tension in the room.

"Periodic lapses that Dr. Vesper is attempting to resolve," Bellamy murmured. "Although I'm certain you have now made the connection between the good doctor and the fact that your wife still lives. He is as remarkably useful to us here in London with Charles Hampton as he's been with Lady St. Martin in India. As it turns out we are making progress all around, if the doctor is to be believed. You were wise to accept my offer of assistance."

"It was a fair exchange," St. Martin responded enigmatically.

A strange smile touched Bellamy's lips and eyes. "Dr. Vesper is waiting in the salon."

"As I would expect."

Bellamy pivoted on his heels, turning to Lilly. "And you, my dear, have you finished the assignment as requested? Or need I even ask?" He gestured casually to the desk before pursing his lips beneath his mustache.

Lilly could scarcely find her voice. "I need more time."

"You've just run out of time, I'm sorry to say," Bellamy said, wandering over to the desk and glancing at the papers strewn across the surface. When he looked up, he pinned her with his gaze. "Perhaps we should all meet with Dr. Vesper in the salon."

Lilly's head buzzed and she clenched her hands together to stop the tumult. Bellamy's decree made no sense, and yet the tendrils of meaning were there if she could only put them together.

Constance, who had been watching the exchange with a curious smile on her face, spoke. "Dr. Vesper. He is such a dear." A small frown marred her smooth brow as she tucked the silk of her night rail beneath one foot. "But I fear we are premature."

His impatience palpable, Bellamy strode over to the divan and stood, legs apart, looming over Constance. "Not now. You are making even less sense than you ever do."

"You are being mean, Isambard." She pouted. "And you know I don't like it when you're mean. What can Vesper do if Julian himself doesn't know what transpired that day."

"What are you babbling about?"

"The truth, of course."

"Not now."

"I think we should tell Julian and his latest lover here all there is to know. I'm certain she"—Constance cast her green gaze over Lilly—"would like to hear how Julian St. Martin murdered his own wife." She sighed, but her eyes flickered eagerly. "Such a chilling, cold-blooded tale."

Lilly lost what little she had left of her bearings. A sensation of falling, the earth disappearing from beneath her, spread out from her brain to her heart like an uncontrollable disease.

He'd killed his own wife. The man who claimed that he loved her. Her voice was hoarse, the words forced from her. "I don't believe that I want to understand any of this," she said.

"She speaks! I was wondering how long before your little inamorata had something to say." Constance addressed St. Martin before smiling slyly at Lilly. "You don't want to know, do you? Are you quite certain?"

Bellamy placed a hard hand on Constance's arm. "Your ramblings are not appreciated. I shouldn't have to remind you that your disobedience will exact a price."

Her full lips curved into a smile. "I know very well how you exact your punishment, Isambard. You learned all your little tricks at the knees of savages. Given your origins, it's not surprising that you took to your lessons so avidly."

His backhanded slap rang through the room. An instant later, a red flower glowed on Constance's creamy cheek, but her eyes hardened into green gems. "Since I've already received the punishment," she spat, cradling her head in the back cushion of the divan, "I believe I deserve to be heard."

Bellamy's response was to pull together the lapels of his smoking jacket before raising his hand to strike again, the expression on his face weirdly beatific. St. Martin moved quickly, suddenly at Bellamy's side. His voice was authoritative. "We're keeping Vesper waiting with all these female histrionics. We have more important matters to attend to."

Bellamy took a moment to consider the claim before lowering his hand. Constance curled defensively into the divan. Lilly could hear Bellamy's heavy breaths, counting each one, watching as he came to a decision and slowly turned his back to Constance.

He stared at St. Martin. "Such as your desire for vengeance against the Crown."

The taller man nodded but said nothing.

Bellamy then settled his gaze on Lilly with unnerving silence. She watched as he produced a cigar from the pocket of his smoking jacket, his fingers clenching reflexively around the stem. "These western women." He shook his head dismissively, coming down from the height of his rage step by step. "In India this type of behavior does not exist, and even if it did, it would not be tolerated. Child marriage, purdah, suttee—would that we should borrow some of these practices," he continued, aiming his commentary directly at Lilly, an intense hatred of women underscoring his words. "What do we have instead? What we have is a squat queen as ruler of our empire." He chewed the end of the unlit cigar savagely. "And she would seek to rob me of my power?" Each word was spit out separately.

The invective was pure madness. Unable to hold back any

longer, Lilly found her voice. "And you would assassinate every member of Parliament as well?" She let the anxieties of the present bleed away, allowing her outrage to come to the surface. "Eliminating the queen hardly resolves your dilemma, demented though it is."

Bellamy chuckled, moving closer to Lilly, St. Martin shadowing him. "Ah yes, I'd forgotten your penchant for brilliant political analysis. Your late husband allowed you far too much freedom." He sucked on the unlit cigar before continuing. "What you forget is that *I am* a company that owns nations. I not only established trade through Asia and the Middle East but I am the ruler of territories vastly larger than Great Britain herself. Ergo, Queen Victoria and her unwelcome political influence present a minor stumbling block, as does her prime minister and his Parliament of lackeys and sycophants."

His skin had lost its usual ruddiness, taking on the white pallor of a snake's underbelly. "Which is why I find your stubbornness, Lilly, so affecting." His eyes never left her face. "And since you've declined to complete the requested drawings for me, I am forced to take action, rather more diverting action, as it turns out. So in the end, you do me no great disservice."

St. Martin spoke. "We are wasting valuable time." He glanced at Lilly and Constance perfunctorily. "What does it matter whether either of them understands your motivations."

Bellamy glanced at the clock. "We can be both efficient and amuse ourselves simultaneously, St. Martin. Surely you learned as much in your time away from England." He strolled toward the doorway. "I shall inform Vesper of a slight change in plans."

"And you," he continued, stabbing the air in Lilly's general direction. "You who are deceiving me at every turn, when you should be grateful that I offered you my name and protection in marriage. And that ridiculous husband of yours—"

He reached for the door handle. "Well I won't ask you again. You've forfeited your chance, my dear. This time I will have the information that I require, whether you are willing or not."

Fighting an overwhelming and irrational urge to run to St. Martin, Lilly didn't move. She watched Constance uncoil from the divan. They were husband and wife. She absorbed a stab of pain, wondering where St. Martin's loyalty lay. To his wife? To Bellamy? Certainly not to her. As if it mattered. She glanced at Bellamy, whose eyes had never left her, and sensed the next hours would be her last.

St. Martin's low voice broke into her tortured thoughts. "I will meet with Vesper in the salon," he said to Bellamy.

"You do that."

"The two women are best left here. They will only get in the way."

Bellamy lifted the cigar to his lips. "You think so? Well, I disagree, St. Martin. I believe both Constance and Lilly will add immeasurably to the evening. And I'm never wrong."

The cavernous salon was meant to be impressive. Lilly had to admit that they made an odd procession into the room with its high ceilings and mullioned windows, the decor deliberately meant to evoke a Gothic past. Bellamy led the retinue, followed by Lilly and Constance, both of whom were flanked by two of Bellamy's men. St. Martin had gone on ahead. Thank God no one had yet discovered the body he had summarily dispatched in the bedroom upstairs nor her small pistol tucked beneath her shirt.

Dim lights illuminated the massive fireplace in one corner and the balconies laced overhead. There was little enough time left for thought or strategy and, agonizingly, her mind flashed to St. Martin.

She wanted to close her eyes against the easy tears beginning to start, and she hated herself. Hated him, most of all. Her conscious, reasonable mind seemed to have shattered, vanished. The little she knew was desperate enough. He had used her from the beginning. He was an assassin, a traitor, who was entangled with Bellamy. And he was married to the woman he had murdered years before.

And yet she loved him, a harsh and inescapable reality that refused to leave her. And hearing him say those words to her had ripped through her body and soul. The irony burned and had she the stomach for it, she would have sobbed aloud. Instead, she looked straight ahead and across what seemed a great distance where St. Martin sat in a high-backed chair. Her spine tensed. There was something not right in his posture, in the way his hands draped over the arms of the chair, in the blankness of his expression. Dr. Vesper stood to the side, his hands behind his back, his thin shoulders set in a straight line.

Bellamy marched ahead. "When I had the house built, I was of course still in India," he said with the peculiar enthusiasm of the nouveau riche. "I originally discovered the taste for high Gothic style which has since become so popular in London."

They had no choice but to listen to his rambling, trailing after him while he pointed out details regarding the marble, the wood, and the manufacture of the windows. Ahead of her Constance appeared bored, her ennui evident in the slope of her shoulders, in her listless movements. Lilly doubted that she sensed the danger she was in and recalled the mention of laudanum.

"I should like the two ladies by the fireplace. Similar to last time," Bellamy said briskly, gesturing to the men at their sides. Before she could protest, Lilly was pushed down on a low upholstered bench next to Constance. One of Bellamy's men was securing her wrists and ankles with thick rope, her trousered legs and shapeless shirt giving her cold comfort.

Beside her, Constance squirmed in her silk night rail. "Is this really necessary, Isambard?"

"You're fortunate that I'm dispensing with the gags this

time," he replied, clearly in a generous mood. "Shriek, scream, or moan, all the better."

Lilly knew she shouldn't ask but couldn't help herself, her bound wrists behind her back already pulsing with pain. "How is this perversion to help your cause? I can hardly supply you with plans when I am deprived of circulation."

Bellamy raised an eyebrow at her audacity, walking in a circle around her as though inspecting a neatly packaged parcel. "All in good time," he said.

Beside her, Constance rolled her eyes. "I presume these games will involve the stable boys." She sighed theatrically. "You are repeating yourself, Isambard."

Across the room St. Martin didn't move. For a panicked moment, Lilly thought he might have been dosed with an opiate far stronger than laudanum. Bellamy picked up the direction of her thoughts.

"You ladies are so transparent," he said, patting Lilly absently on the shoulder with a meaty hand. "Now I know that somehow you believe that St. Martin will rush over to you and cut you loose. It will be deliriously satisfying to watch you sob in disappointment when you discover that I have something quite different planned." He shoved both hands into the front pockets of his smoking jacket. "Actually, it's quite the opposite of what you might expect."

Lilly stared up at him, focusing all her contempt and hatred at the man. He seemed to relish her fury and helplessness. She knew she was going to die—not pleasantly, and not just yet.

Constance wriggled beside her. "I can hardly wait," she drawled lazily. She leaned into Lilly conspiratorially, the waft of her heavy perfume cloying. "I'm certain you're still desperate to find out what Julian did to me so many years ago." She glanced up at Bellamy and said cheerily, "Why not tell her, Bellamy? It will add to her discomfort, and that's what you're looking for after all. As with so many other women in the past, Lilly here is clearly infatuated with my husband."

"An interesting idea," Bellamy responded idly. He rummaged around in the pocket of his jacket to resurrect his cigar. Flynn stepped out of the shadows, the flare of a match announcing his presence. Lilly's stomach lurched, watching as the large man applied the flame to Bellamy's cigar. Hauling a satisfying draught of smoke into his mouth, Bellamy released first one and then a second ring into the air between them. "Very well then," he said finally. "Why don't you tell the story. I think there's a certain piquancy in allowing the wife to do the honors."

Flynn had disappeared into the shadows while Constance turned around the best she could to face Lilly. Her green eyes shone, the pupils dark and dilated. Lilly spared a quick glance at St. Martin and Dr. Vesper at the opposite end of the room. The doctor seemed intent on an entirely different task and in an entirely different world, totally removed from the mayhem that was unfolding before his eyes. And St. Martin—she could feel the chill coming off the huge, empty hearth behind her. Something was urgently wrong.

Constance's lilting, singsong voice stoked her rising panic. "Well you understand, when we were first married, Julian almost immediately carried me off to the wilds of Lahore. Imagine someone like me banished to the colonies, and naturally I couldn't possibly anticipate how outrageously boring my existence would become after the whirlwind of London. Tediously boring to begin with made worse by the fact of his leaving me alone for long stretches of time. Do you recall, Bellamy? How beastly he was to me?"

Without waiting for a reply, she continued coyly. "Not that I didn't find my own amusements, you understand." She was a breathtakingly beautiful and careless woman, and Lilly had no doubts that endless numbers of men would find her endlessly beguiling. St. Martin had. "And one day he returned home unexpectedly and came upon something unexpected. What a surprise!" she said with a girlish giggle. Her face fell almost immediately, her lips forming a pout. "What's worse, he seemed not to care. Can you imagine?" Her vanity was obviously of outsized proportion, thought Lilly, dreading the words that would come next.

"But that was only the beginning. There was much political nastiness, which I never did understand except to discover, from among my numerous lovers, that Julian was always somehow in the middle of it all." She frowned, wriggling her bound hands behind her back. "Isambard—these ropes are chafing my skin. I'd prefer that this time you leave no marks."

Bellamy continued to smoke in a leisurely fashion, glancing at the gaping hearth behind them from time to time. When she didn't receive a response, Constance shook the hair back from her face, forgot about her bound hands, and continued. "So I decided one day that I'd had enough."

Had enough of her husband's indifference, his inattention, his frequent absences.

"I proceeded to go to Isambard, to ask for his help," she supplied, smiling to reveal small white teeth. "I wanted out. And I wanted revenge." She said the last word so softly that Lilly thought she'd misheard. Mesmerized by Constance's account, the pulsing pain in Lilly's wrists and ankles faded away.

"He arranged to have it look as though I'd been kidnapped by an Afghanistan tribe." She wrinkled her nose in disgust. "But you see it wasn't so at all. It was one of Bellamy's own officers who had me in his clutches." She shivered dramatically before smiling brilliantly. "All a façade, you understand, except that Julian never knew. And he believed that when he took aim to kill the man to get me back, that he missed his target. And killed me instead." Triumph shone from the glittering green eyes. "Silly man. Julian St. Martin never misses. He should have known."

The declaration hit Lilly with the force and precision of a rapier's point. Constance smiled as though hugging a secret to herself. Then she raised her striking eyes to Lilly. "I wanted him to suffer for his neglect of me. And he has. Two long years believing that he was responsible for my death and that one of his own, a British officer, was involved in the plot to kidnap me."

"Which nurtured his disillusionment with the Crown to a fever pitch and brought him directly to me," Bellamy finished. Lilly couldn't see him standing behind her, but knew that he was leaning against the mantel of the empty fireplace. "And which brings us all here today."

He walked around the back of the bench to face her directly. She stared speechless, the complexity of his delusions only maximized by the perversity of his plans. The sensation of her burning wrists and ankles returned to her at the same time as the jagged pieces of a new reality slid into place.

You've lost, Lilly. You just don't know it yet. He can drill a dime at twenty paces. Which nurtured his disillusionment to a fever pitch. St. Martin was never after the Koh-I-Noor. Bellamy intended for him to assassinate the queen. Her mind went numb. She looked up at the mullioned windows that had yet to leak morning light. Dear God, what time was it?

Her eyes darted over to St. Martin who sat still in the chair. A wave of nausea rolled through her. Vesper stood directly in front of him, murmuring something indecipherable, a watch in his hand arcing evenly, back and forth, in front of St. Martin's heavy-lidded eyes.

Bellamy reappeared at her side and crouched down low, the spirals of cigar smoke curling into the space between them. "Did you enjoy Constance's story? She's a high-born slut, no different from my mother apart from decades of aristocratic inbreeding. She is close to slumbering again, one of the perils of her addiction to opiates; she never knows how much is enough, and clearly, nor does Vesper. My mother was much the same."

Constance remained silent beside her, and Lilly wondered whether she had indeed fallen asleep under the effects of the laudanum. Better for her, Lilly thought with an unaccountable spark of compassion.

"Are you afraid?" Bellamy asked absently.

"What do you think? I'm not generally accustomed to being bound and held prisoner."

"You have traveled far, Lilly Clarence Hampton, from your sheltered widow's weeds."

"Don't bother delaying on my account. Tell me what you intend to do."

"Imagination is far worse than reality, so I won't spoil the effect," Bellamy said at length. "If you divulge how to access the entranceway through which the queen is expected to travel in a few hours' time, I shall let you go."

It took an extreme act of will not to hurl her rage at his head, but holding back was the only option. She refused to capitulate. "No," she said with finality.

He sighed and then smiled. "As I suspected. You will require extra inducements, which I'm certain, under the influence of Dr. Vesper's expert guidance, St. Martin will be eager to supply."

Her mind grappled with this new threat. To keep her tenuous grip on her sanity, she rubbed her ankles and wrists together, the numbness giving way to pain. For the second time, she refused to react.

Throwing his cigar into the fireplace behind her, Bellamy rose to his full height. "Vesper. Are we ready?" The question catapulted throughout the room and through her nerve endings.

Vesper responded with a quarter turn and with an expression Lilly recognized, the timepiece in his right hand, his face in shadows cast by the gaslight. He was a weak man who, caught by forces outside his control, had been shown his place. Looking at her from across the room, there was something like compassion in his eyes. But it was probably all her imagination, his gaze hidden by spectacles.

Without glancing at Bellamy, Vesper turned to face his subject. "Can you hear me, St. Martin?" His voice reverberated with unexpected authority.

"By way of explanation," Bellamy interrupted at her side, "Vesper is expert in a new science that induces trance-like states in subjects through their fixation on a bright object."

Lilly's mouth went dry, robbing her of her breath. "Hypnotism," she whispered, horror leaching into the farthest corners of her mind. To ensure that St. Martin would do Bellamy's bidding—and assassinate the queen.

"Of course, you would be familiar with the process," Bellamy said with heavy sarcasm. "You are entirely too well informed for a woman, as we've already established. Architecture, politics, and now science. You see what good comes of a woman's inappropriate interests?"

Lilly closed her eyes against the onslaught—how much more of the madness could she absorb?

"You then understand that hypnotism is a neurophysiological process wherein a subject's attention is focused upon the suggestions made by the hypnotist—in our case, the accommodating Dr. Vesper."

Lilly opened her eyes to watch Vesper suspending the watch in front of St. Martin who remained somnolent in the chair. Beside her, she sensed a change in the cadence of Bellamy's breathing, a perverse excitement warming the room. A rustle of movement, Bellamy's men in the shadows, added to the gathering storm.

"Similar to our last meeting, if you will, doctor," Bellamy exclaimed pompously. "With one minor but most diverting variation."

Gas lamps simmered in the quiet of the salon, their light casting elongated shadows. Vesper summoned a barely perceptible nod, his narrow shoulders tightening.

"The variation I would suggest is that St. Martin make a choice. A most difficult choice."

Lilly closed her eyes.

"I would suggest," Bellamy continued, excitement infusing his words, "that he choose between Lilly and his wife. Because"—he paused dramatically—"it has not escaped my no-

tice that he has developed a certain affection for our widow
here. Truth be told, I hadn't anticipated that particular outcome. Precisely the opposite, as a matter of fact. I had intended that he threaten, not seduce, her." He snorted at the
misfortune. "Nonetheless, we will leverage what we can."

Bellamy's breathing accelerated. Vesper did not respond
directly except to redirect his question to St. Martin. "Can
you hear me?" His voice was sure and calm.

A change came over the room, a heavy pall descending
from the high ceilings, suffocating in its closeness. Lilly
stared in mute horror. St. Martin remained still, relaxed as if
in sleep, and then, the heavy-lidded eyes opened. The dark
eyes Lilly imagined she knew so well. Only she didn't.

"Please answer if you can hear me," Vesper said.

"I can." The voice was his, achingly familiar.

"There are two women in the room with us. Please indicate that you can see them, there by the fireplace, sir."

St. Martin flexed his hands, still suspended loosely from
the arms of his chair. Strong, elegant hands that had brought
her excruciating pleasure, thought Lilly, and hands that had
killed for her.

She didn't want to look at Bellamy, repelled by the harshness of his breathing, the rise and fall of his barrel chest on
the outlines of her vision.

"That is very good. You can hear me then," Vesper continued calmly. "And you see the two women by the fireplace."

St. Martin nodded.

"What I am requesting of you, sir," Vesper said slowly,
enunciating each word precisely, "is that you cross the room
to their side."

Constance had slumped beside her, the fall of her dark hair
obscuring her face. Perhaps it was better that way, Lilly thought,
one less woman for Bellamy to terrorize. She felt a strange
compassion welling in her chest, mingling with the anguish
and fear that threatened to drown her.

The doctor continued, using the same mesmerizing monotone, distancing himself from what he was about to do. "Once you are at their side, I want you to . . ." He paused and Lilly knew that they had come to a gaping void. "I want you to," he repeated, "choose one of them to kill. With your bare hands. Do you understand?"

In response and in one fluid motion, St. Martin came to life, rising from the chair. He looked neither left nor right but approached Lilly with a studied calm and a lethal, instinctive intent. And so rapidly that she had not time to recoil even if she could.

He had chosen. Without a moment's hesitation. A shadow appeared above her, then coalesced into nightmare shapes before reassembling themselves. Broad shoulders, strong arms, powerful elegant hands were poised to descend around her neck.

Then his face so close she could feel his warm breath. The familiar heat of his skin against her collarbone. If she could, she should have raked her fingernails down his forearms, twisted from his grasp, howled with outrage. The pain of survival would have sharpened her defenses.

But she could do none of those things. Instead, she summoned the last dregs of courage in her soul to look into his eyes, toward infinity and certain death. The pressure around her neck tightened, and then didn't. Miraculously she sucked in air, one breath coming after the next, like pearls on a silver chain. And his eyes said trust me.

And she did.

Chapter 21

Instead of utter desolation, she felt exhilaration pumping her heart, pushing through the fear and agony that had held her back far too long. He loved her. She saw it in his eyes, those dark, fathomless eyes that now seemed as transparent as glass. Deep in her mind, a spark fluttered to life and she heard her own voice break through the silence.

"I shall do it," she said.

The four syllables fell from her lips with decisive clarity. Something flickered in St. Martin's expression, but his hands did not fall away from her neck. Not yet. Until Bellamy spoke.

His voice was harsh with barely suppressed excitement. "Tell him to cease, Vesper. She's no good to me dead."

Vesper's voice echoed from a cave far away. "Enough, St. Martin." Lilly closed her eyes, feeling the warm pressure around her neck ease.

From the corner of her vision she saw Bellamy, perspiration glossing his brow, his lips obscenely parted. The scent of a diseased mind emanated from his skin. He watched avidly as St. Martin crossed the room and returned obediently to his chair.

"Clearly, death holds no appeal. I thought so," the man who had nearly become her husband said. Her gorge rising, she fought back her rebellious stomach, fighting to maintain her equilibrium. She would not waver, her skin still tingling from St. Martin's touch.

"I demand to go with him," she said abruptly. "To the Crystal Palace. I shall not share the last of the information otherwise."

St. Martin pretended not to hear, his broad shoulders retreating from her view before he sat down in the chair and returned to his somnolent state. Beside her, Constance murmured in her sleep and Lilly once again wondered about the netherworld that now held them all prisoner.

Bellamy plucked a handkerchief from his jacket pocket and mopped his brow. "You are not in the position, literally and figuratively," he said, looking down at her bound hands and feet, "to make demands, Lilly."

"Neither of you, and that includes Seabourne, can do this without me. Besides which"—she jutted her chin toward the windows to the east—"morning is not far off."

Bellamy seemed to give her claim some consideration. Constance had slumped farther on the bench until she was almost completely horizontal, the white silk of her nightgown floating around her. "I suppose I should take some time to prepare myself as well for my meeting with the queen," he murmured agreeably. "Although it would be interesting to see St. Martin murder his wife a second time, had we but the hours at our disposal. It all has a delightful symmetry, I suspect." He smoothed his mustache regretfully. "Then again, good things take time. It's not every day that the major shareholder of the British East India Company presents the world's most precious diamond to the Queen of England."

He snapped his fingers. "Flynn, see to it that the carriages are prepared." Then he turned toward Vesper. The first light of dawn illuminated the two figures at the farthest reaches of the salon, a deadly tableau. "Well done, doctor. You have acquitted yourself admirably. I don't have to tell you to ensure that St. Martin is prepared for the next act in our drama."

He then straightened the lapels of his smoking jacket. "And Flynn. Rouse my valet to confirm that he has everything perfectly prepared for this morning's ennobling ceremony. I shouldn't want to disappoint our queen. And return Lady St. Martin to her rooms." He grimaced sourly at the prone figure before lifting his head to finish. "As for Mrs. Hampton and Lord St. Martin, take them to the carriage house until we are set to proceed." As an afterthought, he added with a final glance at Vesper, "But the doctor will remain here. Given St. Martin's demonstration of perfect obedience, his work is done."

Lilly had no choice but to follow Flynn, her ankles freed but her hands still bound behind her back. Flynn did not speak to her until they had left the house by the servant's entrance. The dawn was beginning to crack over the horizon, pink streaks decorating the dark sky. He stepped back to let her go first, surveying the knots that bound her hands behind her back with something like pride. "That should keep you from getting into trouble," he said, pushing her into the carriage house with a hard hand on her back. He deliberately avoided opening the two large doors that accommodated carriages entering and exiting the house. Trying not to stumble and thankful for her sturdy boots and breeches one last time, Lilly cursed him under her breath, all the while wondering where her newfound knowledge of profanity came from as she ducked under the low side entrance.

Her eyes quickly adjusted to the absence of light. The overall design echoed the main house, the high mullioned windows allowing in the first light of day. She counted seven gleaming carriages arrayed in their stalls. Flynn pushed her to the back of the building, his footsteps echoing behind her along the stone floor.

As massive as an oak tree, he glared at her with simmering resentment. Flashes of their last encounter flickered through her mind's eye. "I'm harmless as you can see," she said with cold civility, her revolver, warm comfort, still tucked safely in her corset. "I shall wait here as requested until Mr. Bellamy joins us."

His small eyes beaded with suspicion. "St. Martin will be here once that doctor is through with him. But this time, he's not got the upper hand." He spat onto the floor for emphasis.

Lilly eyed the bandaged shoulder but wondered who else would be posted outside the carriage house doors. Her own shoulders were numb with pain, her arms soldered in place behind her back for what seemed like hours. She watched the lumbering man retreat and didn't release a sigh of relief until the door slammed behind him.

She wasn't alone for long with her thoughts. Too soon, the door opened once again and before she saw St. Martin she sensed his presence. He grabbed her arm and turned her around so suddenly that she cried out softly. Her eyes were accustomed to the dimness now and she could see the unexpected heat in his eyes as he stared down at her.

"What in hell's name were you doing?"

"I was doing what's necessary."

"You are putting yourself in danger for no earthly reason. Why did you insist on accompanying us to the Crystal Palace?" He asked the question slowly, as though struggling to control his voice. But he didn't allow her to respond. "There's only one reason and it is that you still don't trust me. Otherwise, you would have played along, relinquished the goddamned final details, and Vesper would have seen to your safety."

"You need me and you know it."

He dropped his hand from her arm and left her standing against the wall, feeling more alone than she'd ever felt in her life. "What will it take to have you trust me?" he asked again. He looked ready to lunge at her, the unmasked fury in his eyes unrecognizable.

"I do trust you," she said through gritted teeth, doing everything to avoid pleading with him. "You had my throat in your hands, if you'll recall. And you did not see terror in my eyes but an altogether different emotion—had you been looking," she said in defeated tones.

The silence between them was heavy, a swollen river flowing with the detritus of both their lives. Constance, Charles, Bellamy. But it didn't matter. Because before she could say anything more, he gathered her to him and held her against the solid wall of his chest, where, this time, she heard the steady beat of his heart.

"I don't care what happens to me now," she said, her words muffled against his shirt. "All I care is that the queen is saved and that you are safe. And neither will happen without me."

He pulled her even closer. "I've never been afraid in my life until this moment. That's what you do to me," he said quietly.

She looked up at him desperately, her own fear stinging her eyes. "We will get through this."

"You will get through this, Lilly." The finality in his voice made her shiver. He touched her face, her skin warming with the contact. "I became involved in lies and subterfuge long before I met you, and I won't have you sacrificed to a cause that isn't worth your life."

She was afraid to say the words, to think the thoughts. "Whatever the cause, you are not a traitor. I don't believe it." Her fists curled stubbornly behind her back. "And I won't let you die. I won't allow it. You haven't a chance without my knowledge."

He pushed her away firmly. "This time I say no."

"Impossible," she scoffed, belligerent in her desperation. "You have spent the last several weeks endeavoring to pry the information from me and now you tell me no?" Her voice rang through the carriage house. He closed the distance between them swiftly and clamped a hand on her mouth. She pushed away from his hand and whispered harshly, "You risk too much, St. Martin. You risk the life of the queen and the future of the British Empire. And worst of all, you risk your life."

The darkness in his eyes had returned, shutting out her entreaties. There was only one thing left to say. "I love you," she said finally, pride as futile as her words and her hands still tied behind her back.

He took her face in his hands, his voice grim. "And I love you, and that's the best and worst thing that's ever happened in my life." She closed her eyes against the torment she saw buried in his empty gaze, drawing strength from the warm fingers on her cheeks. She pressed her forehead to his chest.

"Lilly, you cannot do this for me, I won't allow it."

"Bellamy will see you dead," she choked out against the linen of his shirt.

"And it won't matter."

"You bastard," she whispered, her rage fighting with her tears. "It will matter—to me. As if I'm of no account."

"Look at me." She did so reluctantly, opening her stinging eyes a bit at a time, afraid of what she might see. "If you reveal the information to me, Bellamy will leave you behind and Dr. Vesper will see to your safety until all this is concluded."

She straightened her shoulders against his logic, ignoring the pain that gripped her and wishing she could wipe the traces of tears from her cheeks. Her bound wrists burned to touch the hard planes of his face with her fingers, wanting desperately to remember the feel of him.

"Tell me now," he said. "I'm asking for the last time."

But time had run out. One of the large carriage doors shuddered open, the rising sun, liquid warmth, silhouetting Constance St. Martin in its borders. Still in her flowing nightgown, she pushed away the hands that pulled her back, floating defiantly into the interior of the coach house. All languor had disappeared, and in its place was a rough intensity proclaiming her profound anguish. "Where are you going, my love?" she asked in a plaintive voice, stretching out a graceful arm toward St. Martin. She looked up at him, stricken, pleading, every line of her body filled with need. "I have just found you again and you me—surely you won't leave me again?"

The last words held a tinge of hysteria. Flynn caught up with her from behind, holding back her flailing arms, pulling her against one of the shining carriage doors. "Now that's enough, my lady. Mr. Bellamy doesn't have to hear about this if you behave and go back to your rooms like a good little lass we all know you can be."

Lilly moved out from the shadows and away from St. Martin just to see Constance raise her hands and, from behind, scrape her nails down Flynn's face. The rest was a blur. The Irishman exploded, his brawny fists lunging for Constance's neck. He grabbed her violently and went for a choke, cursing profanely.

St. Martin was fast, leaping forward to smash an uppercut from the heel of his right hand into Flynn's jaw, driving it upward and weakening his grip on Constance. She shrieked hysterically as she was freed, her hands clawing wildly, grabbing for the pistol that dangled from the Irishman's waistband.

Amid the screams, Lilly watched St. Martin put a knee to Flynn's spine. He found his thick right arm and jammed it backward into a lock against his back, almost breaking his wrist in the process and no doubt opening the wound on his shoulder. Flynn howled his outrage, the cacophony intensifying with every one of Constance's shrieks.

Lilly's gaze was fixed on the heavy pistol in Constance's shaking, white hands. Lilly took a careful step toward her. "Please lower the weapon, Constance," she said steadily, alarmed by the wildness in the woman's eyes. She received a startled green gaze. "You!"

"I mean you no harm. Please believe me. I can do you no harm." With great difficulty, she raised her tied arms behind her back.

"She's being truthful with you, Constance. Don't hurt yourself or anyone else," St. Martin said, keeping his hold on Flynn.

Constance's eyes glittered strangely. "I want you back, my love," she said, as a child might declare she wanted a sweet. The demand was mournful, hanging in the air along with the dust motes dancing in the golden morning sunlight.

Then there were voices and shouts everywhere, Bellamy's men spilling through the open doorway and into the carriage house. They didn't stop to consider, someone huge hitting Constance violently from behind. She fell forward, protesting, screaming, the pistol still clutched in her hand. The shot rang out as she was pinned to the floor, a powerful male torso on top of her, arms like iron wrapped around her waist. The screams stopped.

And when Lilly looked up, she saw the wide doors of the carriage house gaping open, and the sun a glorious ball of fire over the horizon, heralding a new day. St. Martin had released his hold on Flynn. He looked calm, controlled, his dead wife lying a few feet away.

Lilly didn't know whether to scream or to cry—because there was nothing left inside.

Chapter 22

The preparations for the opening of the Great Exhibition were unprecedented in their complexity. In addition to the structure of the Crystal Palace itself, the interior of the building was enormous. With eleven miles of stalls and a decorative color scheme that required the labor of five hundred painters, assembling the interior alone required the constant work of two thousand men for three months. Exhibits ranged from entire railway engines and enormous pistons to galleries filled with linen cloth, patented invalid chairs, and galvanized walking sticks. And yet, until the opening day, visitors had to content themselves with seeing horse-drawn moving carts, screened from view by vast wooden hoardings.

Disgorged by Bellamy's carriage behind one of the hoardings, Lilly and St. Martin, flanked by Flynn and three of his men, moved into the small entranceway that ran parallel with the main hall. Approximately forty yards away lay the entrance to the room that would display the diamond and from where the queen and Prince Albert would proceed to the official opening of the Great Exhibition of 1851. The massive and ornate opening ceremonies would include a procession with the Royal Family, leading military officials, and the Duke of Wellington. Thirty thousand ticketed guests would fill the Crystal Palace to capacity while half a million others stood outside in Hyde Park. The queen and prince consort would ascend to a specially built, velvet-draped dais in the central transept, and would stand while the great organ played "God Save the Queen." The prince would then read briefly from the Commissioners' report for the Exhibition followed by a prayer from the Archbishop of Canterbury.

Lilly played the scene in her mind, knowing with dread certainty that Bellamy would conspire for it not to take place. It had never been the diamond that he coveted—it was merely symbolic of his will to power. It was the queen who would be removed from her dais, not the Koh-I-Noor.

They walked in silence until they found themselves once again standing in the narrow corridor off the main hallway, which, it seemed to Lilly, they had only left hours ago. It did not surprise her to see Bellamy, resplendent in a severely tailored day coat, relieved by a peacock blue waistcoat and matching striped trousers, waiting for them. He stood beside the two smaller diamonds that were already ensconced, like exotic birds, in their parrot cage with its gilded bars. The gems were lit from below with dozens of gas jets, catching the light with tiny mirrors scattered around the base. Next to the cage, rising like a multifaceted stalagmite toward the roof panes of the Crystal Palace, stood a gushing, glassy fountain, a symbol for the Koh-I-Noor's crystalline beauty.

Bellamy glanced impatiently at his pocket watch and immediately turned to St. Martin. "You will be working with a revolver known as the British Bulldog," he said without preamble and a glance at Flynn who would presumably produce the weapon at the appropriate time.

"A Webley and Scott, notable for its large caliber of ammunition and small, concealable size." St. Martin completed the description.

Bellamy returned the watch back into the pocket of his waistcoat, frowning. "We don't have much time before the queen's arrival. Your wife, with her seemingly inexhaustible appetite for drama, has made us late."

She was also dead. Lilly tried to stop shaking, her small revolver cold against her breast. She couldn't think about Constance right now. It wasn't long before Bellamy turned his
attention to her. "I'm certain you don't intend to slow the
proceedings," he said. "It would be most unwise. We could
have pulled this area apart ourselves but, of course, that
course of action would have alerted the authorities almost
immediately."

She pulled herself up sharply. "May I at least first hear
what you have planned?" she asked. Her hands had finally
been freed and she resisted the urge to hurl herself at Bellamy
and pummel him with his fists until he disappeared into the
hard marble beneath his feet. She took a deep breath and a
quick glance at St. Martin, whose expression gave nothing
away. It was as though she didn't exist.

Bellamy stopped to consider, striking a fashionable pose in
front of the fountain, one foot in front of the other. "And
why not? I can afford to be generous at this point in time,
after all." He paused for dramatic effect, assembling his glorious future for the telling. "Once Victoria has been eliminated, courtesy of Lord St. Martin, Parliament will be in uproar
and the entire country will be thrown into instability. Hardly
the time to contemplate uncertain and dangerous new legisla-
tion concerning the colonies. Particularly when the assassin is
from an illustrious aristocratic family and has worked clandestinely on behalf of the Crown."

St. Martin would be hanged as a traitor.

"Everyone will understand now how disgruntled
Lord St. Martin is with the Crown and its involvement, however indirect, with the demise of his wife. And with the
British debacle that was the Kabul Massacre. Guilt can twist
the most loyal man, let us not forget." He spoke as though
St. Martin were not in the room. "And we have Dr. Vesper
providing additional evidence, if required. You yourself witnessed the control he has over the man who was once considered the Crown's personal grim reaper—and I'm being kind."

He surveyed the room pointedly, gazing up at the gushing fountain and around the smooth glass walls. "Now, Mrs. Hampton, we'll have no more procrastination. I should think that your near death experience late last night should make a convincing case for your cooperation." He glanced at her disdainfully, making her conscious of her disheveled hair, her wrinkled shirt and boy's breeches. "You look like a street urchin from the stews of London. It's difficult to believe that you hold the key to my success, here in this transparent glass room where I can't imagine you have been able to structure a clandestine entranceway."

She could feel St. Martin's intense gaze on her, and she struggled to ignore it. Courage was what she needed at the moment, not his concern weakening her resolve. It had started with Charles agreeing to Bellamy's traitorous schemes, but by rights it would all end with her. Squaring her shoulders, she walked aggressively toward Bellamy, her head held high, her tone dripping condescension.

"I'm surprised you don't know or hadn't thought about Japanese screens—because they have appeared over the years, quite frequently, in the shipping lists of the British East India Company, usually destined for Tonkin or Siam rather than Europe," she said. "Essentially, they are eight- or nine-foot screens made into leaves that principally serve to divide a room or sequester some part of it, as for ornament when placed against walls."

Understanding gleamed in Bellamy's eyes and he stroked his mustache reflexively. "A double glass wall."

She strode over to the south-facing wall and placed her flattened palms against the surface. It had nothing to do with locks, latches, or bolts, but rather the perfectly calibrated amount of pressure. Not too much, not too little, but exactly right. Pushing sideways rather than forward, the panels slid to the side like a horizontal veil pulled out of the way.

Behind lay a small room leading to a narrow staircase. Lilly knew that farther back was a hallway that connected directly to Apsley House on the edge of Hyde Park, the Duke of Wellington's residence, from which the queen and her consort would proceed.

If she was expecting applause, she received none. Bellamy stepped quickly to her side and looked into the yawning space revealed by the open partition. He glanced at the shadowed area adjacent to the stairway. "The perfect place—providing perfect sightlines for your target, St. Martin." His eyes measured the distance to the diamond cage. "With your aim, sixty feet is child's play."

Flynn was close behind. "Ten minutes, sir."

Bellamy nodded and gestured to St. Martin. "Get in," he said. "And a few moments before Her Majesty's arrival, you will receive the revolver from Flynn, not before."

"The panel will remain open, I assume," St. Martin said in an empty voice that didn't seen quite real. "Shattering the glass would ruin both my aim and the effect."

Bellamy patted the fine silk of his waistcoat. "You won't miss, St. Martin, I'm sure of it. And in case the impossible does happen, remember that I have Mrs. Hampton here as guarantor." Flynn grabbed her arm, hauling her none too gently into the foreground. "You miss and Mrs. Hampton dies, instantly, and by your hand as it will turn out. Fleet Street won't get enough of the scandal this time."

Lilly felt hope drain from her soul. She looked ahead and past St. Martin and into a future that was not to be. It took every ounce of courage she possessed to watch him step over the partition to stand by the stairs, his lean body simultaneously strong and relaxed, years of experience priming him for what was to come.

Wisely, Flynn kept his distance, but she knew with sickening certainty that in a few short minutes, he would train a second revolver upon her. Her chest felt dull and heavy with numbness, her body weary and defeated and slowly relenting while her head refused to give up the fight.

Fleeting images passed through her mind, blood pounding

in her ears drowning out the water from the fountain and from the sounds of footsteps coming closer. A strong hand closed around the nape of her neck and the room blurred for a moment before she found herself stepping through the open glass partition like an apparition walking through a wall.

Wedged next to Flynn, she could not bear to look at St. Martin, concentrating instead on the pistol that the Irishman had rammed under her rib cage on her left side, just a hairbreadth away from her own revolver tucked inside her bodice. In the distance she could hear footsteps and the far-off sounds of voices coming nearer. The Royal entourage would enter the hall from the main entrance, greeting Isambard Kingdom Bellamy before securing the way for the queen's entrance via the hidden access from Apsley House.

Beads of sweat trickled down her spine, between her breasts. Perhaps only a few seconds left to live. She wanted nothing more than to run to the back of the stairwell and into St. Martin's arms, but life was spectacularly unkind and there was no time left.

Bellamy moved into her sights, puffed up like a peacock watching as one of the queen's royal guards and an employee of the British East India Company entered with the velvet cushion bearing the Koh-I-Noor. It seemed to grow under Bellamy's covetous gaze, its sharp facets catching the light pouring through the glass walls of the Crystal Palace.

He smiled, stroking his mustache, his plans falling neatly into place. Lilly felt her hand move, clutching the fabric of her shirt at her breast, pretending anxiety for Flynn's sake when she knew only cold, hard conviction. She felt the jab, a reminder, in her ribs. But her hand continued to move, emerging from under her shirt, her revolver in her hands.

She came up faster than she'd ever thought possible and pointed at the exact moment that Flynn turned to give St. Martin his Webley with which to assassinate the queen. She saw his look of surprise before she fired quickly, once, then twice. Something dark flew in the air between them, and she knew she had hit him, hit him squarely at close range, the spurt of liquid on her skin, watching as he tumbled backward before collapsing to the floor in a smear of blood.

She expected death, a hot explosion in the side of her rib cage, but it didn't come. Then all she heard was screaming and shouting, hysterical voices coming from everywhere mingling with the sound of the water fountain beneath it all and someone yelling to keep the queen away. Desperately, she looked behind her for an instant to see St. Martin, pistol raised, a look of the coldest calm on his face.

And Bellamy's booming voice, his lips red beneath the dark of his mustache. "Remember Dr. Vesper's commands. Your will is not your own, St. Martin." His words rang out. "Kill the queen or Lilly dies."

No, she wanted to scream but couldn't, because a heartbeat later, St. Martin put a bullet into the head of the man standing precisely sixty feet away from him. Bellamy's bulk was pressed against the cage of the Koh-I-Noor, his eyes widened in surprise at his impending death or the beauty of the diamond, no one would ever know.

Chapter 23

It took well over three months before St. Martin stopped telling her that she had nearly gotten herself killed on his behalf—not nearly a good enough reason.

"I had no choice. There was no way I would see you die, hanged as a traitor," she said, contented at last. They lay in each other's arms for a long time, ignoring the world around them, although every now and then he would whisper into her hair, "You shouldn't have been there in the first place." And she would laugh and press her lips along his hard jaw. "I belong at your side and you at mine. No matter what the circumstances. And do recall, you're the one who returned my revolver to me. I merely chose to use it."

Summer had come and gone in London along with the thousands of visitors wending their way every day through the Crystal Palace. Lilly's name had been quietly cleared and the attempted assassination of Queen Victoria by Isambard Kingdom Bellamy discreetly buried in the annals kept deep in the bowels of Whitehall. Seabourne had been stripped of his post and his estates, dispatched back to India to live out his days in exile. Duleep Singh, the Maharajah of the Punjab, had presented Her Majesty with the Koh-I-Noor, and Charles Hampton had been posthumously knighted for his contribution to architectural design.

And Lilly and St. Martin were both at peace, with themselves and each other. Lilly worked single-mindedly on her drawings, her spirit cleansed of her unhealthy ambitions so closely tied to Charles. Playing freely with innovative designs and unwilling to give up her newly discovered confidence, she was involved with several smaller commissions where she used her own name and her own ideas.

And St. Martin, freed from the guilt of his past, from his headaches and nightmares, concentrated on building a life for them together.

They lay in companionable silence, as a long morning stretched into afternoon, in the coolness of the sheets and the warmth of their bodies, his pressed to hers, the merging of hardness and softness, of planes and curves. He lay sprawled beside her, her blond head resting on his torso, one languid hand stroking his chest. Her eyes were heavy with fulfillment, wide and blue against her pale, translucent skin.

"I just have one question," she said dreamily.

"Only one? That's unusual for you, Lilly." She could hear his smile.

"Well, actually, two."

His hand drifted leisurely down her smooth back as though he couldn't become accustomed to the freedom of touching his wife, wherever and however he wished. Her skin was warm cream.

"I cannot concentrate on my question if you continue doing that," she said, her eyes darkening with desire. "You see I've nearly forgotten where I was going with my queries." She frowned charmingly. "Now I recall. Poor Dr. Vesper. Has he returned yet from India with his family?"

"He has and as I understand it, they are settling in at the house on Weymouth Street."

"I do hope he will have given up on that mesmerism nonsense. I think a wife and children are just what his home needs, an opportunity to blow away all of those nasty cobwebs." Along with a contented housekeeper and Jenny, the scullery maid, newly returned to health. It was a bleak chapter in St. Martin's life, and he hoped Lilly would never know the flexibility of conscience that his work too often required. She was alive and she was his, despite death and chaos, and that was all that mattered.

"And your second question?" he asked lightly, turning away from his dark thoughts, "before I lose track of where you're going with all this."

"Your scar, above your eyebrow." She traced it with a lingering touch, faint worry etching her forehead. "Please don't tell me it's the result of some horrendous injury inflicted by a knife or worse."

St. Martin grabbed Lilly's hand and kissed her open palm. "Then I won't," he lied smoothly. "Actually, the story is innocuous. I simply fell from a tree and hit my head on a rock when I was seven."

Her gaze said that she didn't believe him. She returned her hand to his chest, threading her fingers with his, her blue eyes intense. "Why did you, or Whitehall, not simply arrest Bellamy at the outset before he had a chance to hatch his plans?"

"That's a third question."

She smiled. "And you will indulge me, I know." She felt the steady beat of his heart beneath the stroking of her hand.

"It doesn't work that way, my love. He was chairman of the British East India Company and its major shareholder. We needed proof and we received it from Bellamy's own lips. At least half a dozen of the queen's Privy Council were on hand to hear it."

She raised her head to look into his eyes. "And to see you save the day." Pride suffused her voice.

"Impossible without you."

Before she could respond, he sealed the statement with his mouth on hers, his hands sliding around her body to cup her buttocks, pressing her hard against him until he felt the playful resistance leave her. Her mouth was soft and yielding, her body melting against his without a will of its own.

"Everything's impossible without you," he said against her lips, words he would repeat to her and to himself at least once a day for the rest of their lives. "My beautiful, talented Lilly."

Postscript

Lilly and St. Martin are, of course, products of my feverish imagination, placed in a historical context filled with power, greed, and ambition that, I hope, tested and pushed their passion to the limit—for your enjoyment.

The Crystal Palace was designed not by Lilly Clarence Hampton but by Joseph Paxton who began life as a gardener and who was ultimately knighted for his brilliant architectural contribution to Great Britain. As Lilly did in *Dangerous Games*, he completed the architectural plans for the Crystal Palace in under ten days and under great duress, designing a radically new iron and glass structure for the Great Exhibition of 1851 that would go on to influence building design throughout the western world for decades to come.

The Koh-I-Noor diamond was indeed presented to Queen Victoria by Duleep Singh in 1851 and subsequently displayed in the Crystal Palace at the Great Exhibition. Apparently, the diamond did not live up to expectations, and many believed, including the queen's consort, Prince Albert, that the gem's brilliance was lacking. As a consequence, Albert had the diamond cut and reduced in size to increase its luster but was still dissatisfied with the results. It was mounted in a tiara and later in a crown and worn by Queen Alexandra, Queen Mary, and finally, by Queen Elizabeth, wife of George VI, where it finally rested atop her coffin as she lay in state in 2002.

Interestingly enough, there is a superstition that the Koh-I-Noor is said to bring disaster to male rulers but great fortune to women of power. I suppose only history, or a good story, will tell.

Everyone knows IT'S HOTTER IN HAWAII,
and in HelenKay Dimon's latest,
that doesn't just mean the weather. . . .

Cassie's head snapped back. "What are you doing?"

The woman asked a *very* good question. "Standing here."

"You were going to kiss me."

For a second there he toyed with the idea, yeah. "Think a lot of yourself, don't you?"

"I know when a man wants to kiss me."

She didn't have to sound so appalled by the possibility. "So, that's a 'yes' on the arrogance thing?"

"Come off it. I saw you."

"Then you need glasses." And a drink. Maybe that would help.

"You're two inches away and swooping in."

"Swooping?" Cal stepped back and well out of swooping range.

Mauling complete strangers was not his style. Neither was making a move on an estranged friend's grieving sister. Make that grieving baby sister. She was somewhere around thirty and hot as hell. Dan probably hadn't slept through the night since Cassie turned fourteen. No sane man who wanted to protect her would.

Cal chalked up the moment of stupidity to the long flight and the shocking news about Dan his brain still refused to compute. Just a heap of pent-up energy with nowhere to go.

Yep. Nothing more than a near-miss brought on by low blood sugar . . . or something.

"Reaction." One he insisted had more to do with the heat of the situation than the length of her legs.

"To what?" Those amber eyes narrowed.

"This," he waved his hand back and forth. "Between us. That and the by-product of the gunfire. It's not real."

Her lips twisted into a look of disgust. "Did your head slam against the floor or something?"

Now she was ticking him off. "Give me a break. Are you trying to tell me this only goes one way?"

"Define *this*." She mimicked his hand gesture by waving her hand back and forth between them.

"Interest."

"In you?"

Now she sounded horrified. A guy could get a complex. "Do you see someone else here?"

"No, but I'm not the one who's lost his mind. That seems to be you at the moment."

"You're trying to tell me—"

"Yes."

"You felt nothing when—"

"Exactly."

"At all?"

"Not even a twinge." She topped the response with a smug smile.

Well, hell. Here he thought they both were fighting back a heavy-duty case of adrenaline-fueled lust. Looked like he stood alone on that score.

Don't miss IMMORTAL DANGER,
the latest from Cynthia Eden,
out this month from Brava. . . .

His back teeth clenched as he glanced around the room. Doors led off in every direction. He already knew where all those doors would take him. To hell.

But he needed to find Maya, so he'd have to go—

"Don't screw with me, Armand!" A woman's voice, hard, ice cold. Maya.

He turned, found her leaning over the bar, her hand wrapped around the bartender's throat.

"I want to know who went after Sean, and I want to know *now.*" He saw her fingernails stretch into claws, and he watched as those claws sank into the man's neck.

"I-I d-don't k-know." The guy looked like he might faint at any moment. Definitely human. Vamps were always so pale it looked like they might faint. But this guy, he'd looked pretty normal until Maya clawed him.

"Find out!" She threw him against a wall of drinks.

Adam stalked toward her, reached her side just as she spun around, claws up.

He stilled.

She glared at him. "What the hell do you want?" She snarled, and he could see the faint edge of her fangs gleaming behind her plump lips.

It was his first time to get a good look at her face. He'd

seen her from a distance before, judged her to be pretty, hadn't bothered to think much beyond that.

He blinked as he stared at her. Damn, the woman looked like some kind of fallen angel.

Her thick black hair framed her perfect, heart-shaped face. Her cheeks were high, glass sharp. Her nose was small, straight. Her eyes were wide and currently the black of a vampire in hunting mode. And her lips, well, she might have the face of an angel, but she had lips made for sin.

Adam felt his cock stir, *for a vampire.*

He shuddered in revulsion.

Oh, hell, no. The woman was so not his type.

Her scent surrounded him. Not the rancid, rotting stench of death he'd smelled around others of her kind. But a light, fragrant scent, almost like flowers.

What in the hell? How could she—

Maya growled and shoved him away from her, muttering something under her breath about idiots with death wishes.

Then she walked away from him.

For a moment, he just studied her. Maya wasn't exactly his idea of an uber-vamp. She was small, too damn small for his taste. The woman was barely five foot seven. Her body was slender, with almost boyish hips. Her legs were encased in an old, faded pair of jeans, and the black t-shirt she wore clung tightly to her frame.

He liked women with more meat on their bones. Liked a woman with curves. A woman with round, lush hips that he could hold while he thrust deep into her.

But, well, he wasn't interested in screwing Maya. Not with her too-thin body. Her too pale skin. No, he didn't want to screw her.

He just planned to use her.

Adam took two quick strides forward, grabbed her arm and swung her back toward him.

The eyes that had relaxed to a bright blue shade instantly

flashed black. Vamps' eyes always changed to black when they fought or when they fucked.

Sometimes folks made the mistake of confusing vamps with demons, because a demon's eyes, well, they could go black, too. Actually, Adam knew that a demon's eyes were *always* black, and for the demons, every damn part of their eyes went black. Even the sclera. With the vamps, just the iris changed.

Usually demons were smart enough to hide the true color of their eyes. But the vamps, they didn't seem to give a flying shit who saw the change. But if a human happened to see the eye shift, it was generally too late for the poor bastard, anyway, because by then, he was prey.

Gazing into Maya's relentless black eyes, Adam had a true inkling of just how those said poor bastards must have felt.

A growl rumbled in her throat, then she snarled, "Slick, you're screwing with the wrong woman tonight."

No, she was the right woman. Whether he liked the fact or not.

So he clenched his teeth, swallowed his pride, and in the midst of hell, admitted, "I need your help."

And keep an eye out for
Kathy Love's newest book,
DEMON CAN'T HELP IT,
coming next month from Brava. . . .

Jo breathed in slowly through her nose. What had she just agreed to? Seeing this man every day? She pulled in another slow, even breath, telling herself to shake off her reaction to this man's proximity.

Sure, he was attractive. And he had—a presence. But she wasn't some teenage girl who would fall to pieces under a cute boy's attention. Not that cute was a strong enough word for what Maksim was. He was—unnerving. To say the least.

But she wasn't interested in him. She decided that quite definitely over the past two days. Of course that decision was made when he wasn't in her presence.

But either way, she should have more control than this. Apparently should and could were two very different things. And she couldn't seem to stop her reaction to him. Her heart raced and her body tingled, both hot and cold in all the most inappropriate places.

"So every morning?" he said, his voice rumbling right next to her, firing up the heat inside her. "Does that work for you?"

She cleared her throat, struggling to calm her body.

"Yes—that's great," she managed to say, surprising even herself with the airiness of her tone. "I'll schedule you from eight a.m. to"—she glanced at the clock on the lower right-hand of the computer screen, "noon?"

That was a good amount of time, getting Cherise through

the rowdy mornings and lunch, and giving him the go ahead to leave now. She needed him out of her space.

If her body wasn't going to go along with her mind, then avoidance was clearly her best strategy. And she'd done well with that tactic—although she'd told herself that wasn't what she was doing.

"Noon is fine," he said, still not moving. Not even straightening away from the computer. And her.

"Good," she poised her fingers over the keys and began typing in his hours. "Then I think we are all settled. You can take off now if you like."

When he didn't move, she added, "You can go get some lunch. You must be hungry." She flashed him a quick smile without really looking at him.

This time he did stand, but he didn't move away. Instead he leaned against her desk, the old piece of furniture creaking at his tall, muscular weight.

"You must be hungry too. Would you like to join me?"

She blinked, for a moment not comprehending his words, her mind too focused on the muscles of his thighs so near her. The flex of more muscles in his shoulders and arms as he crossed them over his chest.

She forced herself to look back at the computer screen.

"I—I don't think so," she said. "I have a lot to do here."

"But surely you allow yourself half an hour for lunch break."

She continued typing, fairly certain whatever she was writing was gibberish. "I brought a lunch with me, actually." Which was true. Not that she was hungry at the moment. She was too—edgy.

"Come on," he said in a low voice that was enticing, coaxing. "Come celebrate your first regular volunteer."

She couldn't help looking at him. He was smiling, the curl of his lips, his white, even teeth, the sexily pleading glimmer in his pale green eyes.

God, he was so beautiful.

And dangerous.

Jo shook her head. "I really can't."

He studied her for a moment. "Can't or won't. What's a matter, Josephine? Do I make you nervous?"

Jo's breath left her for a moment at the accented rhythm of her full name crossing his lips. But the breath-stealing moment left as quickly as it came, followed by irritation. At him and at herself.

She wasn't attracted to his man—not beyond a basic physical attraction. And that could be controlled. It could.

"You don't make me nervous," she said firmly.

"Then why not join me for lunch?"

"Because," she said slowly, "I have a lot of work to do."

Maksim crossed his arms tighter, and lifted one of his eloquent eyebrows, which informed her that he didn't believe her for a moment.

"I don't think that's why you won't come. I think you are uncomfortable with me. Maybe because you are attracted to me." Again the eyebrow lifted—this time in questioning challenge.